VANGUARD

Book One: Ark Royal
Book Two: The Nelson Touch
Book Three: The Trafalgar Gambit
Book Four: Warspite
Book Five: A Savage War of Peace
Book Six: A Small Colonial War
Book Seven: Vanguard

VANGUARD

(ARK ROYAL, BOOK VII)

CHRISTOPHER G. NUTTALL

The characters and events portrayed in this book are fictitious. Any similarity to real persons, living or dead, is coincidental and not intended by the author.

ISBN-13: 9781523862917
ISBN-10: 1523862912

http://www.chrishanger.net
http://chrishanger.wordpress.com/
http://www.facebook.com/ChristopherGNuttall

Cover by Justin Adams

http://www.variastudios.com/

All Comments Welcome!

DEDICATION

To the men and women of Britain's armed forces.

AUTHOR'S NOTE

I wrote *Vanguard* to be as stand-alone as possible; the only major character to have appeared before is Prince Henry, who was a fairly major character in *The Nelson Touch* and *The Trafalgar Gambit*. All you really need to know about him is that he was a starfighter pilot during the First Interstellar War (with the Tadpoles) who got captured and played a major role in peace talks. Since then, he has been assigned to Tadpole Prime as Earth's Ambassador.

As always, reviews, comments and suchlike are warmly welcomed. Please feel free to forward spelling corrections and suchlike to me.

Finally, please follow my blog and/or mailing list for future releases. I've discovered that Facebook doesn't share my posts with *all* of my followers.

Thank you

CGN

PROLOGUE

"Captain," Commander Katy Shaw said. "We are ready to go where no man has gone before."

Captain Francis Preston snorted, rudely. HMS *Magellan* and HMS *Livingston* had been probing the tramlines before Tadpole space for the last six months, only to find nothing beyond a pair of uninhabited worlds that would probably be turned into joint colonies. Nothing to sniff at, to be fair - the crew would be able to claim a bonus from the Survey Service - but nothing to shake the universe either.

"Raise Captain Archer," he said, sitting upright in his command chair. "Inform him that we will jump through the tramline in" - he glanced at his console - "ten minutes."

"Aye, sir," Katy said.

Francis nodded, then looked around the bridge. The younger members of the crew, their enthusiasm undiminished by six months of nothingness, looked excited, while the older crewmen were checking and rechecking their consoles as they prepared for the jump. It was rare for a previously undiscovered tramline to throw up any surprises, but several survey ships *had* set out on exploration missions and vanished, somewhere in the trackless wastes of interstellar space. Who knew? The tramline could lead to anything.

"Captain Archer acknowledges, sir," the communications officer said. "He says he still thinks you cheated at cards."

"Sore loser," Francis commented. He and Captain Archer had played cards for the right to take point as the survey ships moved onwards and he'd won. "Tell him to hold position and wait for our return."

"Aye, sir," the communications officer said.

Francis learned forward. "Take us into stealth," he ordered. "And then set course for the tramline."

He let out a breath as the display dimmed, slightly. There was no way to *know* what was at the other end of a tramline without jumping through, which was why survey ships tended to operate in pairs. If *Magellan* failed to return, *Livingston* would head back to the nearest military base at once, rather than try to follow her sister ship. It would be tough on *Magellan* if she needed assistance, but standing orders permitted no ambiguity. Maybe she'd fallen right into a black hole - it was theoretically possible - or maybe she'd run into a hostile alien race. It was the latter thought that kept the Admiralty's planners up at night. Humanity's first encounter with an alien race had almost been its last.

But the odds against meeting another spacefaring race are considerable, he reminded himself, firmly. *It was sheer luck that we ran into the Tadpoles when they were at relatively the same stage of development.*

He pushed the thought aside as the display flickered, warning him that they had entered the tramline. "Drive online, sir," the helmsman reported. "Gravity flux nominal. I don't think there are any surprises waiting for us in this tramline."

"Good," Francis grunted. He glanced at the green-lit status display, then up at his XO, who nodded. "Jump!"

The starship shivered, slightly, as she jumped down the tramline and into the unexplored system. Francis let out a breath he hadn't realised he was holding as the display flickered and then rebooted, displaying a standard G2 yellow star. Most transits were routine, thanks to the wonders of modern technology, but an unexplored tramline might have an unexpected gravimetric flux that could cripple or destroy a ship. The odds were staggeringly against it, yet there was one tramline, right on the other side of explored space, that had eaten every starship that jumped down it. *No one* had returned to tell the tale.

"Jump complete, sir," the helmsman said. "There were no problems."

"Good," Francis said. "I..."

"Captain," the tactical officer interrupted. "I think you should take a look at this!"

Francis rose from his command chair and hurried over to the tactical console. There were at least two planets within the system's life-bearing zone, both surrounded by the yellow icons of unidentified ships, space stations and radio sources. *Hundreds* of icons were swarming through the system, some clearly heading to an asteroid field and others making their steady way towards a gas giant. He felt his heart start to pound in his chest as the computers struggled to match the unknowns to something in its memory...and failed. They were staring at a whole new spacefaring race.

"Cloak us," he snapped. Stealth mode rendered the ship almost undetectable, but there was no point in taking chances. Standing orders were very clear. No alien race, particularly one that could pose a genuine threat to humanity, was to know the survey ship was present until the various human governments could decide what to do about it. "Tactical analysis?"

"Impossible to be sure at this distance, sir, but I'd say their tech base is on a par with ours," the tactical officer said. "I'm definitely picking up drive fields...they've got bases scattered right across the system."

Katy leaned forward. "Are they using the tramlines?"

"I'm not sure," the tactical officer admitted. "There're three more in the system itself..."

Francis closed his eyes as he thought, rapidly. A race on the same level as mankind - and the Tadpoles - should certainly know about the tramlines that allowed starships to jump from system to system without having to cross the gulf of interstellar space. Mastering drive fields should certainly give them the technology to locate the tramlines and jump through them...unless, of course, they'd somehow managed to miss one or more applications of the technology. Humanity had certainly missed at least one before the First Interstellar War.

"We didn't see any sign of them in the previous system," he mused. "Did we?"

"No, sir," Katy said. "We'll go through the data again, but we were thorough. I don't think we missed anything."

"And if they don't have access to the tramlines, they won't be able to reach the system," Francis said. He opened his eyes and studied the display. "They won't be able to reach us."

"Or they may have decided the system was useless," Katy pointed out. "There was only one planet, sir, and it made *Pluto* look big."

Francis shrugged. There were quite a few human groups that would have considered the system a perfect place for a settlement, one nicely isolated from the temptations of the modern world. But then, maybe they *didn't* have access to the tramlines…or, perhaps, to the weaker tramlines the Tadpoles had learned to access. They might not have been able to progress much further even after they left their system.

Or they might have been able to access other systems through the other tramlines, he mused, *and merely decided to leave a seemingly-useless system alone.*

He glanced at the communications officer. "Have you been able to pull anything useful from their radio chatter?"

"Not as yet, sir," the communications officer said. "I was expecting something visual, but everything we've picked up appears to be encrypted."

"Or they're so alien that we can't understand their chatter," Katy offered. "It took us months to glean *anything* from captured Tadpole databases."

Francis nodded, slowly.

"Tactical," he said, "do you believe we are in any danger of being discovered?"

"No, sir," the tactical officer said. "Unless they have some detection system I've never heard of, Captain, we should be safe."

Francis felt a stab of disappointment. Standing orders strictly forbade making any attempt at First Contact without heavy reinforcements on call, just in case the encounter turned violent, unless there was no other choice. If the aliens had discovered *Magellan*, he could have attempted to communicate with them and ensured his place in the history books…

"Then we will reverse course and jump back out of the system," he said. "Once we link up with *Livingston*, we'll make our way back to the nearest naval base. The Admiralty will put together a contact mission and, hopefully, we'll be on it."

"Aye, sir," the helmsman said.

Katy frowned. "The nearest large-scale base is a Tadpole base, sir."

Francis nodded. The Tadpoles had shown no real interest in the pre-space Vesy, but he was sure they'd be more than interested in a spacefaring race. And he was fairly sure they wouldn't try to keep the information for themselves. They just didn't seem to have the same capability for deception as humans.

He took one last look at the display, watching the alien ships, then nodded to himself.

"We'll be back," he said, as *Magellan* approached the tramline. "And we'll have a great many friends with us."

CHAPTER ONE

"Welcome back, Susan," Mrs Blackthorn said. "Or should I call you *Commander*?"

"Susan is fine," Commander Susan Onarina said, as she clambered out of the car. "It would feel strange to have you address me by rank."

"Hanover Towers is diminished by your absence," Mrs Blackthorn assured her. "But we are proud of your success."

Susan kept the doubt off her face with the ease of long practice. She would have been surprised if Mrs Blackthorn remembered her as anything more than a trouble-maker, one of the girls who had been sent to her for disciplinary action. Her father had been a much-loved, but rather roguish immigrant, her mother a shop-girl with few prospects...Susan had been a commoner in a school where a good third of the students had aristocratic, government or military connections. She had a feeling the headmistress had probably downloaded and read her school reports just so she could pretend to remember Susan.

"I'm glad to hear it," she lied, smoothly. School hadn't been *that* bad, all things considered, but she'd never really seen it as a gateway to wealth, power and success. *That* had come at the Luna Academy. "And I'm glad to be back."

She sighed inwardly as she looked up at the towering school. It had struck her as a castle, when she'd first arrived as a twelve-year-old, but to her older eyes it looked as if its builders had been trying too hard. Four towers, two for boys and two for girls, surrounding a mansion, set within the Scottish Highlands. She winced in remembered pain at memories of long hikes over the mountains, although she had to admit that some of them had been almost enjoyable. There was definitely something to be said for a long walk followed by fish and chips in a cafe near St. Andrews.

And I never tried to skive off, she thought, ruefully. *Father would have been disappointed in me.*

"I'm sure you remember the way," Mrs Blackthorn said, breaking into her thoughts. "But I'd be happy to escort you, if you wish."

"Please," Susan said. She rather doubted she'd be allowed to wander the school alone, even if she *had* been invited. Hanover Towers took its security seriously. The guards at the gates had checked her paperwork twice and then searched the car before allowing her to enter the complex. "It's probably changed since I was last here."

"The more things change, the more they stay the same," Mrs Blackthorn said, primly. "Follow me."

Susan nodded, curtly, as she caught sight of their reflection in the mirrored door. They made an odd couple; Mrs Blackthorn prim and proper, her entire bearing projecting the image of aristocracy boiled down to its essence, Susan herself tall and dark, wearing her naval dress uniform and her dark hair tied into a long braid that fell over her shoulder and down past her breasts. It hadn't been easy to blend in, not when she was the daughter of an immigrant; she'd been sent to the form mistress twice for fighting before she'd found a group of friends of her own. The Troubles had ensured that the ugly curse of racism still bubbled, just under the surface...

She sucked in her breath as they entered the Welcome Hall, where a large portrait of Sir Charles Hanover hung in a place of honour, flanked by portraits of King Charles IV and Princess Elizabeth, the heir presumptive to the throne. Susan had *met* the princess, during a formal visit to the Luna Academy, but she couldn't say she *knew* the lady, while too many of her schoolmates *could*. She sighed, remembering old pains, and then pushed them away firmly. Far too many of her former schoolmates had died during the war.

"I've arranged for the entire school to be present during your speech," Mrs Blackthorn prattled, distracting Susan from her thoughts. "And then I thought you might want to have a more informal chat with some of the

CHAPTER TWO

"Thank you for coming at such short notice, Commander," Commodore Sir Travis Younghusband said, once he'd called Susan into his office and pointed her to a chair. "I knew you were due at least nine days of leave and I apologise for disrupting it and calling you to London."

"Thank you, sir," Susan said. It had to be bad. Senior officers were rarely apologetic, even if they *had* dragged her all the way to London from Scotland. The only consolation was that she probably wasn't in trouble for something. "Hopefully, it will impress on the little children the importance of a naval career."

"And how you can be jerked around at will by some jerk of a staff officer," Sir Travis said, dryly. He'd been a starship officer himself before transferring to the personnel department, Susan recalled; he probably knew *precisely* how she was feeling. "Do you think there were any good prospects among the Hanover seniors?"

"I didn't have enough time to take their measures, sir," Susan said, truthfully. "There were the usual handful of stupid questions, but a year at the academy would knock them into shape or get them on the shuttle back home."

"Quite, quite," Sir Travis said. He leaned back in his chair, his face taking on a grave expression. "Do you know Commander Bothell, Gordon Bothell?"

Susan hesitated, then shook her head. "I believe there was a Bothell in the class above me at the academy," she said, "but I don't recall much about him."

"It probably wasn't the same person," Sir Travis said. "Commander Bothell left the academy four years before yourself. But your paths may have crossed at some point since you graduated and took that posting to *Warspite*."

"I don't recall, sir," Susan said. If Bothell had left the academy in the same year she'd started, he'd almost certainly have become a lieutenant before she'd graduated herself. It was unlikely they'd share confidences, if they ever met. "May I ask what this is about?"

Sir Travis sighed. "Commander Bothell went on leave two weeks ago," he said. "He was due to report back to the spaceport four days ago, but failed to show. We ran through the standard procedures - we checked the local hospitals, police records, even sent a car around to his house - and drew a blank. Bothell appears to have completely vanished."

Susan blinked. The chaos caused by the Bombardment of Earth had helped quite a few people to vanish - hundreds of thousands of records had simply been destroyed and entire communities had been uprooted - but that had been over thirteen years ago. Why would a naval officer simply *vanish*? She'd been in the navy long enough to know that accidents happened, that young midshipmen might oversleep after their first visit to the red light district…and yet, a *Commander* should have known the dangers. Had something happened to him?

And what, she asked herself, *does it have to do with me*?

"Commander Bothell was serving as the XO of HMS *Vanguard*," Sir Travis said, flatly. "His sudden absence leaves us with a hole that needs to be filled. *Vanguard's* second officer has been filling in the gap as best as he can, but he's the tactical officer; the battleship needs both slots filled. I know you were slated for *Edinburgh*, but would you be willing to take up the post on *Vanguard* instead?"

Susan thought fast. *Vanguard* - the Royal Navy's giant battleship - would be an order of magnitude more complex than HMS *Edinburgh*, perhaps almost as complex as HMS *Formidable*. It was a daunting prospect, all the more so as her experience as a senior officer was almost entirely based on cruisers. And yet, if she did well, it would be a boost to her career. There would be a good chance of receiving a command slot during the next round of promotions.

And if I turn it down, she thought grimly, *I'll never be offered promotion again.*

"I would be honoured," she said, out loud. "How long was Commander Bothell on *Vanguard*?"

"Nine months," Sir Travis said. He picked a datachip off the desk and held it out to her. "I suspect he will have had plenty of time to organise everything to suit himself, while you'll have to do everything in a hurry, but his efficiency reports are first-rate. You shouldn't have any problems taking his place. In the event of him turning up, of course, he will not be permitted to return to *Vanguard*."

Susan nodded, curtly, as she took the chip. A day or two late, returning from leave, *might* be overlooked, but a full week would raise a whole string of uncomfortable questions. If Commander Bothell didn't have a very good excuse for not reporting in - for not even contacting the Admiralty to request compassionate leave - his career would come to a screeching halt. He'd need a great many patrons in high places to save himself from a dishonourable discharge. She couldn't help feeling as though she was stepping into someone else's shoes, without the prior preparation she'd expected on *Edinburgh*, but it was one hell of a challenge.

"I understand, sir," she said.

"Good," Sir Travis said. "*Vanguard* is scheduled to jump out of the system in a week to join a set of war games with the Americans. You'll have that long, I think, to get used to your new posting. The Admiralty would take a dim view of the battleship being late for her first true deployment."

"Yes, sir," Susan said. She glanced at the datachip in her hand, then tucked it away in her jacket. "When do you want me to leave?"

"We've booked a flight for you from Heathrow, departing in two hours," Sir Travis said, bluntly. Any thoughts she might have had about visiting her father vanished like new-fallen snow. "My staff has arranged a car to take you to the spaceport."

"Thank you, sir," Susan said. A civilian would have found it a gross inconvenience, but like most naval officers, she travelled light. She could draw everything she needed from the battleship's stores, once she arrived. "I look forward to the challenge."

Sir Travis smiled. "I'm glad to hear it, Commander," he said. He rose and held out a hand, which she shook firmly. "And I wish you the very best of luck."

Susan saluted, then turned and made her way out of the office and down the stairs to the vehicle pool. A black car was already waiting for her, a junior midshipman in the driver's seat. Susan concealed her amusement as he jumped out of the car, gave her the snappiest salute she'd seen since she left the academy and then opened the door for her. *She* would have resisted assignment to Earth with all her strength - a lack of spacefaring experience would tell against the young man, when the promotions board considered who to advance up the ladder - but if someone wanted it, who was she to tell him no?

She climbed into the back of the car, then closed the privacy blinds and activated the computer terminal as the car hummed to life. It would take at least forty minutes to reach the spaceport, no matter what happened; indeed, if traffic had returned to its pre-war norms, it might take longer, much longer, to get to Heathrow. The computer terminal lit up; she keyed a communications code into the panel and waited. Five minutes later, her father's face appeared in the display.

"Susan," he said. "I thought you were going back to school!"

Susan had to smile. Romeo Onarina, her father, had immigrated to Britain from Jamaica, serving in the army before collecting his citizenship papers and marrying her mother. He'd been in London during the bombardment, somehow keeping his wife alive, only to lose her five years later to a pointless accident. And yet, somehow, he'd found the strength to carry on. He was the strongest man she knew.

"I was recalled to the Admiralty," she said. "They're sending me back to duty."

Her father's face fell. "That quickly?"

"I'm due to lift off from Heathrow in less than two hours," Susan said. "I'm sorry I won't be able to see you."

"Duty calls," her father said. He cleared his throat. "You'll write to me, won't you?"

Susan nodded. Some of her fellow cadets had bitched and moaned about the requirement to write home at least once a week, yet *she'd* never begrudged it. Yes, the time *could* have been used to study for one of the innumerable exams, but she loved her family. The three of them had been happy together in a world that eyed immigrants with suspicion. She'd been scared of losing touch back when she'd gone to Hanover Towers, let alone leaving Earth and heading to Luna. Her family was all she had in the world.

"I will," she promised. "And I'll try and call again before we leave orbit."

She closed the connection, then dropped the datachip into the terminal and began to study the battleship. HMS *Vanguard* had been the topic of some debate during the years following the Anglo-Indian War, although it was generally agreed that the pre-war mix of fleet carriers and destroyers was no longer adequate. *Warspite* had blown an Indian carrier into a powerless hulk with a single hit, after all. Besides, with the recent improvements in point defence, it was unlikely that any starfighter could get close enough to a starship to launch its missiles before it was destroyed.

And the fighter jocks still walk around as if they have rods up their butts, she thought, as she skimmed through the data. *Don't they know we lost a third of our pilots during the first year of war?*

She pushed the thought aside and kept reading the files, only looking up when the driver took the car through the checkpoint and into the military section of Heathrow Spaceport. Susan thanked him as he parked outside the terminal, recovered the datachip and hurried into the building. Thankfully, there were none of the elaborate security procedures for military personnel; the officers scanned her ID, checked her fingerprints and DNA code and then motioned her through the barrier. It was a relief; every time she passed through the civilian side of the terminal she was *always* singled out for close inspections. And it never ceased to grate.

The scars of war run deep, she reminded herself, as she glanced around the terminal. Dozens of enlisted soldiers, spacers and airmen lounged around, reading datapads or trying to catch up on their sleep, while officers headed for their private lounge. *And no one will forget in a hurry.*

She picked up a handful of items at the NAAFI, then entered the officer's lounge and sat down to wait. Her flight was announced only thirty minutes later, suggesting that the shuttlecraft had been waiting for her; the military, at least, wasn't wedded to the strict timetables followed by civilian craft. She walked through the terminal, past a handful of enlisted spacers and through the gate. It still struck her as rude to stride past the spacers - they had arrived first, after all - but she *was* their senior officer. She wasn't allowed to treat them in any other way.

"Welcome onboard," the shuttle crewman said. She was relieved he didn't go into the faux-stewardess routine practiced by far too many military crews. It had been funny the first time, but after ten or so repeats it just became annoying. "We should be docking with HMS *Vanguard* in three hours, forty minutes."

Susan took her seat, buckled herself in and closed her eyes, trying to sleep. It had been a long day and it would only get worse, once she actually boarded the battleship. The children back at Hanover Towers would find it hard to adapt if they ever joined the navy. It certainly *felt* as though they were crossing time zones, even though - technically - the Royal Navy operated on GMT. Space Lag was a very real threat.

She must have dozed off, because the next thing she knew was hearing the pilot announce the approach to *Vanguard*, Susan unbuckled herself, rose and peered through the nearest portal as the giant battleship came into view. It would be her only chance to see an exterior view of the ship for weeks, unless she went EVA or borrowed a shuttle - and besides, she was fascinated. The images in the files couldn't compare to a real starship.

Vanguard was massive, she noted; the files stated that the battleship was five kilometres long from prow to stern. It was easy, as the shuttle flew closer, to pick out the four immense turrets towards the prow of the ship and, in the distance, the four *rear* turrets. She'd served on *Warspite*, with its immense plasma cannon, but *Vanguard's* main weapons were much nastier. She doubted that anything could survive long enough to ram the ship, if the captain directed every turret that could bear on the approaching vessel. The smaller weapons and point defences studding the hull looked almost like afterthoughts.

"She looks like a dumbbell," one of the spacers said, behind her.

It wasn't inaccurate, Susan thought. The giant battleship *did* look like a dumbbell; indeed, she had to admit the ship looked even uglier than the old *Ark Royal*. But then, beauty was of no concern, not when survivability was far more important. The fleet carriers that had fought in the Battle of New Russia had been pretty ships, designed to impress the viewing public, but they'd failed their first combat test rather spectacularly. *Warspite* hadn't been very pretty either.

She drank in the details as the shuttle approached the airlock hatch. The hull was covered with plates of armour, each one three or four times the size of the shuttle; if they were damaged, according to the files, they could be easily replaced with new panels drawn from the starship's stores. A boffin had taken the solid-state armour that had protected *Ark Royal* and improved on it, producing a compound that was both immensely tough and far more flexible than its predecessors. And lighter too, if she recalled correctly. *Ark Royal* had about the same grace and agility as a pig in mud - she'd often been outraced by alien starships - but *Vanguard* should have no difficulty keeping up with the rest of the fleet. Her drives were so powerful, according to the notes, that they'd almost torn the ship apart, the first time they'd been powered up. She couldn't help thinking that was a problem that should have been corrected a long time before the navy actually started *building* the ship.

But we'll probably be glad of the extra speed if we run into real trouble, she thought, morbidly. There were two known alien races out in the darkness and one of them, at least, was very definitely on the same level as the human race. And if there were two races, there would almost certainly be more. *Lose half the engine rooms and Vanguard can just keep going.*

A dull thump ran through the shuttle as she docked with the battleship, followed by a flicker in the gravity as the two artificial gravity fields merged. Susan rose to her feet at once - as the highest-ranking officer, she was entitled to embark and disembark first - and strode towards the hatch, which hissed open. She made a mental note to review procedures, even though it should be perfectly safe. There was a *reason* starships had airlocks, after all.

"Commander Onarina," a familiar voice said. "Welcome onboard HMS Vanguard."

Susan smiled as she saw Lieutenant-Commander Paul Mason. "Paul," she said. "It's been a long time since *Warspite*."

"It has indeed," Mason said. He snapped off a salute, then relaxed. "I hear you've been promoted?"

Susan smirked. "Who let the cat out of the bag?"

"I believe it was mentioned in dispatches somewhere," Mason said. He'd always been a joker, although several years as an officer had tempered him somewhat. "Captain Blake wishes to see you at once, Commander. Then I have to show you to your office and answer your questions."

Susan nodded. "You've been filling in for Bothell?"

"Yes, Commander," Mason said. He didn't sound annoyed, although Susan would have been surprised if he hadn't been a little irked by the whole arrangement. Mason would have been acting XO for three weeks, only to be pushed back when his new superior arrived. "I have a briefing for you personally, once you've spoken to the captain."

"I see," Susan said. It was never easy to meet a classmate from the academy when one was of superior or inferior rank. They'd started out as equals, after all. Hell, she was mildly surprised that Paul hadn't been promoted ahead of her. "Please will you take me to the captain?"

"Of course, Commander," Mason said. He nodded to the plaque on the bulkhead - the image of a roaring lion, with the words *We Lead* written underneath - and then led her towards the intership car. "I believe he's actually been looking forward to meeting you."

Susan frowned. It had barely been five hours, if that, since she'd accepted the posting. Even if Sir Travis had contacted Captain Blake at once, he wouldn't have had long to anticipate her arrival. Of course, he *might* have been sent a list of prospective XOs and ordered to pick one... she shook her head. There was no point in worrying about it. Captain Blake had probably served with Commander Bothell long enough to be annoyed at someone else coming in and taking the posting.

I'll have to review their files, she told herself. They wouldn't tell her everything, but at least they'd give her a starting point. *And then interrogate Paul when I have a moment.*

"This is the bridge," Mason said. "And the Captain's Ready Room is right here."

"Thank you," Susan said. She pressed her fingertips against the scanner. "I'll meet you here, afterwards."

CHAPTER THREE

Captain Sir Thomas Blake looked…*nervous.*

Susan studied him, as closely as she could, as she waited for the captain to stop flicking through pages on his datapad and look up at her. He was handsome enough, she supposed, for a man in his late forties; his short brown hair had yet to turn grey, while his face was lined enough to give a hint of maturity without displaying his age. The uniform he wore was expertly tailored, giving an impression of strength without revealing any paunch he might have had. And yet, there was something about his bearing that belayed his appearance. It wasn't something she could put her finger on, but it was there.

She hastily reviewed what little she knew about the captain, silently cursing her decision to study the starship itself rather than her new commanding officer. She'd read everything she could find about HMS *Edinburgh*, from her post-commissioning reports to her personnel files, but she just hadn't had time to do the same for *Vanguard.* Offhand, she honestly couldn't recall any officer being given so little time to prepare for a new assignment, although she knew it must have happened in the past. Commander Bothell would hardly be the first officer to fail to report back to duty. An accident on shore leave…

The Blake Family was well-connected, if she recalled correctly; they enjoyed the honour of having two of the Royal Navy's former heroes among their family. Maybe they weren't a first-line aristocratic family like the Fitzwilliam Family, but they definitely had connections at the highest levels. Wasn't there a Blake on the Privy Council? She rather suspected there was, although she had no idea just how closely related the councillor was to the captain. It was quite possible that one was from a cadet branch of the family. But whatever connections he had, they had proved enough to grant him command of *Vanguard*. The giant battleship was hardly a garbage scow.

"Commander," Captain Blake said. His voice was flat, rather than the commanding baritone prospective officers had been taught to use at the academy. "I must say I was expecting Commander Bothell to return from Earth."

"Yes, sir," Susan said, puzzled. Surely Captain Blake *knew* that *something* had happened to his XO. The Admiralty wouldn't have forced a new XO down his throat unless his chosen XO was unavailable for some reason or another. "I received this assignment on very short notice."

"Commander Bothell was a good man," Captain Blake said. It took her several seconds to realise he was talking about his former XO in the past tense, as if the officer was dead and gone. "You have a pair of very big shoes to fill."

"Yes, sir," Susan said. *Was* Commander Bothell dead? If so, how did Captain Blake know what had happened? Or was the Captain merely treating him as if he were? It was something to raise with the Admiralty, if she had time. "I look forward to serving as your XO."

"A very good man," Captain Blake continued. "He knew what he could handle on his own, without input from me. I shall expect the same from you."

"Yes, sir," Susan said.

"Your file is quite bland," Captain Blake added, after a moment's pause. "Why *are* you qualified to serve as my XO?"

"I was in line for *Edinburgh*, sir," Susan said, unsure if she should feel insulted, embarrassed or concerned. "I already had my promotion."

"But you have not served as an XO previously," Captain Blake said. "Commander Bothell was my XO on *Thunderous*, prior to our joint transfer to *Vanguard*."

Susan puzzled over it for a long moment. It was rare, very rare, for a command team to remain in place for over two years, let alone survive a transfer to a new ship. The only time she recalled it happening had been Admiral Smith and Captain Fitzwilliam and *that* had been in wartime. There were simply too many opportunities for favouritism or for one career to overshadow the other. Had Commander Bothell deserted because he'd felt his career had stalled? It was far from impossible.

"No, sir," she said. Captain Blake had started to look impatient. "I don't pretend I know everything, sir, but I am willing to learn on the job."

"You *have* to learn on the job," Captain Blake said, curtly. "If you fail to satisfy me, Commander, you will be returned to Earth once we complete our exercises with the Americans."

"I understand," Susan said. She could see his point, but there was that undertone of...*something*...that bothered her more than she cared to admit. "I will do my best to satisfy you."

"Very good," Captain Blake said. "I believe Commander Mason has a briefing for you. He worked closely with Commander Bothell, so he is best-placed to bring you up to speed. Add your name to the watch roster, but make sure you are supervised for the first couple of watches."

"Aye, sir," Susan said, tightly. *That* was an insult, although she had a nasty feeling the captain could have justified it if she'd called him on it. *She* was no midshipwoman, fresh out of the academy and barely able to tie her shoelaces together; *she* was a naval officer with fifteen years of service under her belt. "I'm sure Commander Mason will be happy to provide supervision, if necessary."

She swallowed her irritation with an effort. "Is there anything else I need to know, sir?"

"You'll be serving on the bridge with me, rather than operating the secondary bridge," Captain Blake said. "I like having my XO where I can see him."

Her, Susan thought, silently. What the hell was going on?

"We are currently waiting for two new middies," Captain Blake concluded. "Once they are onboard, I'll be inviting my new officers - including yourself - to dinner prior to our departure. I trust you will be able to attend?"

"Yes, sir," Susan said. The odds of any officer *declining* a dinner with his commanding officer were about as low as the Admiralty promoting a midshipwoman to Grand Admiral as soon as she graduated from the academy. "I would be delighted to attend."

"Very good," Captain Blake said. "Dismissed."

Susan saluted, turned and marched out of the cabin, her mind spinning. What was *wrong* with Captain Blake? And why were all of her instincts twitching in alarm the moment she turned her back on him? She could understand a senior captain being concerned about an untrained XO - although she had served as *Cornwall's* XO for two months when her superior had had to leave the ship for a brief period - yet his conduct had been far from professional; indeed, it had been outright insulting. Just what had happened between the captain and his former XO?

"Commander," Mason said, as she stepped onto the bridge. "Do you want the grand tour or should I show you directly to my - your - office?"

"I think it would be better if you showed me to my office," Susan said. She needed a stiff drink - and a chat, where no one else could hear. "I assume it's near the bridge?"

"Near the *secondary* bridge," Mason said. He led the way through the airlock and down into Officer Country. "You'll discover that a great many cabins and offices are actually scattered through the hull, Commander, rather than concentrated in one place. *Vanguard* is built to take a shitload of damage and keep going. There's no prospect of a single hit managing to take out the entire command crew."

Susan snorted. "Does that actually happen outside bad movies?"

"*Aliens* were fictional only fifteen years ago," Mason reminded her. "And so were space pirates."

"I suppose," Susan conceded.

She rolled her eyes as they reached a stairwell and walked down to the lower decks. The idea of space pirates had been the stuff of trashy romance novels ever since humanity had advanced into space, rather than a real-life problem. It was impossible to keep a small starship operating without a nation or a very large corporation providing backing. And yet, on her first voyage, *Warspite had* run into a small group of pirates. It was unlikely there would be any others, she was sure, but the threat had been noted.

And it helps convince Parliament to increase the military budget, she thought, cynically. *As if there weren't enough real threats out there.*

"This is your office," Mason said, opening a hatch. "As you can see, Commander Bothell ran a very tight ship."

Susan shook her head as she took in the scene. The office wasn't just clean and tidy, it was organised to sheer perfection. *Everything* had its place, from the terminal on the desk to a handful of pens, a drinks machine and a large painting of the Battle of Pegasus, a copy of an original Justin Adams. She'd actually seen the original, she recalled, when it had been hung in *Warspite's* wardroom, two years after the battle. Her first commanding officer had been adamant that they hadn't been *that* close to the Indian carrier.

"He was a little OCD," Mason commented, as the hatch hissed closed behind them. "I was surprised when he failed to return from his shore leave."

"So was the captain," Susan commented. She sat down on one of the uncomfortable chairs and motioned him to take the other one, facing her. "Paul…can we talk bluntly, off the record?"

"Of course," Mason said. "Naval Regulation 538-362-3273 clearly states that two officers who shared a class at the academy may speak freely to one another, regardless of their formal ranks."

Susan smiled. "There's no such regulation."

Mason looked downcast. "You'll be astonished how much you can get away with just by quoting non-existent regulations."

"I would be astonished if *anyone* fell for *that* one," Susan said. She shook her head. "It's practically a licence for the breakdown of naval discipline."

"Perhaps," Mason said. "But it's also useful to have an informal connection, from time to time, even if it *was* shaped in the academy."

Susan shrugged. "What's wrong with the captain?"

Mason gave her a long look. It was, she knew, an awkward question. Asking a junior officer to pass judgement on a senior officer was a breach of naval etiquette, even if it went no further. A captain might pass judgement on an admiral, if he or she served on a court martial board, but anyone junior? It simply didn't happen. Hell, even if it was perfectly legal to report one's superior officer for misdeeds, it wasn't impossible that the whistleblower's career would come to a screeching halt. Betraying one's senior officers, for whatever reason, wasn't something that endeared a person to his future superiors.

"You don't need to answer," she said, "if you don't want to answer."

She kept her expression blank with an effort. Paul Mason had been more than *just* a joker, he'd been the most outgoing person in their class. She still smiled at the thought of how he'd made a pass at her, then befriended her when she'd shown no interest...and at how he'd constantly pushed the limits, just to see how far they could go. Hell, he'd cheerfully bragged of having a foursome in New Sin City. She found it hard to imagine *anything* that could silence him.

"I haven't actually had much contact with him," Mason said, finally. He glanced up at the ceiling, as if he was suddenly unwilling to meet her eyes. "Commander Bothell handled almost everything, Susan. He was practically the *real* commanding officer on the ship. The captain would come onto the bridge, but he wouldn't stand watches or *anything* unless there was something important, like a visit from a visiting dignitary. Princess Elizabeth visited us for the launch ceremony and the captain was practically kissing her ass in public, yet the moment she departed he went back to his ready room and Commander Bothell resumed command."

Susan rubbed her eyes. "And no one noticed?"

"I rather doubt it was entered in the reports," Mason said. "Commander Bothell was the one who should have filed any complaints, if necessary, and I assume he didn't say a word."

"*Vanguard* is meant to be the most powerful ship in the fleet," Susan said. "Why didn't she get a commanding officer..."

She shook her head. The answer was obvious. Captain Blake's connections had been more than enough to get him moved to *Vanguard*, a transfer that would probably be worth more than a promotion to Commodore. And his record probably wasn't bad. He was old enough to have served in the war and, presumably, he'd earned credit merely for surviving. Hadn't John Naiser managed the jump from starfighter pilot to command track in the depleted years, following the war?

"I see," she said. She wasn't sure *how* to proceed. If she contacted the Admiralty and reported the budding nightmare, Captain Blake's connections would kill her career, even if the Admiralty agreed with her. But if she kept her mouth shut, she would be compliant in…in what, precisely? Allowing someone to claim the rank without actually doing his bloody job? "What was Commander Bothell like?"

"Competent," Mason said.

Susan frowned. "You say that as though it was a bad thing."

"He did his job," Mason said. "And yes, he did most of the hard work of commanding this ship. He was approachable, always willing to listen, and yet he had no spark of insight or genius. I would honestly have said he was…well, like Fisher."

"That's bad," Susan said. Fisher had been one of their fellow cadets, back during their first year at the academy. Her family had made her join the navy and it showed; she had no enthusiasm, no inclination to actually do her best and no real urge to succeed. She'd passed her exams, by some dark miracle, but she hadn't returned the following year. "He was in command of the ship?"

"Yes," Mason said. "To all intents and purposes, he was the true commanding officer."

Susan ran her hands through her hair. If she'd known what she was getting into, she would have taken the risk of declining the promotion. It was clear the Admiralty hadn't known; they'd have sent an inspection team if they'd had good reason to think there was a major problem. And there *was* a problem. How could *she* step into the shoes of a man who had been effectively commanding a battleship?

"If he deserted," she mused, "why?"

"I don't know," Mason said. "He was always a very straight-laced officer. I would have expected him to complete his term, then retire. There was never the slightest hint of impropriety, Commander. He certainly never went to Sin City while we were orbiting the moon."

Susan frowned. "A wife? A family?"

"None," Mason said. "Susan…he actually gave me his ticket to Luna, two months ago. Just *gave* it to me."

"I don't believe it," Susan said. "He just *gave* it to you?"

"Yes," Mason confirmed. "He said I could have it, if I wanted it."

Susan shook her head. A ticket to the moon, which meant Sin City as far as most crewmen were concerned, might be sold, or used as a gambling stake, but not just given away. The crew would be given a handful of travel vouchers every so often, normally as rewards for good service. If *she'd* had one, she wouldn't give it up for anything.

She scowled down at the deck, thinking hard. Commander Bothell might have deserted...or he might have suffered an accident...or he might have been murdered. Could the *captain* have murdered him? He *had* talked about the XO in the past tense, after all. Or...or was she just being paranoid. Senior officers took loyalty seriously, as they should. And if Commander Bothell had been doing most of the work, his sudden desertion had left Captain Blake in a fix. He couldn't have wanted Susan when she lacked the experience to fill Commander Bothell's shoes.

"Then I'd better do my best to do my job," she said.

"I'm happy to accept any further travel vouchers," Mason said.

Susan gave him a rude gesture, then stood and walked over to the desk. The drawers were locked, but a touch of her fingers to the scanner opened them. Inside, there were a handful of papers, a small selection of Cadbury's chocolate bars and a navy-issue pistol. Susan picked it up and studied it, thoughtfully. The weapon felt to have been crafted for a specific person, even though it was a standard design. Further inside, there were two small packets of ammunition and a cleaning kit.

"Interesting," she mused out loud. "Was Commander Bothell a shooter?"

"Not as far as I know," Mason said. His voice became more formal. "But we *are* encouraged to practice on the firing range. Christopher - Major Andreas, the Marine CO - keeps score. There's a bottle of ship rotgut in it for the person who has the highest score, each week."

"I see," Susan said. It was a wise precaution. The Tadpoles had tried to board *Ark Royal* during the war. Having the crew armed and ready to fight back would, it was hoped, make it harder for the Royal Navy to lose ships to boarding parties. "I'll speak to him later."

She took a breath. "I think I'm ready for that tour now," she said. She'd have to file *something* to the Admiralty, even if the file remained sealed. "Is there anything I need to handle before the end of the week?"

"Yes, Commander," Mason said. "Two more middies are due here later this afternoon, unless there's *another* delay. I think you have to greet them, even if you have not yet assumed your post."

"Understood," Susan said. She rose from behind the desk. "You can take me on tour now, Paul."

"Yes, Commander," Mason said.

CHAPTER FOUR

"Hey, George," Midshipman Nathan Bosworth called. "They summoned you back today too?"

"Yep," Midshipwoman George - no one ever called her Georgina, certainly not twice - Fitzwilliam said. "How does it feel to be back at the academy?"

She smiled as they walked past the guards and into the academy itself. It had been a week since their formal graduation ceremony, a week since she'd watched her uncle give the final address before the newly-minted midshipmen were given their rank badges and a week's leave before they were dispatched to their new assignments. She stepped to one side as a crowd of cadets ran past, snapping off salutes as they saw George's uniform bars. It was truly said that the academy was one of the few places where midshipmen were saluted.

"Look at those youngsters," Nathan said. "Doesn't it make you feel *young*?"

George snorted. She was twenty; she'd signed up for the academy as soon as she'd turned sixteen, despite her father's half-hearted protests. He might have expected her to become a proper lady, to be presented to the king at her coming out party and hunt for a rich or well-connected husband at a series of balls, but she was damned if she was allowing the aristocracy to turn her brains to mush. She would sooner follow Prince Henry and renounce her title than surrender to the demands of her birth.

And her father, to his credit, had allowed her to go rather than continuing the fight.

"You're twenty-two," she said. Nathan's mother had insisted that he stay in school until he turned eighteen. "I don't think you're *that* old."

"I'm glad you feel that way," Nathan said. "But compared to some of the newer cadets, I *feel* old."

"Cling to that feeling," George advised. "You'll need it when we go back to the bottom of the pecking order."

The cadets were probably a little confused, she thought. They looked *young*; they had both cut their hair close to their scalps, as the academy required. George's dark hair and pale skin contrasted oddly with Nathan's blond good looks. And yet, they were wearing midshipmen uniforms and carrying weapons. Technically speaking, they no longer *belonged* in the academy.

She sighed, inwardly, as they made their way along the corridor. There were four years at the academy, imaginatively called First to Fourth Year. The seniors, the Fourth Years, ruled the academy; they were, to all intents and purposes, senior officers. And they could be nasty at times, bullying and harassing the younger cadets. Her uncle, when she'd asked, had pointed out that life onboard ship could be a thousand times worse, even though midshipmen and lieutenants were expected to be more mature. It was better to weed the ones who couldn't hack it out of the academy before they graduated and wound up on starships. But she'd never been entirely convinced of the logic.

"Maybe we'll be promoted quickly," Nathan said. "You can't be promoted for at least a year, unless you do something staggeringly awesome."

"I don't think you can do *anything* that will get you promoted up a grade before the earliest legal opportunity," George said. She'd looked it up; only one person had ever been promoted from midshipman to lieutenant in less than a year and that person had had to step up when her superiors died in an accident. There *had* been acting officers, of course, but they didn't stay in their temporary ranks. "We'll be middies for at least a year."

They turned into the commandant's office and paused outside the hatch. It was rare for a cadet to visit the commandant and, when it happened, it was almost always the final interview before a cadet was expelled. The office was in Officer Country, to all intents and purposes; cadets were not supposed to enter without special permission. But they'd been recalled to the academy, just to receive their new assignments...

She took a step forward and pressed her hand against the scanner. It hissed open, revealing the commandant's secretary, the formidable Mrs Kale. The cadets whispered that she'd been around since the days of Nelson, quietly steering the Royal Navy as it changed from a seafaring to a spacefaring force. Even if she was much younger, and logic suggested she couldn't be much older than fifty, she was still respected and feared. She'd been in her post for years and knew where all the bodies were buried.

"Cadet...*Midshipwoman* Fitzwilliam, reporting as ordered," George said.

"Take a seat," Mrs Kale ordered, once Nathan had identified himself. "The commandant will call you shortly."

George nodded and sat down. The seats were uncomfortable - she had a nasty feeling that that was deliberate, to remind troublemakers that they were in trouble - and she found it hard to speak, knowing that Mrs Kale was sitting there, listening to every word. She waited for the commandant to tell her where she was going, feeling her heartbeat starting to race. If she got a poor assignment, right out of the academy, her career might never get off the ground.

Unless you ask for help, her thoughts reminded her. *But you wanted to see what you could do on your own.*

She scowled, inwardly. Her uncle was the First Space Lord! It would be easy to ask him to make sure she got a dream assignment - or, for that matter, for a senior officer to *assume* the First Space Lord would intervene in her favour. But she'd know, even if no one else did, that she'd done nothing to deserve it. She wanted to *earn* her place in the Royal Navy. Her pride would admit of nothing less.

The hatch hissed open. "You may go through," Mrs Kale told them. "Leave your holdalls on the chairs."

Her expression softened, just slightly. "Good luck."

George nodded as she rose, then walked through the hatch. Commandant McWilliams was seated behind his desk, his cold stare sending shivers down her spine as he studied her for a long chilling moment before turning his attention to Nathan. She came to attention and saluted, only relaxing - slightly - when he returned the salute. They might be officers now, but they had a long way to go before they reached *his* exalted rank.

"You may be seated," the Commandant said. "Congratulations on your graduation."

"Thank you, sir," George said.

She sat down and waited, resting her hands in her lap. Whatever she got, be it an assignment to a mining scow or a survey ship, she would take it and be glad. A survey ship wouldn't be bad, even if she might wind up stuck in survey for the rest of her career. There was always the prospect of being the first person to meet a *third* alien race.

"You both graduated with high marks, both theoretical and practical," the Commandant said, shortly. "Your *practical* experience is limited, but there are...*problems* creating truly realistic training scenarios. Accordingly, you are both being assigned to HMS *Vanguard* as junior middies. I trust you both find this acceptable?"

"Yes, sir," Nathan said.

George echoed him a second later. There was little prospect of becoming first middy on *Vanguard* - if she recalled correctly, there were at least six or seven midshipmen assigned to a battleship - but it had its compensations. As long as she didn't screw up, she'd remain firmly on command track, rather than being diverted into survey or - horror of horrors - staff work. There was no way to know if her uncle had had a quiet word with the personnel department or not, but at least her grades provided justification for the assignment. She knew, without false modesty, that she'd done well.

"Mrs Kale has your travel details," the Commandant added. "You'll have an hour before your shuttle departs, so I suggest you use that time to send messages home before you arrive on *Vanguard*. You'll be very busy right from the start."

He paused. "I won't give you much advice, because you should have been paying attention in class. However" - his expression hardened for a second - " you should recall that you are *very* junior and inexperienced officers. You must *earn* the respect of the crewmen under you if you wish to proceed. *Listen* to personnel who are more experienced than yourselves, even if you outrank them. Your rank badges do not make you little gods. A single mistake can kill you."

George nodded, not daring to speak. She'd been taught to check everything, time and time again, because space was merciless. And yet, she knew all too well that a single mistake, something that could easily be overlooked, something that would be perfectly safe on Earth... could get them killed in space. She wondered, absently, just how long it would be before she was trusted to work on her own, then dismissed the thought. Having someone else check her work was just common sense.

"Thank you, sir," Nathan said.

"Good luck," the Commandant said. He rose. "Dismissed."

George and Nathan saluted, then turned and marched out of the office. Mrs Kale, without looking up from her computer terminal, held out a pair of datachips. George took hers, picked up her holdall and headed out of the hatch. Nathan followed her and, as soon as the hatch had hissed closed, he wrapped her up in a tight hug.

"*Vanguard*," he said. "A *battleship*!"

"It could be worse," George agreed, mischievously.

She pulled her reader off her belt and slotted the datachip into it. They had a shuttle flight in an hour, as the Commandant had said; she scanned the list of requirements quickly, then nodded to herself as she shut down the terminal. There was no need to make a run to the stores before they arrived on the giant battleship. She had two full changes of clothes with her - as well as extra underwear - and she shouldn't need anything else immediately. Her reader had enough books loaded to keep her content for years.

"I need to pick up an extra uniform," Nathan said. "Coming to the store?"

George sighed. "What happened to your spare?"

"Don't ask," Nathan said. "I mean it. *Really* don't ask."

"What happens in Sin City, *stays* in Sin City," George said. She'd been twice, but she hadn't cared for it very much. Cadets and spacers - and everyone else - were welcome, as long as they had money to spend.

Ironically, it was also the safest place on the moon. *No one* was fool enough to tangle with the city's authorities by mugging the guests. "Let's go."

She picked up some extra chocolate and sweets at the store, then followed Nathan down to the airlock. The shuttle docked on schedule - she was surprised to discover that there were a handful of crewmen waiting to board the craft too - and she hurried onboard. Maybe it was her imagination, but the crewmen looked tough, unwilling to suffer fools gladly. How could she give orders to them?

"It's only a short flight," Nathan said. "There's hardly any time to sleep."

"I'm too excited to sleep," George said. It was true. Everything she'd done, over the last four years, had been building towards this moment. "I'm going to read."

She opened her reader as the hatch banged closed and the shuttle took off, accessing the other files on the datachip. There was surprisingly little about *Vanguard* herself, save for a handful of deck plans that looked to be intentionally vague and a great deal of buzzwords that seemed designed for public consumption. She'd been told, back at the academy, that much of the information freely available online was inaccurate in many ways, but it didn't look as though the academy wanted *her* to be any more informed. But then, she *was* only a midshipwoman *en route* to her first posting. No doubt she'd be filled in when she arrived.

"There's very little on the command crew," Nathan observed. "And the XO slot is completely empty."

George frowned as she checked her own reader, then nodded. "It's missing completely," she said. Were they meant to look it up for themselves, while they were at the academy? Had they just failed a test? Or had something else happened? "Maybe they want to surprise us."

"Seems a bit of a petty surprise," Nathan observed. "Is that normal?"

"I don't know," George admitted. She'd tried asking her naval relatives for details of their first duty postings, but none of them had been particularly specific. Perhaps midshipmen didn't do anything spectacular; her uncle, at least, hadn't been particularly successful until the First Interstellar War. "It could be a bureaucratic mix-up."

"Or it could be a test to see how we react," Nathan speculated. "Prince Henry might have come back from Tadpole Prime to serve as XO. Or maybe it's Stellar Star herself!"

"I very much doubt it," George said, primly. The thought was amusing, but it was the kind of thing that only happened in bad movies, the ones written and produced by hacks who thought they could substitute nudity for storytelling. Given how much nudity was available on the datanet, she had a feeling they were wasting their time. "Every time you hear uncontrolled laughter rippling out of the officers' wardroom you just *know* they're watching Stellar Star."

She glanced through the rest of her reader, but found nothing else beyond basic facts she could have downloaded from the public database, if she'd wished. Shaking her head, she opened one of the latest novels from her favourite writer and settled down to read. Her uncle had been the one to introduce her to wet-navy stories and, after she'd gotten used to the tropes, she'd found she rather enjoyed them. It seemed odd to think that sailing on water could be as dangerous as travelling through interstellar space, but it could be...

There are no storms in space, she thought, wryly. *And fewer enemies.*

The intercom bleeped. "If I could have your attention please," the shuttle pilot said, "we are currently approaching HMS *Vanguard*. Passengers are reminded that we are landing in Shuttlebay Four; all passengers are to walk through the hatch and then remain within the reception bay until collected by greeting parties. Please make sure you take all personal possessions with you upon disembarking this craft, as we will be proceeding to HMS *Rubicon* shortly."

"As if we brought much," Nathan muttered.

"Good thing my sister didn't come," George muttered back. "Anne has more clothes in her room than everyone in our class, put together."

"That's a lot of clothes," Nathan said. "How much money did she waste on them?"

George shrugged. It was impossible to say just how rich her family actually was, not when half of their wealth was invested in everything from land to asteroids and industries. Her father and grandfather had steered the family through the chaos caused by the bombardment, although they'd taken quite considerable losses after the floodwaters had ravaged Earth. And, as long as some of her more idle cousins didn't get their hands on any of the steering levers, the family should be wealthy and powerful for a very long time to come.

And Anne could buy expensive gold bikinis and handbags for years without putting a serious dent in her trust fund, she thought, darkly. She'd never gotten along with her sister, who had always preferred to emulate their mother. But then, it *had* been her sister who had convinced her to shorten her name to *George*. *Father may give her money, but he'll never give her the keys to the kingdom.*

She stared down at the deck, despite the urge to stare as the shuttle approached the massive battleship. Nathan was one of her friends, one of the few who hadn't seen her as a rich bitch or as the ticket to promotion, yet even *he* sometimes showed flickers of envy. And the hell of it was that he had a point. *She* had enough money in her trust fund to get out of just about *anything* short of mass murder. There was no way she *had* to work a day in her life if she didn't want to.

"She's impressive as hell," Nathan said. A dull thump echoed through the shuttle as the craft touched down in the shuttlebay. "Ugly, too; she looks like someone crossed a hammer with a dumbbell."

"Our new home," George said.

She rose, picked up her holdall and headed for the hatch, feeling an odd twinge of nervousness. She'd been scared when she'd gone to boarding school - it was customary for aristocratic children to go to boarding school - and uncertain when she'd gone to the academy, but this was different. A screw-up at the academy might get her expelled, if it was bad enough; it wouldn't get someone dead. Here, the slightest mistake could cost the lives of her shipmates. She hesitated at the hatch, then stepped out of the shuttle and looked around the shuttlebay. A handful of other shuttles were sitting on the deck, but there was no one in sight. She followed the lines drawn on the deck through a large airlock, Nathan tagging at her heels, and into a larger room. A marine stood at the far end, weapon in hand. It was clear that *no one* was to go into the battleship without an escort.

The hatch opened with a hiss, revealing a dark-skinned woman wearing a commander's uniform. George stared, impressed. The woman's bearing said, very clearly, that she was not someone to mess with. She was followed by a tough-looking midshipman who gave her a brief once-over, then scowled at her. George shivered. Judging by his age, he was almost certainly the First Middy.

"Midshipman Bosworth, Midshipwoman Fitzwilliam?"

"Yes, Commander," Nathan said.

"I am Commander Onarina," the Commander said. "Welcome onboard HMS *Vanguard*."

"Thank you, Commander," George said.

"This is Midshipman Fraser," Commander Onarina added. "He will see to it that you're bedded down in middy quarters and give you a basic orientation. I'm afraid you'll have to hit the ground running, but your grades suggest you should be up to it."

George swallowed. The look in Fraser's eyes promised nothing, but trouble.

"Thank you, Commander, Nathan said.

"I'll speak to you all later," Commander Onarina added. She studied them both for a long moment, then straightened. "Dismissed!"

CHAPTER FIVE

"Were we ever that young and innocent?"

"Young, perhaps," Mason said. "Innocent…I think not."

Susan shook her head as the two new middies headed down the corridor, following the First Middy. The boy - it was hard to think of him as being twenty-two - looked mature enough to cope, but there was a question mark over the girl. Her file clearly stated she was twenty, having joined the navy at the earliest possible age. She'd made it through the academy, naturally, but she might well lack the maturity of someone with more life experience. Still, she'd known what she was getting into when she signed up. Susan made a mental note to keep an eye on her, then turned to Mason.

"So," she said. "You want to complete the tour?"

"Of course, Commander," Mason said.

He led the way down the corridor towards the rear turrets, chatting all the time. "The boffins came up with a new material for our internal hull," he explained, cheerfully. "In theory, if you were to detonate a nuke inside our hull, the damage would actually be minimal. No one's tried, naturally. I don't think I'd care to be the person who proposed *that* to the Admiralty."

"It would be an alarmingly realistic test," Susan agreed. "And even if the hull survived, what about the control systems?"

"That's the real question, Commander," Mason said. "The ship has countless redundancies built into the command network. In theory, we can lose four-fifths of the grid and keep operating, although there are obvious limits. There are three formal command stations within the hull - the bridge, the secondary bridge and the CIC - and we can steer the ship from Main Engineering, if necessary. She's built to take a shitload of damage, really."

"Let's hope we don't have to test it," Susan mused. "What's the real danger?"

"You're familiar with plasma cannons, I assume," Mason said, as they stepped through a series of airlocks. "*Warspite's* giant cannon was merely the first in a series of increasingly dangerous weapons. Ours are far more powerful than *Warspite's* and our rate of fire is a great deal more rapid. The real danger, however, is overheating the guns or losing containment within the plasma chamber. If the former occurs, we'd have to shut down the guns to allow them to cool; if the latter, we'd have to vent the plasma into space or risk an explosion."

"It wouldn't be as bad as a nuke," Susan pointed out.

"No," Mason agreed. "But it *would* ruin the gun completely, perhaps even melt the turret. I don't think our engineering crews could repair the damage without a shipyard."

"And it would have to be a shipyard that had the right parts in stock," Susan said. "One of the reports I glanced at said there were shipping problems."

"There are," Mason confirmed. "Each of the main guns needs to be crafted specifically for a battleship. We couldn't tear a *Warspite*-class cruiser apart to replace the missing gun."

He waved a hand as they passed through the last airlock and into the turret. A handful of crewmen were sitting at consoles, practicing their tactical skills against simulated targets, just in case the turret had to engage targets independently. It wasn't likely, given how much redundancy was built into the system, but it was a wise precaution. Susan had to admit that Commander Bothell had done an excellent job of preparing the battleship for war. She just wasn't sure about the captain.

"We can engage multiple targets simultaneously," he said, "or concentrate our fire on a single target. Even a Tadpole superdreadnaught wouldn't be able to stand against our fire for long."

Susan glanced at him. "Long enough to ram us?"

"No, according to the simulations," Mason said. "In practice...let's just say no one wants to try it and find out."

He shrugged. "Put a light cruiser like *Warspite* up against us and we'll blow her out of space casually," he added. "She won't even scratch our paint! Starfighters...they shouldn't be able to inflict much damage, save for stripping our hull of weapons and sensor blisters...and even then, we have hardened replacements in stock. It won't be easy for *anyone* to stop us from reaching our destination."

"I'm glad to hear it," Susan said. She took one final look around the turret, noting the access hatches that allowed the crew to perform repairs while the ship was underway, then followed him back through the airlock, making a mental note to return at some point and explore the turret thoroughly. "Where next?"

"Engineering," Mason said. "I think you'll like it. We have six fusion cores, each one powerful enough to keep the ship moving on its own..."

Susan couldn't help feeling tired, two hours later; Mason had shown her everything from the fusion cores to the bridge, sickbay and tactical compartment, his personal domain. *Vanguard* was lavishly equipped, compared to a cruiser; Susan rather suspected that the Admiralty intended to use the battleship as a flagship, if all hell broke loose. *Vanguard* would tend to draw fire - she was hardly unnoticeable - but she had the greatest chance of surviving a modern-day fleet battle. The war would have gone very differently if *Vanguard* had fought in the Battle of New Russia.

"I'll be happy to cede the post to you whenever you want it," Mason said, as he led the way to her cabin and opened the hatch. "Commander Bothell's next duty slot was tomorrow morning" - he glanced at his watch - "seven hours from now."

Susan nodded, frowning as they walked into the cabin. It was larger than she'd expected, easily big enough to swing a cat; a giant painting of a starship she didn't recognise hung against the far bulkhead, illuminated by a lamp mounted on the overhead. A small bookshelf, embedded in the bulkhead, housed a dozen paper books; beside it, a coffee machine bleeped for attention. Another portrait - she smiled as she recognised the king - hung above the drinks machine. She would have bet ten pounds that the XO's safe was hidden behind the portrait. It was practically *tradition*.

She looked into the sleeping compartment and frowned. The bed had been changed, probably by one of the stewards, and her holdall had been placed at the foot of the compartment, but the remainder of Commander Bothell's possessions had been left in place. He looked to have been something of a packrat, judging by the books on the shelves. It was rare for any naval officer to bring physical books onto a starship when they could load thousands, if not millions, of eBooks onto a datapad. She could download the complete works of *anyone* and read them during long deployments and boring watches.

"I'll have to get his possessions boxed up," she said, tightly. She'd slept in uncomfortable places before - her midshipwoman quarters had been cramped, smelly and thoroughly unpleasant - but she'd never slept in someone else's room. "I wish I knew what had happened to him."

"I'm surprised no one has come to collect them," Mason said. "Surely, *someone* must want to go through his possessions to look for clues."

Susan nodded, slowly. "I'll put in a request for an investigative team, then have his possessions put in storage if they're not interested. I can't see them *not* wanting to take a look."

"Technically, they should have sealed the quarters," Mason said. "But there's been a marked *lack* of interest in inspecting his possessions."

He cleared his throat. "When do you want to take up your post?"

"I'll assume the position formally tomorrow, when I take my first watch," Susan said. Seven hours...she could take a nap, then read her way through the personnel files, just to make sure she knew who she was supposed to be commanding. It would mean hitting the deck running, but she could handle it. "If that suits you..."

"Well, I'm *sure* I can serve as the *acting* XO for another few hours," Mason said, mischievously. "But I don't think I want the job permanently."

Susan frowned, inwardly. The Paul Mason she recalled had been ambitious, as ambitious as herself. And he had every right to be irked at her coming in and taking a position he might have thought to be his by right, although it was common for officers who were promoted to XO to be transferred to a whole new ship. But he hadn't tried to put up a fight or even show passive resistance. It worried her more than she cared to admit.

"I'll see you on the bridge," she said. She cast a longing look at the sleeping compartment, then back at him. "It's been a long day."

Mason nodded, then strode out of the compartment. Susan sighed, then sat down in one of the comfortable chairs. It struck her, looking around, that Commander Bothell hadn't *entertained* in his cabin. The space might be vast, compared to a junior officer's cabin, but there were no sofas, no tables, nothing that suggested he ever had guests. Her old XO on *Cornwall* had been fond of playing poker with the other senior officers - his cabin had been comfortable, if shabby - but Commander Bothell's cabin was his private place.

She shook her head in amused disbelief. It had only been nine hours since she'd been at the school, telling the teenaged children what they could expect if they joined the navy. And now she was taking up a new post on *Vanguard*, preparing to depart the system in just under a week. It wasn't what she'd been led to expect.

Rising to her feet, she padded into the bedroom and checked the compartments under the bed. The steward hadn't removed anything; Susan cursed under her breath as she poked through Commander Bothell's uniforms, then placed her holdall on the bed and removed fresh clothing for the following day. She'd have to have HMS *Vanguard* sewn onto her jacket, she reminded herself; the stewards would see to it, if she told them when they took her jacket to be cleaned. Or she could just draw new supplies from the ship's stores.

Gritting her teeth, she undressed and stepped into the shower compartment. Thankfully, *someone* had taken the original towels and replaced them with fresh ones, along with a small selection of navy-issue toiletries. She showered quickly, donned fresh underwear and walked back out into the cabin. Her body wanted sleep, but she knew she had to complete a number of tasks before she closed her eyes. Sitting down at the desk, she tapped the terminal and accessed the starship's communications network. Sending a sealed message back to the Admiralty wasn't difficult, although it ran the risk of drawing attention. If someone was monitoring her traffic…

And maybe you're just being paranoid, she told herself, firmly. *You have no reason to suspect foul play.*

She shook her head. She'd had captains she would follow into the gates of hell itself and captains who had been blustery tyrants, but she'd never known one like Captain Blake. It was hard to believe the Admiralty knew of his failings...unless Commander Bothell had been meant to keep him under control. No, that made no sense. The Admiralty wouldn't take chances with the commanding officer of a full-sized battleship. If Captain Blake had been deemed unsuitable for the post, he would have been reassigned, no matter what connections he had.

And that leaves me with a dilemma, she thought. *Just what do I do about it?*

"Record the message, then encrypt it for the personal attention of the First Space Lord, to be released if *Vanguard* is declared missing or lost," she ordered.

"Acknowledged," the terminal said. "Key the switch to record."

Susan tapped the console. "Sir, if you are receiving this message..."

She ran through a long explanation of everything that had happened since boarding *Vanguard*, from her meeting with Captain Blake to her inspection of Commander Bothell's office and concluded with an apology for not sending the message directly to the personnel department. It would have destroyed her career, she knew, even if Captain Blake had been proven unfit for command. She would have been lucky not to be shunted sideways to an asteroid mining station until her enlistment expired.

And yet, she mused, *doesn't that make me a coward?*

She brought up Commander Bothell's logs and skimmed the last few entries. It didn't take her long to decide that Commander Bothell had been detailing *everything* - his logs included references to bringing supplies onboard and a brief mention of a fight in the middy cabin - and yet, there were surprisingly few *personalised* details. Commander Bothell had no thoughts or feelings of his own, judging by his logs; there was nothing to say how *he'd* reacted to the problems facing the Royal Navy's first battleship. He'd been nothing more than his captain's right hand.

"Odd," she said, out loud.

She'd read some XO logs back at the academy and most of them had included observations and cheerfully irreverent comments. The tutor had explained that the XOs sometimes needed to vent, secure in the knowledge that no one would read their logs and take note of the comments they made, sometimes, about their commanding officers. Their personalities had shone through their words. But Commander Bothell had no personality, as far as she could tell. He spent a dozen paragraphs covering the dispute over which starship should have first dibs on a shipment of spare parts, yet no time at all covering his personal feelings. She was honestly starting to wonder what he'd been trying to hide.

Unless he suspected someone would be reading his logs, she thought. There had been one XO log that had included grumbles about a captain who refused to move on, keeping the XO and everyone below him firmly in place. She doubted his commanding officer would have been particularly amused if he'd read it. *Could the captain have been reading over his shoulder?*

It wasn't a pleasant thought. Traditionally, personal logs were inviolate, unless there was an internal security investigation underway, but the captain could unlock any file on the ship, if he chose. Someone who wanted true privacy would need to bring their own laptop onto the ship, which was against at least four different regulations. If Commander Bothell had believed that Captain Blake was reading his logs…

Definitely not a pleasant thought, Susan told herself. *And I'd better be careful what I write myself.*

She saved the message, knowing it would be transmitted to the archives on Nelson Base, then tapped out another message for Commodore Younghusband. He'd tell her what he wanted done with Commander Bothell's possessions, if he didn't want to send an investigative team to *Vanguard*. She had a feeling he'd probably just want them all boxed up and shipped back to Earth, unless something had popped up to suggest it was more than an open-and-shut case of desertion.

Shaking her head, she rose and strode over to the king's portrait, pulling it back to reveal the hidden safe. It hadn't been programmed to accept her fingerprints, she discovered; it rejected them the moment she pressed her fingertips against the scanner. She made another mental note to have the safe reprogrammed, then looked at the bookshelves. Commander Bothell, it seemed, had been fond of the science-fantasy books that had been common, before the Troubles. It suggested a whimsical nature that was at odds with his logbook entries. She opened one at random and smiled at the description of life on Mars. Two hundred years of exploration had turned up nothing to suggest that Mars had ever been inhabited, even by single-celled creatures. The only beings living on Mars were human settlers.

There was no answer from Younghusband, but she hadn't expected one. She checked her message file, just to make sure no one else was trying to contact her, then walked back into the sleeping compartment and set the alarm. Five hours of sleep was less than she needed, but she was used to getting by on very little sleep. She'd have enough time to dress, freshen up and eat something before making her way to the bridge and officially assuming her post as XO. And then...

This is a career boost, she told herself. Serving as *Vanguard's* XO should be a great step forward, opening up the prospect of commanding a fleet carrier or one of the newer battleships, when they came online. Either one would be regarded as the quickest way to become an admiral, although she knew her connections were too weak to guarantee it. *I should make the most of it.*

She scowled at the thought. There was something wrong with the captain, the former first officer had vanished under mysterious circumstances...she had the nasty feeling she'd been dropped in a cesspit. Perhaps she had been assigned to *Vanguard* purely so someone *without* serious connections could take the fall, when the situation - whatever it was - finally exploded. Captain Blake *had* to have some connections in *very* high places, while no one would give a damn about *her*.

Even paranoids have enemies, she thought, gloomily. *Paul might be my only ally on the ship and he's nothing more than a lieutenant-commander.*

She climbed into bed, turned out the light and closed her eyes. The situation might look better tomorrow, when she assumed her post...and, even if it didn't, she'd have the advantage of a few hours of sleep. Who knew? Maybe Captain Blake had just been having a very bad day. It couldn't be easy to lose a trusted XO, certainly not to desertion...hell, it would make

Captain Blake look very bad, even if he *hadn't* driven Commander Bothell to flee the service. His trust had been betrayed…

Sure, she thought, as sleep dragged her down into the darkness. *And I'm the Queen of England.*

CHAPTER SIX

"So," the first middy - Charles Fraser - said, addressing Nathan. "You two have never served on a starship before?"

"No," Nathan said. "Not unless you count *Rustbucket*..."

"That's *no, sir*," the first middy corrected. "And no, no one counts *Rustbucket* as a *real* starship."

George swallowed. Fraser was huge, intimidatingly huge...there was an air of barely-restrained violence around him that terrified her, even though she'd met no shortage of extremely dangerous men when they visited her family. His hair was cropped short; his face was battered and ugly, twisted into a perpetual scowl, as if he were smelling something disgusting under his nose. The tutors at the academy had been tough, particularly the unarmed combat instructors, but Fraser chilled her to the bone.

She followed him down the corridor, trying hard to keep from glancing around as they passed through a series of airlocks. *Rustbucket* had been fantastic - a decommissioned spacecraft turned into a training zone for cadets - but *Vanguard* was a true starship, humming with light and power. A dull *thrumming* echoed through the hull, reminding her that they were on an active starship about to power up its drives and head out into the great unknown. Dozens of crewmen walked past the midshipmen, some pushing trolleys loaded with sealed packing crates. George stared at them in silent fascination, wondering what they were doing. Shipping spare parts to the engineering decks, perhaps, or transporting ration bars to the galley? There was no way to know.

"This is middy country," Fraser said, as they stepped through yet another airlock hatch. "No one is supposed to enter, save us. Don't be surprised, however, when the XO makes an inspection every so often. We got in deep shit when Commander Bothell made an inspection and this new XO may be just as nit-picking."

"Yes, sir," Nathan said.

"Gym through there," Fraser said. He jabbed a finger at a green hatch. "Shared with some of the senior crew, but we have priority. You're meant to spend at least an hour a day in there, working to build up your muscles and generally staying healthy. Emergency stores in there" - he pointed at another hatch - "but don't take anything unless you desperately need it, as I am required to account for all the supplies. The XO may ask pointed questions."

George frowned. *Of you or of us?*

Fraser stopped outside a larger hatch. "These are our sleeping quarters," he said. His gaze crawled over George, sending shivers down her spine. "I trust that neither of you are claustrophobic?"

"We wouldn't have made it through the academy if we were," George said, refusing to allow him to intimidate her any further. "We've been in some very cramped spaces."

"I am the first middy," Fraser said. He leaned forward, his dark eyes meeting hers. "You will address me as *sir*."

George was tempted to refuse - they were of equal rank, technically - but she knew he had far more experience of shipboard duty. Besides, he *was* the first middy. She'd be under his supervision - and command - until one of them was promoted to lieutenant and moved to a private cabin.

"Yes, sir," she said, reluctantly.

Fraser eyed her for a long moment, then keyed the hatch switch. It hissed open, revealing a tiny space, barely large enough for ten bunks and ten tiny cabinets. George felt a sinking feeling as she saw a sleeping midshipman in one of the bunks, even though she *knew* not all of the midshipmen would be on duty at the same time. The compartment was so tiny that Fraser alone seemed to take up most of the space; hell, she had a nasty feeling that the only place to change was in the middle of the cabin, where everyone could see them. There were only a handful of thin curtains covering the bunks!

"There are two showers and two toilets at the far end," Fraser said. "As junior midshipmen, it is your duty to clean them every day. I will check your work and woe betide you if it is not perfect."

Nathan blinked. "I thought such duties were shared..."

"You're fit for little else at the moment," Fraser told him, curtly. He opened one of the doors to reveal a shower, barely large enough for a single person. "Wash the decks, empty the bins, check the flushers...we'll go through the rest of it later."

He turned. "You have the bunks here, nearest the hatch," he added. "Do *not* wake anyone else when you get up in the morning; some of us have to work shipboard nights. If you want to read books, play games or listen to music, make sure you wear headphones and keep your mouths shut. No one will be even *remotely* sympathetic if you get punched in the nose by a person you woke up, believe me.

"We have our own table in the wardroom, which you'll see when I give you the basic tour of the ship. Do not eat elsewhere and do not invite anyone to eat at our table without my permission. If you want a snack in the middle of the night or something along the same lines, and you can't be bothered going to the wardroom, there are ration bars in the side compartments. Remember, you have to replace any you take. Again, if you eat or drink in here, don't wake up the sleeping ugly midshipmen."

"Yes, sir," Nathan said.

"You each have one locker for your personal clothes and other such shit," Fraser added, pointing to the lockers. "Those are your *private* compartments - no one, not even the XO, will look in them without a good reason. If you need more space, tough shit. Any fancy dresses you happened to bring" - he shot George a nasty look - "will have to be spaced."

George nodded, not trusting herself to speak.

"Midshipwoman Fitzwilliam, unpack your holdall and then wait in here," Fraser concluded, shortly. "I'm going to have a little talk with Midshipman Bosworth."

"Yes, sir," George said. Judging from the look on Nathan's face, he welcomed the idea of a private chat with the first middy about as much as George herself. "I'll remain here."

She watched Fraser and Nathan leave the room, then opened her holdall and emptied it out onto the bunk. Her two spare uniforms were easy enough to hang up in the locker, but it was harder to sort out her underwear and the handful of personal effects she'd brought with her until she realised she was meant to just leave them on the bottom. It didn't strike her as being very efficient, but naval uniforms were designed to be durable as well as uncomfortable. She slotted a photograph of her parents and sister into the locker door, then reached for the chocolate on the bunk, just as the hatch reopened.

"Ah, chocolate," Fraser said. "Put it in the general stash."

George stared at him. "I bought it..."

"And now it's in the general stash," Fraser said. He inspected her locker, his eyes darkening at *something*. "Anything sent to us from Earth goes into the general stash. We'll share it out later today."

He smiled at her shocked expression. "Come with me," he ordered. "We'll give Bosworth his chance to open his bag and hide his stash."

"Yes, sir," George said. There was no point in arguing, she suspected. "Where are we going?"

Fraser led her through the hatch, down the corridor and into a small compartment. A table, chair and terminal sat, perched against the far corner; the remainder of the room was barren, completely bare. There weren't even any pictures on the bulkheads. The hatch hissed closed behind them; Fraser caught her, spun her around and pushed her against the bulkhead. She tensed, unsure if she should try to fight or not, as he glowered down at her. Up close, all alone, he was far more intimidating. She would have thought that was impossible.

"I want you to understand something," he growled. "Your family name means *nothing* on this ship. I don't give a damn if you're the heir to the Barony of Cockatrice or the next in line to inherit Buckingham Palace. Your name means *nothing* here. Do you understand me?"

"Yes, sir," George stammered.

"I am the first middy," Fraser said. He loomed over her, far too close for comfort. "That means you do as I say, whatever it is. I am *god*, as far as you are concerned. I don't give a shit if you like me or not. My job is ensuring you fit into the crew before you make a typical maggot mistake and get someone killed. Do you understand me?"

"Yes, sir," George managed.

"You are young, absurdly young," Fraser added. "Your family probably saw to it that you entered the academy early, even though the recruiters prefer prospective cadets to complete their basic schooling and enter the academy at eighteen. Don't expect any respect from me, or any of the other midshipmen, until you earn it. Do you understand me?"

George merely nodded, fighting to keep her legs from trembling. Her uncle had never told her about *this*, never implied that she would be intimidated by the first middy. And yet, some of the stories she'd read from the wet-navy era had been far worse. Midshipmen could be whipped to a bloody pulp by their superiors, if their superiors were having a bad day.

"If I catch you being derelict in your duties, or using your family name as a weapon, I will administer punishment duty," Fraser said. "Space is unforgiving, *Fitzwilliam*; this isn't *Rustbucket*, where the worst that can happen is you getting roundly mocked by your peers or kicked out for gross stupidity. A mistake here... well, you'll be lucky if all that happens is you meet the wrong end of my fists."

He stepped backwards. "Did you manage to unpack everything before I collected you?"

"Yes, sir," George said. It was hard, so hard, to keep her voice level, but she managed it. "I have everything put away, save for the chocolate."

"And that's going to be shared out tonight," Fraser said. "We're all in this together, Fitzwilliam. I won't tolerate anything that smacks of elitism among the middies. Elitism breeds resentment."

George blinked. "Like one of us being the first middy?"

"I'm the senior midshipman," Fraser said, simply. Oddly, he didn't seem inclined to bite her head off for cheek. "I didn't get this post through connections, merely through endurance."

"Yes, sir," George said.

Fraser nodded. "This room - and the privacy tubes - are the only places where we get any actual *privacy*," he said. He nodded to the terminal.

"You'll have a time slot each day to use the terminal to write messages and suchlike, if you have the chance to actually use it. You can trade personal time with the other middies, if you wish, but you're not allowed to use the terminal outside your designated slot. Unless, of course, you're studying for exams. *Those* take priority."

He smiled, rather coldly. "Any questions?"

George studied him for a long moment. "Is there anything else I need to know?"

"Plenty," Fraser said. His smile turned into a leer. "Once the ship is underway, we'll give you the *formal* welcoming ceremony. After that, you'll be one of us…assuming, of course, you survive."

He turned and strode out of the hatch. George stared after him, feeling her thoughts whirling in confusion. *No one* had told her *anything* about *this*. She wondered, briefly, if she should send a message to her family, just to ask what was going on, but she knew it would be counted as whining. Her uncle had made it very clear, when he'd told her that she'd been accepted at the academy, that he expected her to earn her rank on her own merits. There was no way he'd do anything about her minor problems. He'd been in the middle of a war.

And he was a midshipman too, she thought, grimly. *He would have gone through worse before being assigned to Ark Royal.*

She pushed the thought aside - she'd been warned, after all, that shipboard life could be difficult even when it wasn't dangerous - and followed Fraser back into the middy cabin, where Nathan was waiting for her. The sleeping midshipman was awake, chatting quietly with Nathan; he shut up, at once, when Fraser glowered at him. George nodded politely to him, then stepped back to allow Fraser to lead them both out of the compartment. She knew she'd have a chance for formal introductions soon enough.

"Luckily, his duty slot starts in an hour," Fraser commented, as soon as the hatch had hissed shut. "*Don't* be late for your duty slots; try to be there five minutes before you're actually *meant* to be there. The officer commanding will *not* be pleased; you'll be lucky if you're spending the next month cleaning the toilets with your own toothbrushes. In your case, you'll be tried and tested on the consoles before they let you take a formal duty slot, but *don't* treat it as anything other than a serious assignment. A bad report from one of the OCs could ruin your career at this early stage."

George nodded. Her uncle had told her the same thing.

"You're both on the day shift until we get you bedded in," Fraser continued. "Get out of your bunks at eight, have a shower, grab something to eat and report to the OC at nine; you'll have a full schedule waiting for you in your mailboxes. You'll get a break for lunch, probably around one or two, then another duty slot until five or six. After that, you're expected to do at least an hour in the gym every day. Make sure you have a more experienced midshipman with you until you're fully checked out on the equipment."

Nathan coughed. "Isn't it the same as the academy's equipment?"

"Yes, but I want you to be fully checked out before you try to use it without a spotter," Fraser said. "Certain machines really shouldn't be used without a spotter in any case, but we don't have the manpower to handle it. Try and see if there's someone else in the area before you start exercising."

George kept her thoughts to herself as Fraser showed them around a handful of compartments; the wardroom, serving food and drink to the crew; the bridge, the nerve centre of the giant battleship; Main Engineering, where the engineering crew kept the ship going; the tactical compartment, where she hoped she'd be working...they were starting to blur together in her head as they stopped outside one final hatch, the hatch to sickbay. A large red cross had been painted on the white airlock.

"The doctor wants to take a look at you two before clearing you for duty," Fraser explained, shortly. George winced. Medical exams at the academy were always unpleasant, even when she hadn't been injured. "Do you think you can find your way back to middy country?"

"I think so, sir," George said. She had her reader; she could download an updated deck plan, if necessary. "If we can't, we'll just ask a passer-by."

"How very feminine," Fraser sneered. His voice lowered. "And you'd be wise not to listen to that helpful passer-by, particularly when the ship is in a holding orbit. Randy was sent halfway to Main Engineering before he realised that the *helpful* crewman was anything but."

He shrugged. "Once you return, I'll introduce you to the other midshipmen and show you how to download your schedules," he added. "And then we can go through some basic lessons before you get some sleep."

George watched him go, then glanced at Nathan. "What did he say to you?"

"When we were alone?" Nathan asked. "He just told me that I'd be expected to work hard if I wanted to be cleared for shipboard duty. Oh, and we are apparently going to be welcomed onboard the ship formally, once we leave orbit."

"Oh," George said. It didn't *sound* as though Fraser had made any attempt to intimidate Nathan. But then, Nathan didn't come from aristocratic stock. His family might have a tradition of naval service, but it was very low-key. "What do you think they have in mind?"

"Probably nothing good," Nathan said. "My father never talked about his time as a midshipman."

George nodded. Her uncle hadn't said much about *his* time as a midshipman either. He was perhaps the most famous officer alive, save only for John Naiser, but he hadn't *become* famous as a midshipman. And John Naiser had *never* been a midshipman. Midshipmen were really nothing more than caterpillars, who *might* become a butterfly sometime in the far-off future. A successful naval officer wouldn't want to look back at his early years.

She sighed, then keyed the hatch. There was no point in trying to escape. It had been made clear to them, back at the academy, that failing to attend regular medical check-ups could lead to relief from duty, if the doctor had reason to believe they were concealing a dangerous medical condition. The hatch hissed open, revealing a giant sickbay. Thankfully, all of the beds within eyesight were empty.

We're near Earth, she told herself. *Any accidents will be taking place down on the surface.*

"Ah, new midshipmen," a cultured voice said. George turned to see a young man wearing a medical tunic emerging from a side door. His office, she guessed. "I'm Doctor Chung, Adam Chung. Welcome onboard."

"Thank you, sir," George said. A doctor wasn't *technically* in the chain of command - it struck her, suddenly, that *she* would have to die before

Doctor Chung could assume command - but it was wise to treat him as a superior officer. “Our medical records should have been forwarded to you.”

“They were,” Chung assured them. “But I prefer to take baseline readings myself.”

He smiled, cheerfully. “Who’s first?”

CHAPTER SEVEN

The midshipmen, Susan noted, looked like rabbits caught in the headlights of an oncoming car.

She kept her expression blank as the captain droned on, despite her amusement. Captain Blake had kept his promise - or his threat - to host a dinner party for the newcomers, inviting Susan, both new midshipmen and a handful of his older officers. The food had been excellent, the wine a pleasant compliment to the meal - although she'd been quick to order the stewards to make sure the midshipmen didn't get more than a single glass each - but the conversation had been minimal. She couldn't help recalling some of the more awkward dance and etiquette lessons of her youth, where boys and girls had stumbled around awkwardly rather than learning the ropes.

"And so I welcome you to the most powerful ship in the Royal Navy," Captain Blake finished. It was customary for the captain to give a speech, true, but not one that lasted longer than five minutes. "And I trust you will serve her faithfully."

He sat down, then nodded to Susan, who rose and lifted her glass. "Ladies and gentlemen," she said. "I give you King Charles, Princess Elizabeth and the United Kingdom of Great Britain."

She winced inwardly as the toast was echoed back by the small crowd of guests. If it had been up to her, more guests would have been invited and the tables would have been spread out, allowing the junior officers to chat without the disapproving presence of their seniors, while she and

Mason could talk to Captain Blake. Instead, there were two tables, parked far too close together. If *Vanguard* had been hosting a diplomatic dinner, she knew, Captain Blake would have a great deal of explaining to do the following morning. It would be difficult for anyone to have a private conversation without everyone overhearing.

"You have done well, filling Commander Bothell's shoes," Captain Blake said, distracting Susan from her thoughts. "I didn't expect so much when I heard you were coming."

"Thank you, sir," Susan said. It hadn't been *hard*, once she'd gotten over the surprise. The ship's various departments had been organised *perfectly*, in line with the very latest naval regulations. Commander Bothell hadn't been a little OCD, he'd been *anal*. "It's a fascinating challenge, but I think I'm getting the hang of it."

"Very good, very good," Captain Blake said. "Do you feel we can depart Sol as planned?"

"Yes, sir," Susan said. "We should have no trouble making our scheduled departure date."

She sighed, inwardly. Commander Bothell had done a *very* good job. *Vanguard* had taken on thirty new crew, including the two new midshipmen, but her various departments were already assimilating them nicely. There was nothing wrong with any of the senior crew, save for the captain himself. He'd spent the last few days either watching over her shoulder or leaving her completely on her own. If it hadn't been for that, she would have honestly been delighted with the state of affairs on *Vanguard*.

"Then I will inform the Admiralty that we will depart on schedule," Blake said. "The war games will not wait for us, unfortunately. We're going to be testing ourselves against the Yanks and *they're* not likely to make any foolish mistakes."

"I hear their planned battleships are bigger than ours," Susan said. "Are we going to be testing ourselves against one of them?"

"Only against a fleet carrier or two," Blake said. "The details haven't been set in stone."

Susan nodded. It wasn't easy to assemble over thirty starships from two different nations in a single system for war games, even if the two nations were closely allied. Something might pop up that would require one or more of the ships to be diverted at short notice or simply force the war games to be cancelled. It would have been a great deal easier to hold the war games in the Sol System, but everyone else - up to and including the Tadpoles - would have been able to watch and take notes.

Not that they won't be able to take notes now, she thought, wryly. *They just have to work harder to spy on us.*

"I wouldn't bet good money on a fleet carrier standing against our firepower," Blake said, darkly. "The Yank carriers were just bigger targets during the war."

"They've built their own version of the *Theodore Smith*-class fleet carriers now, sir," Susan reminded him. "Those ships have quite heavy armour..."

"Not enough," Blake said. "Fleet carriers have too many vulnerable points. And even if they didn't, our cannons are rated to burn through anything. They'd be fools to let us come within weapons range."

"And they'd find it hard to outrun us," Susan agreed. "Their only real hope would be slowing us down with their starfighters."

She kept her face blank as the stewards appeared, carrying great trays of spotted dick, sticky toffee pudding and real fresh cream, shipped directly from Earth or one of the lunar dairy farms. The discussion might have been interesting, it might even have been fun, but there was something about the way the captain spoke that bothered her. As if...he was reciting lines from memory, rather than actually thinking before he spoke.

"Their missiles could do us some real damage," she said, carefully. "If they took out a couple of our drive compartments..."

"The point defence will keep them back," Captain Blake said. He took a spoonful of pudding, then looked at her. "What do you make of the new middies? Particularly the girl?"

I think I'm glad you're not the one who has to work with her, Susan thought. It wouldn't be *easy* for the girl, not when her family was both a blessing and a curse. She had the nasty feeling the captain would practically have fawned on her, just in the hopes of pleasing her uncle. *And I notice you changed the subject very quickly.*

"They look to be good kids," she said. "It'll take them a while to get rid of that baby fat and turn into decent officers, but they'll make it."

It was true enough, she admitted privately, but she had other concerns. The first middy was competent enough, she supposed, yet it was clear he was brooding over his lack of promotion. Indeed, there was no *written* reason why he *hadn't* been promoted, but after meeting him Susan suspected his superiors had noted that he had a chip on his shoulder and chosen to leave him as a midshipman. And yet, the longer he stayed as a midshipman, the lower the chances of actually getting promoted. It was a situation that was just tailor-made for resentment.

There, but for the grace of God go I, she thought. She'd feared she too would be stuck on the very lowest rung, able to climb to the top if she could only reach the second rung. *I'd better keep an eye on him.*

"I will need a new steward," Captain Blake said. "If I were to offer one of them the post..."

He allowed his voice to trail off, suggestively. "It would be bad for their careers, sir," Susan said, keeping her voice level. She was starting to have an idea why Commander Bothell had deserted. Even if the captain thought he was doing some poor midshipman a favour, it would turn into a disaster. "They need to hit the deck running, not waste their time serving as stewards."

"I suppose," the captain said. "I expect you to keep me informed of their progress."

"I'll have a full report for you just prior to departure," Susan assured him. "And I won't hesitate to send one of them back to the academy if they fail to come up to snuff."

She wondered, absently, if he'd even bother to *read* the reports. The earlier documents she'd sent for his signature had come back, signed and dated, within minutes. If she'd wanted to organise a criminal ring, dedicated to stealing naval components and selling them on the black market, it would have been easy. And if the captain had signed the paperwork, he'd take the fall when the audit finally caught up with them.

"I insist on being consulted first, before anyone is sent back," the captain said. "See to it."

"Yes, sir," Susan said, irked. As XO, the responsibility was hers. The captain seemed inclined to second guess her on matters that were *her* responsibility, while allowing her free rein on matters that were technically *his.* "I'll make sure you are aware of any issues prior to sending them back to the academy."

Which would be the end of their careers, she thought, tiredly. *Poor kids.*

She took a bite of her pudding and discovered, not entirely to her surprise, that it was very good. The captain, it seemed, had ensured that *Vanguard* had a very good chef, a civilian given a temporary naval commission, rather than someone who'd been through the navy's cooking course. Although, she remembered, there was the old joke about the course being so hard that *no one* actually passed...

"You hired a good cook," she said, changing the subject herself. "Where did you get him?"

"Poached her off Lord Hunter," Captain Blake said. He sounded pleased, even though it had probably been no more challenging than offering the cook more money. "She is skilled, isn't she?"

And she shouldn't be here at all, Susan thought. *Is she even qualified to serve on a starship*?

She made a mental note to check it out later, then pushed the thought aside. Given all the other problems she had to solve, it was very much a minor issue right now. A cook couldn't cause anything like as much trouble as a poorly-trained midshipman or an older officer who had been nursing a grudge for the past five years...

"Ask her for the remainder of the pudding," the captain said. "She always makes more than strictly necessary."

"Yes, sir," Susan said.

George had attended more than her fair share of formal dinners; indeed, some of her earliest memories were of attending Christmas dinners at Buckingham Palace, once the war damage had been repaired. She'd never really liked them, even though the food had always been excellent; the combination of poor speakers who were madly in love with their own voices and society dames who were happy to prattle on about the need for marriage and countless grandchildren had long-since curbed her enthusiasm for eating out. She knew how to conduct herself at High Table, at least, but she would do everything within her power to decline an invitation.

But we didn't get much of a choice, she thought, sourly. *We couldn't decline an invitation to the captain's table without being dead.*

"I bet you're used to this sort of food all the time," Fraser muttered, leaning close so only she could hear. "Fancy dinners all the time, hey?"

"Not at all, *sir*," George muttered back. If she'd had any doubts about just how much Fraser disliked her, she would have lost them after he'd constantly given her the hardest and most demeaning tasks to do. He rode the other midshipmen hard - she had to admit he had middy country well organised - but he reserved the worst of his attitude for her. "I've been eating academy food for the last four years."

She glanced up towards where the captain was sitting, next to the XO and his tactical officer, Paul Mason. The captain had looked at her several times, she thought, and the only reason anyone would pay attention to *her* was because of her name. It wasn't *fair*, she told herself, tiredly. If only she'd been allowed to use a false name at the academy. Prince *Henry* had gotten away with it and *he'd* been the heir to the throne!

"Yes, I suppose that *would* explain the smell in the toilets," Fraser said. "Make sure you give them an extra clean tonight."

"Yes, sir," George said, resignedly.

She cursed under her breath. As much as she hated to admit it, she was starting to think that Fraser believed there were *thirty* hours in a day, instead of twenty-four. Between preparing for her role in the tactical department, reading endless briefing notes and exercising, she hardly had any time to handle the chores Fraser seemed determined to bury her in. Nathan did as much as he could, but Fraser had made it clear that *she* was to handle her own chores.

It would be so easy just to leave, she thought. Fraser had taunted her with the prospect of being put off *Vanguard* just before she left Sol, but she'd looked it up and he'd been right. If she failed to impress her superiors, she *could* be returned to the academy. It would mean the end of her career, at least on starships, but it was a possibility. *And a word of complaint from me in the right ears would ruin him.*

She gritted her teeth. It would be easy, so easy, but she was damned if she was letting him win. Her semi-cousin had gone through hell to join the Royal Marines; his stories had chilled her to the bone, even though she'd known *she* had no intention of joining the marines. And for all Fraser's best efforts, he wasn't working her anything like as hard as the marine recruits. Why, she even had twenty minutes to herself every day!

I can take it, she thought, scowling. *Whatever you pour onto me, I can take it.*

"Dismissed," the captain said, quietly.

George rose to her feet and followed Fraser, Nathan and two of the other midshipmen out of the compartment. The captain hadn't spoken a word to any of them, but she saw him watching her - again - as she walked through the hatch and out into the corridors. It had been an awkward dinner, she knew; too close to the senior officers for comfort, too formal to allow any real chatter. Even Fraser hadn't had the nerve to speak out loud.

"We leave in two days," Fraser said, after he pulled George and Nathan into the private compartment. "I am required to ask now, for the record; do either of you want to leave this ship?"

"No, sir," Nathan said.

"No, sir," George echoed.

She thought she saw a flicker of disappointment on Fraser's face, but it vanished too quickly for her to be sure. Had he really wanted to drive her into quitting, despite the risks it raised for his career? Or did he genuinely believe her inexperience made her a danger to the ship and her crew? Fraser seemed nothing more than a bully, yet much of his advice, however presented, was sound. She had the feeling he genuinely worked to care for the midshipmen under his supervision.

And he's an asshole, she thought. *It doesn't excuse anything.*

"Very well," Fraser said. "You've had most of your orientation, so tomorrow you join the main duty roster. Bosworth, you will report to the helmsman at 0800; you'll find the full details in your message box. Try not to ram the ship into any asteroids or it'll be taken out of your salary."

"Sir, the odds of us hitting an asteroid are staggeringly low," Nathan protested.

"And the odds of encountering alien life, fifteen years ago, were *also* staggeringly low," Fraser pointed out, curtly. "You're not immune to incompetence or bad luck just because you're flying a battleship instead of a starfighter."

"I've never flown a starfighter in my life," Nathan said.

"Try one of the simulators while you're at Sin City," Fraser said. "You can fly down the Death Star trench, if you like, shooting off missiles all the while. Or, if you have a friend in the training centre, you can borrow one of their simulators."

He cleared his throat. "Fitzwilliam, you will report to the tactical compartment at 0800 tomorrow," he said, addressing George. "I would suggest you made every effort to impress Commander Mason, but it's probably a waste of time. He'll just take one look at your name and approve you for active service."

"I don't think he will, sir," George said. "My uncle would go ballistic."

Fraser's face darkened. George knew, immediately, that mentioning her uncle, the First Space Lord, had been a mistake. Admiral Sir James Montrose Fitzwilliam had spent half of his term in office battling officers who put family names ahead of service records - he'd admitted there was a certain level of hypocritical humour in the whole affair - but his success had been somewhat limited. The Old Boy Network pervaded the entire navy.

"Your uncle's opinion doesn't matter," he snarled. "You'll report to Commander Mason and you'll make damn sure you do a good job."

"Yes, sir," George said.

"Good," Fraser said. His voice calmed, slightly. "I want you both to exercise, then scrub the toilets before you go to your bunks. Remember to reset your alarms and *don't* wake anyone when you get up."

George nodded. Nathan *had* accidentally awoken a midshipman on their second day, who had brutally cursed him out. Fraser had assigned extra push-ups for punishment, promising that the next punishment would be a great deal worse. George believed him. After having been jerked awake far too often at the academy, it was hard not to feel that anyone who accidentally woke up a midshipman deserved the harshest of punishments.

"Go," Fraser ordered. "And report to me, tomorrow, after you complete your first duty shifts."

George groaned. Unless she was very quick, she would have hardly any time to eat before starting her *second* duty shift. Maybe she could smuggle out a pair of ration bars and eat them on the way back to the tactical compartment. Or maybe that was a bad idea. There was no regulation against eating in the corridors, but it was frowned upon. Fraser had threatened them with being ordered to mop the corridors before, after all.

I shall survive, she thought, eying Fraser. *And I will not let you drive me away.*

"Yes, sir," she said.

CHAPTER EIGHT

It said something about the designer, Susan thought, that *Vanguard's* bridge was easily the largest in the fleet. *Warspite's* bridge had been cramped, *Cornwall's* bridge had only been marginally larger, but *Vanguard's* was easily ten times larger than her cabin, even though it was crammed with consoles, holographic displays and a handful of comfortable chairs for visiting dignitaries. She sat in the XO's chair, next to the command chair, and watched as the crew made hasty preparations to depart Sol. The omnipresent sound of the drives was growing louder, as if *Vanguard* herself was keen to depart. Susan found it hard to blame the giant battleship.

She tossed the captain a sidelong glance, careful to keep her thoughts to herself. It was standard procedure for the captain to be on one bridge and the XO to be on the other, just in case something went wrong, but Captain Blake had repeated his insistence that Susan join him on the main bridge. There *were* captains who would cheerfully allow their junior officers to watch as the ship jumped out of the system, knowing it would be their first trip away from Earth, yet *she* was an experienced spacer. She'd made her first jump on *Warspite*, over a decade ago. It just didn't make sense.

"Captain," Lieutenant Theodore Parkinson said. The communications officer looked up from his console. "All five of our escorts report ready to depart on schedule."

"Good," Captain Blake said. He glanced at the timer. "Inform them that we will depart in ten minutes, barring accidents."

Susan frowned, inwardly. Captain Blake should *also* be informing *Earth* of his intended departure, just in case the Admiralty wanted *Vanguard* to remain in the system for some reason. Most captains hurried to notify their superiors, just to enjoy the moment when they were truly independent, free of outside authority, but Captain Blake seemed oddly hesitant to cut his ties to Earth. She'd wondered if he had a wife or mistress on Earth, yet - as far as she could tell - he'd spent all his time in his cabin. And the ship's manifest didn't imply that the captain had a...companion on the ship.

Unless he's bonking a crewwoman, she thought, darkly. It would be a major scandal if he was, she knew, even if it was truly consensual. A senior officer could not have a relationship with a junior officer - or a crewman - without raising the spectre of favouritism. *But the only person who seems to see him regularly is his steward.*

She sighed to herself. A week of going through Commander Bothell's notes hadn't turned up anything interesting, beyond a handful of notes on the ship's tactical performance that she intended to study once they departed Earth. There was still no reason for his absense... she was honestly starting to wonder if he'd gone swimming in the ocean and drowned, the undercurrents carrying his body well away from the mainland. The Admiralty had ordered her to box up his possessions and send them back to Earth, but they hadn't shown any interest in searching his cabin or interviewing any friends he might have had amongst the crew. If, of course, he'd *had* friends. Commander Bothell's log entries had made him sound like a human computer, rather than a living breathing person.

Pushing the thought aside, she looked down at her console as the flood of departmental updates began to appear in front of her. *Vanguard* was a well-oiled machine, she had to admit; there had been no real problems in the week since she'd assumed the post and started to assert her authority. The suspicious part of her mind insisted that she only needed to wait for the penny to drop, but it was hard to see what was likely to go wrong. Commander Bothell had done a *very* good job.

And they wouldn't assign halfwits to a battleship, she reminded herself. Collectively, *Vanguard's* senior officers had over a hundred years of experience in their various fields, while the junior officers had been at the top of their years at the academy. *I barely need to do anything.*

"Commander," Captain Blake said. "Perhaps you would care to take the conn?"

Susan blinked in surprise. Very - very - few captains, at least in her experience, would give up the pleasure of commanding their ship as they entered or departed the Sol System. The only time it had *ever* occurred, in her experience, had been when *Cornwall* had been carrying the Second Space Lord back to Earth and *he'd* been a renowned commanding officer in his youth. But for Captain Blake to give it to *her*? It might have been a generous gesture, yet she couldn't help thinking that it was worrying. She'd seen nothing to suggest the captain was a generous person.

"Yes, sir," she said. It *was* a honour - and it would have been a greater one if she hadn't been sure there was a sting in the tail somewhere. "It would be my pleasure."

She cleared her throat. "I have the conn."

"You have the conn," the captain confirmed.

Susan braced herself as she studied the display. Technically, the captain should have left the bridge, just to avoid confusion, but he was still sitting in his command chair, watching her through dark eyes. Was this some sort of test? Or was he blind to the implications, to the suggestion he didn't trust her to handle it? Or...she glanced down at her console, then cleared her throat again. All she could do was carry out her duty and hope for the best.

"Helm," she said. "Lay in a direct course for the tramline to Terra Nova."

"Aye, Commander," Lieutenant David Reed said. He was a thin bespectacled man, a man who would have looked more natural in a university than on a starship's bridge, but his records suggested more than *mere* competence. "Course laid in."

Susan smiled, despite her worries. Reed would have had the course plotted out hours ago, along with several other potential courses, or she'd eat her uniform jacket. Hell, helmsmen were *encouraged* to play with their consoles when they weren't actually required to work, just to keep their skills sharp. *Vanguard* wasn't anything like as manoeuvrable as a cruiser or a destroyer, let alone a starfighter, but his skills might make the difference between life and death for the entire crew.

"Communications, inform Earth that we will depart in" - she glanced at the timer - "five minutes, then copy our primary datacore to Nelson Base," she ordered. The sealed message she'd prepared would be included in the dump, but it wouldn't go any further unless she was declared dead or missing. "And then make one final check with our escorts."

She sensed, more than heard, the captain stirring beside her, but he said nothing. *Vanguard* didn't need an escort - the idea was absurd, given that she was the most powerful ship in space - yet she would have one until the war games were completed. It made sense to travel in convoy, she supposed. She hadn't been on *Warspite* for her maiden voyage, but she'd heard stories from the old sweats. Losing power immediately after jumping through a tramline could have killed the entire crew.

"Aye, Commander," Parkinson said.

Susan nodded to herself. Parkinson wasn't just hyper-competent, judging by his file, but wasted in his current post. There were only a hundred communications officers who could talk to the Tadpoles, all of whom had been assigned to the embassy on Tadpole Prime after completing their training. She honestly wasn't sure *why* Parkinson had been assigned to *Vanguard*, unless *someone* at the Admiralty was anticipating either joint operations or another war. Even if *he'd* hoped for his own command, one day, it was unlikely the Admiralty would let him. There simply weren't enough officers with his skills.

I must talk to him at some point, she told herself. *And make sure he doesn't resent his position.*

"All ships confirm," Parkinson added, after a moment. "And Nelson Base has sent us a good luck message."

"Good," Susan said. If she'd been the commanding officer, she would have been delighted at the simple message. In theory, starship commanders were the masters of their ships but in practice the Admiralty could overrule any commanding officer in the Sol System. And yet, now, they were ready to head out beyond the tramline. "Helm, take us out of orbit and straight for the tramline."

"Aye, Commander," Reed said.

Susan felt the battleship *quiver* beneath her feet, but there was none of the faint sense of acceleration she recalled from her earlier posts. The doctors insisted the crews were imagining it - a compensator accident would kill the entire crew instantly, if the system failed - yet starship crewmen were equally insistent that the sensation was real. But on *Vanguard*, there was almost nothing. She eyed the console, half-convinced they weren't moving at all; it insisted the battleship was departing orbit and heading directly for the tramline. Maybe there was something different about the drives...

Or maybe the ship's too large to produce the sensation, she thought. She'd experienced it on a fleet carrier, but no carrier - not even the legendary *Ark Royal* - was anything like as solid as *Vanguard. It could be spread through the hull...*

"Picking up speed now, Commander," Reed reported. "Tramline ETA: five hours, forty minutes."

"Understood," Susan said. *Vanguard* was fast, but she needed to build up her speed gradually. A smaller ship had a very good chance of making an escape before the battleship caught up with her. "And our escorts?"

"Matching course and speed," Mason reported. He sounded oddly concerned. "Commander, a courier boat left orbit five minutes after our departure, heading for the tramline. She's matching our course and speed."

Susan glanced at Captain Blake? Coincidence? It wasn't as if the Admiralty could ban courier boats leaving orbit, even if the latest battleship was *also* leaving orbit. But a courier boat should have been easily able to outpace *Vanguard*, reaching the tramline well before the battleship. Matching course and speed was odd, to say the least.

She looked back at the display. "Do you have an ID on the boat?"

"She's civilian, Commander," Mason said. "British-flagged, but civilian."

"Spies," Captain Blake said. "Is she within active sensor range?"

Mason hesitated. Susan cursed under her breath. Was Captain Blake resuming command? If so, he should say so. It was confusing now...and, if all hell broke loose, it might well be lethal. They couldn't afford a disagreement over who was in command of the battleship if energy starships appeared and opened fire.

"She's not using active sensors, sir," Mason said, finally. "I don't think she'll be able to pull much from our hull."

Susan studied the display, thinking hard. The media? No one outside the Admiralty, as far as she knew, had any reason to suspect that *anything* had gone wrong on *Vanguard*. There had been no alert issued for Commander Bothell, no suggestion that he might have deserted... there was no reason for the media to be taking an interest. Or maybe there was. The battleship *was* going to take part in war games, after all. The media might be interested in seeing just what the Admiralty had done with the billions of pounds invested into shipbuilding by Parliament.

Captain Blake leaned forward. "Is she within weapons range?"

Susan stared. Was Blake *mad*?

"She's within missile range," Mason said, carefully. Susan couldn't help thinking he sounded nervous. Firing on hostile ships was one thing, but firing on a civilian courier boat - a *British* civilian courier boat - was insane! "I don't know what ECM countermeasures or point defence she's carrying. Hitting her might be tricky."

"I see," Captain Blake said.

Susan tensed. She couldn't allow the captain to fire on a civilian craft, not even if there was good reason to suspect it was carrying spies - or the media. It would be a black eye the navy would never recover from, tainting the career of everyone on the ship. She'd be lucky not to be hung if she allowed him to open fire. Relieving the captain of command would probably cost her everything - it would certainly be the end of her career - but it was preferable to allowing him to kill a handful of civilians...

"Keep a sharp eye on her," Captain Blake ordered. "If she comes closer, ready a marine boarding party. She shouldn't be dogging our heels."

"Aye, sir," Mason said.

Captain Blake rose. "Commander, you have the bridge," he said. "Inform me ten minutes before we jump through the tramline."

"Aye, sir," Susan said.

She kept her face expressionless as the captain strode off the bridge, despite the sweat trickling down her back. Who'd been in command? If they'd come under attack...

And, just for a moment, you were convinced he was going to fire on a civilian ship, she thought, as she settled into the command chair. *Would Paul have opened fire on his command?*

It wasn't a pleasant thought. Mason had clearly been shocked, but orders were orders...and yet, firing on a civilian craft could easily get him in deep shit. There were illegal orders, after all, and blowing the courier boat out of space probably counted. And yet, what could she do about it? Anything she did could easily be construed as mutiny. It was a nightmare. She wanted to believe the captain had just been testing his crew, but it was impossible to convince herself that that was the truth. For a moment, the captain had teetered on the brink of ordering an atrocity.

And there's no way to prove it, either, she thought. *If I took it to the Admiralty, his connections would be enough to get any charges dismissed.*

She cursed under her breath. All she could do was watch, wait...and pray that she could stop him before he went too far.

"I can't see anything," George complained. "There's nothing there."

Fraser laughed, unkindly. "You've been watching too much Stellar Star," he said. "The tramlines are *not* visible to the naked eye. Much like Stellar's clothing."

George felt her cheeks redden as she stared out of the observation blister. Fraser had told Nathan and her that their presence wasn't desired on the bridge, but - after much angry grumbling - he'd reorganised their training rotas so they could be in the observation blister during transit. She would have enjoyed it more if he hadn't spent half the time telling them just how many favours he'd had to call in to get them half an hour of free time.

She grunted as Fraser elbowed her in the back. "Did you watch the movies?"

"The naval personages in my family used to roar with mad laughter every time they came on, sir," she said, without looking back. "They thought they were hilarious."

Fraser snorted. "Even *Stellar Star VII: The Republic Kicks Arse*?"

George shrugged. "My parents never let me watch that one."

"I'll have it shown when we have a moment," Fraser said. "Really, that girl gets around the navy. She has a dozen aristocratic titles, five separate starships under her command..."

"And she's a champion Olympic diver too," Nathan put in. "The scene where she jumps fifty miles down to the water..."

"Would probably not be survivable," George said. She'd done *some* diving in school, but the idea of falling over fifty *miles* before hitting the water...it was absurd. "And how much of her clothing did she lose along the way?"

"All of it," Nathan said.

George rolled her eyes. "Why am I not surprised?"

Fraser cleared his throat. "You might want to watch carefully," he said. "We're about to jump."

"Thank you, sir," George said.

She stared out into the darkness. The stars burned constantly - there was no atmosphere in space to produce the twinkling effect - but they seemed to be fighting desperately to push back the shadows. There was a religion, she recalled, that believed the darkness between the stars belonged to the devil, while the suns belonged to God. The adherents prayed nightly for the light to drive back the darkness...and claimed that the *prevalence* of darkness was caused by human sins...

"Ten seconds," Fraser said. "Nine...eight..."

George tensed, feeling a hint of nervousness. It would be her first jump...what if something went wrong? The Puller Drive rarely failed, but when it did the results were spectacular. In five seconds, she'd be in another star system - or dead. She braced herself...

...And a faint sensation of...*something*...washed through the ship.

"I saw nothing," she complained. She'd expected the stars to blink out, then return. "I..."

"Some of the stars are in a different position," Fraser pointed out dryly, as she turned to face him. He smirked. "Welcome to Terra Nova, home-world of idiots, morons and lunatics who hate everyone from Britain, particularly government officials. The greatest export is sane people who want to live somewhere - anywhere - else; the greatest import is guns and ammunition. It is, in short, a shithole."

Nathan frowned. "Are we going to be landing there?"

"I rather doubt it," Fraser said. "Didn't you hear the part about them hating everyone from Britain? If you go to the surface, you'll be cut into tiny pieces and shipped around the globe."

"Yuck," George said.

"Quite," Fraser agreed. His smile turned into a leer. "And, now you've made your first jump, it's time to welcome you formally to the crew. Your initiation starts this evening."

"Oh," Nathan said.

They shared a look. Fraser had been dropping increasingly unpleasant hints over what was lying in store for them over the last four days, ranging from suggestions that they should bring clean underwear to make sure they were wearing bulletproof clothing. George was sure he was exaggerating, but she wasn't looking forward to the coming ordeal.

And yet, she was damned if she was letting him win.

"We'll be there," she said.

CHAPTER NINE

"You know," Mason said. "I really thought he'd do it."

Susan nodded, tightly. It had taken some finagling to find a time when Mason and she could talk in private - he was the second officer, after all, and she wasn't sure she wanted to risk leaving the captain on the bridge - but she'd had no choice. She couldn't keep the whole affair to herself or she'd go mad. Or, for that matter, do something stupid. It was just possible she was on the verge of making a terrible mistake.

"I thought he'd do it too," she confessed, as she poured them both mugs of coffee. It hadn't taken her long to locate the still - there was one on every ship, producing alcohol of dubious taste and worse quality - but she'd resisted the urge to take some of the booze for herself. "I thought I'd have to relieve him on the spot."

"It would have been easy to prove you had a right to relieve him," Mason pointed out. He took one of the mugs and nodded his thanks. "Everything on the bridge is recorded."

"That wouldn't have saved my career," Susan said. She took a chair and sipped her coffee, grimacing slightly at the taste. No one would award her points for coffee-making, whatever else she did. "What's *wrong* with him?"

It wasn't a question she dared ask anyone else. Hell, if she hadn't known Paul Mason at the academy, she wouldn't have dared ask him either. But he was the only person she thought she could trust on *Vanguard*; certainly, he was the only person she *knew* personally. And besides, he'd served under

Captain Blake for longer than anyone else, with the exception of some of the senior crewmen.

And Commander Bothell, she thought. *But I'm starting to think I know why he deserted.*

"Well, we *did* spend our time watching dirty movies together," Mason said. "He has a dark sense of humour in private."

Susan quirked an eyebrow. "And the truth?"

Mason shrugged. "I don't know him, outside of the moments we meet on the bridge," Mason said. "There were a handful of formal dinners, but otherwise Commander Bothell handled everything - and I mean everything. I think he was captain in all but name."

"I'm starting to think you're right," Susan said. "But it makes no *sense*."

She'd downloaded a copy of the captain's file while she'd been on Earth, although she hadn't had a chance to read it until she'd settled into her new post. Captain Sir Thomas Blake had a honourable record; his connections were among the best she'd seen, but he'd definitely acquitted himself well. He'd served in the war, surviving several battles with the Tadpoles, and then commanded a ship during the brief Anglo-Indian War three years later. It was a surprise that he hadn't been pushed up to Commodore or Admiral, yet it wasn't uncommon for commanding officers to resist promotion if they thought they could get away with it. A starship command was far more exciting for a dedicated officer than a desk job, even if the desk job came with considerably greater authority.

And Commander Bothell was with him for over a decade, she mused. *What were they doing together*?

Mason snickered, suddenly. "Do you think he's been replaced, somehow? A robot? Or an enemy spy?"

Susan rolled her eyes. "You've been watching too many bad movies," she said. "How could a robot have passed through the medical screening? Or an imposter duplicate the captain's DNA?"

"Maybe the captain didn't report for his routine exam," Mason said. "And if someone could get a spy into a ship, surely they could replace the DNA records on file too."

"If they have that sort of penetration they've already won," Susan pointed out. And yet, there was something about the idea that refused to die. Commander Bothell might have been the only person close enough to Captain Blake to recognise a replacement. What if someone *had* replaced the captain with an imposter? "They wouldn't *need* to replace the captain."

"It wouldn't be easy to replace someone more senior than a starship commander," Mason said, smoothly. "The Admiralty runs regular security checks."

Susan shook her head. Even if someone *could* duplicate the captain, right down to his fingerprints and DNA code, far too many things could go wrong. The command implants lodged within the captain's hand would have to be removed and reprogrammed, particularly after the incident on *Ark Royal.* Susan didn't know *precisely* what had happened, but it had to have been serious. New security measures had been introduced in record time. Hell, coming to think of it, the captain's DNA would be checked against his relatives. Alarms would sound when it was clear there was no match.

"I think you have a great career ahead of you as a low-grade movie producer," she said, finally. "But this is *reality.*"

Mason looked disappointed. "Reality is *boring.*"

"You're on a starship travelling through another star system, en route to war games with our cousins," Susan said. "What's *boring* about it?"

She dismissed the thought with a wave of her hand. "I don't understand it," she said. "The captain's file makes him out to be an experienced officer, yet the man we saw on the bridge was hardly *experienced.* He shouldn't have been promoted above midshipman, if that."

"His connections *are* very good," Mason pointed out. "Someone could have covered for him."

Susan rather doubted it. The Old Boys Network was good - very good - at making sure that most promotions went to those with the correct connections, but it was dominated by serving officers who understood the stakes. A decent officer would get a boost, true, yet a well-connected officer without competence would be pushed into a cushy desk job rather than being allowed to take command of a starship. The near-incident on the bridge only illustrated the wisdom of that policy. One disaster ran the risk of tearing the Old Boys Network apart.

It isn't enough to make sure that the right people get the right jobs, she thought, with a twinge of the old bitterness. *They have to be the right people for the right jobs.*

"Maybe," she said. "But they'd be taking one hell of a risk."

"They might not know," Mason pointed out. "Officially, there are no question marks in the captain's file."

Susan eyed him. "You've been studying the file too."

"Yeah," Mason said. "And unless there are aspects sealed away above my clearance, Commander, there's no reason to doubt that Captain Blake can handle his post."

Susan stared down at her coffee. "If there was an accident...I mean, something that happened to him."

Mason looked relieved. "I thought you were considering arranging an accident for him."

"I think the Admiralty would not be amused," Susan said, dryly. Captains had died before, in accidents, but they'd always been carefully investigated. Anyone who attempted to assassinate a commanding officer would wind up hung. "Even if he *is* a potential danger."

She cleared her throat. "If something happened to him, over the last decade, wouldn't it have been noticed?"

"There's no accident recorded in his file," Mason said. "And the only time he was in sickbay for anything more than a routine check-up was when he was badly scalded as a young officer, back during the war. There wasn't anything more to the incident."

"And he just got put back to work," Susan said.

She frowned. Back when she'd been roped into rebuilding work on Earth, she'd read a paper by a noted psychologist predicting that the human race would recover quicker than anyone expected, despite the *lack* of psychiatric help. Susan had found the paper rather amusing - civilian psychologists had never struck her as anything more than money-grubbing hypocrites - but the author had had a point. It was hard to believe that there was something uniquely terrible about losing one's home and family to rising floodwaters when hundreds of thousands of other people were in the same boat. These days, no one wasted thousands of pounds on expensive mental treatment. They just got back to work.

"I've been injured too, in combat," Mason pointed out. "It didn't do me any harm."

"It didn't do you any harm," Susan repeated, sarcastically. "Really?"

"Oh, yes," Mason said. "I may have spent three months in a hospital on the moon, but there were some really cute nurses and a doctor who had an enormous..."

"I don't want to know," Susan said, quickly. Given how often Mason had visited Sin City, while they'd been at the academy, she was surprised he'd done as well as he had on his exams. "And I'm sure *that* wasn't on the approved list of treatments."

"It should be," Mason said. "Do you know one of the nurses used to..."

"No," Susan said. She was no prude, but she'd heard enough exaggerated stories of sexual conquests during her time as a midshipwoman to take them all with a grain of salt. Besides, she hadn't been able to fund trips to Sin City for herself. "And I don't want to know either."

Mason shrugged. "So," he said. "What are we going to do?"

"*You're* not going to do anything, beyond keeping copies of my notes," Susan said. It was heartening to realise that Mason was prepared to risk his own career to help her, but she wasn't about to let him throw away his prospects for nothing. "I'll keep an eye on him and stay on the bridge as much as possible."

"He does seem willing to let you handle everything," Mason noted. "Has he actually been *on* the bridge since the...incident?"

Susan shook her head. As XO, it was her job to organise the duty rosters for bridge crew, but by long-standing tradition the captain had the right to choose whatever shift he liked. Somewhat to her surprise, although not entirely to her dismay, Captain Blake hadn't chosen *any* duty shift for himself. She'd organised a rotating shift consisting of herself, Mason, Reed and Parkinson, but she had no idea what the captain had in mind. Ironically, she knew she would have been relieved if the captain had openly stated he wouldn't be taking shifts when the ship wasn't actually heading into a combat situation.

"Maybe you could just claim the role by default," Mason said. "How long would you need to be an *acting* captain before they had to promote you anyway?"

"There's no fixed limit," Susan said. In theory, anyone could be promoted to any rank, as long as it was an *acting* rank, but in practice it was rare for any such rank to be automatically confirmed. "I could be the effective commanding officer for years and still not automatically succeed Captain Blake."

"Something has to be done," Mason said. "We're heading out for war games, remember, with Admiral Boskone in command. I wouldn't put good money on *him* not noticing Captain Blake's...issues. He'd go through the roof."

Susan nodded, curtly. She'd heard of Admiral Boskone. He'd been a Commodore during the Anglo-Indian War, then promoted to serve as commanding officer of the border guards for two years. He had a reputation for being a sharp-tongued bastard, although no one doubted his tactical skill. She rather doubted he would be pleased if the Royal Navy lost the war games because of *Vanguard's* commanding officer.

"Maybe I should speak to him bluntly," she mused.

Mason looked up. "Admiral Boskone?"

"Captain Blake," Susan corrected. She looked down at her mug and scowled. "Tell him that he needs to buck up before Admiral Boskone takes a good hard look at his records."

"It would cost you your career," Mason said, bluntly. "Never make a weak man look small, Susan. He'll never forgive you for it."

Susan sighed. The relationship between captain and XO had been laid down for centuries, ever since the days when the Royal Navy had been messing around in boats instead of flying starships. An XO was supposed to be the captain's *alter ego*, watching his back, taking as much of the day-to-day burdens off his shoulders...and, when asked, providing uninhibited commentary and advice. Her superior officer on *Cornwall* had never contradicted the captain in public, but she'd heard him disagree - sometimes quite loudly - with the commanding officer in private. And *his* career had never been harmed. He'd been earmarked for CO of a cruiser when Susan had left the ship for the final time.

Of course, she thought, *a commanding officer is supposed to have been an XO. He'd understand what the job entailed, even if he didn't like being contradicted in private.*

She scowled. "So what *do* I tell him?"

Mason met her eyes. "You can't tell him he's being an ass, because that could cost you everything," he said. "A simple comment in the margins of your personal report would be enough to damn you to Rockall. And you can't report him because that would probably be enough to damn your career anyway. The captain's connections will bring you down, unless you make a secretive approach and that could easily backfire. All you can really do is wait until he crosses the line, then hope you can relieve him before he causes a *real* disaster."

Susan glared at him. "You mean like nearly blowing an innocent courier boat out of space?"

"It may not have been entirely innocent," Mason pointed out. "She vanished shortly after we passed through the tramline."

"Maybe," Susan said, doubtfully. "But even if she was crammed to the gills with reporters, it wouldn't justify blowing her out of space."

She looked down at her hands. There was no reason for the courier boat to shadow *Vanguard* and her escorts all the way to the tramline, not when the courier could easily have given the warships a wide berth. No, it suggested that the courier and her crew were interested in the battleship itself, which was worrying. And yet, they could learn nothing through optical examinations of the ship's hull, certainly nothing that wasn't already public. She'd been careful to monitor off-ship traffic, but there had been nothing save for their final transmission before entering the tramline.

"All we can do is wait, then," she said. She stood and poured herself a second mug of black coffee. "What do you make of the new midshipmen?"

"Reasonably capable," Mason said. "Not a patch on us, of course."

"Of course," Susan agreed.

Mason smiled. "Fitzwilliam has a good head on her shoulders for tactical problems, it seems," he added. "Asks good questions, never makes the same mistake twice...Bosworth asked about one of the unpredictable tests and seemed a little put out when I told him it was meant to help him prepare for the unexpected, not what we *knew* we'd be facing."

"It does tend to catch people by surprise," Susan agreed. "I fought a ship that was protected by forcefields and carried long-range energy weapons."

She smiled at the memory, although it had been embarrassing at the time. An outside-context enemy would be a complete surprise, she'd been told; the *real* purpose of the test was to see how quickly she reacted to an unexpected threat, rather than something she understood and trained to face. Forcefields were the stuff of science-fantasy, like jumping through space without tramlines or sending messages at FTL speeds, even though the boffins kept claiming that they *should* be possible. But no one had produced a working forcefield, let alone a portable tramline generator. She wouldn't hold her breath waiting to see one.

"Yeah," Mason said. "I won ten pounds on that battle."

Susan gave him a cross look. "I won *fifteen* on yours."

"No wonder you were buying the drinks that night," Mason said, wryly.

"Back to the subject at hand," Susan said, "do you anticipate any major problems?"

"With our two new midshipmen?" Mason shrugged, then allowed his voice to become more formal. "They've got a lot of baby fat to lose, Commander, and much of what they learned at the academy hasn't prepared them for the reality of shipboard life. But they're good kids and have a reasonable chance of actually *mastering* their responsibilities before we go back to war."

Susan *looked* at him. "Do you think we're going to be fighting another war?"

"Humans are always fighting wars," Mason said. "The Indians are probably still smarting over the thrashing we gave them, while the Russians are brooding and the minor powers are plotting their own advance into space. And then there're the Tadpoles. They might decide to restart the war at a moment's notice."

"I hope you're being paranoid," Susan said.

"Maybe," Mason said. "But you have noticed that the government has been pouring one-third of our total revenue into the navy and shipbuilding? I don't think we were spending so much on the military during the Troubles, when we were fighting for our survival. Even now, ten years after the last war, they're still building up the fleet. Someone expects trouble."

He paused. "Not that I'm complaining," he added. "The more starships in active service, the greater the chance for a command of my own."

"I can understand that," Susan said. "I feel the same way too. A command of my own…that would be a dream come true."

She finished her second mug of coffee, then rose. "If you don't mind, I have to be on the bridge in two hours…"

"…And you want a catnap," Mason finished. He rose, putting the mug down on the table as he walked towards the door. "I'll speak to you soon, all right? You're not alone here."

"As long as the captain doesn't know it," Susan said. She met his eyes for a long moment, trying to convey her message. "There's no point in *both* of us going down in flames."

CHAPTER TEN

"You know," Nathan commented, as he looked around the tiny compartment, "this looks like a prison."

George said nothing. She was too nervous to speak. Fraser's hints of what was coming worried her, even though - so far - all that had happened was that they'd been pushed into a small compartment and told to wait while the older midshipmen prepared for the initiation. It was unlikely either of them would be physically hurt - the navy took a dim view of midshipmen hurting themselves while they were meant to be on duty - but she had a nasty feeling that they were in for some humiliation. She'd tried looking up initiation rites in the files, only to discover that each ship had its own. There had been nothing on what might be lying in wait for them.

"It won't kill us," Nathan said. He was trying to be reassuring, George realised. "I'm sure it won't hurt, either."

"Hah," George said. The files had suggested that initiation rites brought crews closer together, but they'd also stated that some crews had crossed the line. Would Fraser? She knew he disliked her, purely because of her name. "I bet you it'll be humiliating."

"Fraser will have survived his own," Nathan said. "I'm sure he wouldn't repeat something that almost killed him."

George snorted. Back at the academy, senior cadets had hazed junior cadets, insisting that they'd been treated in the same way when *they'd* been junior cadets. But there, the academy staff had kept it under firm control, ensuring that it didn't go too far. Here, on *Vanguard*, the person who was meant to supervise was Fraser. And *he* was clearly not inclined to be *nice*.

"We shall see," she muttered. The tension in her stomach had only grown worse. "And if we don't survive?"

"I'm sure they'll give us a decent funeral," Nathan said.

George gave him a one-fingered gesture. Someone dying during an initiation rite - a hazing, in less polite terms - would be a major scandal, but was Fraser too far gone to realise it? He would have to be insane to actually risk their lives, yet he might well believe they could cope with more than they could. After all, he'd been a midshipman for over five *years*. They'd barely been midshipmen for over a fortnight.

The hatch hissed open. Midshipman Randor - everyone called him Randy - Miles and Midshipman James Pettigrew stepped through, wearing long dark robes that made them look like wizards, rather than starship crewmen. George wondered, as she stood, just how they'd managed to bring the clothes onto the ship, then decided the answer was probably simple. If all of the midshipmen had brought one set, they wouldn't need any more.

"From this moment on, you do exactly as you're told, without hesitation," Randy said, sternly. "Do you understand me?"

"Yes, sir," Nathan said.

George hesitated - Randy hadn't given any sense of being genuinely *randy*, but she had the feeling he liked her no better than his superior - and then nodded in agreement. There was no point in disagreeing, not now. It would be better to save her energies for later in the initiation rite. She held herself as steady as she could, refusing to let any sign of fear show on her face despite his proximity. Beside her, Nathan did the same.

"Strip," Randy ordered.

Nathan choked. "What?"

"Strip," Randy repeated. "And that was your one warning."

George glowered at him. He expected her to strip, as though she was a prisoner in a maximum-security prison? Or, for that matter, Stellar Star in one of the innumerable times she'd been captured by a handsome enemy soldier? It was absurd...she could just walk out, refusing to take part... and yet, all the files agreed that spacers rarely respected anyone who refused to go through the initiation rites. They were part and parcel of living in space.

And he's probably seen me naked already, she thought. Hell, she was used to being naked in front of her fellow midshipmen. She'd seen *him* naked a few times too. *And I won't be giving him a show.*

She kept her eyes on him, defiantly, as she stripped off her shirt and trousers, followed by her bra and panties. They were navy-issue, she knew; there was nothing there to excite even the most depraved pervert. Resting her hands on her hips, she met his eyes as she stood there, as naked as the day she was born. Nathan was naked too, she presumed, but she refused to look away from Randy. He'd have to do more than merely order her to strip if he wanted to break her.

"Turn around," Randy ordered. George gritted her teeth, but did as she was told, keeping her hands on her hips. Her movements would be as asexual as possible. "Put your hands behind your backs."

George obeyed, then tensed as she felt a plastic tie being wrapped around her wrists, binding her hands firmly in place. She opened her mouth to protest, only to grunt in surprise as someone dropped a black hood over her head. It was hot and uncomfortable; she felt a flicker of panic before realising she could still breathe normally. Someone gripped her arm - standard female grab area, the irrelevant part of her mind noted - and turned her around, pulling her out of the hatch. She knew they couldn't be going far - somehow, she doubted the XO would be amused if two naked midshipmen were stumbling blindfolded through the corridors - but it was disconcerting. Where were they going?

She heard a hatch hiss open and braced herself as she was half-pulled into the compartment. It was still dark, inside her hood, but she could hear several people breathing, although it sounded oddly muffled. Perhaps she was imagining it? She'd endured a sensory deprivation chamber as part of her tests, back at the academy; it hadn't taken her long to start imagining she was hearing voices, even though she'd *known* they were imaginary. Hell, she'd known what she was going to face and it had still been a hellish experience. Perhaps they'd just shoved her in a closet and left her there, bound and helpless. She might be alone...

"On your knees," Fraser's voice said. It was hard to be sure, but it sounded as though he was standing right in front of her. "Now."

It wasn't easy to get down on her knees with her hands bound behind her back, but she managed it, somehow. The sound of breathing grew louder, as if the person was right next to her...or if her own breathing was echoing in her ears. Being blindfolded was more disconcerting that she'd realised. God alone knew where Nathan was, let alone the others...

"We are gathered here today," Fraser said, "to welcome two prospective crewmembers to our ship."

George giggled. She couldn't help herself. Fraser sounded like a man on the verge of performing a wedding ceremony, not someone presiding over an initiation rite. But, a second later, someone slapped her ass hard enough to sting. She bit her lip to keep from crying out at the sudden shock.

"They must be of stout heart and stouter body to serve on this ship," Fraser continued, dramatically. George heard the sound of a glass clinking and wondered, feeling a flicker of alarm, just what Fraser was drinking. "Are they ready to drink the nectar of the gods?"

"Yes," Randy said.

George tensed as she felt hands fiddling with her hood, pulling it up so her mouth was exposed. She half-expected to feel a cup being pressed to her lips, but instead she felt something warm and slimy. He had to be out of his mind! Forcing her to perform oral sex was so far beyond the line that Fraser's court martial would be the shortest formality on record, even if it *did* ruin her career. A sudden surge of anger shot through her; she opened her mouth, then bit down as hard as she could. She tasted rubber and plastic as she spewed out the remains onto the deck.

"Well, there goes a good hose," a female voice said. She sounded as though she was trying not to laugh. "Good thing you didn't actually..."

"Shut up," Fraser said. He didn't sound angry, somewhat to George's surprise. But then, he'd *wanted* her to think he was going to place his cock in her mouth. "Clearly, they are *not* ready to drink the nectar of the gods."

A ripple of laughter ran around the compartment. George tried to estimate just how many people were standing around her - all seven midshipmen? - but it was impossible to be sure of anything, save for Fraser and Randy. And Nathan. There were two other midshipwomen on the ship, yet she didn't know them that well. Their duty shifts rarely coincided enough to allow her to have a proper chat.

"They must be tested," Fraser intoned. "They will rise."

George tried to rise, but it was impossible to get off her aching knees with her hands bound behind her back. Eventually, someone took her shoulders and helped her to her feet, then pulled her forward. The deck felt colder, somehow, beneath her bare feet, although she wasn't sure if that was normal. Being without shoes on duty was probably worth an infraction or two. She walked for nearly ten minutes before she was pulled to a halt, confusing her. They wouldn't really have gone outside middy country, would they?

"The prospective midshipmen will now walk the plank," Fraser said. He sounded more distant, somehow. "Midshipwoman Fitzwilliam, walk forward."

George hesitated, then took a step forward. The deck changed beneath her feet, becoming a piece of springy plastic. It wobbled under her weight; she stopped, unsure just where she was or what she should do. Walking the plank only happened in bad pirate movies or the books her uncle had loaned her, back when she'd expressed an interest in joining the navy. There had been initiation rites in them too, she recalled, although they tended to include floggings until the victim's back ran with blood. At least Fraser didn't seem to have read *those* books.

The plastic shifted again as she took another step. Where did it lead? There wasn't a pit in the ship, was there? Unless someone had taken up some of the deck plating, allowing her to plunge down an entire level. She froze, suddenly convinced that that was *precisely* what Fraser had done. If he'd been drinking, he might not have the sense, any longer, to realise it was a terrifyingly bad idea. She could break a leg or worse...

"If she is of stout heart," Fraser said, "she will walk forward."

I'm not letting you beat me, George thought. She took a step forward, and another, and another...and then the plank gave way. There was no time to do more than take a breath before she toppled forward and landed, face-first, on something soft and yielding. She was stunned, she realised dully, but unharmed. *Fuck you, you bastard. I fucking won.*

"She is of stout heart," someone said. It sounded like Randy, but George was too stunned to be sure. "Help her up."

George felt hands helping her back to her feet, then pulling at her hood. It came free, revealing a makeshift plank hanging over a comfortable mattress. She looked around to see Fraser, Randy and Honoraria grinning at her. All three of them were wearing black robes.

"Turn around," Honoraria said. "You're nearly done."

"Thank you," George said, as Honoraria cut the plastic tie away from her wrists. Her wrists ached; they were covered in ugly red marks, which she did her best to smooth away. "Is that it?"

"More or less," Honoraria said. Fraser and Randy turned and walked away, while Honoraria passed George a black robe of her own. "You did better than me, I think. I pissed myself when I walked the plank."

She snickered. "And you *really* did a number on the hose."

George pulled her robe over her head, hoping the aches in her wrists would be gone by the morning. She had the feeling any marks would be difficult to explain to her superiors, even though *they* would have presumably gone through the same rites themselves. Honoraria watched her calmly, then held out a hand. George shook her head as she took a step forward, making sure she could walk properly. Her legs didn't feel as though they were working right.

"If you need a few minutes to gather yourself," Honoraria whispered, "we can tell them we're powdering our noses."

"No, thank you," George said. She walked through the hatch and down the corridor towards the sleeping compartment. "How did you walk me around?"

"We went around the corridor a few times while everyone else hastily changed the room," Honoraria explained. "Couldn't take you out of middy country, of course."

"Of course," George echoed.

Honoraria led her into the sleeping compartment, which was cramped. The remaining midshipmen were crammed together, cheering loudly. Someone put a glass in her hand as Fraser called for a toast; she lifted it to her lips and took a careful sip, only to have Honoraria grab the glass and tip it upwards so she drank more than she'd intended. It tasted like paint stripper, she decided; she gagged on the taste, feeling her mouth going numb, then pushed the glass aside before she could drink any more. Turning up for duty with a hangover would be disastrous.

"Just take a sobering pill before you turn in for the night," Honoraria advised. "That's what I did."

"Hey, you did great," Randy said. He slapped George on the right shoulder, hard enough to sting. "I don't think there's been a better show since..."

"Since that one with Midshipman Flowers," Honoraria said. She giggled as she took another swig of her drink. "He started to pray, loudly, right in the middle of the plank. It tipped and he almost hit the bulkhead."

"Yeah, that was funny," Randy agreed. "And *Nathan*! You did great too!"

George looked at Nathan, who was sporting a black eye. "What happened to you?"

"He pushed forward too fast," Fraser said. "Nearly got decked by accident."

"Never mind," Honoraria said. "I meant to ask, George, why George? Did you read too many Enid Blyton books as a little girl?"

George flushed, hesitating. She wasn't sure she wanted to tell them *that* little story, even though it was nothing *too* embarrassing. It would only remind Fraser of why he disliked her in the first place. Who knew if the other midshipmen felt the same way too? But they'd accepted her now...would that change, she asked herself, if she reminded them of her background?

"It's a stupid story," she said, finally. "Do you really want to hear it?"

"It can't be worse than Midshipman Lombardi's claims about the Swedish Woman's Swimming Team," Randy said. "Although that story *did* keep us warm at nights."

"Shut it," Fraser growled. "I want to hear the story."

"Very well," George said, throwing caution to the winds. "When I was young, my mother tried to groom me for the season. I'd..."

She broke off as Randy laughed, the others joining in a moment later. The aristocratic girls who had their seasons in London were sweet dainty things, too fragile to stand up to a gust of wind...or so she'd charged, during one of many arguments with her sister. George had been born and bred to the aristocracy, yet she knew she could hardly pass for a debutante attending court for the first time. The combination of short hair and muscled body would get her laughed out of London, if she'd chosen to go.

"She tried to groom me for the season," George repeated. "And every day, she would whine and moan and call me *Georgina.* I came to hate it. And eventually I only started answering to *George.*"

Fraser leaned forward. "Because you want to be a man?"

"Because I'd like to be more than a pretty bauble on some man's arm," George said, keeping her anger under tight control. She just *knew* he'd make fun of her. "Because I want to be something for myself, not for my family."

"And yet your connections make it hard for anyone to know what you've earned," Fraser pointed out. "Did you *actually* score so highly on your exams or did someone twist them in your favour?"

"My family would not arrange for me to get high marks," George said.

"I hope you're right," Fraser said. He met her eyes, just for a second. There was a dark burning hatred and resentment flickering in his gaze, then he raised his voice. "I hope that those of you who are on duty in an hour haven't been drinking. If you have, go to sickbay now and ask for a pill."

"Oh, sir," Randy moaned.

"No excuses," Fraser said. "Unless *you* want to explain why you're half-drunk on duty."

George shuddered. The XO was a formidable woman. She had no doubt that anyone who turned up drunk on duty would regret it for the rest of their short and miserable lives.

"Come with me," Fraser ordered. He led her out of the sleeping compartment and into the private room. It was a mess, pieces of plastic and rubber scattered on the floor. Her uniform - and Nathan's - had been neatly folded and placed on the shelf, next to a handful of unmarked bottles. "You're going to clean this compartment, then the sleeping compartment, once the remaining middies hit their racks."

George opened her mouth to protest - she was on duty in seven hours - then closed it again. There was no point. She'd gone through the whole rite, yet Fraser still didn't like or trust her. All she could do was keep going and hope he'd get over it, eventually.

"Yes, sir," she said. She thought about asking him if she could recover her clothes, then decided it was pointless. "I'll get right on it."

CHAPTER ELEVEN

"Bridge, this is the Secondary Bridge," Susan said. "Confirm disconnect from main command network."

"Disconnection confirmed," Lieutenant Theodore Parkinson said. "I have the conn."

"Very good," Susan said. She glanced at the secondary tactical console. "Commander Mason, run Tactical Program Alpha-One."

"Aye, Commander," Mason said. "Tactical Program Alpha-One running…now."

Susan smiled to herself as the main display lit up with a handful of red icons: a Tadpole fleet carrier and seven escort ships. Humanity didn't have *much* data on their performance - the Tadpoles were as careful about live-fire exercises as their human counterparts - but MI6 had made a number of very good guesses. She reminded herself, firmly, that the spooks might be wrong. The Tadpoles had held the firepower advantage through most of the war, after all, and produced a whole new starship design in record time.

And we'd better hope we don't go back to war against them, she thought, as the enemy ships shook down into formation and slipped into an intercept course. *They were disturbingly formidable enemies.*

"Midshipwoman Fitzwilliam," she said. "Tactical analysis?"

The young woman started, clearly surprised by the question. "Ah… they're planning to swamp us with starfighters?"

"Certainly looks that way," Susan agreed, deadpan. "And the reason they're not launching starfighters?"

Midshipwoman Fitzwilliam frowned. "They know we don't have any of our own, so they're conserving their life support packs rather than launching a CSP."

"Good," Susan agreed. She raised her voice. "Red alert! All hands to battlestations!"

"Battlestations, aye," Mason said, as alarms howled through the compartment. "Enemy carrier is launching starfighters. I say again, enemy carrier is launching starfighters."

Susan sucked in her breath as the display sparkled with deadly new icons. The Tadpoles hadn't drawn any distinction between fighters and bombers, back during the war; their plasma weapons had burned through thin-skinned human ships and ripped through their innards with ease. Now, with solid-state armour the order of the day, it was quite possible that the Tadpoles had designed a bomber-class starfighter of their own. They'd need *something* to give them an edge against heavily-armoured ships.

"Alter course," she ordered. Now the Tadpoles had launched their starfighters, they'd be doing everything they could to stay out of the battleship's range. "Lock in a pursuit course and ramp up the drives."

"Aye, Commander," Midshipman Bosworth said. He'd taken the helm console, after completing the first set of exams. "Pursuit course laid in."

Susan smiled, grimly. No one was entirely sure just how fast the newer classes of Tadpole starships could move, but unless they'd made a radically new breakthrough it was unlikely the fleet carrier could outrace *Vanguard*. Her escorts could, she assumed, yet they'd have to abandon their charge in order to escape. Their enemies had to hope their starfighters would be enough to cripple the battleship before she forced her way into weapons range.

"Enemy starfighters approaching engagement range," Midshipwoman Fitzwilliam said. She sounded nervous, even though it was only a simulation. But then, a poor showing during a simulation could slow her career, perhaps even torpedo it. "Point defence is online, ready to fire."

"Fire at will," Susan ordered. "I say again, fire at will."

The enemy starfighters fell out of their ordered formation, then ducked and weaved their way into a chaotic pattern that made it harder to score a direct hit. Civilians would stare at the formation and call it madness - no officer would propose it for a flypast unless he wanted to be relieved of duty and reassigned to yet another mining complex - but it was the only way to have any chance of survival. A single hit with a plasma cannon, even a glancing hit, would be enough to obliterate a fragile starfighter. Flying a predictable course meant certain death.

And the odds of scoring a hit are lower than the civilians assume, Susan thought, as *Vanguard's* point defence opened fire. *Space is vast and starfighters are tiny.*

"Five enemy starfighters destroyed," Midshipwoman Fitzwilliam reported. Her voice was rising, slightly. "The remainder are closing in on our hull."

"Stand by to switch point defence to antimissile duty," Susan ordered. She'd programmed the simulation, but she'd added an element of randomness to the situation. It was just possible that the enemy starfighters would have missiles as well as plasma guns. "All hands, brace for incoming..."

"Ah...missiles away," Midshipwoman Fitzwilliam said. She sounded hesitant, too hesitant; Susan made a mental note to discuss it with her later. Certain reports took priority, even if it meant interrupting one's senior officers. "Impact in nine...eight...seven..."

Susan nodded, tightly. Starfighter missiles weren't designed for long-range engagements, which gave them an edge; they were both smaller and faster than the weapons carried in *Vanguard's* missile tubes. Hitting them was tricky, even when they were making no attempt to evade enemy fire. No human could hope to perform the targeting calculations in time. It was left to the point defence computers, which had a random pattern generator deliberately confusing their fire. There was a very real chance of taking hits...

The display flashed red as three missiles struck home. "Contact nukes, Commander," Mason reported. "Damage to decks..."

"Dispatch damage control teams," Susan ordered, coldly. "Combat damage?"

"Turret Three is offline, along with a number of point defence cannons and sensor nodes," Mason said. "Tactical datanet has already adjusted to compensate."

Susan nodded. One of the many flaws in pre-war ship design had been a conviction that the datanet would remain operational, if the ship took damage. Successive battles had taught the Royal Navy the folly of that assumption, but it hadn't been until after the war that any sort of permanent fix could be contemplated. The endless series of redundancies built into the network allowed the overall system to adapt to anything less than the destruction of the entire hull...although, she had to admit, if the ship took heavy damage, the command network was likely to be completely irrelevant.

She sucked in a breath as she studied the display, leaving Mason and his subordinates to handle the damage control teams. The enemy starfighters were swooping around, ready to try to pour fire into the gash in the hull. It would have worked against another ship, even the legendary *Ark Royal*, but *Vanguard's* designers had woven armour through her decks, rendering the effort pointless. The damage control teams were already sealing off the exposed sections; the enemy starfighters could pour their fire into the gash to their heart's content, without doing serious damage. Even another nuke could be contained.

Unless they come up with something new, she thought, grimly. There *was* an element of randomness built into the simulation, after all, with concepts taken from all manner of pre-space books and movies. Who knew *just* what could go wrong? *And if it does...*

"Enemy escorts are peeling off," Mason reported. "They're turning to face us."

"Midshipwoman Fitzwilliam, target the escorts with our main guns," Susan ordered. If the Tadpoles were foolish enough to come within her range, she was happy to take advantage of it. But then, they didn't have much choice. "Continue targeting the starfighters with point defence."

"Aye, Commander," Midshipwoman Fitzwilliam said. A handful of red icons separated themselves from the other starfighters and raced away, back towards their carrier. "I think..."

She broke off. Susan sighed.

"Spit it out," she ordered.

"I think they're the bombers," Midshipwoman Fitzwilliam said. "They'd need to rearm."

"Tag them as priority targets, when they return," Susan ordered. Midshipwoman Fitzwilliam was almost certainly right. The Tadpoles would *have* to rearm their bombers if they had any hope of winning the battle. "Try to take them down before they have an opportunity to launch their missiles."

"Aye, Commander," Midshipwoman Fitzwilliam said. She paused. "Enemy destroyers are entering weapons range."

Susan leaned forward. The Tadpoles had to know *Vanguard* could run their carrier down, given enough time; their only real hope was to slow the battleship - or *ram* her. *Ark Royal* had killed a Tadpole superdreadnaught through ramming the enemy ship, after all; there was no way to be *sure* what would happen if a destroyer rammed a battleship, but she suspected the impact would, at the very least, cripple the bigger ship.

"Fire," she ordered.

The Tadpoles had designed the plasma cannons, but human scientists had taken the original concept and run with it. HMS *Warspite* had mounted a giant plasma cannon, easily five or six times more powerful than the largest weapon the Tadpoles had designed and used it, a decade ago, to cripple an Indian carrier. And *Vanguard's* plasma cannons were larger still, designed to avoid many of the problems that had made *Warspite* a flawed tool at best, a one-shot weapon at worst. The turrets spat out fire at a terrifying rate.

Targeting isn't perfect, she thought, as one enemy destroyer blew apart under *Vanguard's* fire. *Standard countermeasures against mass drivers work just as well against our cannons.*

"Turret One reports overheating," Mason said. "Their magnetic bottles are threatening to lose containment."

"Tell them to discontinue firing and run an emergency cooling routine," Susan ordered, sharply. The simulation erred on the side of caution, when it came to predicting just how many shots could be fired before the weapons started to run into problems. It would be better to have more shots to fire in combat, rather than less. "If necessary, tell them to strip out the magnetic bottle and replace it with a fresh one."

"Aye, Commander," Mason said.

"Two more destroyers taken out," Midshipwoman Fitzwilliam said. The exultation in her voice made Susan smile. Had she ever been so young? "The remaining destroyers are opening fire."

"Order the point defence to take out their missiles," Susan said. The Tadpoles were playing it smart, she noted; they wanted to force her to cope with multiple threats at the same time. But *Vanguard* was practically *designed* to handle multiple threats. "Turrets are to continue engaging the destroyers; close-range weapons are to handle the starfighters. Random pattern fire."

"Aye, Commander," Midshipwoman Fitzwilliam said.

Susan gritted her teeth as the destroyers launched a full salvo of missiles towards the battleship. They'd be easier targets than the starfighter missiles, but she would be astonished if they were contact nukes. It was much more likely they were bomb-pumped laser warheads, which would make them far more dangerous. Powerful laser beams wouldn't be enough to cripple the ship, but there was always the prospect of hitting something vital and causing a chain reaction. *Vanguard* was designed to keep such disasters from happening, yet the countermeasures had never been fully tested. The only way to be sure was to take the ship into battle.

She smiled as another enemy destroyer blew apart, the remainder still ramping up their drives as they closed in on the battleship. They'd find it easier to score hits at that range, but it was clear they also intended to ram. Midshipwoman Fitzwilliam, thankfully, seemed to have them under control; the final destroyers barely had time to launch a second salvo of missiles before they were blown into vapour. But their last shots might still prove disastrous…

"Direct hit, prow superstructure," Mason reported. More red icons flashed into existence on the status display. "Damage to inner hull…"

"Enemy starfighters concentrating on our rear," Midshipwoman Fitzwilliam added. "They're slipping into missile range."

"Launch a shipkiller keyed for remote detonation," Susan snapped. It wasn't a standard tactic, certainly not with fleet carriers or smaller ships, but those starfighters needed to be stopped. Besides, *Vanguard* had an excellent chance of surviving the tactic without taking damage. "Now!"

Midshipwoman Fitzwilliam's fingers danced over her console, but it was clear she hadn't anticipated the order in advance. It took her several minutes to set up the firing command and, by then, the enemy starfighters had already started to launch their missiles. The computers insisted that five of them had been taken out, but two survived long enough to slam into the hull and detonate. Susan felt her lips thin in disapproval - she couldn't help being reminded of Mrs Blackthorn - at the results. It had been far from perfect.

That's what simulations are for, she reminded herself, sternly. *Sort out these problems before we actually have to take the ship into battle.*

"One of our drive compartments has been disabled," Mason reported. "Main Engineering requests permission to shut it down completely."

"Granted," Susan said. *Vanguard* was overpowered, after all. They could survive losing a single drive compartment. "Order the entire section sealed off."

"Aye, Commander," Mason said.

Susan nodded as she looked at the display. There was little hope of repairing the damage to the drive compartment, certainly not quickly enough to matter. She'd have the damage control teams concentrating their efforts on damage that *could* be repaired in a hurry. The battleship wouldn't have any difficulty making her way back to a shipyard, where the drive compartment could be replaced with ease. It might need to be rebuilt from scratch, but it could be done.

"Enemy carrier coming into range," Midshipwoman Fitzwilliam said. Thankfully, she hadn't come to pieces over her failure. *That* would have severely hampered her career. "She's locking her weapons on us."

"Open fire," Susan ordered.

She allowed her lips to curve into a nasty smile as *Vanguard* opened fire, slamming plasma bolt after plasma bolt into the enemy carrier. It was anyone's guess just how much armour the Tadpoles had been adding to their latest generation of fleet carriers, but even *Vanguard* would have had problems standing up to such an immense weight of fire. And the fleet carrier, like almost all fleet carriers from before the war, mounted almost no heavy weapons on its hull. *Ark Royal* had been the only ship on both sides that had been effectively a fleet carrier and a battleship rolled into one.

And even the latest fleet carriers try to avoid combat, she thought. *The Indians learned that lesson the hard way.*

She watched, feeling a flicker of cold delight, as the enemy carrier was systematically ripped apart. The simulation had assumed a heavy layer of armour, but not enough to save the carrier; *Vanguard* inflicted too much damage, within a minute, for the carrier to have a hope of escape. A final salvo slammed deep into her hull, setting off a chain reaction that blew the entire starship into flaming debris. Susan, who had watched far too many recordings from the Battle of New Russia, couldn't help thinking that it was only just.

"Enemy starfighters are converging on us," Midshipwoman Fitzwilliam reported. "I think they're going to ram!"

"It isn't as if they have anywhere else to go," Susan said. The Tadpoles had never surrendered, although she knew a handful of prisoners had been taken in the early days of the war. Even if they *did* surrender, keeping the prisoners alive and reasonably healthy would be tricky. *Vanguard* just wasn't equipped to take non-human prisoners. "Take them out, if you can..."

The final enemy starfighters closed in, firing desperately. Two launched missiles, but the remainder just slammed into the hull. Susan quietly assessed the damage and concluded, to her relief, that it was minimal. The only serious damage had been losing the drive compartment and she would have had to lose two more before it became a major problem.

And the damage was only simulated, she thought. *A real battle might inflict much less.*

Her thoughts darkened. *Or much more...*

She tapped a code into her console, ending the simulation. The displays froze. She'd have to reconnect the secondary bridge to the main command network before leaving the compartment, but that could wait. Right now, she needed to address the crew.

"That went well," she said. She glanced from face to face. Mason looked calm and composed, while the two midshipmen looked nervous. They knew they were on the verge of having their performance dissected. "Midshipman Bosworth, Midshipwoman Fitzwilliam, go have a mug of coffee and a bite to eat, then report to my office in one hour. We'll go through your performance then, once I've had a chance to study the reports."

"Yes, Commander," Fitzwilliam said.

Susan watched the two midshipmen hurry out the hatch, then glanced at Mason. "Thoughts?"

"I want a mug of coffee too," Mason said. "Please…"

"Get back to work, you slacker," Susan said, without heat. She checked the time display and smirked, coldly. "You've got another two hours in the tactical compartment before you get a break."

"Blast," Mason said.

He cleared his throat. "Bosworth didn't try to alter course to bring other turrets to bear on the enemy, although it could be argued that he wasn't *ordered* to do anything of the sort," he said, more seriously. "Fitzwilliam took far too long to fire the shipkiller. That could have cost us quite badly if we'd been in a real engagement."

"True," Susan agreed. "But it isn't exactly a standard tactic."

"No, but it's one we're going to have to use," Mason said. "And we *did* use it during the war."

Susan nodded. The Tadpoles had designed their starfighters to take advantage of human weaknesses, but they'd missed one of the implications of nuclear-armed missiles. They could be geared to produce an EMP, which crippled plasma containment fields and destroyed any Tadpole starfighter unlucky enough to be caught in the blast. It hadn't taken them long to improvise countermeasures, but a couple of minor battles had ended badly for them because their starfighters had practically been wiped out in the first few seconds.

"We'll add it to the enhanced training routines," she said, keying another command into her console. The displays came back to life as the secondary bridge reconnected to the command datanet, showing *Vanguard's* slow crawl towards Marina. "And I'll see you tonight, for dinner."

"Yes, Commander," Mason said. "Have fun castigating the midshipmen."

"It's not fun," Susan said, dryly. The midshipmen had made mistakes, but neither of them had screwed up too badly. "It's meant to be a learning experience."

CHAPTER TWELVE

"It feels as if we're waiting to see the headmaster," Nathan said, after they'd drunk a mug of coffee each and made their way to the XO's office. "As if we're waiting…"

"Shut up," George said. She'd felt nervous before the initiation rite, but this was worse. She had failed to anticipate an order, let alone prepare for it. The XO had good reason to be annoyed with her and, she was morbidly sure, Fraser would rub it in for the next couple of weeks. "This isn't *anything* like going to see the headmaster."

"A good thing too," Nathan said. He didn't sound unhappy, but he hadn't screwed up as badly as George. "Back at my old school, they…"

"I don't want to know," George said. She stopped outside the XO's office long enough to brace herself, then pressed her fingers to the buzzer. "The worst a headmaster can do is expel you or send you to one of the borstals. That wouldn't be too bad. But here…we could be kicked off the ship."

"I don't think it would come to that," Nathan said. "If they kicked us off right now, we'd be trying to breathe vacuum."

The hatch hissed open before George could think of a rejoinder. She scowled at Nathan instead, then led the way into the compartment. It was larger than she'd expected, larger than the midshipman sleeping and communications compartments put together…and yet, at the same time, there was something oddly impersonal about it, as if the XO hadn't had the time to make the space *hers*. The only personal touch was a photograph of a dark-skinned man, a light-skinned woman and a mixed-race girl who couldn't have been older than seven. It took her a moment to realise that it had to be the XO, long before she'd joined the navy.

"Stand at ease," the XO ordered. She was sitting behind her desk, but she wasn't wasting time with petty power games. George's uncle had told her that anyone who pretended to read a datapad while you were waiting was either an asshole or insecure. "So tell me...what went wrong during the simulation?"

"I fucked...ah, messed up," George said. "I should have had the shipkiller programmed for launch before we engaged the enemy."

The XO lifted her eyebrows. "Really?"

George nodded. It would have been easy to make excuses, but she had the nasty feeling that the XO wouldn't be impressed if she started explaining, as patiently as she could, why it wasn't her fault. Certainly, she'd had no *reason* to anticipate the order, yet - in hindsight - it was an obvious tactic. *Vanguard's* armour could shrug off a contact nuke. A proximity detonation wouldn't even scorch the hull. Why *not* use a shipkiller to swat starfighters like bugs?

"One advantage of simulations," the XO said, after a pause, "is that they allow us to discover such mistakes without being in real danger. How unpleasant do you think it would have been if it was a real engagement?"

"It would have been very unpleasant, Commander," George said. She tensed, wondering just what her punishment would be. Fraser's imagination was both innovative and sadistic, but the XO had many more opportunities for making her life miserable. "They might have fired more missiles into the gash in the hull."

"They might, yes," the XO said. She glanced at a datapad, resting on her desk. "You're due in the tactical compartment this afternoon, are you not?"

"Yes, Commander," George said.

"You have two tasks," the XO told her. "First, I want a detailed analysis of the whole engagement, from start to finish. I want you to outline ways it could have gone differently, for better or worse. Do not hesitate" - her voice hardened - "to consider mistakes I made, or might have made, as well as your own. I will not be offended by a critical remark, provided you can justify it."

George swallowed. "Yes, Commander."

"Your second task is to practice reprogramming the system on the fly," the XO added. "The best tactical officers can program a command macro within seconds, minutes at most, simply by using pre-programmed shortcuts. Commander Mason will assist, if you need assistance."

And I had better need it, George thought.

She shifted uncomfortably. The academy had insisted, time and time again, that everything had to be done by the book. Her tutors had practically *sworn* that everyone on the ship, from the commanding officer to the ship's boy, read the manual before doing anything. And yet, none of the officers she'd met seemed inclined to follow the book completely. Even Fraser, as much as he might rebuke her for the slightest mistake, didn't seem bound by the rules.

The XO met her eyes. "You have a question?"

George swallowed, again. "Commander," she said," at the academy we were taught to avoid shortcuts."

"Welcome to the real world," she said, not unkindly. "It doesn't matter, on this ship, if your salute is perfect or sloppy, or if your uniform isn't folded exactly right. However, it does matter, very much, that you complete your tasks as rapidly as possible. Failing to adapt as quickly as possible to a changing situation can be disastrous."

Her eyes narrowed. "Do you understand me?"

"Yes, Commander," George said.

The XO looked at Nathan. "And do *you* feel you could have done anything differently?"

"No, Commander," Nathan said.

George resisted the urge to elbow him. She had the feeling the XO wouldn't have asked if there had been *nothing* he could have done better. His tasks had been easier than hers, but he'd still had problems. And yet, she couldn't say that out loud, not now. She'd been too busy worrying over her mistakes, while drinking coffee, to consider Nathan's mistakes…

"There are two points you should have considered, at least," the XO said, coolly. "The first was that you could have rotated the ship, allowing the disabled turret to be replaced by one of the active turrets, the ones that couldn't bring themselves to bear on the enemy ships. Why didn't you consider it?"

Nathan paled. "I didn't receive orders to rotate the ship…"

"No, but you could have *suggested* it," the XO pointed out. "Or you could have simply done it for yourself, without orders. The helmsman has authority to angle the ship to bring more weapons to bear on her targets."

She paused. "The second point is that you kept charging after the enemy carrier, even when the enemy destroyers reversed course and attempted to ram," she added. "Why was *that* a mistake?"

"It shortened the range between us and them," Nathan said, after a moment. "They didn't have as far to go to ram us."

"Correct," the XO agreed. Her voice hardened. "A destroyer ramming us would be bad, don't you think?"

"Yes, Commander," Nathan said. "However…"

He broke off. The XO fixed him with a stern look. "However?"

Nathan hesitated, then pressed on. "However, reducing our speed or even altering course would not have been effective," he said. "I think the enemy would still have had a good chance to ram."

"They might well have had a chance," the XO agreed. "*However*, your task is to make *their* task as hard as possible. Winning more time, even a minuscule amount of time, might have made the difference between our survival and destruction. *Your* task, during your time in the helm compartment, is to practice evasive manoeuvres. The next battle we face may be real."

"Yes, Commander," Nathan said.

The XO nodded. "We have a fortnight before we arrive at Marina for the war games," she added, after a moment. "I want the two of you ready to move to another department at that point. You should have had enough experience at tactical and the helm to take a place on the duty roster by then."

"Yes, Commander," George said.

She allowed herself a moment of relief. She'd enjoyed working in the tactical section, but as an officer on the command track she was expected to have at least a basic working knowledge of how the other departments functioned. Where would she go next? The helm, swapping with Nathan? Or engineering? She didn't have the specialised training of an engineering officer, but she could assist the Chief Engineer for a month while learning how he ran his section.

"And other than that," the XO said, "how are you fitting into the ship?"

George hesitated. She thought the other middies had accepted them - they were certainly much more friendly nowadays - but Fraser still hated her, still looked for excuses to assign her to unpleasant or humiliating tasks. And yet, it wasn't something she wanted to complain about, not to the XO. It would just allow Fraser the chance to prove she *didn't* belong in the navy. There was no room in the fleet for shirkers, whiners and cheats.

"We're getting used to it, Commander," Nathan said. "It's a great deal harder to find our way around the ship, as the deck plans don't quite match up with the reality, but we're learning."

The XO smiled. "The builders had problems turning the original set of plans into reality," she commented. "*Vanguard* was the first in her class, after all. Hopefully, the other ships will be easier to build now the plans have been modified to respect appearances."

She looked at George. "And you, Midshipman Fitzwilliam?"

"I've been getting used to the ship, Commander," George said. She was *not* going to tell the XO about Fraser. "It's definitely very different from *Rustbucket*."

"It would be," the XO said. "Everything works here."

She rose. "Thank you both for coming," she concluded. "You can now report to your next duty station."

"Thank you, Commander," George said.

She glanced at her watch as soon as they were outside the cabin. The XO had timed it well; they had barely seventeen minutes before they were expected at their next duty station. She checked the pair of ration bars in her uniform jacket, then glanced at Nathan. He was looking oddly pensive.

"It didn't occur to me to rotate the ship," he said. "Do you think that's going to look bad on my record?"

George frowned. In hindsight, it *had* been a stupid mistake. Outside the annual fleet display, when the king would review every Royal Navy starship in the system, there was no reason for a battleship to remain upright at all times. It wasn't a wet-navy ship, after all; it didn't matter to the crew if the ship was the right way up or not, assuming such terms had any meaning in space. Nathan could have rotated the ship easily, knowing that the point defence subroutines would compensate for the sudden shift in position.

"You made it during a simulation," she said, as reassuringly as she could. "I don't think it will be counted against you, as long as you learn from the mistake."

She sighed, inwardly. They really needed more time on the simulators, but between their duties and Fraser constantly finding them new tasks it was unlikely they'd be able to find time to do *anything*. She briefly considered appealing to reason, yet Fraser didn't seem to be particularly reasonable. There were times when George honestly wondered if he had a split personality, when he'd do something decent for the middies and then turn around just to remind her how horrible he could be.

"I hope you're right," Nathan said.

"Let's get a move on," George said, banishing thoughts of Fraser for the moment. She could outlast him, if nothing else. "We'd better be in the tactical compartment before the deadline."

Susan felt an odd sense of...worry...as she stopped outside the hatch leading into the captain's cabin. She hadn't been invited to visit; hell, the only times she'd *seen* the captain were when he'd been in his office or on the bridge. And, she had to admit, it suited her just fine. Better the captain recluse himself than do something drastic. She still wasn't sure if he'd been seriously considering firing on the courier boat or if he'd merely been testing his crew.

She braced herself, then pressed her fingers against the buzzer. The hatch slid open at once, something that puzzled her. It was possible, she supposed, that the captain had keyed her into the lock, but the automatic system should have denied her access until the captain authorised it, assuming he was in his cabin. Unless something was wrong...her hand reached for the pistol on her belt, before she told herself, quite firmly, that she was being silly. The captain was unlikely to be in real trouble.

The cabin was larger than her own, according to the ship's blueprints, but it was so crammed with clobber that it looked smaller. Captain Blake, it seemed, was a bit of a packrat. Boxes and suitcases lay everywhere, some lying open, others closed and firmly locked. She stepped forward carefully, taking a moment to admire a painting placed neatly on the bulkhead, looking around for the captain. He was sitting in a stuffed armchair, drinking from a steaming cup and reading a book. It snapped closed before she could make out the title.

"Commander," Captain Blake said. "What brings you to my humble abode?"

"I thought you would appreciate a personal report on the new midshipmen," Susan said. She found it impossible not to glance around, taking in the piles of books, chessboards and several objects she didn't recognise. Judging by what was in view, the captain had enough clothes to outfit the entire senior staff. "They're fitting in very well."

"I'm glad to hear it," Captain Blake said. "One would expect no less from the daughter of Admiral Fitzwilliam."

"Niece, sir," Susan corrected. "She's his niece."

"He clearly had a hand in raising her," Captain Blake said. "I served under him, you know, back on the border guard. He was a good officer."

Susan shrugged. She'd only met Admiral Fitzwilliam once, shortly after the Anglo-Indian War. The Admiralty had awarded the Victoria Cross to the entire crew of *Warspite* and the task force's CO - Admiral Fitzwilliam - had been the one to pin the plaque underneath the ship's commissioning plate. She rather doubted he remembered her. To him, she would have been just another wet-behind-the-ears midshipwoman.

"She probably deserves some sort of reward," the captain added. "What do you think?"

"I don't think that would be appropriate, sir," Susan said. "She has a long way to go before she's ready for promotion."

It was hard to keep the irritation out of her voice. She hadn't had as much time as she would have liked to observe the new midshipmen, but there had been no suggestion that Midshipwoman Fitzwilliam was ready to use her family name to get her way. There was certainly no sign she was a spoiled aristocratic brat like too many girls she recalled from school. But too much favouritism, too soon, could easily change a decent girl into a complete bitch. She'd seen that happen at school too.

"There will be dinners, of course, when we reach Marina," the captain said, after a moment. "Perhaps she could be invited. As the junior deck representative, of course."

That would be more of a punishment, Susan thought. *She* would have hated it, back when she'd been a junior officer: too low-ranking to relax and enjoy the meal or to sneak off early, before the innumerable speeches. *We should be saving that for someone who's been really bad.*

"The opportunity is traditionally offered to the first middy," she said, instead. She had her concerns about *him* too, but it was just possible he wouldn't see the assignment as a punishment. "But the Americans may not wish us to bring midshipmen."

Captain Blake frowned. "Traditionally, one *does* bring a midshipman or two."

"The Yanks may have different customs," Susan said. She'd reviewed the arrangements for a handful of diplomatic dinners on *Formidable*, but they'd been supervised by trained staff from the Foreign Office. Dining with an American Admiral and his staff, hopefully, would be rather less stuffy. "Besides, there are twenty-one of our ships due to attend and thirty-seven of theirs. That's nearly sixty captains alone."

And Admiral Boskone may not be too pleased if he sees you, she added, silently.

"True," the captain agreed. He looked down at the deck, resting his hands on his knees as he considered. "However, we must make sure she has an opportunity to shine."

He glanced up. "Assign her to the shuttle crews, once she's finished her time in the tactical department," he ordered. "That will broaden her mind a little too."

Susan nodded, slowly. It *was* the sort of experience young officers needed, although it tended to come *after* they'd mastered their bridge duties. And yet, it *could* be justified, if the captain remained insistent. Young officers needed to learn how to command, sooner or later, and any mistakes made in the shuttlebay wouldn't reflect too badly on the rest of her career.

And it will give her a break from bridge duties, she thought. *I've wanted to alter the training patterns for a while now.*

"Midshipman Bosworth will also require a set of non-bridge duties," she said, out loud. "I .."

"Choose one you feel suits him," the captain said, waving his hand dismissively. "I leave it with you."

Social-climber, Susan thought, rudely. At least the captain wasn't making noises about having poor Midshipwoman Fitzwilliam assigned to his personal staff. That would probably have killed her career as surely as if she'd committed mutiny in the heat of battle. It would certainly have made it impossible for anyone to take her seriously. *And do you really think Admiral Fitzwilliam will look kindly on you for coddling his niece*?

"Yes, sir," she said. "And I'll inform you when we have a complete set of tactical plans for the war games."

CHAPTER THIRTEEN

"Jump completed, Commander."

"Thank you, Mr. Reed," Susan said. "Tactical?"

"Picking up low-level signals from Marina II, but nothing threatening within immediate detection range," Mason said. "Unless it's in stealth, of course."

Susan nodded, curtly. Marina was unusual; a G2 star located roughly midway between British and American space, but not one that had given birth to either habitable planets or an asteroid belt. There was a low-level terraforming program underway on Marina II, yet without a clear settlement plan it had to be regarded as highly speculative. But then, America had plenty of small groups that wanted their own planet and were prepared to pay for it. The system was really too close to other inhabited systems to be passed lightly to a potential future enemy.

"Send our IFF to Admiral Boskone," she ordered. Unless there had been a delay, the admiral and his task force, returning from the borders, should have reached Marina ahead of *Vanguard* and her small flotilla. "Inform him that we will reach Marina in roughly ten hours from now, then order the screen to flank us."

"Aye, Commander," Parkinson said.

"Helm, set course for Marina," Susan added. "Engage."

"Aye, Commander," Reed said. Another low quiver ran through the battleship as the drives came online. "Drives online. All systems functioning at optimal levels."

Susan nodded, tightly. Commander Bothell hadn't hesitated to replace any components that were showing signs of wear and tear, despite increasingly irked complaints from the beancounters back on Earth. Military gear was tough, designed to endure months of harsh treatment, but she couldn't find any fault with Commander Bothell's procedures. A faulty component was one that might break in the midst of a battle, regardless of the bureaucratic complaints. It was cheaper to replace a drive motivator than an entire battleship.

And we can do without them burning out as we're trying to run, she thought, as the display slowly began to fill with icons. The star and its five daughter worlds were easy to detect and track, but she knew from long experience that any starships might well have altered course or changed position before their emissions had been detected and logged. *If the Americans happen to be planning an ambush...*

She smiled at the thought, then frowned. Admiral Boskone was reputed to be a hard-ass; he might well have asked the Americans to try to sneak up on *Vanguard* or sent one of his own ships to do it. The mission would have been chancy during a live-fire exercise - the near-disaster during the last set of war games had been enough to convince the Admiralty to change the rules with astonishing speed - but now, it risked nothing more than embarrassment for one side or the other. And it was unlikely that the Americans would have had any trouble predicting *Vanguard's* rough location. She would have been surprised if there hadn't been a stealthed picket in the previous system.

"Run out a shell of recon drones," she ordered, curtly. It would be costly, yet most of the drones could be recovered and refurbished. The beancounters wouldn't be pleased, but they wouldn't be pleased by anything less than the spacers leaving all their shiny new toys in the wrapping so they could be returned to the shop, if necessary. "And alter their positions randomly, so we're wrapped in a sensor haze."

"Aye, Commander," Mason said. He looked up from his console. "You're expecting someone to start playing silly buggers?"

"You never know," Susan said. "You never know."

She leaned back in the command chair and reached for her datapad. Someone had insisted, years ago, that military service was ninety-nine percent boredom and she was inclined to agree. There was little they could do, save for exchanging recorded messages, before they reached the fleet, gathering in orbit around the second planet. If they'd been at war, she would have made sure they were creeping around the system, but now? All she could really do was wait and catch up with her paperwork.

At least the midshipmen are taking advantage of the crawl to track the location of the other ships, she thought, calmly. *They won't be bored, at least.*

Civilians rarely grasped, at least in her experience, just how immeasurably *vast* a star system truly was. Every starship in human service - and the Tadpoles as well, she assumed - could have fitted comfortably into the volume of space occupied by Earth, with plenty of room left over for future construction. A fleet twice the size of the Royal Navy could be lurking within the interplanetary void and, as long as its crewmen were careful, *Vanguard* wouldn't have a hope in hell of spotting them. Naval starships travelled at immense speeds, by earthly standards, but it still took hours to cross the interplanetary gulfs.

She sighed inwardly as she skimmed down the list of reports. A note from the Boatswain that two crewmen had been brawling, probably under the influence of too much shipboard rotgut; they'd be on reduced wages for a week as punishment. Several other notes from the mess, complaining about crewmen slipping into the compartment for extra meals; she sighed and made a mental note to have a few sharp words with the chefs. The beancounters might *try* to assign a set daily ration of food to the crew, but it worked about as well as the pre-Troubles attempts to calculate just how much a child should eat. She much preferred the post-Troubles insistence that children - and crewmen - should eat as much as they wanted, then be encouraged to exercise to burn it off.

Boring, she thought, crossly. She glanced at the timer in some irritation. The midshipmen were supposed to receive their new duties, but that meeting wasn't scheduled for another two hours. If the captain was doing his bloody job, he could have taken the conn while she handled the midshipmen...she shook her head, crossly. *If I keep reading this crap while I'm on duty, I'll fall asleep in the command chair.*

"Commander," Lieutenant Charlotte Watson said. "I think I may have something here."

Susan rose and stalked over to the sensor console. She didn't know Lieutenant Watson as well as she would like, but the officer had served on *Vanguard* since before the battleship had been commissioned and there was *nothing* about her sensor suite that Watson didn't know. Mason had told Susan, back when they'd been discussing the younger officers, that Charlotte had won several prizes for detecting cloaked ships; indeed, reading between the lines, Susan had a suspicion her old friend rather fancied Charlotte. Given her pale skin, green eyes and short red hair, it was hard to blame him.

And he outranks her, Susan thought. *He can never say it out loud.*

"Show me," she ordered. She trusted Mason to be professional. "What do you have?"

"There's just a faint energy trace here," Charlotte said. She tapped an icon on her display; the trace was far too close to the battleship for Susan's comfort. "It's inching closer, I believe; I'm fairly sure the pattern is too ordered to be natural."

"Trying to get into firing position," Susan mused. She was almost insulted. The Royal Navy had not only *invented* the tactic, it was also the only power to use it to take out an entire supercarrier. "Unless, of course, it's a random spike of background energy?"

"It would be more *random*, Commander," Charlotte said. "That's a ship, not something *natural*. And it's in *just* the right position to minimise the danger of being detected by the screen."

Susan - again - cursed the captain under her breath. They had been urged *not* to light up any targets until they got too close, if only to deny any watching observers hard data on just what would draw the Royal Navy's attention, but she knew from her service on *Warspite* that letting a cruiser get too close was asking for trouble. The captain was the one who should have made the call, not his XO. And yet, she was the one on the spot.

She studied the display for a long moment, thinking fast. Assuming the trace was a cruiser with a hull-mounted plasma cannon, like *Warspite*, she was almost within firing range. And, even if it *was* just a drill, letting her within firing range would count as a loss. She could blow a *Warspite* out of space with ease, but *Warspite*-class ships were cheaper than battleships. *Vanguard* might survive the hit, yet she'd definitely need a repair yard...

And if the Yanks have somehow extended the range of the plasma cannon, she might already be taking aim, she thought. *We'd lose without ever knowing what we were playing.*

"Light her up," she ordered, reluctantly. It was highly unlikely that the American starship would actually open fire - they might pick up hints she was charging her cannon - but Susan didn't know for sure when the mystery ship would enter firing range. "And stand by point defence."

Mason looked up, sharply. Susan understood his surprise. The Americans were unlikely to open fire, true, but accidents happened. Better to be safe than sorry.

"Illuminating target...now," Charlotte said. There was a pause. "Gotcha!"

Susan smiled as the trace became an icon on the display. "What do we have?"

"American vessel...reads out as a modified *Galveston*-class light cruiser," Charlotte said. It was easy to hear the gloating tone in her voice. "Originally, a missile-armed ship, but judging from her emissions she's probably been refitted to carry a plasma cannon. They didn't build her straight from the keel up."

"Probably saw her as a temporary expedient," Mason commented. "We were nailing armour plate to fleet carriers after New Russia."

"It didn't do much good," Susan recalled. "We lost two more carriers during the Battle of Earth."

"At least they put up a better fight," Mason said. "It would have been a great deal worse if the Tadpoles had arrived on the heels of their victory at New Russia."

"Picking up an IFF," Parkinson said. "She's USS *Truxtun*."

Susan frowned. "What's a Truxtun?"

Mason grinned. "Named for Commodore Thomas Truxtun," he said. "Fought in the quasi-war with France, if I recall correctly. One of his namesakes helped provide missile defence to Britain and France during the latter stages of the Age of Unrest, when they were launching cruise missiles over the Mediterranean. My grandfather served in the Royal Navy during that time and used to tell me a great many stories."

"You *would* know that," Susan said. She cleared her throat. "Communications, inform *Truxtun* that we caught her, fair and square, and that her senior crew are welcome to dinner sometime during the war games."

"Aye, Commander," Parkinson said.

Susan allowed herself a tight smile. The test - she knew it had been a test - had been passed with flying colours. Unless, of course, *Truxtun* had a secret weapon up her sleeve...she smiled at the thought, then shrugged. The remainder of the cruise to the planet would probably be quite peaceful.

"Mr. Mason, you have the bridge," she said, when the time came to meet with the midshipmen. "Alert me at once if anything changes."

"Aye, Commander," Mason said. "I have the bridge."

Susan nodded, then rose and hurried through the hatch. The two midshipmen were already waiting outside her office, five minutes too early. They'd picked up that habit at the academy, she knew; she'd been the same, back when *she'd* graduated. Better to be early and look eager than late and look slapdash. Both midshipmen looked tired, sadly; she recalled that from her own experience too. They'd be spending half their time training and the other half learning from the older midshipmen. Sleep was an optional extra.

"Come in," she said, as they stumbled to attention. They'd learn many more shortcuts as their careers progressed, if they didn't decide they weren't cut out for shipboard life after all and request reassignment. "You both did well on the last set of tactical exercises."

"Thank you, Commander," Midshipman Bosworth said.

"Indeed, now you have your helm badge, you can be reassigned," Susan added. It looked, very much, as though both midshipmen were trying not to yawn. She didn't blame them, although she hated the thought of what her first commanding officer would have said if she'd yawned in his face. "Midshipman Bosworth" - the young man straightened to attention - "you will be reassigned to the engineering compartment, under the supervision of Chief Finch. I don't expect you to transfer to an engineering track, but it is vitally important that you learn the ins and outs of main engineering."

"Aye, Commander," Bosworth said.

"Snatch a cup of coffee, then report to Chief Finch at 1700," Susan ordered. "He'll give you your duty roster for the next fortnight, barring accidents. Good luck."

"Thank you, Commander," Midshipman Bosworth said.

Susan switched her attention to Midshipwoman Fitzwilliam. The young woman was looking tired, too tired. She was trying to hide it, obviously, but she really was pushing her limits too far. Susan felt a flicker of concern, despite her reluctance to treat Midshipwoman Fitzwilliam as anything other than just another junior officer. It was quite likely the poor girl would fall asleep at the worst possible moment.

"Midshipman Fitzwilliam, you have been assigned to the shuttlebay, under the supervision of the Boatswain, Chief Petty Officer Simon Williams," she said. She'd intended to send Midshipwoman Fitzwilliam directly to the shuttlebay, but given her current state that was likely to be dangerous. "You're due to report to the shuttlebay at 0800, so go back to middy country and get some sleep. I expect you bright-eyed and bushy-tailed tomorrow morning."

"Aye, Commander," Midshipwoman Fitzwilliam said.

"You are both relieved of all other duties until you have your new duty rosters," Susan added, after a moment. "Once you do, coordinate with the first middy to fit your midshipman duties around your assignment duties. I expect you to handle any clashes calmly and professionally."

"Aye, Commander," Bosworth said.

Susan glanced from one to the other, wondering if she should take a closer look at just what was going on in middy country. Technically, she had the power to inspect every compartment in the ship, but tradition said that middy country was to handle its own affairs unless they got *right* out of hand. Tradition had its place, she had to admit, yet there were limits. Maybe the Boatswain would make a formal complaint that would prompt an investigation.

And if that happens, it's already too late, she thought. She'd heard of wardrooms that went bad, but it had never happened on her watch. Her career might be permanently tainted, certainly if civilians wound up judging the navy. *Something else needs to be done.*

"I will speak with you after the war games," she said. "Do you have any questions?"

"Yes, Commander," Bosworth said. "Do you know if there will be any shore leave on Marina?"

Susan wondered, absently, just who'd put him up to that question. It had only been three weeks since *Vanguard's* crew had enjoyed two weeks of shore leave; even the midshipmen had had a chance to visit Earth, if they wished. And even the newcomers would have enjoyed a week of leave before they made their way to *Vanguard*. The only person who'd had their shore leave cut short was Susan herself.

"I believe the Americans have a handful of shore leave domes on the planet, but facilities are very limited," she said, resisting the urge to tell him off. "We will see what arrangements can be made after the war games."

"Yes, Commander," Bosworth said.

"Dismissed," Susan said.

She watched them go, unable to keep herself from feeling concerned. Midshipman Bosworth looked tired, but Midshipwoman Fitzwilliam looked *exhausted*. It wasn't impossible that she was having problems coping with her duties - some midshipmen took on too much during their first few months on active service - yet she should have had the common sense to admit she was having problems. Too stubborn…or too convinced she wouldn't be believed? It was impossible to do anything without her saying *something…*

Perhaps I will inspect middy country after all, Susan thought. *I could do it as part of the preparations for any formal dinners.*

The intercom chimed. "Commander, this is Parkinson," a voice said. "Admiral Boskone has sent us a message packet."

"Download it to my console," Susan ordered. If she was lucky, she'd be able to read it without having to ask the captain. "Was there anything else?"

"No, Commander," Parkinson said. "But I have been picking up more chatter from the fleet's communications officers. There's a lot of favour-trading going on."

Susan groaned. "Why am I not surprised?"

"I can see if they want anything from us," Parkinson offered. "And see if they have anything *we* might want."

"Try," Susan ordered. Communications officers *talked*. It was what they did. "But don't promise anything."

She closed the channel as the message packet appeared on her terminal, already decrypting itself. Not an eyes-only message for the captain, then. Admiral Boskone was apparently a man of few words. He intended to inspect *Vanguard* when she entered orbit, before the war games began. Reading between the lines, Susan suspected he wanted to discuss his tactical concepts too.

And find out what we can do, she added, silently. *He won't have seen a battleship before.*

Rising to her feet, she headed for the hatch. The captain would have to be warned, of course, and the ship prepared for a high-ranking guest. Somehow, she doubted the captain would stick up for his position, no matter what regulations and custom said. She just hoped he wouldn't spend the entire time kissing the admiral's ass. Admiral Boskone wasn't supposed to like flattery, but she had no way to know for sure.

And lock me out of the room, she thought. *How am I supposed to do my job - and cover for him - if I don't know what's going on?*

CHAPTER FOURTEEN

"You've been a bad girl," Fraser said, as George stepped out of the shower. "Going to the shuttlebay at *this* point in your career."

George groaned. Fraser had been mercifully absent when she'd returned to middy country and climbed into her rack - even *he* wouldn't disturb someone asleep in their rack - but he'd been coming back off-shift when she'd been woken by her bedside alarm and hurried into the shower. Thankfully, he hadn't been around to realise she hadn't taken a shower *before* hitting her rack or he would have made a fuss about it. Cleanliness wasn't just next to godliness, as far as the navy was concerned; it was well *above* godliness.

She reached for her underwear and pulled it on, doing her best to ignore him. A good night's sleep had made her feel better; she could dress, snatch something to eat and then make her way to the shuttlebay five minutes before her due time. Fraser snorted rudely and started to undress. He'd taken the night shift for himself and would need to catch at least six hours of sleep before his next duty shift began.

"I imagine this will look very bad on your record," Fraser said, as George snapped her jacket into place and checked her appearance in the mirror. At least she didn't look as though she was on the verge of collapse any longer. "A midshipman shouldn't be flying shuttles…"

"It could be fun," George said, crossly. Was he right? She was *meant* to rotate through the different duty compartments, but the XO might have intended to give her a break between tactical and the helm. Or, perhaps, to see how quickly she adapted when dumped into a whole new environment. "At least I'd have the chance to go outside."

"Mind you don't ram the ship," Fraser needled. He stepped to one side as she walked past him, careful not to brush against her. "They'll take it out of your salary."

George shrugged and opened the hatch. If the shuttle *did* crash into the battleship, which was at least theoretically possible, she rather suspected no one on the craft would survive the experience. Crews were meant to wear shipsuits and keep their helmets within easy reach, but the impact would probably vaporise the shuttle. She stepped through the hatch, half-expecting Fraser to call her back for some more makework and was mildly surprised when the hatch closed without him saying a word. No doubt, the nasty part of her mind noted, he thought being assigned to the shuttlebay was enough of a punishment for being born to the wrong family.

Bastard, she thought. *Stupid fucking bastard.*

She pushed her annoyance aside as best as she could as she walked into the wardroom. It was swarming with crewmen, but the middy table was empty, as always. They opened their ranks to allow her to walk up to the serving line, leaving her feeling alone in a crowd of older men and women. It seemed absurd, somehow, to think that she had to give them orders when any one of them had more experience of shipboard life than herself. She was surprised a few of them hadn't applied for the academy in the hopes of becoming officers themselves.

"We like recruiting mustangs," her instructor had said. One of her fellow cadets - Nathan, she thought - had asked why there were small numbers of older recruits scattered amongst the teenagers. "They already know the most important lessons we teach here."

George shook her head, ate her breakfast and hurried down to the shuttlebay. She'd explored it once, back when Nathan and she had been learning how to navigate through the giant battleship, but now it was her duty station. It was heaving with life; dozens of crewmen were moving shuttlecraft up to the launch hatch, while others were inspecting and repairing a number of other craft. The shuttlebay itself, she recalled from her exploration, was actually a massive compartment in its own right, honeycombed with smaller hangers so shuttles could be worked on while others were launched into space. There didn't seem to be anything out of place.

She looked around, then headed for the shuttlebay office. Regulations, if she recalled correctly, insisted that *someone* had to be on duty at all times. If the Boatswain wasn't there - he'd know she was coming, but he might have other duties - the deck officer would be able to page him for her. Three crewmen - two young men and a young woman - stepped past her as she reached the hatch, chatting easily amongst themselves. George felt a sudden stab of envy at their camaraderie. She was getting on better with the other crewmen, but Fraser's harassment was making it harder for her to befriend anyone.

The hatch hissed open, revealing a cramped office overlooking the main shuttlebay. She could see the darkness of space in the distance as the main doors opened. There was something out there in the shadows... she tensed, then relaxed as she realised it was just another shuttlecraft coming in to land. She watched with admiration as the shuttle glided through the doors and landed neatly on the deck, shuttlebay crewmen hastily rigging up an atmosphere tube rather than taking the time to close the hatch and repressurise the bay. It had to be a very important guest...

"That's the admiral's shuttle," a voice said.

George jumped. She'd been so fascinated by the shuttlecraft that she hadn't noticed the two men in the compartment. She turned and saw an older man, easily old enough to be her father, sitting in one of the chairs. There was something about his face that put her instantly at her ease, a sense that he would always be kind and friendly. His uniform marked him out as the Boatswain. The dark haired man next to him was only a year or two older than George herself.

"Jack, dismissed," the Boatswain said. He rose and saluted. "Chief Petty Officer Simon Williams, Midshipwoman."

"Midshipwoman George Fitzwilliam," George said, automatically. She was meant to give orders to someone who'd been in the navy longer than she'd been alive? Hell, someone who'd been in the navy longer than her uncle? She shifted awkwardly, unsure what to say or do. Maybe Fraser was right. Maybe it *was* a punishment for something. "The XO ordered me to report to you."

"I believe she wanted you checked out on a shuttle," the Boatswain said, calmly. At least he didn't *sound* as though he was mocking her, although she suspected he'd be smiling on the inside. But then, he'd probably seen hundreds of young officers coming and going. "It's quite a useful skill to know."

"I haven't flown a shuttle since the academy," George said. That *had* been only a couple of months ago, but she was grimly aware that she barely had a hundred hours of flying to her name. A dedicated shuttle pilot would have racked up *thousands* by the time he was qualified to serve in the navy. "I have my certificate, but..."

"We can work on that," the Boatswain assured her. "If you'll come with me...?"

George nodded and allowed him to lead her out of the compartment.

Susan couldn't help the sweat trickling down her back as the admiral's shuttle landed neatly in the shuttlebay, the crew hurrying to affix an atmospheric tube to its airlock. She'd warned the captain as best as she could, without crossing the lines, but she had no idea what would happen when Admiral Boskone and Captain Blake met face to face. Hell, she had no idea what the destroyer captains had been saying to the admiral. It was odd, very odd, for a flotilla commander *not* to enjoy himself passing orders to the screen. Captain Blake wouldn't get any closer to fleet command until he was promoted.

If he ever is, she thought. The airlock hissed open, revealing a tall man walking down the tube and into the ship. *And if the admiral finds out I passed the screen orders in his name, we're all likely to get in deep shit.*

"Admiral Boskone," she said, straightening to attention. "I'm Commander Susan Onarina, executive officer. Welcome onboard HMS *Vanguard*."

The admiral saluted the flag and the portrait of King Charles, then turned to Susan and returned her salute. His skin was slightly darker than the average, his black eyes hinting at Indian blood somewhere in his family tree. Probably quite distant, Susan suspected; he wouldn't have been promoted if there was any suggestion he had close ties to India, particularly after the Anglo-Indian War. He was bald, the complete lack of facial hair suggesting he'd had his skin treated to prevent it from growing back. That, in Susan's experience, was unusual. Very few men seemed willing to destroy their prospects of having a beard, even though naval officers were supposed to be clean-shaven at all times.

"Thank you, Commander," Boskone said. His voice held a very definite trace of London, although she couldn't hear any traces of an upper-class accent. But he would have some connections, she was sure, if he'd made it above Commodore. "I look forward to a tour, after the meeting."

"Of course, sir," Susan said. *Vanguard*, at least, was in good shape. She'd have hated to give him a tour when the ship was right out of the shipyards. "If you'll come with me?"

She led him into the intership car, answering his questions as best as she could. Boskone was a carrier admiral, it seemed; from what he said, she suspected he had his doubts about the battleship concept. But at least he didn't seem inclined to reject the whole idea out of hand either. The death of INS *Viraat* proved, all too clearly, that naval warfare had changed since the First Interstellar War.

And it changed then too, she thought, as they reached the captain's office. *Or, at least, the weapons we used to fight changed.*

She pushed the thought aside as the hatch hissed open, revealing that *someone* had cleared up the office. A bottle of wine sat on the captain's desk, escorted by three glasses; Susan wondered, inwardly, if she was going to be drinking or if the captain intended to invite someone else to the meeting. Or he might have assumed the admiral would be bringing an aide. The captain himself rose, walked around the desk and saluted the admiral. Susan had to admit that, for once, he looked almost like a captain.

"Admiral Boskone," Captain Blake said. "Welcome onboard *Vanguard*."

"Thank you, Captain," Admiral Boskone said. He took a seat, without being invited, and held out a datachip. "This won't take long, I hope. Put the files on the display."

"My steward has taken the liberty of preparing a meal," the captain said, as Susan took the chip and slotted it into the terminal. "I was hoping to speak with you..."

"After the games, one hopes," Admiral Boskone said. "We received word, only a week ago, that one of the American carriers attached to the border guard suffered a critical reactor failure. Admiral Pournelle intends to dispatch one of his carriers, accompanied by screening elements, to the border to replace her while she limps back to New Washington. We will only have that carrier present for five days before she has to depart."

Susan winced. Accidents happened, she knew, but a critical reactor failure? Losing one reactor would be worrying, yet unless there was something odd about the carrier's design she should still be capable of carrying out her duties. But then, if *she'd* lost a reactor, she'd want it repaired as soon as possible. And if she wasn't entirely sure what had happened, she'd want her other reactors checked too.

"Admiral Pournelle has a reputation as a skilled tactician," Admiral Boskone added, as Susan opened the files. A holographic representation of the Marina System popped up in front of them, surrounded by tactical icons. She couldn't help noticing that a handful of the icons represented facilities that were actually nothing more than sensor buoys. "But he doesn't have actual *experience* in commanding a fleet in combat. This is the closest either of us will get to gaining that experience unless another war starts. I don't intend to waste it."

"Yes, sir," Captain Blake said.

"The first war game will involve us attacking the American-held system," Admiral Boskone explained. "Task Force Churchill will split into two formations; Churchill-One will advance towards the gas giant, while Churchill-Two will advance on Marina itself. The overall objective will be to defeat the Americans before they can push us back out of the system."

Susan frowned, inwardly. Her experience of actual combat was limited, but it struck her that Admiral Boskone was taking a serious risk in splitting his forces. The Americans might just manage to catch one of the formations and bring superior force - vastly superior force - to bear on it before the other formation managed to intervene. But it wasn't her place to say so.

"I don't expect to be able to *keep* the system," Admiral Boskone added, dryly. "But I do want to take out the facilities before we have to leave."

"Yes, sir," Captain Blake said.

"I believe they'll concentrate on defending Marina itself," Admiral Boskone said. "Accordingly, you'll take command of Churchill-One and attack the gas giant facilities with maximum force. *Vanguard* will lead a fleet consisting of three cruisers, two escort carriers and five destroyers. The remainder of the fleet will attack Marina itself and attempt to pin down the Americans. We will not, of course, be aiming for a decisive battle."

"Because it would lead to our decisive defeat," Susan said, before she could stop herself.

Admiral Boskone smiled. "Quite right," he agreed. "Churchill-Two will be fighting a long-range engagement, rather than pushing forward as hard as possible. The Americans will find themselves forced to remain in place, rather than advancing themselves to deal with you."

It sounded workable, Susan conceded. The time delay would actually work in their favour, for once. Even if the Americans tracked the British ships as soon as they came out of the tramline, they'd still need to commit themselves very quickly if they wanted to save the gas giant's facilities. She glanced at the display, running through the calculations in her head. It would take at least an hour for a signal from the gas giant to reach Marina...and four hours for any ships, *leaving* Marina, to reach the gas giant. And that was the *optimistic* scenario, for the Americans. It might easily take them longer to realise the danger.

She glanced at the admiral, feeling a flicker of admiration. If he wasn't planning to actually *keep* the system, and he didn't have the firepower to be certain of victory, his options opened up. Wrecking the system's industries wouldn't do any immediate damage to Marina, but it would make it harder for America to continue the war until victory. Or, at least, that was what he would argue in front of the umpires.

We always assumed that wars would be short, she thought. It had been a prevalent assumption, back before First Contact. *But the First Interstellar War lasted over two years, with both sides capturing and recapturing dozens of star systems.*

"Your precise orders are on the chip," Admiral Boskone said. "I will, of course, expect you to adapt them to your situation, then forward the orders to your subordinate commanders. Set up a provisional chain of command too, in case something happens to *Vanguard*. I'm sure she'll draw a great deal of fire."

"The Yanks did try to sneak up on us, sir," Captain Blake said. There was nothing in his tone to suggest he'd been in his cabin while Susan held command. "Our sensors picked them up before they could get into firing position."

"Very good," Admiral Boskone said. He nodded towards the fleet lists. "But I'm sure the Americans would happily trade a cruiser for a battleship."

Susan nodded. It was cruel to suggest that a starship, even a small cruiser, was expendable, but it was true. The Royal Navy had taken eight years to construct *Vanguard*, learning a great deal about the process along the way; the United States Navy would have taken less than a year to produce the cruiser. By any reasonable standard, the trade-off would have been heavily-weighted in America's favour.

Particularly when all that's really at stake are bragging rights, Susan thought. By long tradition, the crews of ships that were 'destroyed' in war games were the ones who bought the beer afterwards. *Admiral Pournelle won't even have to consider truly sacrificing the ship.*

Admiral Boskone rose. "Your XO has promised me a tour of the ship," he said. "I'll expect a report from you, Captain, by the end of the day, detailing your planned formation and chain of command. Once we start the games, you'll be on your own."

Susan nodded. Once the two formations had diverged, any orders from the admiral would be hopelessly out of date by the time they arrived. Captain Blake would hold formal command…

She groaned, inwardly. She could cover for him on the bridge, but it would be far harder when she needed to issue orders to the rest of the formation. They'd be in Captain Blake's name, yet if one of the commanding officers needed to talk to him personally…she cursed, inwardly, as she rose too. She'd need to give the admiral his tour, then hurry back to inspect the captain's planned dispositions. Mason would need to hold the conn for a great deal longer.

At least we rotated other officers through the slot, she thought, silently congratulating herself on her foresight. *He can be relieved if necessary.*

"We'll start with the bridge, Admiral," she said, out loud. "If you'll come with me...?"

CHAPTER FIFTEEN

"Long-range sensors and IFFs confirm it," Lieutenant Charlotte Watson reported. "We have an audience."

"Then we'd better not fall on our faces in front of them," Susan said. She'd known that the war games weren't exactly a secret, but the presence of seven starships from seven different nations, watching the proceedings, was more than a little alarming. Britain and America wouldn't be the only nations who'd draw lessons from the games. "Communications, send them the standard warning."

"Aye, Commander," Parkinson said. "Message sent."

Susan nodded. Lacking an Earth-type world, Marina was technically an open system, even though the Americans had a solid claim on both Marina itself and the gas giant. There were no legal excuses for chasing the watching ships out of the system, even if the war gamers had had the time to play hide and seek. Perhaps it would have been better to hold the games in the New Washington or Britannia systems, but one of the other objectives was to test the fleet's logistics skills. They couldn't do *that* in a settled system.

They won't be able to see the data we exchange, she thought, as she settled back into the command chair and glanced at the timer. Thirty minutes until kick-off, when the first war game would begin in earnest. *And they won't have seen the pre-game planning sessions either.*

She forced herself to wait, resisting the temptation to review the operation plan for the umpteenth time. Thankfully, Mason and the tactical staff had been able to review it and offer suggestions of their own, but it had still taken her longer than she'd wished to complete the document and forward it to Admiral Boskone. Captain Blake had been no help whatsoever; he'd sat in his cabin and drunk his wine, she assumed, while she did the work. And the hell of it was that she almost wished he'd *stay* there while the war game played out.

"Captain on the bridge," Mason said.

Susan cursed, inwardly, as the hatch hissed open behind her. She rose from the command chair and turned; the captain was striding into the compartment, looking supremely confident as he nodded to her, then took the command chair. It wasn't going to be easy, Susan realised, when it became clear he wasn't going to take the conn. The bridge crew wouldn't know who to look to for orders.

And we're not departing Earth this time, she thought. *We're going into battle against a cunning foe.*

"Captain," she said. "You have the conn."

Captain Blake blinked, his confidence clearly flickering out of existence. "I have the conn," he said. "Remain on the bridge."

"Aye, sir," Susan said. She would have preferred to go to the secondary bridge - it was her duty station, if the shit hit the fan - but there was no point in arguing. The post-battle assessment would make the captain look very bad, if they lost, yet it probably couldn't be blamed on her. "The war game will start in" - she glanced at the timer - "ten minutes."

"Excellent," the captain said. If Susan hadn't been able to see the undertone of concern, even fear, she might have relaxed. As it was, all she could really do was worry. "Inform me when the games begin in earnest."

Susan sighed inwardly and took her seat, keeping one eye on the long-range sensor display as two new starships blinked into existence. The Russians had kept a low profile for the past ten years, but now there were no less than *three* Russian ships watching the war games. Susan had heard rumours that the Russians had been building up their military, *despite* the staggering losses they'd taken in the First Interstellar War, yet there had been very little hard data. Now, it was clear the Russians were *very* interested in watching the games.

The timer reached zero. A low buzzing sound ran through the compartment.

"The exercise has now begun," Susan said. She keyed her console. "Exercise protocols; I say again, exercise protocols. All duty stations confirm."

The captain gave her an odd look, which she ignored. Regulations didn't stipulate that *all* duty stations had to sound off, but Susan knew it was better not to take chances. Lighting up an American starship that was trying to creep up on *Vanguard* was one thing; accidentally blowing her out of space was quite another. Even if it didn't start another human-on-human war, it would be the end of the entire crew's career. She didn't dare risk a blue-on-blue.

"Signal from the flag, sir," Parkinson said. "We are to proceed as directed."

Susan glanced at the captain, who nodded. "Set course for the gas giant," she ordered. The Americans had promised not to track the ships as they made their way away from Marina, but in their place she would have been able to make a very good guess at their location. "Best possible speed."

"Aye, Commander," Reed said. "We will enter firing range in five hours."

"Good," Susan said.

She glanced down at her console. All duty stations had confirmed that the exercise protocols were up and running, ensuring there was no risk of a friendly fire incident. There would be no shortage of arguments after the engagement, she was sure, which the umpires would have to sort out, but at least there would be no real danger. *Vanguard's* crew might cover themselves with glory, or wind up with egg on their faces...she pushed the thought aside, annoyed. Right now, a friendly fire incident was the least of her worries.

"Maintain course and speed," she ordered, turning her attention to the display. "Inform me the moment any American ships are detected."

She sighed inwardly. Sneaking up on the gas giant would be easy, but Admiral Boskone had specifically ordered the fleet not to use any cloaking devices or stealth systems. She wasn't sure if he wanted to keep the latest cloaking devices secret from the Americans, or if he intended to use them later, yet it hardly mattered. The Americans would have no trouble detecting the task force as it approached its target.

Unless he's hoping the Americans will attempt to defend the gas giant and discover, too late, that their homeworld is under attack, she thought. It made a certain kind of sense, although it had a whiff of the trying-to-be-clever stench she recalled from the academy. Grand plans that depended on the enemy reacting in a certain way, she'd been taught, were doomed to spectacular failure. *But then, if they get caught between two fires, they might not be able to react in time to deal with even one of them.*

She tossed the possibilities around in her head, while keeping an eye on the captain. She'd half-expected him to slip back into his Ready Room, but instead he stayed on the bridge, just like a *real* captain. Susan felt a bitter stab of pain, mixed with an emotion she didn't care to identify. There was something to be said for being the *de facto* commanding officer, but, at the same time, it wasn't her responsibility. *She* was just meant to take as much as possible of the burden of running the ship off his shoulders.

"I'm picking up two cruisers orbiting the gas giant," Charlotte said, suddenly. "Both of them just lit up their drives."

Susan glanced at the display. Unless the Americans had developed something completely new, the cruisers had shown themselves almost as soon as they should have seen *Vanguard* and her escorts. It made little sense, which worried her. She'd have been happier if she'd come up with an explanation for their behaviour, even if it were wrong. As it was, they'd given up the advantage of stealth for nothing. Neither ship would last long enough to get into firing range.

"Launch a spread of probes beyond the screen," she ordered. The beancounters would howl - *again* - but she was damned if she was allowing the Americans to distract her from another threat. "And monitor sensors for any signs of turbulence."

"They may be defending the planet," the captain said. He sounded hesitant. "Admiral Boskone predicted as much."

Susan frowned. It was still too early to get any solid lock on the remainder of the American fleet - or, for that matter, Admiral Boskone. Theoretically, Churchill-Two was blazing towards Marina at unimaginable speeds, but there was no way to know for sure, now the formation was out of sensor range. The icons on the display were really nothing more than guesses.

But reasonable ones, she told herself. *The Yanks wouldn't have sought a deep-space engagement unless it couldn't be avoided.*

"We have to be careful," she said. "Who knows what's lying in wait for us?"

She leaned back in her chair and forced herself to relax. The gas giant was growing larger on the display, but it would still be nearly an hour before they could engage their targets. Maybe the American ships intended to bug out, leaving the facilities to be destroyed. No one would ever accuse the Americans of not being brave - there was no shortage of glorious last stands in American history - yet standing and fighting would only add two destroyed cruisers to the list of smashed facilities. She couldn't have blamed the American commanders for bugging out in search of reinforcements.

"I'm not picking up any additional ships near the gas giant," Charlotte reported. "But all of the facilities are altering position."

The captain looked up. "Running?"

"No, sir," Susan said. *Vanguard* could give a cloudscoop a twenty-four hour head start and still catch it within an hour. "They're trying to evade any KEWs we might be launching."

Which isn't something I'd care to try in those facilities, she added, silently. *Their drives are little more than glorified station-keeping reaction thrusters.*

She glanced at the tactical console. "Commander Mason, do you have a firing pattern locked into the computers?"

"Aye, Commander," Mason said. He sounded confident, although if the facilities continued a random evasion pattern they were likely to be hard to hit at such a distance. "We can smash most of the facilities with buckshot unless they have some pretty good point defence..."

"Captain," Charlotte interrupted. "Both American cruisers just blasted out of orbit. They're heading straight for Marina."

Susan blinked. It looked almost as though the Americans couldn't make up their minds. And yet, they'd had ample time to run the calculations and come up with a plan. Hell, they could have traded long-range fire with the squadron before turning and running for their lives. A shot or two fired for the honour of the flag would look better on the after-action reports.

We're being screwed, she thought. *Something isn't right.*

"Launch a second set of probes," she ordered. "And then order the screen to spread out and deploy active sensor nodes. There's no point in trying to hide. They already know where we are."

"Aye, Commander," Charlotte said. Parkinson echoed her a second later. "I..."

She broke off. "New contacts," she said, as red icons blinked on the display. "Starfighters, right behind us!"

Susan stared. Starfighters couldn't cloak. They were simply too small to carry *any* form of stealth gear; hell, their drives were easy to detect even at long range. And yet, the Americans had somehow slipped over a *hundred* starfighters into range without being detected. How the hell had they done that?

She glanced at the captain. He was frozen, staring at the display as though he couldn't believe his eyes. Susan swallowed...she'd been issuing orders, on the assumption he would just watch, and yet...he jerked free, staring up at her with wild eyes. He looked as if he were having a panic attack.

"Evasive action," he ordered, his voice quavering. "Get us out of here!"

"Aye, Captain," Reed said. "Taking evasive action."

Susan opened her mouth, but she honestly wasn't sure what to say or do. There was *no* point in trying to evade, not when the starfighters were easily twice as fast as the destroyers on their best day. *Vanguard* was solidly armoured, too; she should have no difficulty surviving the first pass and taking a colossal bite out of the American ships. Unless... new red icons popped onto the display, as if some malevolent entity had held them in reserve until it was too late. The Americans had arrived in force...

"Captain," Charlotte said. "The entire American task force is bearing down on us."

That's how they did it, Susan thought, numbly. *They decided to abandon the planet entirely, trusting that we wouldn't bombard it. Instead, they focused on the gas giant and now they've caught us with our pants down.*

"Alter course," the captain ordered. "Thrust us away from them..."

"Enemy ships are opening fire," Mason reported. "Missile ETA roughly two minutes after the starfighters..."

Susan swore inwardly. This was no skirmish, this was an outright attempt to defeat Churchill-One in detail.

"Stand by point defence," she snapped. "Launch buckshot at the facilities; cover as many possible locations as you can."

"Aye, Commander," Mason said.

"Incoming message from Captain Nottingham," Parkinson said. "He's requesting permission to deploy starfighters."

"Do it," Susan snapped.

"Belay that order," Captain Blake said. She could hear panic in his tone. "They'll just be destroyed..."

Susan cursed as the American starfighters lanced into the formation. Dozens died, picked off by point defence, but the remainder survived to press the attack against the escort carriers. It only took a handful of missiles to take them both out, leaving Churchill-One without any starfighter cover of its own. The remaining destroyers lasted only minutes after the escort carriers, leaving *Vanguard* alone. And she didn't have a hope of outrunning her tormentors...

"Reverse course," Susan ordered. Should she relieve the captain? Admiral Boskone was likely to explode with rage when he reviewed the engagement report, if only because the best opportunity for relieving the captain had long since vanished. "Take us right into the teeth of their fire."

The captain emitted a little moan, but said nothing as the battleship slowly turned and advanced towards the American ships. Clearly, the dispassionate part of Susan's mind noted, the Americans had underestimated the battleship. The damage was mounting up, but it wasn't *serious*, while their fleet carriers and escorts were slowly entering *Vanguard's* range.

"Fire as soon as we bear," she ordered, quietly. The Americans had realised the danger, but they'd have real problems getting out of range before it was too late. "And don't let up."

"Aye, Commander," Mason said.

"Two of our drive rooms have been disabled," Reed warned. "Our speed is dropping."

"Keep us going as long as you can," Susan ordered. The Americans had a chance to scatter, and they might well save some of their fleet, but they were going to know they'd been in a fight. "Open fire."

"Aye, Commander," Mason said. "Firing...now."

Susan sucked in a breath as the main guns opened fire, sweeping two American destroyers out of space before concentrating on one of the fleet carriers. The American carriers had their own protective armour, but it wasn't enough to stand up to *Vanguard.* Susan allowed herself a moment of vindictive glee as the carrier's icon dimmed on the display, then watched coldly as the other fleet carrier came under heavy fire. Her crew were either more experienced or better led, she noted; they managed to keep the carrier going until she was out of *Vanguard's* effective range. She was badly damaged, but two of her launch tubes were still intact. She'd be able to recover the starfighters from the other carrier, although *keeping* them might be tricky. The Americans might need to land their starfighters on the hull and hope they could be recovered before their life support packs ran out.

And their packs may be lower than normal, she thought. *If they launched the starfighters on unpowered ballistic trajectories...*

She had to hand it to Admiral Pournelle. The tactic had been innovative and, against a fleet carrier, it might well have proved decisive. Pournelle couldn't have *known* Captain Blake would freeze, when put to the test, so he'd thrown a sucker punch at the entire squadron. The only thing that had saved Churchill-One from a curbstomp battle had been *Vanguard's* armour.

And we lost all of the squadron, she reminded herself. Fleet carriers took five years to build, but still...it had been a costly victory. *Admiral Boskone may not consider the trade-off worthwhile.*

"Captain," Parkinson said, formally. "I'm picking up a surrender signal from Admiral Pournelle. He's striking the flag."

"I think we won," Mason added. He sounded pleased. "They really shouldn't have let themselves get so close."

Susan gritted her teeth. After killing one fleet carrier, two cruisers and seven destroyers - and crippling another fleet carrier - it was quite possible that Admiral Boskone wouldn't look too closely at the combat records. Part of her was almost relieved; she wouldn't have to explain why she hadn't either relieved the captain of command or reported his...*problems*...to superior authority. And yet, at least it would have ensured she didn't have to hide anything any longer.

"Signal to all decks," she ordered, tightly. "Well done."

The display flickered as the 'destroyed' ships came back to life. Her crew would probably be swimming in beer, once they returned to Marina. She had no idea if American crewmen were paid more than British crewmen, but there was nothing else to spend money on while cruising between the stars. And besides, by any reasonable standard, they'd won.

And the captain froze up, she thought, grimly. Maybe they *had* won, but Captain Nottingham was likely to have a few harsh things to say about the whole affair and so were the other commanding officers. How could she blame them? *Now what the hell do I do*?

CHAPTER SIXTEEN

"If this is punishment," George murmured to herself, "I need to be naughtier."

The Boatswain looked up from his console. "Pardon, Midshipwoman?"

George felt her cheeks heat. It was against regulations to fly a shuttlecraft with less than two crewmen, unless it was a major emergency, but she'd been so enraptured by the vision of interplanetary space that she'd forgotten the Boatswain was there. Being out in space, away from the cramped interior of *Vanguard*, was fantastic. She was honestly tempted to request a permanent transfer to flying shuttles and to hell with trying to reach command rank.

"I'm sorry, Chief," she said. "My mind was wandering."

"As long as it doesn't wander us straight into another ship," the Boatswain said, dryly. "And as long as you don't lose touch with the fleet."

George nodded, embarrassed. The first war game had been followed by a dozen others, ranging from deep-space ambushes to defending the planet against an invading fleet. She'd been torn between enjoying her birds-eye view of the engagements and envying Nathan and the other midshipmen for serving in the engineering, tactical and helm departments when there were so many interesting things going on. The experience they were gaining, just from unpredictable fleet games, would be invaluable later in their careers.

But at least I've been getting better at issuing commands, she thought. *Even if I still make mistakes from time to time.*

She glanced at the Boatswain, who seemed to be paying attention to his console. He'd saved her from making a number of mistakes, although he'd often let her make the first mistake and only then explain why it *was* a mistake. The shuttle crews knew what they were doing, after all; George could issue generalised orders, but never specific ones. She hadn't realised just how little she'd known of shuttle operational procedures - everything from flying to maintenance - until she'd gone to work in the shuttlebay.

"You're an officer," the Boatswain had said. "You find an enlisted crewman who knows how to do any specific task and order him to do it."

Her console pinged. "Emergency message," she said, feeling a sudden flicker of tension running down her spine. A *real* emergency message, too. "I'm plotting a course."

"A pilot - an American pilot - has bailed out of his starfighter," the Boatswain said, his fingers dancing over his console. "He suffered a power surge, apparently. His plasma cannons are threatening to overload."

George winced as she gunned the engines, sending the shuttle hurtling towards the source of the distress call. Starfighter plasma cannons had a tendency to overload if they were allowed to overheat through rapid fire, although she wasn't sure just what the Americans had been shooting at with live weapons. Perhaps it was a drill…no, every distress signal sent as part of a drill had to be clearly marked as such. The Royal Navy couldn't afford the risk of growing too used to fake distress calls.

American protocols might be different, she thought, as her sensors flashed an alert. The starfighter was very definitely overheating. *No, it isn't a drill.*

"Prep the airlock," she ordered. The pilot had thrown himself into space, rather than remain with his craft. An explosion must be imminent. Very few spacers would take the risk of being lost forever, although the risk was very limited compared to the certainty of being toasted if he stayed too close to the doomed starfighter. "Does he have an EVA pack?"

"Doesn't look like it," the Boatswain said. "He's not in any sort of controlled flight."

George hesitated. Technically, she should remain at the helm, but the Boatswain was a far superior pilot. And this wasn't a drill…

"I'm going to grab him," she said, as she checked her shipsuit. It wasn't anything like as reliable as a full-sized spacesuit, but it would suffice. She snapped an EVA pack into place as she spoke. "Take us away from the craft as soon as I've got a firm grip."

"Understood," the Boatswain said.

George nodded, locked her helmet in place and hurried to the airlock. The inner hatch hissed open, revealing a cramped compartment barely large enough for three or four grown men, assuming they were wearing nothing more than their underwear. Her lips quirked in amusement - it reminded her of one of the more absurd Stellar Star movies - as she fastened her tether to the airlock, then keyed the hatch. It hissed open, allowing the atmosphere to gust out into interplanetary space. She tumbled out with it, rather than trying to stay in the airlock. There was no time to be careful.

For a moment, the sheer vastness of the universe held her in its grip. Groundhogs never understood; hell, there were spacers who hated the very *thought* of going EVA. It was so immense and she was so tiny…even *Vanguard*, the largest ship in the fleet, was nothing more than a mote of dust compared to the Milky Way alone. All of a sudden, she understood why there were promising cadets at the academy who'd washed out after their first EVAs…

She pushed the thought aside as she scanned space for the American pilot. His suit wasn't visible to the naked eye, but her helmet HUD could track the distress beacon. She keyed her EVA pack on an intercept course, hoping she had a long enough tether to reach the pilot without having to ask the Boatswain to alter the shuttle's trajectory. He came into view faster than she'd believed possible, tumbling helplessly through space… she caught hold of his arm, praying he wasn't panicking. Panic killed, her instructors had warned her…

"Hit it," she said.

The tether grew taut; she half-expected it to snap before she realised it was pulling her and the American away from the starfighter. She twisted, trying to see it with her naked eye, but she couldn't pick it out, even with the HUD pointing her in the right direction. Something *twinkled* against the darkness…

"She lost containment," the Boatswain said. "She's gone."

George was almost disappointed. She'd expected something more spectacular, although anything bigger might have killed both of them. Shaking her head, she keyed the tether and allowed it to pull them back into the airlock, which hissed closed as soon as they were through the hatch. She motioned for the American to keep his helmet on as the gravity took hold of them, then checked the telltales on his suit. Everything seemed fine…she waited until the air pressure equalised, then took off her own helmet. The American followed suit moments later.

"You're an angel," he said, in a strong accent she recognised from the movies. "That could have been very bad."

"Someone else would have come to get you," George said. The American was darker than the XO, although his eyes were a rather odd purple. Hadn't that been a fashion in America, once upon a time? "Are you all right?"

"Merely annoyed with the deckhands," the American said. He stuck out a hand. "Malcolm, Malcolm Douglas."

"George Fitzwilliam," George said. She shook the American's hand, then led him into the cabin. It didn't look as though the American recognised her name, but she couldn't put a name to the highest-ranking American naval officer either. "We'll have you back to *Enterprise* in a jiffy."

"No hurry," Douglas said. He glanced around the cabin, then winked at her. "Can I buy you a drink in the bar?"

George hesitated. "I don't know if I'll get any shore leave," she said, finally. Even if shore leave *was* authorised for the midshipmen, Fraser might find an excuse to keep her from getting a few hours away from the ship. "But if I do, I'll give you a call."

"There's supposed to be a good bar on the surface," Douglas assured her, as he took one of the rear seats. "I don't think there's anything else for the settlers to do, save watch the terraforming package do its job."

"Poor bastards," George said. The settlement was tiny. Having a hundred crewmen visiting for shore leave would probably overwhelm the facilities. "But I'll give you my private v-mail address and you can message me."

And hope Fraser doesn't find out about it, she added. There was very little true privacy in middy country, but they treasured what little they had. *He'll tease me about it for hours.*

She took her seat and powered up the drives, checking the sensors to make sure they had a clear flight path to *Enterprise.* A pair of shuttles were heading towards where the starfighter had been, although George would have been surprised if they recovered more than a handful of atoms. There were certainly no large chunks of debris to inspect. She gunned the drives and sent the shuttle racing towards the American carrier while the Boatswain called ahead for landing clearance.

"We'll make sure to copy all our files to you," she called back, as the American carrier grew larger in front of them. "Do you want anything else?"

"The investigators will no doubt let you know," Douglas said. He remained seated until the shuttle had actually docked, unlike some of the others they'd flown around the fleet. "And thank you, once again."

"You're welcome," George called.

She watched Douglas step out of the hatch, then closed and locked it before separating from the American carrier and heading back into space. The American ship didn't look *that* different from a British carrier, although she couldn't help noticing that she had eight flight decks instead of six. George wasn't sure if they allowed the Americans to launch more starfighters or served as easier targets for enemy fire. A warhead detonating inside the launch tubes might not destroy the ship, but it would certainly render the tube unusable.

"We have to head back to the mothership," the Boatswain said.

George sagged, despite herself. Going back to *Vanguard* meant going back to Fraser, going back to enduring his torments. She kept telling herself not to give up, she kept telling herself that she'd win his respect, yet... yet sometimes it felt as if she were fighting an uphill battle, one she was doomed to lose. Perhaps she should go to the XO after all...

The Boatswain coughed. "Would you like to talk about it?"

George blinked. "Talk about what?"

"Whatever is bothering you," the Boatswain said. "I can tell you're having problems."

"I'm not," George lied. "I just..."

"I don't think you fell instantly in love with that Yank," the Boatswain said. There was something in his tone that suggested she'd disappointed him. "You certainly didn't fall so deeply that the mere thought of losing him depressed you."

George blushed, furiously. "It's not like that," she said. "I...I liked him, but..."

The Boatswain smiled. "So what *is* bothering you? I am here to advise."

That, George knew, was true. The Boatswain was a father to the men and women under his command, particularly the ones young enough to be his real children. She'd heard him offering them advice, ranging from quiet words of encouragement to pointing out, sternly, just where they'd gone wrong. And yet, advising *her* wasn't his job. She was, technically, his superior officer...

And perhaps it was time to throw caution to the winds.

"I have a problem," she admitted. "The first middy hates me."

Once she started to talk, the entire story seemed to just *leap* out of her mouth. The Boatswain listened, saying nothing, as she described how he'd treated her, from the extra duties to penalising her for even the slightest mistake. Fraser didn't seem to treat *Nathan* the same way, even though Nathan was just as green as George herself...

"He's screwed," the Boatswain said, when she'd finished.

George stared at him. "How?"

The Boatswain met her eyes. "How long has Fraser been a midshipman?"

"Six years," George said. She'd looked it up. "But only six..."

"Most midshipmen are promoted to lieutenant within their second or third year of service," the Boatswain noted. "It keeps a steady turnover of midshipmen in middy country - the midshipmen who are not promoted are often reassigned, in the hopes they'll have a chance to shine on another ship. The post of first middy is therefore passed down as the senior midshipman jumps up the ladder."

He clicked the autopilot on, then turned to face her. "A midshipman who remains in that rank for longer than four years has a problem," he added. "Have you ever heard of the lemon car dilemma?"

George shook her head, wordlessly.

"It was something of a problem when I was a kid," the Boatswain said. "If you wanted to buy a new car, well, it could cost something around twenty thousand pounds. Most of us couldn't hope to afford it, of course;

there were laws against lending money to people with poor financial prospects. That was after the economic crash, of course..."

He shrugged. "Assuming you *did* manage to buy a new car, its value instantly declined by at least a third," he told her. "Why do you think that was the case?"

George considered it. "Because it was no longer *new*?"

"True," the Boatswain said. "But there's another reason. No one would *sell* a new car unless there was something wrong with it. Therefore, no one would *buy* a second-hand car when it had barely been used. The more pristine it seemed, the more suspicious they'd be..."

"And a midshipman who's served six years without being promoted... people assume there's something wrong with him," George said. She saw what he'd meant, now. "There's no hope of either being promoted or being transferred?"

"Correct," the Boatswain said. "And young Mr. Fraser has the added humiliation of watching younger midshipmen being promoted ahead of him."

George stared down at her hands. "That doesn't excuse him for picking on me!"

"No, it doesn't," the Boatswain said. He met her eyes, evenly. "People lie; not just to others, which is *marginally* understandable, but to themselves. Mr. Fraser has become convinced that the *reason* he hasn't been promoted is because countless others, all far less qualified than himself, are being jumped ahead of him. He's told himself that so often, I suspect, that trying to convince him otherwise would be a waste of time. He hates you because he thinks you'll be promoted as soon as it's legally possible. And you'll take a slot he could have filled himself."

"But no one is using influence on my behalf," George protested.

The Boatswain looked...*irked*. "Can you *prove* it?"

"You can't prove a negative," the Boatswain said. "Mr. Fraser knows he isn't likely to see promotion, not now he's been a midshipman for too long. And the hell of it is that he *isn't* a bad first middy, as long as he keeps his head out of his ass. He really should have been promoted a long time ago."

George met his eyes. "Why wasn't he?"

"That isn't a question I can answer," the Boatswain said. "And I *advise*" - his voice hardened - "you to be careful who you ask."

"I could *order* you to tell me," George said.

Oddly, the Boatswain seemed pleased by her remark. "I would have to refuse," he said, "but at least you thought of it."

George looked down at her hands. Who *could* she ask? The XO wouldn't answer, she was sure, and she didn't dare ask the captain. Commander Mason had seemed nice enough - and he *had* served on *Vanguard* for two years - but she doubted they could sit down and have a pleasant chat. And none of the midshipmen would know, not if there *had* been a steady turnover. If something had happened, early in Fraser's career, they might not know what it had been…

"I won't order you to do anything," she said, "but please could you tell me what I should do?"

"You have several options," the Boatswain said. "You *could* always complain to your relatives."

"That would let him win," George said, stubbornly. "I want to make it on my own."

"He *has* to," the Boatswain said. He took a breath. "You could just tough it out, if you wish, or you could challenge him directly."

George frowned. "A challenge?"

"Midshipmen are expected to settle any disputes amongst themselves," the Boatswain said, simply. "That's what the first middy is *for*. Bringing in higher authority…well, let's say that rarely ends well for everyone. It's only done in the worst possible situations."

"And this isn't?"

"No, it isn't," the Boatswain said. "There was a scandal, ten years before the war, when a first middy was prostituting the midshipmen under his command."

George stared at him. "How…how did that happen?"

"It's amazing what you can get away with if you have the nerve," the Boatswain said. "I suspect the newcomers assigned to the ship were bullied into working for him. He was hanged, along with three of his accomplices, and most of the ship's crew were dishonourably discharged. Fraser, whatever his faults, isn't anything like them."

"No," George agreed. She'd been naked in front of Fraser, but he hadn't tried to *do* anything to her. The academy tutors had made it clear that relationships between midshipmen who shared the same sleeping compartment were forbidden. "He's not that bad."

"Then you can get through to him," the Boatswain said. "But some people need to be smacked in the face before they learn."

George sighed. She had a lot to look up in the files, it seemed. "Why?"

"Human nature," the Boatswain said. "We are programmed to respect strength and determination. Submission, surrender, appeal to higher authority...we emotionally scorn them, even when rationality tells us otherwise. Why do you think there are so many remakes of *Captain America*?"

"He never surrenders," George said.

"He *never* surrendered," the Boatswain said. "*That's* why we like him. Even when he was a skinny little runt, he never surrendered."

CHAPTER SEVENTEEN

"He froze up in the middle of a fucking war zone," Susan hissed.

"The battle was won," Mason pointed out. "And we acquitted ourselves well in the later battles."

Susan bit off a curse she *knew* her father would have slapped her for saying out loud. The captain had been lucky, amazingly lucky. Any halfway competent post-battle analysis would have turned up proof that Captain Blake had frozen, but Admiral Boskone had been too pleased to order a full investigation. The mock skirmishes that the Royal Navy had lost would draw much more attention, at least for the next few months. And then...

"If we take it to the admiral," she said, "what happens next?"

"We get in deep shit for not reporting it earlier," Mason said, bluntly. "Or we get steamrollered by Captain Blake's connections for daring to question his competence."

Susan stared down at her hands, feeling helpless. She knew how to deal with crewmen, junior officers and balky machinery, but the academy had never taught her how to deal with a captain who was...what? A coward? Mentally unstable? Promoted well past his competence level? All of a sudden, she thought she understood *precisely* why Commander Bothell had deserted. He'd spent the last five years of his career covering for his superior.

"Someone will run an analysis of the first engagement eventually," she said, grimly. "And when they do, they'll realise just how badly we screwed up."

Mason shrugged. "Both sides made mistakes," he pointed out. "If the Americans had launched from further out, they might have had a good chance to blow us out of space before we caught up with their carriers."

"We should have reacted faster," Susan said. "We *cannot* afford another incident like that in a combat situation."

She glared at the deck. The recordings from the engagement should be enough to justify relieving Captain Blake of command - she had no doubt that Admiral Boskone would be furious, if they were brought to his attention - but her career would probably be doomed too, no matter what happened to the captain. Even someone who understood her position would ask why she hadn't alerted the Admiralty earlier, even if she hadn't relieved the captain of command personally.

And if someone doesn't understand my position, she thought, *I can bend over and kiss my career goodbye.*

"You could ask the doctor to take a look at him," Mason suggested. "The doctor could relieve him of command..."

"The doctor would have to satisfy a medical board that the captain was dangerously unfit for command," Susan reminded him. She picked up her datapad and opened the captain's file, checking to see when he'd had his last routine check-up, then cursed as she realised Doctor Chung's predecessor had carried out the examination shortly before leaving the ship. "And we'd need grounds to urge the doctor to order an exam."

"We have grounds," Mason said. "He froze up in combat."

"Which could easily be justified as being surprised," Susan sneered. She rose and paced around the cabin, trying to think. What the hell should she do? "If we take this to the admiral, we just have to explain too much."

She kicked the bulkhead, hard. A rock and a hard place...stay where she was and await the inevitable moment when someone ran an analysis and exposed the captain's failings or report the captain, knowing it would probably destroy her career. Even if she didn't lose her rank, officially, what commanding officer would want a sneak under his command? It wasn't a rational objection, but she knew it would be made. *No one* would accept an XO who'd betrayed her commanding officer.

"I think the bulkhead's designed to stand up to laser warheads," Mason said. "But keep kicking it if you wish."

Susan shot him a nasty look. "Do you have any other suggestions?"

Mason scowled. "Try and ask Doctor Chung to carry out an examination anyway," he said, after a moment. "It could be billed as part of the war games…"

"The captain wouldn't buy that argument," Susan said. "And Doctor Chung wouldn't be keen on cooperating."

She sighed, inwardly. Captains were notoriously hard to force into sickbay for a medical examination, something that had puzzled her until she'd realised that the ship's doctor was the only person who could legally relieve the captain without a very good reason. No captain would gracefully submit to an examination; no doctor would willingly abuse their position, knowing that it would cost them far too much. Captain Blake couldn't be pushed into having a medical exam for at least another three months, unless he suffered an accident…

The buzzer rang. Susan blinked - she wasn't expecting visitors - and snapped out the open command. The hatch hissed open, revealing the Boatswain. He was carrying a small bag under one arm, which shifted as he snapped to attention.

"Chief," Susan said, surprised. "What can I do for you?"

"I have the latest reports for you," the Boatswain said. He was an older man, old enough to pass for Susan's father. He'd spent nearly twice as long as Susan herself in the navy. "If you wish to inspect them…?"

Susan picked up on the unspoken message and nodded. "Paul, I'll talk to you later," she said, briskly. "Meet me after your next duty shift."

"Aye, Commander," Mason said.

"Chief," Susan said, once the hatch had hissed closed behind Mason. "How long have you served on this ship?"

"I was assigned to her five years ago, back when she was really nothing more than a framework, Commander," the Boatswain said. "They built the armoured hull around me."

Susan had to smile. *She'd* served on four starships before transferring to *Vanguard*, but *she* was an officer and officers were almost always transferred after their first promotions. A crewman, on the other hand, or a non-commissioned officer might spend his entire career on a single ship. The Boatswain was unusual in having been transferred around, although - if she recalled correctly - his previous ship had been decommissioned and sold to Japan.

She hesitated, then took the plunge. "Chief, I need to ask you a question, off the record," she said. "What happened to Captain Blake?"

The Boatswain studied her for a long moment. Susan understood his concern. Asking a crewman, even a senior chief, about the captain wasn't just a severe breach of military etiquette, it was technically against regulations. But if there was anyone on *Vanguard* who might know what had happened to the captain, it was her longest-serving crewman. The Boatswain would have heard all manner of rumours as they filtered through the hull...

"I heard there was an...*incident* on his last command," the Boatswain said, finally. "He wasn't the same afterwards, or so I heard."

Susan frowned as some of the pieces fell into place. An *incident* covered a multitude of possible disasters, but if one of them had shocked the captain so badly he'd developed mental health problems...it might explain a great deal. She'd assumed he'd been promoted to a point just above his level of competence, yet if he had *been* competent no red flags would have been raised. There would have been no *reason* to raise them.

She met his eyes. "Do you know what happened?"

"No, Commander," the Boatswain said. "Commander Bothell was the only other transfer from his former command, I believe, and he was a very private man. Highly competent, very capable, but not inclined to sit back and just chat."

Susan nodded slowly. None of the senior officers had known Commander Bothell very well, although they'd clearly respected him. And Commander Bothell had clearly been loyal to his commanding officer, right up until he'd deserted. Or suffered an accident. There was no way to know, but he'd left Susan with an ungodly mess.

And what would I do, she asked herself, *if a commanding officer I respected and admired needed me to cover for him*?

"Thank you," she said. She'd have to find a way to get the captain into sickbay for an exam, even if it risked her career. There was no other choice. "Now, I assume you didn't just come to talk to me about shuttlecraft reports?"

"No, Commander," the Boatswain said. "You may have a problem in middy country."

There had been a joke at the academy, George recalled, about some mythical entity called 'free time.' Younger cadets had been sent on snipe hunts, the joke went, for scant hours when there was nothing to do, but kick back and relax. She hadn't really understood the joke until she'd been commissioned and assigned to *Vanguard*, where free time was almost non-existent for junior midshipmen. It had taken hours of haggling with Nathan and Midshipman Walter Haworth to get even an hour of free time.

She slipped into the privacy compartment, hoping desperately that no one had seen her enter, and locked the hatch behind her. By long tradition, no one entered a locked privacy compartment unless the ship had to rush to battlestations; she'd heard stories of half-dressed crewmen trying frantically to pull on their clothes while rushing to their duty stations. None of the stories were actually true, she suspected, but it hardly mattered. Anyone who saw her entering the compartment - alone - might start off a new series of rumours.

The bunk looked clean, but she decided it would be better to sit on the deck instead as she pulled out her datapad and connected it to the starship's datanet. She wasn't surprised to discover, as she thumbed through the files, that a large number were classified well above her pay grade, yet the basic personnel files were open to all. Her own file contained little more than a note of her academy rankings - any notes made by her superiors were hidden from her - but anyone who had more than a little experience in data-mining could probably draw lines between her and her uncle. The name alone was a bit of a giveaway.

It's not like we're the only people with the name Fitzwilliam, she told herself, crossly. *But we are the first ones any naval officer will consider.*

Shaking her head, she looked up Fraser's file and frowned. Fraser had been assigned to *Vanguard* for three years, something that puzzled her until she realised he'd actually been on the ship while she was still in the shipyard. She tried to parse out a reason for his assignment to an incomplete ship, but nothing came to light. Whatever notes his superiors had attached to his file, and she was sure there had to be *something*, weren't open to her. His previous assignment had been a carrier…and he'd been transferred, instead of being promoted.

Odd, she thought. Had something happened to deny Fraser promotion? *Did he screw up or did someone screw with his career*?

The file offered no clues. Fraser couldn't have screwed up royally or he would have been reassigned to a mining station or simply dishonourably discharged from the Royal Navy. But if he'd made an enemy amongst the senior officers…even a mere second lieutenant could cripple a midshipman's career, if he said the right words in the right ears. And reassigning him to an incomplete starship might have been a deliberate slap in the face. But, no matter what she did, she couldn't find any further data from the files.

She gritted her teeth, then brought up the complete registry of midshipmen assigned to *Vanguard* and worked her way through their files. Fraser was the longest-serving by over two years, she noted; the other midshipmen had been promoted and transferred within two years of their assignment. The Boatswain had been correct, she saw; indeed, he'd understated the situation. Fraser was doomed to remain first middy on *Vanguard* for the remainder of his career.

Unless he requests a transfer himself, she thought. *But being a midshipman for so long would ensure he wouldn't get a post on another starship.*

Her frown deepened as she worked her way through the files. Every midshipman who'd been promoted had also been reassigned, without fail. That was standard procedure - and lucky, very lucky, for Fraser. Tradition might insist that whatever happened in middy country *stayed* in middy country, but she didn't think *she* could have resisted the temptation to punish him, once she gained promotion. His bitterness had only been made worse by watching junior officers rising above him and being reassigned. He probably wouldn't have taken it so hard, she thought, if they *had* stayed on *Vanguard*.

She saved the files on the datapad, then skimmed through the file covering the official regulations - and unofficial traditions - of midshipmen in the Royal Navy. All sorts of things were condoned, if they were kept within reasonable limits; higher authority didn't *like* being forced to take note of problems in middy country. Fraser would be in deep shit if something happened, even if it hadn't been his fault. He was, after all, the first middy. Whatever happened in middy country was his responsibility.

Then I have to handle the matter myself, she thought. Complaining would ruin both of their careers, no matter what else happened. *And...*

She gritted her teeth as she rose, checked the compartment to make sure she hadn't left anything lying on the deck, then opened the hatch and strode through without a backwards glance. No one was standing outside, much to her relief, but she passed two crewwomen who grinned knowingly at her as she walked up the corridor. Her cheeks burned red with embarrassment, knowing just what sort of rumours would be running through the ship. If someone had seen her *enter*, Fraser and the other midshipmen might already have heard...

They'll forget about it, she told herself, as she reached middy country. The hatch hissed open, revealing an empty corridor. *It isn't as if we don't have anything else to talk about.*

She hesitated outside the hatch to the sleeping compartment, feeling her heart starting to race in her chest. She was no coward - she wouldn't have passed through the academy if she'd been a coward - and yet she was afraid. Part of her just wanted to give in, to duck her head and endure until she was promoted up and off the ship, but she was too stubborn. She couldn't imagine her uncle bowing the head to anyone. The only senior officer he'd spoken of with respect had been Theodore Smith.

The hatch hissed open. Fraser stood there, looking annoyed. She caught sight of Nathan and Walter behind him, Walter half-naked as he undressed for the shower. They both glanced at her, Nathan trying to convey a warning message with his eyes. No doubt Fraser had realised she'd traded some of her assignments for an hour of relative peace.

"So," Fraser said. "Had enough of pleasuring yourself?"

George pulled herself up to her full height. *Someone* had to have seen her entering the privacy compartment, alone. She wondered who, then decided it didn't matter. Rumours grew in the telling as people added new details, then reported those details as fact. No doubt she'd discover tomorrow that she'd taken part in a threesome with two other midshipmen.

"No," she said. "But I've had enough of you."

Fraser's eyes widened, but he showed no other sign of surprise. Instead, he stepped closer until he was looming over her. Even standing upright, she was still a head shorter than him; she had to fight to keep from stepping backwards as he pushed his way into her personal space. There was little of *that* on a starship, but he was deliberately trying to intimidate her.

"I challenge you to meet me in the gym," she said, tossing down a gauntlet. "The winner will be first middy."

His face went blank. Technically, she *couldn't* take his position, but if she beat him in a fight she'd be first middy in all but name. And, by the unwritten code of conduct, if he refused her challenge, she'd be first middy anyway. He'd be furious - she had nothing at stake, beyond being beaten in the fight - and yet he couldn't refuse, not in front of the rest of the middies.

"It strikes me that you have nothing to lose," he said, finally. "What can I possibly win?"

George forced herself to meet his dark eyes. "The right to be first middy?"

His eyes flared with anger and she knew she'd won. He couldn't refuse her challenge, not now, even though the best he could hope for was keeping his place. No one would respect him if he declined the challenge. And yet, with the odds so uneven, he wouldn't gain much through victory. Unless, of course, he gained pleasure out of beating her to within an inch of her life.

"Very well," he said, tightly. "We will meet tomorrow afternoon. I can alter the duty rosters to ensure we both have an hour's free time. I trust that will be suitable?"

"Of course," George said. There was no backing out now, not for either of them. "I look forward to it, *sir*."

Fraser showed his teeth. "I look forward to it too," he said, as he walked past her. She tensed, expecting a blow, but felt nothing. "Until then, go do your duties."

"Yes, sir," George said.

Nathan caught her arm as she stepped into the sleeping compartment. "Are you mad?" He demanded. "He'll kill you!"

"I once saw him thrash a midshipman bloody," Walter offered. "The poor guy spent a week in sickbay."

"I'm just sick of him," George said. Now she'd issued the challenge, she felt cold - and terrified. The combat training she'd had at the academy had been very limited. She'd certainly never been expected to fight hand-to-hand. "And just because he hasn't been promoted is no reason to take it out on me."

CHAPTER EIGHTEEN

"Daddy," Victoria Windsor called, as she peered through the bedroom door. "You have a priority call from the swimming pool."

Ambassador Henry Windsor - who was no longer His Royal Highness, at least in his own mind - groaned as he pulled upright. It had been a late night at the embassy complex on Tadpole Prime and he'd only managed to get to sleep - he glanced at the clock mounted on the wall - three hours before his oldest daughter had woken him. His tiredness insisted he should tell her to ask the caller to wait and go back to bed. And yet, it *had* to be an emergency. A call from the swimming pool meant that he, in his role as Earth's ambassador to the Tadpoles, was being summoned to meet with their representatives.

Unless they forgot to check the time when they called, he thought, sourly. The Tadpoles, living below the waves, didn't really understand why humans worked during the day and slept at night. *But they wouldn't call me directly unless it was important.*

He stood and grabbed his dressing gown, pulling it on over his swimming trunks, then shoed his daughter back to her bedroom as he hurried down the corridor and into the secure room, where a human face was on the screen. Charles Potter was, technically, Henry's assistant, although he seemed to spend most of his time engaging in bureaucratic wars with the other embassy staffers rather than doing his job. Indeed, Henry had had to speak to him quite sharply when the man had tried to insist that Henry and his family should live in the embassy itself, rather than the mid-sized house in Human Town. It wasn't as if he *needed* to be in the embassy to do his job.

"Charles," he said, sitting down in front of the terminal. "What's up?"

Potter's face twitched at the deliberate informality. "Mr. Ambassador," he said, stiffly. It had taken Henry a year to stop Potter addressing him as 'Your Highness,' even though he'd put the title aside. "We picked up a priority call from the swimming pool. They request your immediate presence."

Henry frowned. "Did they say why?"

"Nothing," Potter said. "And the discussion boards are clear."

Henry felt his frown deepen. The Tadpoles were not human and, like their human counterparts, they worked hard to avoid misunderstandings that could easily lead to a renewed conflict. If something had happened to restart the war, he was sure the embassy would have seen *some* signs of it…and there had been nothing. The only issue he'd had to handle that had been more than merely routine, over the last two years, had been the joint exploration program and even *that* had been a minor matter. When one race wanted the lands and the other the sea, it was hard to find anything to fight over.

"Inform them I will be there presently," Henry said. The Tadpoles wouldn't be impressed - they probably wouldn't even *notice* - if he turned up fashionably late. "And then have the courier boats prepped for immediate departure."

"Of course, Mr. Ambassador," Potter said. "I'll also call the senior representatives…"

"You better had," Henry grunted. Maybe it was nothing, but it was better to be safe than sorry. Besides, if he'd been woken in the early hours of the morning, his staff might as well be awakened too. "I'll call ahead when I leave the swimming pool."

He closed the channel and turned, just in time to see Janelle Windsor entering the chamber carrying a steaming mug of coffee. A decade of married life - and three beautiful young children - had only enhanced her beauty, as far as he was concerned. And, unlike far too many of the other wives, she actually knew how to support her husband. Bringing coffee when he desperately needed it was only the icing on the cake.

"Victoria said you needed this," Janelle said. "Is it going to be bad? Another Simon?"

"I hope not," Henry said. He drank the coffee quickly, despite the heat, then hurried down to the door. "Last time was quite bad enough."

He winced at the memory. Simon Barlow, the son of one of the embassy staffers, had made the mistake of swimming in the ocean, only to be killed in passing by a handful of Tadpoles. Human outrage had been met with Tadpole incomprehension; the humans had been horrified at a young child's death, the Tadpoles had honestly been unable to understand why the humans were so outraged. To them, children were expendable. Only a relative handful of juniors survived long enough to grow into adults and enter society. The whole affair had left a nasty taste in everyone's mouth. Henry had kept his daughters on Tadpole Prime, but he never allowed them to leave Human Town. The other parents felt the same way too.

"Good luck," Janelle said.

Henry nodded, discarded his dressing gown and walked out the door. The heat struck him like a physical blow, reminding him that Tadpole Prime was significantly hotter and wetter than anywhere on Earth, at least outside the tropics. Overhead, the skies were darkening; it wouldn't be long before the first rainstorms began, drenching the small settlement in rushing water. They'd designed the buildings to redirect water down to the ocean, but even so...it was a very odd settlement.

And it takes a very odd set of humans, he thought, *to live here.*

He smiled at the thought as he passed two of the French staffers jogging around the settlement before the rainstorm began. Both of them wore nothing more than bikini underpants, their breasts bobbing merrily as they moved. He reminded himself, firmly, he was a married man, even though there weren't many people in the settlement who wore more than shorts or swimming trunks. Anyone who tried to walk outside, wearing a suit and tie, was likely to get heatstroke sooner rather than later. The long-term settlers had just had to get used to near-nudity.

There were no dangerous animals on the island - the Tadpoles had cleared them out, years ago - but there was a metal fence surrounding the complex anyway, mainly to keep the children inside. Henry nodded to the guard at the gate, who opened the door to allow him to hurry down to the swimming pool. It was, perhaps, the strangest complex on the island, a structure that reminded him of an iceberg pushed up against a tropical beach. The Tadpoles had designed it as a place both races could meet and talk, but most humans found it uncomfortable. Henry wasn't *sure*, but he had the feeling the Tadpoles found it uncomfortable too, although for different reasons. A moist atmosphere, too wet for humans, might well be too dry for the aliens.

He glanced up as thunder rolled, directly overhead, then started to run as the rain started to pelt down. The pathway dissolved into a slippery mess, but he kept his balance with the ease of long practice as he reached the door and hurried inside. A pair of staffers stood there, one holding a headphone set that connected directly to the settlement's computers. Henry hated to think of how much money had been spent on the network, just to get something that was as near to truly intelligent as possible. But there was no choice. There was no other way to talk to the Tadpoles.

"The triad has been in the swimming pool for the last half hour," Mariko said. She was Japanese - and one of the smartest people Henry had met, although at twenty-five she was easy to underestimate. Her assignment to the embassy, perhaps the most vital duty station in the galaxy, spoke well of her. "They've been waiting for you."

Henry frowned, concerned. The Tadpoles didn't really understand human diplomacy, but it was unlike them to enter the negotiating chamber until their human counterparts had arrived, something to do with their social structure. If they'd changed the rules...he nodded to them both, placed the headset over his ears and hurried through the inner door. The Tadpoles were waiting for him.

He came to a halt as the triad surfaced, their dark eyes staring at him. The first humans to meet the Tadpoles face to face had thought they were staring at sea monsters - and, up close, it was easy to see their point. A Tadpole was a vaguely humanoid creature, but there were so many flaps and folds of leathery dark skin that it was hard to be sure. Indeed, there were people who steadfastly believed that the Tadpoles had no legs. He didn't wrinkle his nose at the faint smell of rotting fish - he was used to it - as he walked over to the swimming pool and sat down, allowing his legs to dangle into the water. There was nothing dangerous under the surface, he knew. The Tadpoles hadn't been able to understand why their human counterparts wanted the water free of smaller creatures - everything from tiny fish to crab-analogues - but they'd happily kept the water clear.

They probably thought of it as an embassy dinner, Henry thought. *And think of us as people who don't like to eat while we're working.*

"I greet you," he said. It was better to use simple concepts when talking to the Tadpoles, if only to limit the risk of screwing up the translation. "I have come, as you requested."

The triad - he was never sure if he was meeting the same Tadpoles, every time - shifted for a long chilling moment, their heads slipping in and out of the water. It was hard, very hard, to tell the Tadpoles apart; indeed, as a communal race, it was vanishingly rare to talk to one of the Tadpoles alone. The researchers assumed the Tadpoles had similar problems telling humans apart, although Henry wasn't so sure. Tadpole eyes were far more capable than human eyes and humans were far more distinctive.

"There have been developments," an atonal voice said, finally. No attempt to add emotion to the speaking voice had succeeded; indeed, reading Tadpole emotions was almost as hard as telling them apart. "A starship has returned from the unknown waters."

Henry blinked in surprise. The unknown waters were what the Tadpoles called the unexplored tramlines on the other side of their space. They'd been quite happy, after the dust had settled from the Anglo-Indian War, to share the costs of exploring the unknown regions, if only to prevent a second disastrous First Contact. Discovering one other intelligent race during their early explorations might have been bad luck, but discovering *two*...

"They have detected a third spacefaring race," the Tadpole voice said. "This race is apparently on the same level as ourselves."

"Wow," Henry said. His thoughts caught up with him a moment later. "Shit."

The Tadpoles had been more advanced than humanity by at least a decade, when the war had begun. And he knew, from bitter experience, that they'd come very close to winning. A new race presented all sorts of opportunities - humanity and the Tadpoles had learned a great deal from one another - but they also posed a threat. There could be no careful contact procedure when the newcomers were spacefaring, nor could contact be broken in an emergency. The First Contact mission would have to be put together very carefully.

"As laid down in the treaty, we intend to put together a task force to make contact," the Tadpole voice said. The triad jumped in and out of the water, sending waves rippling through the pool and splashing over the edge. "We invite you to add warships and contact specialists to the fleet."

Henry nodded. The treaty had gone into great detail about just *how* any new self-spacefaring race was to be approached, although the *next* First Contact - on Vesy - had been botched from start to finish. Both races were to be informed, defences were to be prepared and the First Contact mission was to be escorted and covered by a powerful task force. The Tadpoles would probably make the largest contribution, as they were closer to the new race, but humanity needed to be represented.

"I believe my people will be happy to uphold their half of the treaty," he said. The Tadpoles hadn't shown much interest in the Vesy, but a spacefaring race was a potential danger by any reasonable standards. "I will communicate with my people and request redeployment."

"All data has been forwarded to your embassy," the triad informed him. "We thank you."

They vanished beneath the water. Henry leaned forward, just in time to see them swimming out into the ocean, down towards their settlements far below the waves. He'd seen their cities through underwater cameras, but he'd never been there and he probably never would. A handful of humans had been modified to allow them to breathe underwater, yet Tadpole Prime's oceans held too many dangers. There were nasty shark-analogues that the Tadpoles treated as pets - and guard dogs.

He swung his legs out of the water and hurried back to the path, passing the headset to the staffers as he walked past. The rain was still falling, but it was slacking off and bright flickers of sunlight were burning through the clouds. He braced himself, then hurried through the warm downpour back towards the embassy. A handful of staffers and senior officials were already making their way into the building.

"Have coffee sent in for all of us," he ordered Potter, as he walked into the main conference room. "It's going to be a long day."

He took his seat at the head of the table and waited for the table to fill. No one had disagreed with the need to set up an embassy on Tadpole Prime, but there had been thousands of arguments over just who should be represented on the planet. In the end, it had been decided that there would only be one embassy, with a dozen ambassadors. Henry considered himself the senior ambassador, but he suspected the others thought he was merely the first amongst equals. Shaking his head at the thought, he opened his terminal and started to read the files as the staffers brought coffee. It was clear, judging from the attached reports, that it had been a pair of *human* starships that had discovered the new race.

They didn't mention that, he thought, amused. *They're more like us than they let on.*

He smiled at the thought, then sat upright as the room was sealed. Eleven ambassadors, four military attaches and two senior staffers looked back at him. He was mildly surprised that none of them had started accessing the files, although it was quite possible that *someone* within the embassy had given his superiors some advance warning. The problem with having a multinational staff, even on an alien homeworld, was that they had divided loyalties.

"You can review the files later, but the short version is that a pair of *human* starships have discovered a third intelligent race," he said, bluntly. "This race is spacefaring and may - I say *may* - pose a potential threat."

The French ambassador leaned forward. "Are you serious?"

"Yes," Henry said. "As you can see" - he brought up the starchart - "the newcomers are located on the other side of Tadpole space, the unknown waters. The survey ships analysed the data as best as they could, but they're unsure if the unknowns have any awareness or understanding of the tramlines. However, as they clearly have standard drives, they *should* be aware of the potentials."

"Unless they just overlooked them," one of the military officers offered. "We overlooked quite a few applications of gravimetric technology ourselves."

Henry nodded. "As we are unsure if this race poses any threat, the Tadpoles intend to make first contact as soon as possible," he said. "They have formally invoked our obligations under the Contact Treaty to request both technological and military support. I intend to send messages to the border guard, requesting a redeployment, but I also intend to take a number of experts from the embassy and join the Tadpole mission."

It took a moment for the implications to sink in. "You intend to go *personally*?"

"They need a senior representative, someone authorised by the Great Powers," Henry said, simply. He *did* have authority to speak for Earth, although there were so many caveats that his power was actually quite limited. "I'm probably the best choice for mission commander."

"And you want to get away from the embassy for a while," the American Ambassador joked.

Henry shrugged. Going on a Tadpole ship was one thing, but boarding a Royal Navy starship would mean spending hours explaining that he was no longer part of the Royal Family, even if he *had* kept the name. But really, what choice did he have? He *was* the best person for the job, certainly the most experienced when it came to contacting alien races. He'd been among the first humans to actually *speak* to the Tadpoles.

Another military officer leaned forward. "Should we prep the embassy for destruction?"

"I don't think there's any immediate threat," Henry said. He could understand why the Tadpoles were jumpy, but there was no evidence the mystery aliens had advanced towards Tadpole space. "Still, best to review our procedures. The Tadpoles nearly reached Earth during the first month of the war, after all."

He sighed, inwardly, as they began to review the files. In all the excitement - and it *was* exciting - he'd forgotten one very simple fact. How the hell was he going to explain his departure to his daughters? Janelle would understand - she was a military officer, even if she was technically a reservist - but his daughters? Victoria was eight, old enough to understand that her father was leaving, too young to understand that he would be back. Hell, she'd spent time crying whenever one of her parents had left the room.

I'll have to go, he told himself. *And all I can do is promise I'll be back.*

CHAPTER NINETEEN

This was not such a bright idea, George thought, as she dressed for the fight. It wasn't much; a shirt, a sports bra, a pair of shorts…neither would provide much protection if she took a hit. She couldn't help feeling sick as the hour drew closer. *But it has to be done.*

She swallowed, hard. Challenging Fraser directly had seemed such a smart idea, before she'd actually gone and done it. The logic was still good, she was sure, but she'd humiliated him in front of the other middies. Trapping him in an untenable position - unable to refuse the challenge, unable to demand something in exchange - had only made him mad. In hindsight, she understood - too late - what her tutors had meant when they'd talked about the dangers of death ground. Trapping an enemy was only a good idea if the enemy couldn't fight their way out of the trap, or maul you badly as you killed them.

You could still back out, a voice said, at the back of her head. *You don't have to go through with it.*

She shook her head, despite the temptation. Unlike Fraser, she had no position to lose, but if she backed out no one would ever respect her again. They'd see her as an empty-headed braggart and they'd be right, the silly little girl who'd allowed her mouth to get her into trouble. She checked her appearance in the mirror, wishing suddenly that she was allowed boxing gloves - she could have slipped something solid into them - and then opened the hatch. Honoraria was standing outside.

"I need to search you," Honoraria said. "Hold your arms above your head, please."

George scowled as Honoraria ran her hands over George's shirt and shorts. "What is the point of this?"

"The fight is bare-knuckled," Honoraria said, as she stepped backwards. "Neither of you are allowed weapons, apart from your hands and feet."

"Oh," George said. Good thing she *hadn't* tried to slip something into her clothing, as scanty as it was. "Are there any actual rules?"

Honoraria gave her a sharp look. "You didn't bother to look them up before throwing down the challenge?"

She went on before George could answer. "You fight with your hands and feet until one of you yields or is knocked out," she added. "Try not to kill him, but otherwise don't hold back and don't have any illusions about fighting a fair fight. If he gives you a shot at his balls, take it."

"I don't want to think about touching his balls," George protested.

"Then you better *had* start thinking about it," Honoraria snapped. "I *know* Fraser; he's tough, fast and very strong. You let him get you in a grip and you're fucked - and not in a good way. Don't even *think* about trying to trade blows because he has a colossal advantage. Get in there - go for the eyes, go for the balls - and keep moving."

She shook her head. "How much unarmed combat training did you take?"

"Just the academy classes," George admitted.

"You're fucked," Honoraria said. "Fraser's been sparring with some of the marines, for heaven's sake. And he survived the experience."

George swallowed. "Shit."

"Quite," Honoraria said. She glanced down at her wristcom. "It's time."

She turned and walked through the hatch. George hesitated, her legs refusing to move properly, and then forced herself to follow Honoraria. She'd never been in the boxing ring before - some of the crewmen boxed, but the marines tended to keep themselves to themselves - yet she didn't feel like looking around. Fraser was standing at the other end of the compartment, wearing nothing more than a loincloth. She couldn't help thinking that he looked like a barbarian hero out of a comic book.

"Well," Fraser said. He eyed her, coldly. She had to fight the urge to just stumble backwards. "Are you ready?"

"Yes," George said. She'd managed to get herself into this mess; if she couldn't win, she could at least make sure he knew he'd been in a fight. She tried not to look at the muscles rippling on his arms as he stepped over the line on the deck and into the ring. "I'm ready."

"Good," Fraser said. He nodded to Nathan, who was standing beside four of the other midshipmen. The remainder of the chamber was deserted. "Nathan will blow the whistle once we're at opposite sides of the ring. From that moment on, if you want to stop, all you have to do is throw yourself to your knees and beg for mercy."

"Yes, sir," George said.

Her legs felt like jelly, but she somehow managed to step over the line and enter the ring, taking up her position. Fraser studied her for a long moment - he was examining her muscles, she reasoned - before swaggering over to the other side. George braced herself as best as she could, trying to recall lessons she'd barely mastered, as Fraser nodded impatiently to Nathan. George's friend gave her a grim look, then blew the whistle.

Fraser met her eyes, trying to stare her down. George felt a sudden flicker of confidence, recalling high-class afternoon teas she'd been forced to endure. The family's elderly relatives might have had only a single brain cell between them, but they practically latched on to any hint of improper behaviour and attacked. He might be able to beat her to within an inch of her life, she thought, yet he couldn't psyche her out. Lying with a straight face was one of the skills she'd mastered as a very young girl.

There was a pause, then Fraser came forward. He wasn't covering himself, George noted, but it was clear that he didn't need to watch his back. She darted forward, trying to win herself some room, then ducked back as he threw at ugly punch at her head. Maybe she was faster than him, but she doubted it was enough. And yet, there was an opportunity...

She threw a punch of her own, realising the danger a fraction of a second too late. Fraser caught her arm, twisted her and practically *threw* her entire body right across the ring. It was all she could do to land properly, without coming down so hard the fight ended there and then; she lunged to the side as Fraser leapt at her, kicking out with his foot. He would never have dared try that against a trained opponent, but he'd probably scanned her file and knew her weaknesses. Unarmed combat had never been one of her skills.

He turned to face her, keeping his fists up in a boxing pose. George clenched her own fists, then moved to the side as he hurled a punch at her throat, throwing a jab of her own at his face. He lifted his arm to block the blow, grunting when she struck him, then slapped out at her chest. The blow stung, but didn't do any serious harm. Fraser snorted and turned again, punching out at her. George jumped backwards, looking for another opportunity to land a blow. She thought she was faster than him, but he was fast enough himself for that not to matter. Fraser paced her, then darted forward. George couldn't move quickly enough to keep him from grabbing hold, spinning her around and hurling her to the deck. She rolled over just in time to keep him from landing on her, jumping upwards and landing a punch right on his nose. It didn't break, she thought, but she was sure he'd *felt* it.

Fraser growled, bloody murder written in his eyes even as blood dripped from his nose and splashed on the deck. George almost broke then, almost threw herself to her knees, but something inside her refused to let her give up. He hurled himself forward, faster than she would have believed possible, and ploughed right into her, shoving her back down to the deck. George cried out in pain as she hit the ground, feeling his hands slamming down on her chest, just above her breasts, as they made their way to her throat. She clawed at him, trying to hit his groin or his eyes; he caught her wrists and shoved them back to the deck, holding them above her head with one hand while the other held her throat.

"Yield," he growled.

George tried to struggle, but his grip was too tight. The weight of his body, pressing down on her, made it impossible to move. She couldn't even draw up her knee to kick him; he simply knew, all too well, just how to hold her down. And the grip on her throat was tightening...

"Yield," he repeated.

Panic boiled at the corner of her mind. He wouldn't actually kill her, would he? But she'd provoked him, and she'd probably ruined what was left of his career, and...she refused to submit. If she could survive a depressurisation chamber at the academy...but a depressurisation chamber had never glared at her with such hatred. The smart move was to give up, and yet..."

"Fuck you," she managed. Her voice sounded odd in her ears, as if there was something wrong with it. "I *won't*."

"You're beaten," Fraser insisted. His weight shifted, slightly. "You cannot win!"

"Fuck you," George said, again. It was growing harder to breath. "I..."

He lowered his head until their eyes met. She stared into the face of hatred, into the face of someone she was *sure* would kill her...and yet she refused to submit. Her body was aching in pain - she had a nasty feeling she had a handful of broken bones - but she wasn't about to give in. They stared at each other for a long chilling moment, then he let go of her throat and rolled off her. George stared at him, one hand moving to rub her throat. It hurt, but there didn't look to be any permanent damage. Indeed, she was starting to think that she might have a great many bruises, yet nothing was actually broken.

Fraser touched his nose, gingerly. "You didn't break."

George stared at him. There was something odd in his voice too, something...*respect*?

She forced herself to sit upright. There were nasty bruises on her chest and bare legs, and her shirt had been badly torn, but otherwise she was intact. And yet, he could have killed her, or won the challenge by beating her head into the deck until she blacked out. It was hard to move, but she didn't want to be too close to him if he changed his mind.

"I could kill you, but I couldn't beat you," Fraser said. He sounded almost as though each word was torn from an unwilling mouth. "Congratulations."

He rose and held out a hand. George took it, feeling her body protest as he helped her to her feet. She honestly wasn't sure if she should go to sickbay or not - or, for that matter, if Fraser should go. Was his nose broken or was he merely having a nosebleed? The pain in her hand suggested she'd hit him quite hard...

You're dazed, she realised.

"Help her to sickbay," Fraser ordered. It took George a moment to realise that Nathan had stepped over the line and come to join them.

"I'll reorganise the duty shifts so she won't have anything until tomorrow afternoon."

"Yes, sir," Nathan said.

George forced herself to walk upright, despite the throbbing pain, as he helped her to leave the gym. She was damned if she was collapsing now...blood was staining her shirt; she glanced at it blearily, trying to determine where she was bleeding, before realising that it wasn't *her* blood. Fraser had been on top of her, hadn't he?

"I don't know if you won," Nathan said, as they stumbled down the corridor, "but I don't think you lost either."

"Yeah," George managed. It was suddenly very hard to stay upright. "There has to be an easier way to earn respect."

The midshipmen, for whatever reason, hadn't bothered to disable the monitors in the gym. It should have been beyond them, Susan knew, but she would have been surprised if someone who had been in the navy for as long as Midshipman Fraser *didn't* know how to evade the watching surveillance recorders where necessary. She'd watched, torn between the urge to intervene and the certain knowledge that events had to play out, as the two midshipmen had fought.

"He wanted her to submit," the Boatswain noted. "It would have been straightforward to knock her out."

Susan nodded, feeling a flicker of pride in her youngest midshipwoman. Demanding respect was futile, but once it was earned...she had the feeling that Midshipwoman Fitzwilliam wasn't going to have any problems with Fraser in future, even though she'd technically lost the bout. Fraser had seen the real *her*.

She looked at the Boatswain. "This was what you wanted, wasn't it?"

"I pushed her in the right direction, yes," the Boatswain said. He didn't bother to try to deny it. "She could let him beat her down, which would destroy her; she could ask her family for help, which would ruin her...or she could try to convince him, face to face, that there was more to her than a name. And she did."

Susan nodded, remembering all the rebukes she'd had for fighting in school. The daughter of an immigrant would always have a harder time than others, even though she'd been *born* in the United Kingdom. Old memories ran deep, after all, and the Troubles had left Britain's collective memory covered in scars. Teaching them to respect her, or at least to leave her alone, had been worth the punishments. But then, it had also disappointed her father...

She pushed the bitter guilt aside as she shut down the monitors. "I believe Midshipwoman Fitzwilliam is still assigned to you," she said. "Make sure she isn't pushed too hard, if Doctor Chung allows her to leave sickbay. Midshipman Fraser is currently attached to the tactical section, I believe. I'll have Commander Mason keep an eye on him."

"He's not a bad person," the Boatswain said.

Susan snorted. There were worse people - far worse people - than Midshipman Fraser serving in the Royal Navy, but that didn't excuse Fraser's conduct. She understood his feelings - she could even sympathise with a man who felt he was trapped in a dead-end position - yet she couldn't condone bullying other midshipmen. *Particularly* one who had a powerful family...perhaps, at some level, Fraser had hoped George *would* call her family for help. A dishonourable discharge would look very bad, but it wouldn't be quite the same as requesting a transfer or early separation.

"Have a word or two with him when you get the chance," she ordered. Fraser's file was odd; he'd been transferred to *Vanguard* before she was commissioned, but there were gaps in the data that puzzled her. It wasn't normal to transfer a middy to an incomplete battleship. He must have made a powerful enemy at some point...a few hints in the right place and his career would be effectively stalemated. "Tell him to buck up and promotion will be considered."

Which will have to be justified, she thought, darkly. Fraser was right; he'd spent too long as a midshipman to be promoted, unless he did something *very* heroic. *But a field promotion might be doable...*

Her wristcom buzzed. "Commander, this is Parkinson. The admiral has sent us a message."

Susan sighed. An order to relieve the captain? An order to attend a court martial? Or...what?

"I see," she said, trying to keep the sarcasm out of her voice. "And it says?"

"He's ordering all captains and their XOs to attend a holographic conference, one hour from now," Parkinson said. "And he wants all ships ready to depart within four hours. The exercises are now officially terminated."

Susan frowned. The war games still had another two days to run, with at least one final full-scale exercise being planned. Cancelling them now... there had to be an emergency, but where? The Tadpole border? Or maybe the Indians had decided to restart the last small colonial war.

"Understood," she said. She felt her frown deepen. Organising the games had taken nearly a year of diplomatic negotiation. Admiral Boskone - and Admiral Pournelle - would need a *very* good excuse for cancelling them before they were finished. "Did he say why?"

"No, Commander," Parkinson said. "But the message is very clear on the importance of departing on schedule."

"Order all stations to prepare for departure," Susan ordered. She'd have to find the captain and invite him into the holographic conference room. "And tell the logistics section to snatch what we need from the fleet train. I have a bad feeling about this."

She glanced at the Boatswain. "See to your department too," she added. "We may need it."

"No major injuries," Doctor Chung said. "But I *advise* you to make your excuses a little less blatantly untruthful."

"Thank you, sir," George said. She stood in front of the mirror and gazed at her naked body, covered in blue and purple marks. They'd vanish quickly, the doctor had assured her, but she'd be aching for the next couple of days. "And I'm sorry."

"Tripping and falling down a hatch tends to leave a different set of injuries," the doctor told her, sternly. "And your hand was quite clearly used to hit something solid."

George thanked him again, then dressed quickly and headed for the door. Outside, Nathan was waiting for her, holding a datapad in one hand.

He rose as she approached. "Do you want the good news or the bad news?"

"The *good* news," George said.

Nathan smirked. "The good news is that the fleet is apparently being reassigned, although no one knows where yet," he said. "The *bad* news is that I'm on toilet duty tonight."

He held out the datapad. It was showing the duty roster.

"He changed it," George said, in surprise. Fraser had delighted in assigning her to the worst jobs, but now they were evenly distributed. "I..."

"I guess you won," Nathan said. He slapped her shoulder. "Congratulations."

CHAPTER TWENTY

It was customary in the Royal Navy, Susan knew, to have all non-emergency meetings face-to-face. The Admiralty believed that actually *meeting* one's fellow officers was good for morale and, perhaps more importantly, made it easier for one to get the measure of one's fellows. Susan had never been so sure about the former, but the latter would have been a very good idea under other circumstances. As it was, she was quietly relieved that Admiral Boskone had ordered a holographic meeting. It was easier to cover any mistakes.

She followed the captain into the conference room and frowned in surprise as she noticed the foreigners who'd been invited to the meeting. The Americans were understandable, she supposed, but Admiral Boskone had invited the French, Russians, Japanese and Indians, even though the Indians had been Britain's enemies only a decade ago. Excitement ran down the back of her spine, warring with fear. The only reason she could think of for gathering *every* commanding officer in the system was alien contact - or alien war.

We're not far from the borders, she thought, grimly. *If the Tadpoles have decided to restart the war.*

"Sit down, Commander," Captain Blake said. He sounded nervous, one hand playing with his tie as he took his own seat. It was very lucky for him that the conference was purely electronic. The Admiral would not be amused if the battleship's commander fidgeted during a physical meeting. "Let's see what Admiral Boskone has for us."

Susan nodded, listening with one ear to a steady string of security updates. The human encryption system was a constant headache for the diplomats; human navies needed to talk to one another, particularly if they had to drop their petty disputes and ally against an outside threat, but no navy was keen on sharing its secrets. It might have saved time and effort if everyone had agreed to send messages in clear - every nation worked hard to crack foreign encryption schemes - yet she knew it wasn't going to happen. Unless, of course, the human race managed to unite…

And pigs will strap on wings and fly, she thought, darkly. *We're perfectly capable of fighting each other at the same time as an outside threat.*

"Gentlemen," Admiral Boskone said. Admiral Pournelle's image stood next to him, although they were on different ships. "I'll keep this brief."

Susan smiled, inwardly. *That* would be a first.

"A long-range exploration mission has stumbled across a third self-spacefaring race," the admiral continued. There were some gasps and muttered exclamations, but fewer than one might have expected. Experienced naval officers knew they wouldn't have been ordered to attend a joint meeting for anything less. "This race does not, as yet, pose an active threat, but they may well pose a *potential* threat. The Tadpoles would like to make first contact as soon as possible."

"Shit," Captain Blake muttered.

Susan eyed him, concerned, then turned her attention to the starchart as it flickered into existence. The unknowns were on the other side of Tadpole space, four weeks from their current location at full speed. It was probable - indeed, it was almost certain - that the Tadpoles would be redeploying their fleet to counter any threat from the unknowns, even though there was no reason to believe the unknowns knew the Tadpoles existed. They were, after all, a very careful race. Their precautions had almost given them an easy victory over humanity.

"In line with our treaty obligations, the fleet will depart Marina and head directly to UXS-468," Admiral Boskone informed them. "We will link up with Tadpole starships and experienced alien-contact personnel in that system, then proceed through the tramline to UXS-469 and onwards to the alien system, where we will attempt to make contact with the aliens. If all goes well, the majority of the fleet will remain in UXS-469 and the aliens will never have to know the fleet was there. But if trouble breaks out…"

"Shit," Captain Blake said, again.

Susan winced. First contact between humanity and the Tadpoles had ended badly and the first contact between humanity and the Vesy hadn't been much better, although the Vesy had posed no real threat. And human history suggested that first contacts would *always* be dangerous. Maybe the unknowns would be friendly, maybe they'd have more in common with humanity than either of the other two intelligent races, but it was equally possible that they might be hostile. They might see the appearance of a starship in their star system as an act of war.

And if they do start shooting, we'll need the fleet to cover the diplomats as they run, she thought, morbidly. *And maybe even win the war in one fell swoop.*

Captain Bunter cleared his throat. "Admiral," he said, "do we have a threat level?"

"Insufficient data," Admiral Boskone said. "The full reports will be forwarded to you, but the analysts believe that their tech level is roughly equal to ours before the First Interstellar War. So far, the only question mark is over their use of the tramlines. They do not appear to have a presence in UXS-469 and there's no hint they actually explore other star systems, beyond their own. However, UXS-469 is a barren system and they may have decided not to explore further."

It would be odd if they had, Susan thought. There was no shortage of barren systems within the human sphere that were useless in themselves, but led to other systems that were far more habitable. The aliens must be aware of the tramlines, surely. And yet, if they weren't, it opened up all sorts of possibility for avoiding further contact, if the unknowns turned out to be hostile. *But they may not think like we do.*

"We will remain on tactical alert, however," Admiral Boskone warned. "The ambassadors on Tadpole Prime have activated the relevant sections of the treaties governing first contact and this fleet will act as a united force. As the senior officer, I will serve as overall CO, with Admiral Pournelle as my second. This will be awkward for all concerned, but under the circumstances we will expect all officers to be professional about it."

Susan hid a smile. It *would* be awkward, not least because Admiral Pournelle's fleet was actually larger. But the treaties governing the allied command structure were clear; the senior officer, by time in grade, would be the overall commander. It had caused problems, back during the war, yet there was no choice. Humanity could not afford to face a new threat while disunited.

"The fleet will depart in three hours," Admiral Boskone concluded. "There will be no time for further war games, unfortunately, but we will be sharing tactical data and testing the command network during the voyage. Hopefully, this will be a completely peaceful contact and the diplomats can handle everything. If it isn't, I have faith that each and every one of you will uphold the finest traditions of the human race."

His image blinked out of existence as the conference came to an end. Susan watched, feeling a strange mix of emotions, as the other holograms vanished. It was odd to attend a conference where hardly anyone had the chance to ask questions, but that wasn't what was bothering her. Alien contact would be a useful feather in her cap, even though she'd just be a passive observer if all went well, yet she didn't see how the aliens *didn't* know about the tramlines. Humanity had been exploring them long before developing realspace drives.

"Interesting," the captain said. "I trust you'll have the ship ready for departure?"

"Of course, sir," Susan said. She'd started preparations as soon as the admiral had contacted the ship, trying to make sure that everything was ready. "We'll be travelling with the remainder of the fleet."

She looked down at the deck. "But I don't see how they can *avoid* knowing about the tramlines..."

"There were ancient civilisations on Earth that never developed the wheel," the captain pointed out, smoothly. "It wasn't until they encountered other civilisations that they realised the concept existed."

Yeah, Susan thought. *And what happened to those civilisations when they encountered superior forces*?

She scowled, inwardly, as they left the conference room and separated, the captain heading to his quarters while Susan headed to the bridge. A self-spacefaring race, even one a decade or two behind humanity, would be a valuable trading partner, although there might be disputes over sharing colony worlds. Humanity and the Tadpoles could share easily, she knew; it would be harder to share a world with another race that wanted the surface, rather than the deep oceans. And yet, if the unknowns truly didn't know how to jump through the tramlines, they were likely to be irked when they discovered just how close they were to Tadpole space.

They won't have much room for expansion, she thought, remembering the starchart. *And if that star is their homeworld, they'll have almost no cushion between the centre of their civilisation and a potential alien threat.*

"Commander," Mason said, when she stepped onto the bridge. "You have the conn."

"I have the conn," Susan agreed. She took the command chair and looked at the display for a long moment. "Status report?"

"All decks report that they are ready to depart on schedule," Mason told her. "We have five shuttles still on deployment, picking up crew from the shore leave facilities, but otherwise we can depart now if necessary."

Susan's lips quirked. Shore leave facilities on Marina were minimal, but she hadn't been surprised when the crew competed eagerly for the handful of slots assigned to *Vanguard*. It was a chance to get out of the metal hull, after all, and enjoy the local company. But it was a problem now, when the battleship had to get underway as quickly as possible. Repatriating any stranded crewmen to Earth would be a major headache.

"Inform me when the shuttles have returned," she said. Admiral Boskone *probably* wouldn't order the fleet to depart ahead of schedule, not when it was unlikely the situation would change in a hurry, but she wanted to be ready. The last thing she needed, right now, was the admiral peering over her shoulder. "And forward me the datapack from the flagship."

"Aye, Commander," Mason said. He leaned forward. "What's happening?"

"Alien contact," Susan said. She suspected the rumours would already be spreading through the fleet, growing wilder and wilder with each retelling. The admiral would probably declassify most of the files, once the tactical staff had run their own analysis, but that would take at least a week. "A brand-new self-spacefaring race!"

"That's one for the record books," Mason said. He grinned, showing his teeth. "This time, we can show people how to make First Contact properly."

"Assuming that that's even possible," Parkinson said. "Just *talking* to the Tadpoles is difficult, sometimes. So much of their culture is completely alien to ours."

"They can't be *that* different," Mason said. "Their technology works along the same lines as ours."

"Their technology isn't *that* different, sir," Parkinson said, "but their culture is *very* different. A human politician who told us about the benefits of socialism would be thrown out on his arse, but to the Tadpoles socialism is a normal way of life."

"That's because socialism doesn't work," Mason said.

"Not for us, sir," Parkinson said. "Our society is structured to fit our nature and fill our living needs. For them, however, socialism and communal decision-making are just a fact of life; they don't need to farm for food when they can just take what they need from the ocean."

He shrugged. "But even among humans," he added, "what's normal in one society may be offensive in another. That's why the diplomats have so much trouble, even now, keeping international relationships on a steady keel."

Susan nodded. She hadn't majored in first contacts - real and imaginary - at the academy, but she knew the basics. There were countless stories and movies about first contacts that turned bad, from aliens finding humans incomprehensibly ugly to one side making a gesture that the other considered hostile. Parkinson was right. If a simple gesture like shaking hands could turn into a major incident, among *humans*, who knew what the unknowns would consider a threat? Or a rude gesture?

"It's probably a good thing you're here," she said. "Do you have any feel for how they'll approach the aliens?"

"Assuming they stick with the planned procedures, they'll monitor alien communications traffic as best as they can, in the hopes of learning their language, then start beaming signals towards the alien homeworld from the outer edge of the system," Parkinson said. "That said, we showed the first contact protocols to the Tadpoles, after the war, and the Tadpoles were mystified. They understood the maths, but they didn't understand some of the other components."

He frowned. "If we manage to build up a shared language, we'll advance forward and attempt a face-to-face meeting. By then, hopefully, we should have a good idea what the aliens look like and other such details. We have cultural exchange packages for them that are quite informative, but hold nothing of military value."

Mason gave him a sharp look. "Are you sure?"

"Reasonably sure," Parkinson said. "They won't be told anything about the human sphere until we know we can trust them, but details on how we live and work can't be used against us. It cuts down on the prospects for misunderstandings later."

"Unless they find our mere existence offensive," Susan pointed out.

"They might," Parkinson said. "Commander, with all due respect, most of our first contact planning is theoretical. The Tadpoles announced their existence by attacking Vera Cruz; the Vesy were force-fed human languages by the Russians, once they were discovered. For all we know, the unknowns might be giant spiders bent on having us for dinner or cyborgs who want us to be one with the collective. Everything we were taught about discussions with aliens started with the warning to leave our preconceptions at the door."

He shrugged. "What do we do if the aliens have two sexes, but only one of them is actually intelligent? Or what do we do if the alien social system is something we find disgusting? Or what if the aliens are telepathic, able to read our thoughts? There's no way to know what we'll encounter until we actually do."

"They'll be in trouble if they try to read *my* thoughts," Mason said.

"I can imagine," Susan agreed. She keyed her console, bringing up the datapacket. "Inform me when the admiral orders the fleet to depart."

"Aye, Commander," Mason said.

Susan skimmed through the datapacket, but had to conclude - reluctantly - that there was very little to use as the starting point for her analysis.

The survey ships hadn't risked returning to the alien system, let alone creeping close enough to the alien planet to gather more useful data. She didn't blame them, either. *Humanity* would take a dim view of someone skulking around the edge of the solar system, even if it *was* a justifiable precaution. If the aliens had caught the survey ships, they might just have started a war there and then.

Though they shouldn't have been able to track the survey ships back to Earth, she thought. It felt wrong to be glad the Tadpoles were between humanity and the new race, but it *was* something of a blessing. *The survey crews would have destroyed their ships rather than let them fall into enemy hands.*

She sucked in a breath as she contemplated the final report. The survey crews *weren't* full-fledged tactical experts, but she couldn't really disagree with their conclusions, save one. She couldn't see any evidence the aliens were using the tramlines, yet she couldn't understand how they'd managed to develop space drives without understanding the potential of naturally-occurring gravimetric lines. Maybe they'd missed it, but still...

They'll copy the idea from us, if they haven't thought of it for themselves, she thought. *And that won't take too long.*

"Commander," Mason said, breaking into her thoughts. "All shuttles have returned to the ship. We're ready to depart."

"Signal the admiral and inform him that we're ready," Susan said, curtly. They still had an hour, but it was possible the admiral would want to depart ahead of schedule. "And then send me a copy of the updated crew rotas. I want to run through tactical exercises while we're on the move."

"Aye, Commander," Mason said.

Susan sighed, inwardly. The admiral hadn't noticed anything wrong with the captain, as far as she could tell, but that might be about to change. *Vanguard's* commanding officer - a man with six years seniority - would almost certainly be put in command of a flotilla, a subunit of the task force. There was no way for Admiral Boskone to avoid it, not without violating naval protocol and giving offense. And the hell of it was that Captain Blake probably wouldn't mind at all...

And I have no idea how I'm going to handle that, she thought. *And I have no idea what I'm going to do if the shit hits the fan.*

"Commander," Parkinson said. "The Admiral has uploaded a revised set of files to the datanet. They're marked for the crew."

"Then forward the files to their inboxes," Susan said. That was quick, but she supposed there really wasn't that much that needed classifying. There was just too little data to be of real use. "Was there anything else?"

"No, Commander," Parkinson said.

Susan nodded, then sat back in her chair, thinking hard. It might be time to start planning for the worst. There was a good chance she'd end up in deep shit, if the Admiralty ever found out, but there was likely to be enough blame to go around anyway…

The unknowns might turn nasty, she reminded herself. *And if they do, we need to be ready.*

CHAPTER TWENTY ONE

"You're being reassigned again, it would seem," Fraser said. There was no malice in his voice, no readiness to mock her. "You're going to Turret Six."

George nodded as she took the datapad. Matters had *definitely* improved in middy country over the last fortnight; Fraser treated her like all the other middies, while she'd made friends with her older comrades. She was still the baby of the ship - *that* wouldn't change until another midshipman arrived - but at least she was no longer being assigned to every demeaning task. And Fraser had actually been giving her useful advice...

She blinked as she read the brief message. "What do I do in the turret?"

"If you're lucky, nothing," Fraser said. "If you're unlucky, which you will be because the XO loves calling snap drills, you'll be controlling the guns as they target enemy starships or hastily replacing overheating components before they explode."

"Ouch," George said, passing back the datapad. At least she had nine hours before she was supposed to present herself at her new duty station. "I'll do my best not to let the XO down."

"That would be a bad idea," Fraser agreed, dryly.

"Hey," Midshipman Tim Williams said. "Do you want to place any bets?"

George shrugged. Everyone on the ship had been arguing - and betting - over the most important topic of the moment, just what the mysterious aliens actually *looked* like. George had heard crewmen arguing that the aliens would be little green or grey men, while others had insisted the aliens would be cyborgs or simply progressed beyond the need for physical forms. She'd been tempted to bet a pound on the aliens looking exactly like humans - the odds weren't in her favour, yet if she won she'd win big - but so far she hadn't joined the betting pool. Gambling onboard ship could be immensely destructive to morale.

"So far, pointy-eared humanoids are doing well," Tim offered. "And bird-like creatures aren't too bad."

Fraser leaned forward. "Birds?"

"Well, we've had aliens who practically live in the sea and we've had humanoid lizards," Tim said. "And if *we're* the mammals, then birds are about the only *genus* that hasn't been represented in intelligent form."

"I don't think those words mean what you think they mean," Fraser said, darkly. "Besides, for all we know, bird-like aliens could be vastly in the majority and we're in the minority."

"Then the odds of this new race being bird-like are high," Tim pronounced. "And so it's a poor bet."

"Only if it loses," George said.

Fraser snorted. "But could birds become intelligent?"

Tim stuck out his tongue. "Could monkeys?"

"Obviously not," Fraser sneered. "You're not intelligent at all."

"Blast," Tim said, without heat. "You've proved the fatal flaw in my grand scheme of universal understanding."

"I think I need to go to bed," George said. She removed her jacket as she walked past them, silently cursing regulations under her breath. She'd have to take a shower before she climbed into her rack and went to sleep. She understood the reasoning - being cooped up with ten unwashed bodies would become hellish very quickly - but it was still annoying. "Or I'll be too tired to see the aliens when they arrive."

"You'll have plenty of time to kip when we're in the next system," Tim said.

"No, she won't," Fraser said. "I heard we're going to stay on tactical alert at all times, at least until we *know* the new aliens aren't going to start a fight."

Tim swore. "Does the captain have any idea what that would do to us?"

"I'm sure he'd appreciate you telling him differently," Fraser said, dryly. "Why don't you march up to his cabin and tell him that we can't handle double shifts for more than a day or two? We'll be sure to visit you in the brig."

"At least I'll get some rest," Tim said.

Fraser snorted, rudely. George hid her amusement - it was nice to see a more humorous side of her former tormentor - as she finished undressing and hurried into the shower compartment to wash. Jokes aside, Tim had a point; the midshipmen would be exhausted if they had to pull double shifts for more than a couple of days, even if normal duties were reduced or suspended entirely. But they had three weeks to get ready before entering the closest system to the alien world…

She felt a flicker of excitement as she washed herself as quickly as she could. Aliens! She might be nothing more than a midshipwoman, but she was still going to make history. People would talk about *Vanguard* and those who served on her in the same awed tone as they spoke of *Ark Royal* and her handful of surviving crewmen. Her uncle might have made himself a hero by serving on *Ark Royal*; she'd have the chance to do the same, for herself. Who knew *what* opportunities would emerge in the next few weeks?

None at all, unless you sleep now, she told herself, as hot air washed down from high overhead. The only advantage to serving on a battleship, as far as she could tell, was a higher ration of bathing water. It wasn't as if the ship was short on water - if worst came to worst, they could mine a handy comet or water-ice asteroid - but there had to be *some* perks reserved for the senior officers. *And you have to impress your new supervisor tomorrow.*

Shaking her head, she pulled on her panties, stepped back into the main compartment and climbed into her rack. Fraser had already left, heading off to his duty shift, while Tim was playing with his datapad. He'd met an American crewwoman during his brief period of shore leave - he'd been the only midshipman to win a slot - and they were still exchanging messages. George wasn't sure if she should envy him or laugh at the growing intimacy.

Good night, she thought, as she pulled the curtain closed. *It'll be morning all too soon.*

The report was clear, Susan discovered, as she waited patiently in her cabin for the others to arrive. *Vanguard's* stockpile of spare parts was well above the levels specified by regulations; indeed, the logistics officers were surprised that no one had attempted to requisition spare parts from *Vanguard* for one of the other ships. They'd have kicked up a fuss, Susan knew, if someone *had*; it was common, alarmingly so, for engineering officers to understate the spares at their disposal. *She* would have been annoyed with any officer who dared try that on *her* ship, but she knew that other XOs weren't so scrupulous. Keeping their ship in working order was their highest priority.

She looked up as the hatch opened, revealing Mason and Parkinson. Mason looked unconcerned - he'd been to her cabin before, several times - but Parkinson seemed unsure of himself. He'd been on Tadpole Prime, she recalled, attached to the embassy. The communications officer would have a greater awareness of social strata than most starship officers, even if none of them questioned who was in charge. It was uncommon for ambassadors to invite their junior staffers to tea and cakes.

"Take a seat," she urged, as warmly as she could. She felt almost as nervous as she'd been the first time she'd donned a spacesuit for a high-orbital jump. "There's tea and coffee in the dispenser."

"I'll be mother," Mason said, as the hatch opened again. This time, Reed and Charlotte Watson stepped into the compartment. "Tea or coffee?"

"Tea for me, please," Susan said.

She rose and padded over to the sofa as the others sat down. Reed seemed surprised by the invitation; Charlotte's expression was completely blank, suggesting she either had a vague inkling of what was up or that she was all too aware that she was the lowest-ranked officer in the compartment. Mason poured tea and coffee, then passed the cups around before sitting down next to Susan. She allowed herself a moment of relief that everyone had come without asking too many questions, then took a sip of her tea.

It isn't as if a meeting of the senior staff is a problem, she told herself, although she knew things could go badly wrong. *But it will look very bad in hindsight.*

"Thank you for coming," she said, as she put her cup down on the table. "There is an important matter we need to discuss."

She paused, knowing that she was about to commit herself. Just hearing what she was about to say - just hearing it and not reporting it - could get her junior officers in trouble, when the Admiralty found out. Susan had gone to some trouble to obscure the meeting from any official logs, but she knew the inboard sensors would have tracked her subordinates as they walked to her cabin. In hindsight, she should have set up a regular poker game as an excuse to have a meeting without arousing suspicion.

And if one of them goes to the admiral, she thought, *the shit will hit the fan.*

"Captain Blake…has lost his nerve," she stated, baldly. In hindsight, the captain's actions suggested a very *definite* loss of nerve. "He froze up on the bridge during war games."

"Indeed," Mason agreed. "The early analysis of the battle made it very clear that we were caught with our pants down, but we still took too long to react."

"There was some confusion over who was actually in command," Reed said. His voice was flat, revealing nothing of his emotions. "We weren't sure who to obey."

"And we only won through luck and the application of brute force," Susan added. "If we'd lost, I dare say Admiral Boskone would not have been pleased."

She tapped the table, meaningfully. "What's going to happen when this ship goes into a *real* battle?"

Charlotte looked pale. "Is that likely to happen?"

"There's an unknown alien race out there," Mason pointed out, coldly. "*Anything* could happen. If the captain were to fire on an alien ship…"

Susan felt cold. How many others had been thinking along the same lines?

"We don't know there's going to be a fight, but we have to prepare for the worst," she said, carefully. "The damage we took in the war games was simulated. Any damage we take in an actual fight will be *real*."

"It might not be so bad," Reed pointed out, with the air of a man desperately trying to find a bright side. "Our simulations assumed the worst, repeatedly."

"Or it might be far worse," Mason said. "For all we know, the aliens have a superweapon that can blow *Vanguard* into dust with a single shot."

"They might," Reed agreed. He looked directly at Susan. "What do you propose we do?"

"We could go to the admiral," Charlotte said. "If we have concerns..."

"We'd have to explain why we didn't do it earlier," Mason snapped, interrupting her. "And relieving the captain of command ourselves could end badly."

Susan nodded. She'd looked up the precedents, such as they were. Only two captains had been relieved of duty by their senior officers in the last hundred years; one for gross misconduct, the other for mental instability. There hadn't been many details in the files, but reading between the lines it had been clear that both sets of officers had had their careers blighted. The Admiralty wasn't keen on senior officers relieving their commanders. It cast doubt on the sheer level of authority granted to commanding officers.

And even reporting the problem to higher authority can end badly, she thought. *Even if we didn't have to explain why we didn't say anything earlier.*

Charlotte took a shaky breath. "So what do we do?"

"I notice Major Andreas and the Chief Engineer weren't invited," Mason said. "Did you have a reason to leave them out?"

"Yes," Susan said. She looked from face to face, hoping they understood. "If the shit hits the fan, I'm going to relieve the captain of command. If necessary, I'll stun him on the bridge and leave him there until after the shooting has stopped. This will not be reported to Admiral Boskone or any of the flotilla until the fighting is over. All I need from you is your acceptance of the change in command."

"You're putting yourself at risk," Mason observed.

Susan nodded. If she relieved the captain in the middle of a combat zone, the best she could hope for was a court martial and a long sentence to Colchester Military Prison. Admiral Boskone *might* review the records and decide to send her back to Earth, rather than passing summary judgement himself. But if he didn't, or if the captain's contacts took his side, she rather suspected she'd be marched to the gallows and hanged. His family would definitely blame her for his disgrace.

"I understand the risk," she said, out loud. She'd never been anywhere near Colchester, but she'd gone through the dreaded Conduct After Capture course at the academy. Being in prison would probably be worse, far worse. "And I will take full responsibility if things go badly wrong."

"Which they will," Mason said. "You're talking about mutiny."

"It isn't quite a mutiny," Reed protested.

"Call it mutiny, barratry or whatever," Susan said, crossly. Captain Blake would *certainly* call it mutiny. "The point is that I am going to relieve the captain of command in a combat zone. The Admiral will not fail to take a dim view of it."

"I can't let you do this alone," Mason said.

"You have to," Susan said. Whatever happened, her career was doomed. Perhaps it was what she deserved, for not reporting the problem as soon as she'd become aware there *was* a problem, but she'd been caught in a trap. "There's no point in throwing your career away right behind mine."

She met Parkinson's eyes. "All you have to do is follow my orders, as if I was in command…"

"You *are* in command," Reed said. "You're this ship's commanding officer in all but name."

"I'm sure that argument will impress the Admiralty," Mason said. "It's quite possible the captain will just lurk in his cabin when the shit hits the fan."

"You don't know it *will* hit the fan," Charlotte insisted.

"We have to prepare for the worst," Susan said, again. "I don't know anything about this new alien race - do you? But we do know that first contact with the Tadpoles went badly wrong and led to a shooting war. I will *not* have this ship found wanting if we have to take her into battle."

She studied the younger woman for a long moment. Charlotte was very good with her sensors, all right, but she hadn't had enough experience to understand the little compromises officers had to make with regulations. Or, for that matter, to realise that doing the *legal* thing could sometimes blow one's career out of the water. She'd have to learn quickly, Susan told herself, or she'd wind up in deep trouble. Politics shouldn't have any bearing on military operations, everyone knew, but they did.

"I understand," Mason said, quietly. "For what it's worth, I won't oppose you when you take command."

Susan nodded, gratefully. It was rare, vanishingly rare - in fact, she couldn't think of a single incident - when a captain was taken out without losing the entire ship. Maybe a fleet carrier could survive something that took out the bridge - there were secondary bridges and emergency control stations - but anything that inflicted serious damage on a cruiser or destroyer would smash the command network beyond hope of repair.

And yet we have procedures for losing the bridge, she thought, darkly. *We just don't have procedures for losing the captain.*

Reed leaned forward. "I assume he refuses to go for a medical exam?"

"I doubt one would pick up on his loss of bottle," Mason sneered. "It isn't a *physical* problem."

"No," Susan said, flatly.

"Then I won't resist your coup either," Reed said. "Are you planning to ask anyone else?"

"Just the senior bridge crew," Susan said. If it had been *entirely* up to her, *no one* would have been told before she actually relieved the captain, but she didn't dare risk a confrontation on the bridge while the ship was under attack. "Whatever happens, no one else is to have advance warning."

"Yes, Commander," Parkinson said. "And I won't resist either."

"I'm not remotely comfortable with this," Charlotte admitted.

"Join the club," Mason snapped.

"But it does have to be done," Charlotte continued, ignoring Mason's interruption. "And if it is to be a joint endeavour..."

"It should be just me," Susan said, flatly. "If worst come to worst, I'm hoping none of you will be considered accomplices."

"We will be," Mason said.

"But I am the XO," Susan said. "It was *my* duty to bring our concerns to higher authority and I did not do so. My career is the only one that should be at risk."

"With all due respect, Commander, your career is *not* the only one at risk," Reed said. "And yeah, maybe we should have complained while we were back home. Now, all we can do is prepare for the worst."

"Very well," Susan said. "But nothing - absolutely *nothing* - is to be done unless the shit hits the fan. I don't want to hear about *anything* that might be related to this until the shit hits the fan. Do you all understand me?"

"Yes, Commander," Reed said.

Susan allowed herself a sigh of relief. There should be no need to take any further precautions, except obtaining a stunner from the armoury and practicing with it. And who knew? Maybe her precautions would not be necessary.

Sure, the pessimistic side of her mind noted. *And perhaps the horse will learn to sing.*

CHAPTER TWENTY TWO

Despite himself, Henry couldn't help feeling a mixture of delight and concern as the shuttle approached the giant battleship. He'd hoped, once upon a time, to vanish into the ranks of the Royal Navy as yet another fighter pilot, but everything that had happened to him - being captured by the Tadpoles and turned into the first *de facto* ambassador - had rendered that impossible. The child in him loved the concept of the battleship; the adult knew he was going to have to explain, time and time again, that he was no longer a Prince of the Realm.

And whoever reinvented the concept of the male being in line to the throne, rather than the firstborn, really needs to burn, he thought. *I will not be King of Britain.*

He scowled at the thought. The only good news, as far as he could tell, was that most of the human ships had been on war games, rather than dispatched from Earth. Admiral Boskone had to be gloating over his luck; the only reporters on the ships would be Admiralty-approved embedded reporters, rather than the dunderheads who made up the vast majority of the media corps. Maybe the ones who'd chased him all over the world *hadn't* been assigned to clearing up the mess in the restricted zones, but at least they wouldn't be on *Vanguard*. He could pass wind without worrying about reading about it on the datanet.

The shuttle slowed as it approached the battleship, then carefully docked itself against one of the universal airlocks. Henry had worried about taking a Tadpole shuttle, but thankfully the Tadpoles had anticipated the problem and borrowed a human-designed shuttle - as well as a pilot - from the embassy before their fleet had departed Tadpole Prime. Living on a Tadpole ship wasn't easy - most of the ship was filled with water, effectively keeping the humans prisoner - but they were going to meet a whole new alien race! Henry would have happily spent the entire trip in a spacesuit, smell and all.

"The hatch is opening," the pilot called. "Ambassador, if you would like to disembark first…?"

Henry sighed, inwardly. He'd signalled ahead, asking for a lack of ceremony, but it was clear that whoever was in command of the battleship had chosen to ignore his request. And to think he'd been careful to ask for his staff to be placed on *Vanguard*, rather than the fleet carrier *Courageous*! Part of it was curiosity - he'd never had the chance to inspect the first true human battleship - but the rest of it was ensuring a degree of separation between the ambassadorial staff and the military commanding officer. It meant nothing to him - he'd been in the military - yet it would be important to others. Besides, it might just convince the unknowns that humanity *hadn't* sent a purely military force to make contact.

And they'd have to be very stupid to believe that, he thought, rising. *But a sensible race would understand the need to take precautions.*

He tugged down his shirt as he walked towards the hatch, feeling oddly uncomfortable in his shirt and trousers. He'd grown far too used to the heat of Tadpole Prime, but he doubted he'd be allowed to walk the battleship's corridors in swimming trunks. Or, for that matter, that his female staff would be allowed to wear nothing more than bikini briefs. He pushed the thought aside, pasted something he devoutly *hoped* was a princely expression on his face and stepped through the hatch. The battleship was strikingly *cold*.

"Britannia, arriving," a voice boomed.

Henry fought hard to keep his face expressionless as he took in the handful of people waiting for him, wearing their dress uniforms. They'd hate him for that alone, he was sure. Unless dress uniforms had magically become more comfortable in the thirteen years since he'd left the navy, which he doubted, there wasn't a single person in the line who wasn't either uncomfortable or itchy. Or both. And to think he'd bloody *asked* for a complete lack of ceremony!

He braced himself, saluted the flag and then turned his attention to the ship's officers. The Captain looked dashing in his uniform, but there was something about his attitude that reminded Henry of some of his odder cousins. Beside him, his XO was a dark-skinned woman, one who seemed preoccupied with a greater thought. At least she didn't seem to carry a chip on her shoulder, as far too many officers - including his younger self - did after life had reminded them, far too often, that it wasn't fair.

"Welcome onboard, Your Highness," Captain Blake said. His file suggested a career officer with good prospects, but the fawning tone in his voice suggested otherwise. Did he really think *Henry* could boost his career? Even *King Charles* would have problems patronising an officer, regardless of his skills. "It is a pleasure to have you on my ship."

"Thank you, Captain," Henry said. Maybe it had been a mistake to ask for *Vanguard*, but he'd expected to meet someone akin to Theodore Smith or James Fitzwilliam. Smith had torn him a new asshole, twice, and he'd deserved both of them. "I look forward to finding my way around her."

"Certainly, Your Highness," Captain Blake said. "But first, let me introduce my officers."

His tone shifted, marginally, as he introduced nine men and women, suggesting that some of them had powerful connections while others did not. Henry committed their names and faces to memory - if there was one good thing about his training, it was that he never forgot a face - and made private plans to talk with them later. Commander Onarina was probably a fascinating conversationalist; there was something about her attitude that reminded him of Janelle, although he couldn't put his finger on it. And Midshipman Fitzwilliam looked like a young and feminine version of her uncle.

Poor girl, Henry thought, as Captain Blake introduced her. His fawning sounded worse than unwanted sexual advances. *She looks as though she hates him.*

"I'll show you to your cabin personally," the captain finished. "We've put your staffers in nearby compartments."

"That's good to hear," Henry lied. Maybe he was a bit older from when he'd served on *Ark Royal*, but he wasn't fat enough to need a whole compartment for himself. "I'll also need to review your tactical staff's work, if that's all right."

"Of course, Your Highness," the captain said. "If you'll come right this way…?"

He didn't seem interested in greeting any of the staffers, Henry noted, as Captain Blake led him through the corridors. *Vanguard* felt different from *Ark Royal*, a sense of newness pervading the hull, even though the hints of paint he recalled from *Theodore Smith's* commissioning ceremony were absent. But then, the Old Lady had been over seventy years old by the time she'd sailed out to do battle against the Tadpoles. *Vanguard* had barely been in active service for *three*.

"I'm looking forward to hearing about the war games," he said, as they reached Officer Country. "I heard they were quite spectacular."

"Indeed they were," Captain Blake said. "My crew acquitted itself well."

He keyed a switch, opening a hatch. For a moment, Henry simply stared. The cabin was huge, easily large enough for thirty or forty sleeping racks. There was a drinks cabinet, a solid desk, a private computer terminal…the bed, he saw to his astonishment, was located in a separate compartment. He wasn't exactly unused to huge bedrooms, but on a starship wasting so much space on one person was absurd!

"Your bags will be brought along, Your Highness," Captain Blake said. "I was hoping we could discuss policy later."

"I need to discuss how best to approach the unknowns," Henry said. It was true enough. The Tadpoles had a basic plan, but human input would be required before the fleet advanced to UXS-469. "My staff will coordinate with the admiral's staff…"

"I believe the admiral intends to invite you to dinner tomorrow night," Captain Blake said, seriously. "I'd be delighted, however, if you joined me in my stateroom for dinner tonight."

It won't get you anything, Henry thought. He scrambled for an excuse, but came up with nothing. Captain Blake might be annoying, yet his dinner invitation couldn't be declined diplomatically. Stopping a war would be easier. *Blast.*

"I would be honoured," he lied, smoothly. "And I look forward to discussing the war games with you."

Captain Blake bowed and retreated out of the hatch. Henry watched him go, then shook his head in disbelief. Admiral Smith hadn't treated him with any deference. Indeed, when he'd discovered that Henry and Janelle had become lovers, he'd scolded Henry for exposing Janelle to the media. Henry's own *father* hadn't torn him apart so effectively. The idea of Admiral Smith fawning...it was impossible to credit. And Admiral Fitzwilliam hadn't been any more inclined to fawn on his well-connected officers.

Not that he had to be, Henry thought. *He was already at the top of the tree.*

The buzzer rang. Henry hesitated, then hurried over to the hatch and pressed the key. It opened, revealing Midshipwoman Fitzwilliam. She was carrying his carryall in one hand, her expression rather bemused. No doubt, given her relatives, she'd expected him to travel with no less than five trunks of clothes, books and assorted junk.

"Thank you," Henry said, taking the carryall. The only thing he'd really needed was his diplomatic outfit and a handful of clothes. A couple of datachips could carry more books and movies than he could hope to read in a year, even if he devoted himself to nothing else. "I hope your uncle is fine?"

Midshipwoman Fitzwilliam looked embarrassed. "He was fine the last time I saw him," she said, so quietly he had to strain to hear her. At least her connections were *useful*. Henry had never found an upside to being a Prince of the Realm and potential Heir to the Throne. "I didn't have a chance to speak to him."

Her graduation ceremony, Henry recalled. The First Space Lord was always the keynote speaker, unless a genuine emergency cropped up. *Her classmates will have known who she was...*

"I'm glad to hear it," he said, feeling a sudden surge of sympathy. "I served under him, you know."

"I know," Midshipwoman Fitzwilliam said. "He spoke of you, a few times. Said you had..."

She broke off. Henry shrugged. The First Space Lord - Captain Fitzwilliam, as he'd been at the time - hadn't had the best impression of him, the first time they'd met. Anything he said afterwards, certainly anything said in private, would be a two-edged sword. And he didn't blame the poor girl for not wanting to repeat whatever she'd heard.

"It doesn't matter," he said. It would have been nice to chat with his former commander, but that wouldn't happen unless he returned to Earth. "Thank you for bringing my bag."

He watched her go, wondering just who'd given her the assignment and why. A midshipwoman wasn't meant to carry bags, fetch tea or any other task more suited to a steward or a crewman. Indeed, it was either a humiliating task, intended as a punishment, or another example of the captain's fawning. He was starting to have the feeling that *Vanguard* wasn't exactly a happy ship.

Shaking his head, he placed the carryall on the bed and walked back to the desk. A line of messages had already appeared in his inbox, mainly concerning plans for making first contact. Captain Blake had been correct, he noted; Admiral Boskone had invited Henry and his staff to dinner the following day. No doubt the captain was congratulating himself on having pulled off a social coup.

Idiot, he thought, coldly. *Let's see what dinner brings.*

It hadn't been an easy two weeks.

Susan had known she was committing herself, when she'd spoken to the other senior officers about her plans. A single word from one of them to the captain, or the admiral, would have brought the entire plan crashing down in ruins, probably taking her career with it. Her tension had only risen the closer they'd come to UXS-468, where they were due to meet up with the diplomats. It hadn't made organising the flotilla any easier.

At least the captain didn't invite his subordinate captains to dinner, she thought, as she stepped into the captain's stateroom. *And he left the midshipmen out of the invitation too.*

She honestly wasn't sure what to make of Prince Henry. His service in the navy and his apparent death hadn't impressed her at the time, although she *did* have to admit he'd worked hard to keep his true identity a secret. Indeed, it had only come out after he'd been reported missing in action. And then, he'd gone off to serve as an ambassador, rather than stay on Earth. She didn't know if she should be impressed - he could have enjoyed an easy life if he'd stayed - or suspicious. For all she knew, a more competent ambassador was pushed aside to allow the prince to shine.

But they wouldn't play games with the ambassador to Tadpole Prime, she thought. *Even if the government was inclined to allow it, the other Great Powers would object.*

"I have wondered what the social scene on Tadpole Prime is like," Captain Blake was saying, as she took her place at the table. "Do you have many parties?"

Susan didn't - quite - roll her eyes. The rich or well-connected brats she recalled from her schooling had bragged about attending parties, about how their dresses had cost thousands of pounds apiece and how they'd been driven all the way to London from Hanover Towers just for a chance to dance with the aristocracy. Maybe Prince Henry had been like that, once upon a time, but she rather doubted it. He'd run all the way to the academy to escape the press.

"I'm afraid we have only a handful of entertainments," the prince said, casually. Too casually. "There aren't really enough of us for a proper social scene."

He smiled. "And my former title means nothing to a society that has representatives from nearly every spacefaring nation on Earth, still less the Tadpoles themselves," he added, his voice lightening. "They don't have any concept of family lines. It's very rare for one of them to *know* who sired him."

Susan hid her amusement with an effort. "What do you make of them?"

"The Tadpoles? It's hard to say anything for sure," Prince Henry said. "There's no real hope of getting agents to give us the inside scoop, as it were. I think, in a few hundred years, we and they will share interlinked space, but rarely actually *talk*."

He cleared his throat. "But I was curious to ask about the war games," he said. "How did they go?"

"We proved the battleship concept," Susan said, when it became clear Captain Blake was not going to answer. "Well, at least we proved it in simulations. But we still have a long way to go."

"We tagged many American starfighters," Captain Blake said. "Covered ourselves from their attacks."

Prince Henry winced. He'd been a starfighter pilot, Susan recalled, a pilot who'd earned his wings when the Tadpoles were introducing the human race to plasma weapons. Nearly a third of *every* starfighter pilot in the human sphere had died in the fighting, most of them picked off by rapid-fire plasma cannons. And *Vanguard* mounted more of them than any war-era Tadpole starship.

"We could certainly win most of the battles of the war, if they were refought," Susan said, feeling a twinge of sympathy. "But we assume the Tadpoles have advanced too. Do you know anything about their innovations?"

"We know they have several more superdreadnaughts," Henry said. "You've seen a couple in their fleet. But we don't know anything about their later innovations. They've been mucking around with focused gravity beams, yet we don't know if they've come up with anything workable."

Susan frowned. "Focused gravity beams?"

"A homemade tramline," Henry said. "Apparently, it's *theoretically* possible."

"That would change everything," Captain Blake said. For once, he sounded completely serious. "If we were no longer bound by the tram-lines…"

"It would," Henry agreed. "If nothing else, it would open up a number of previously inaccessible stars. But we don't know if they've actually had any real success. They certainly haven't told us anything."

Captain Blake leaned forward as the stewards entered. "And you know this how?"

"Careful intelligence work, much of which is classified," Henry said. "And quite a few details are well above my level."

Susan considered it, thoughtfully. It was the Tadpoles who'd discov-ered ways to use tramlines humanity had dismissed as being too weak to allow a starship to jump from one star system to another. If there was any race who could invent a workable FTL drive, it was the Tadpoles. And yet, there *was* a tramline in place; they merely enhanced it. It would be a great deal harder to craft one from nothing…

The Holy Grail, she thought. *Everyone wants an FTL drive and an FTL communicator…*

"I think you'll enjoy the food, Your Highness," Captain Blake said. Susan was almost grateful for the shift from the awkward topic. "I had it brought specifically for diplomatic dinners."

The Prince smiled. "How did you know I'd be coming?"

"I didn't," the captain said. His lips twitched in amusement. "I expected to host Admiral Boskone and his staff after the war games."

"I see," Prince Henry said. His expression darkened. "I hope everything goes peacefully, Captain, but if it doesn't…"

"You needn't worry, Your Highness," Captain Blake said. The confidence in his voice was almost convincing. "We're ready for anything."

Susan kept her peace, but she desperately hoped he was right.

CHAPTER TWENTY THREE

"Jump completed, Commander," Reed reported. "We have entered UXS-469."

Susan nodded, feeling an odd shiver running down the back of her spine. There was little of importance in UXS-469, but it linked directly to an alien star system...had Admiral Smith and his crew felt the same way too, when they'd taken *Ark Royal* deep into Tadpole space to wage war?

We're not here for war, she told herself, firmly. *We're here to make peaceful contact with our new friends.*

But the shiver wouldn't go away.

She pushed the thought aside and studied the display as starship after starship blinked into existence. Sixty-one human starships, including five fleet carriers; forty-one Tadpole starships, including three fleet carriers and five superdreadnaughts. It was the single most powerful fleet to be deployed, ever; she had no doubt they could smash through both fleets if they were sent back in time to the First Interstellar War. Coordinating the fleet was a major headache - she'd lost count of the number of soothing messages she'd had to send to various commanding officers - but it was still formidable. If the newcomers wanted a fight, they'd rapidly find themselves in serious trouble.

"Long-range sensors are clear," Charlotte reported. "There's no sign of any activity within the system."

Susan scowled. She'd argued - or, rather, primed the captain to argue - that the fleet should enter UXS-469 under cloak. *She* wouldn't be too happy if she saw an immense fleet entering the Terra Nova System, a single jump from Earth, and she saw no reason to assume the aliens would disagree. But Captain Blake had been overruled. If the newcomers had no access to the tramlines, there was no point in keeping the fleet cloaked and, if they *did*, they'd probably be nervous if they detected a cloaked fleet. Susan privately suspected the argument was nonsense, but there was no way she could push her point any harder. The absence of starships, settlements and navigational beacons within UXS-469 *did* suggest that the aliens either couldn't reach the system or considered it useless.

But there's at least one other tramline that should be usable, if they could get here in the first place, she thought. *And it leads directly to Tadpole space.*

"Keep us at tactical alert," she ordered. She had to bite down the impulse to issue orders to the screen, but Admiral Boskone held that authority. "And make sure we remain linked to the fleet command network."

"Aye, Commander," Mason said.

Susan glanced down at her console as the fleet slowly advanced into the system, leaving the tramline behind. They'd crawl to the other tramline, if they followed the plan, and then send scouts through before the contact ship made its own jump. If the aliens were waiting on the other side, with bad intentions, the scouts would detect them before it was too late. And yet, no one thought that was likely. Guarding an entire tramline was beyond the capabilities of every human navy, working together.

"Orders from the flag," Parkinson reported. "The fleet is to advance along its planned course."

Susan sucked in a breath. Admiral Boskone and Admiral Pournelle didn't see any reason to delay, then. She found it hard to blame them - a successful first contact would put both men in the record books - but she still felt inclined to be cautious. Or perhaps it was the Tadpoles, insisting on an early first contact. Given how badly they'd reacted to a botched first contact, they probably had good reason to want to establish friendly contact before there were any incidents.

And there were incidents on their homeworld that caused problems, she thought, grimly. *If we hadn't been talking to them, would we have had another war?*

"Very well," she said, slowly. "Helm, take us away from the tramline as planned."

She leaned back in the command chair, silently grateful the captain wasn't on the bridge. The fleet surrounding *Vanguard* was powerful, enough firepower to cover a retreat if necessary, yet the nasty sensation at the back of her mind refused to go away. Perhaps it was simple proximity to the alien tramline, perhaps it was just stress caused by her contingency planning…but she still felt worried. She hadn't felt so concerned since the tactical exercises she'd done at the academy, where her grade had depended on beating her fellow cadets…

"Sensors," she said. "Are there no contacts at all?"

"Nothing apart from the fleet itself, Commander," Charlotte assured her. "We have every inch of space for light-seconds around the fleet under constant observation. We'd know if a single atom of space dust was out of position."

"Good," Susan said. She didn't feel any better, but there was nothing she could do about the sensation bothering her. "Continue to monitor local space."

Gritting her teeth, she forced herself to relax. There was no *evidence* that they weren't alone in UXS-469, there was nothing to suggest they were being watched…and yet, the hairs on the back of her neck continued to prickle. Maybe it was just psychometric…

But we've taken all the precautions we can, she thought, grimly. *We're ready for anything…*

"That's a Tadpole fleet carrier," Gunner Fitzroy Simpson said. He was a short man, with a muscular body and a kindly face that reminded George of her first teacher. "See if you can draw a bead on her."

George nodded, angling the targeting system so the main gun was pointed directly at the Tadpole starship. She wasn't *quite* out of effective range, but the magnetic bottles that kept the superhot plasma in position would probably start to degrade before they struck the Tadpole starship's hull. No one was quite sure just how heavily the Tadpoles armoured their latest generation of fleet carriers, yet George was sure they'd know they'd been kissed. The battleship's plasma cannons were an order of magnitude more powerful than any the Tadpoles had been known to deploy themselves.

"I'm targeting her drives," she said. She rather liked the gunners, although they kept themselves to themselves when they weren't on duty. "That should cripple her even if it doesn't destroy her."

"Very good," Simpson said. He tapped another icon on the screen. "And what do you make of *that* target?"

"Armoured superdreadnaught," George said. She closed her eyes as she recited from memory. "Probably immune to long-range fire."

"Probably," Simpson agreed. "We might scratch her hull, but burning through her armour would require a steady bombardment."

George nodded. She'd studied the final battle of the war, between *Ark Royal* and a Tadpole superdreadnaught, and she'd been struck by just how confident the Tadpoles had been that they could burn through the Old Lady's armour before she rammed their ship. But they'd underestimated the extra layers of armour that had been woven over the ancient carrier before committing themselves to a death ride. *Vanguard* might have been able to kill *Ark Royal* before it was too late - the gunners were rather reluctant to discuss possibilities with her - but anything lesser would have died with the Old Lady.

"They'll have upgraded their weapons," she said, slowly. "Won't they?"

"Probably," Simpson said. He didn't sound concerned, which surprised her. "We keep updating our own weapons too."

"That's true," another gunner said. Peter Barton was only a year or two older than George, young enough that she'd caught him glancing at her once or twice when he thought she wasn't looking. "Why, I've heard the boffins are coming up with a one-shot weapon that will blow a superdreadnaught into dust."

"Let us hope not," Simpson said, dryly. "A weapon that can turn one of their ships into dust can easily do the same to ours."

George nodded in agreement. She'd heard rumours - everyone heard rumours - that Britain and every other spacefaring nation was throwing money into all kinds of advanced or unusual weapons programs. There hadn't been anything concrete - half the rumours had been concepts stolen from various science-fantasy programs - but she was certain there was *some* truth to the rumours. The human race couldn't afford to let the Tadpoles have a breakthrough that rendered the Royal Navy nothing more than scrap metal.

"We'd be back in the days of tin-can ships," Simpson added. "Cramped little pieces of metal, one-hit wonders. And he who brought the most to a fight would win."

"I saw one of those ships in London," George recalled. "They were tiny!"

She smiled at the memory. Her mother, perhaps intent on keeping her from joining the navy, had taken her to the Imperial War Museum as soon as it reopened after the floods, where the family name had been enough to convince the curators to allow her to crawl around inside HMS *Victory*, the first true British warship. She'd been ugly, nothing more than a handful of modules buckled around a plasma drive and her crew crammed into quarters that made middy country look huge, and yet she'd been truly fascinating. But Simpson was right too. A single warhead - a conventional warhead, rather than a nuke - would have been more than enough to vaporise the ship.

"My grandfather used to fly on them," Simpson said. "He said *we* have it easy."

"We don't have it easy," Barton protested. "Changing the plasma conduits is hard work."

"Back then, if they sprang a leak, they were in deep shit," Simpson said. "And they didn't even have artificial gravity. They floated around the ship and strapped themselves down when the time came to change course."

"Might have been fun," Barton insisted. "You can do a *lot* in zero-gee."

"They didn't have muscle regenerators either," Simpson pointed out. "You spend a few months on one of those ships, you'll be as weak as a kitten."

George shivered. The early fears that lunar colonists would be unable to return to the homeworld had proved unfounded, but muscle decay had proved a very real problem, forcing the colonists to exercise daily if they ever wanted to go back home. There were a handful of asteroid colonies without gravity, where the inhabitants could fly around like birds…at the cost of never being able to enter a gravity field again. They'd looked inhuman, she recalled from her studies; so thin and delicate that she'd be afraid to *touch* one. She had no doubt that humans belonged in space, but there was no need to strip the human race of its ability to live on a planet.

Simpson cleared his throat. "That's enough target practice for one day," he said. "Why don't you and Peter inspect the tubes?"

"Yes, sir," Barton said.

George carefully deactivated the console, then stepped back. There wasn't any *real* prospect of accidentally opening fire on a nearby starship, she'd been assured, but caution had been drummed into her at the academy. The turrets were designed to act on their own, if necessary, although she found it hard to imagine the ship taking so much damage the turrets couldn't be controlled from the bridge. What would happen, she wondered, if each of the eight turrets engaged eight different targets?

"This way," Barton said. "Coming?"

"Yep," George said.

Barton pulled back a hatch, allowing them to climb into the tubes surrounding the gunnery station. The temperature seemed warmer, although George had never been sure if it genuinely *was* hotter or if it was just the awareness that she was far too close to a dozen containment fields, each one holding enough superhot plasma to vaporise an entire section of the hull. If there was a leak, she'd been told when she'd first started her work in the turret, she'd be vaporised so completely that no one would ever know she'd been there.

"We need to check the containment systems here," Barton said. "Make sure there's nothing older than a couple of months."

"Understood," George said. "Is the venting system online?"

"Just in case," Barton confirmed. "I don't think the gunner will thank us if we accidentally vent a containment chamber."

George nodded - if nothing else, the chamber would have to be carefully inspected, then refilled - and started to check the field components, one by one. Barton did the same on the other side of the section, making notes as he worked. A couple of components were reaching the end of their service, even though they didn't need to be replaced immediately. George had a feeling Simpson would make sure they were replaced a week before regulations *insisted* they had to be replaced. Simpson hadn't risen to his current post by taking chances.

"Some of these parts can be broken down and refurbished, then sold to civilians," Barton commented. "Or turned into mines."

"Pretty dangerous work," George said. "Who'd want them?"

"Less dangerous than you might think," Barton said. He glanced up at her, his face shining with sweat. "There's a shitload of redundancy built into each of these little beauties. We replace them because our demands change randomly, but a civilian power system wouldn't have so many shifts in demand. Or we can just use them to construct mines."

George made a face. Minefields were normally wasted in space, although mining the skies over a couple of worlds had delayed the Tadpoles by a few hours. On the other hand, if an enemy force could be lured into the minefield…she saw the idea, but she wouldn't have wanted to try it. A single mistake could turn the minefield into a deadly trap for both sides.

And civilians talk about mining the tramlines, she thought. *It just isn't possible.*

She finished her section, then moved over to recheck Barton's work. She'd found it annoying, back when she'd started at the academy, but there had been enough early problems for her to understand the value. He'd check her work, just in case she'd missed something; she worked her way through her section and decided he'd done everything right. But then, with Simpson riding herd on him, she doubted he'd dare to make a mistake. The gunner's disappointment would be worse than a screaming fit.

"So," Barton said, as he finished. His voice was casual, too casual. "When do you expect your next shore leave?"

George laughed, despite herself. "I have no idea," she said. She was an officer, to all intents and purposes and he was a crewman; he certainly shouldn't be trying to pick her up. And yet, she had to admire his nerve. "It depends on where the ship goes, doesn't it?"

———

"Welcome to the bridge, Your Highness," Captain Blake said.

Henry groaned, resisting the urge to shoot a murderous look at the captain's back as he relieved his XO. He'd told Captain Blake seven times - at least - that he was no longer in the line of succession, yet the man kept insisting on addressing him as *Your Highness.* He wouldn't have minded *Sir*, or *Flying Officer* - it had been his rank when he'd left the navy - or *Mr. Ambassador* but *Your Highness* was nothing more than a reminder of the past, a past he'd put firmly behind him.

And Victoria is going to grow up without being in line to the throne, he told himself, as he stood at the back of the bridge. *And any reporter who even looks at her funny is going to be hit with a harassment suit.*

He smiled at the thought - putting a reporter through legal hell would have given him no end of pleasure - as he studied the display. UXS-469 looked deserted, save for the joint fleet; a handful of scouts were already racing towards the alien tramline. There was no sign of any unknown starships, yet he understood why so many officers were concerned. Logically, the newcomers should have access to the tramlines. Why hadn't they picketed UXS-469, if nothing else? It was what both humanity and the Tadpoles would have done?

Perhaps this is the very edge of their space, he thought. *And the world we're approaching is their version of Cromwell or Pegasus.*

"As you can see, Your Highness, all is in order," Captain Blake said. "There's no sign of alien contact."

"That is always good to hear," Henry said, keeping his expression blank. He'd learned to hide his true feelings early in life, although living on Tadpole Prime had weakened his control. There was no point in maintaining a poker face when the Tadpoles wouldn't have noticed - or cared - if he'd thrown a tantrum. "Let us hope things stay that way."

"Ah, yes," Captain Blake said. He nodded towards an unoccupied console. "If you'd care to take that..."

Henry nodded and strode over to the chair. He had no idea how his father endured so many ceremonies without either strong drink or mental conditioning - or why his sister actually *wanted* to be Queen. Didn't she have enough problems as a princess? If she put on even a little weight, she was fat; if she slimmed down, she was terrifyingly thin...

"Captain," the sensor officer said. "I'm picking up something odd, behind us."

The XO sat upright. "What?"

"I'm not sure," the sensor officer admitted. Her already pale face seemed to pale further. "It could be a sensor distortion field. I can't see it directly, but there are hints from the other ships…"

"Alert Admiral Boskone," the XO ordered. She shot a sharp glance at Henry. "Captain, I recommend we move to red alert."

"We don't know what the contact is," the captain objected.

Henry groaned inwardly. He'd flown starfighters, not starships, but even *he* knew that the mystery contact was too close. And it was blocking their line of retreat. If that was a coincidence, it was a very dangerous one. The fleet needed to know what was creeping up behind it, now…

The display flared with red light. "I'm picking up active sensors, multiple sources," the sensor officer snapped. "Sensor analysis calls them targeting sensors."

"Red alert," the XO snapped, hitting a control on her console. Alarms started to howl. "All hands to battlestations. I say again…"

"Incoming missiles," the sensor officer said. "They've opened fire!"

CHAPTER TWENTY FOUR

"They've opened fire?"

Susan barely had time for the captain's stunned question. The unknowns - and she doubted they'd run into a *second* unknown race - had carried out a near-perfect ambush. They had to have detected the survey ships, part of her mind noted, and lurked in UXS-469 until more starships arrived. And then they'd attacked. Unprovoked, they'd attacked.

"Stand by point defence," she snapped. Launching missiles from long range was an exercise in futility, which suggested the aliens had something nasty up their sleeves. "Alert the screen; order them to adjust formation and prepare to repel attack!"

"They can't," Captain Blake stammered. He sounded as if he were on the verge of panicking again. "They shouldn't even be here! Run the first contact protocols - we have to *talk* to them!"

Susan gritted her teeth, pulled the stunner from her belt and stunned the captain before he could hope to react. He collapsed on the deck, unconscious. It was unfortunate, part of her mind noted, that he'd seen fit to invite Prince Henry to the bridge. The bridge crew might keep quiet about a pre-planned mutiny, but the prince might be experienced enough to recognise what she'd done. And yet, he might also understand *why* she'd done it.

"I am formally relieving the captain of command," she stated, for the record. "If any of you wish to object, you may insert a note into the ship's log."

She sat down in the command chair, resting the stunner in her lap. None of the senior officers would object, she was sure, but the juniors might do something stupid. And then there was the prince, a wild card. She was tempted to order him off the bridge, yet she knew she didn't dare take the risk of him going straight to the marines. The last thing they needed was a shootout on the bridge.

"Admiral Boskone has ordered all starfighters launched," Parkinson reported. "He's also attempting to use the first contact protocols, but the unknowns are not responding."

"Shooting at someone is also a form of communication," Mason noted. "It says they don't want us around."

"Launch sensor probes," Susan ordered. It was hard, very hard, for the tactical sensors to get a lock on their foes. Their sensor stealth system wasn't a *perfect* cloaking device, but it seemed capable of keeping active sensors from gaining a hard lock on enemy hulls. "And..."

"Incoming starfighters," Charlotte snapped. "They're launching starfighters of their own."

"Order the point defence to concentrate on the missiles," Susan ordered. The enemy missiles *had* to carry something nasty, something *far* nastier than a standard nuke. They *had* to know the defenders would swat most of the missiles out of space before they could enter attack range. "Can you get me a target breakdown?"

"They're concentrating on the bigger ships," Charlotte said. "*Courageous, Enterprise*, the Tadpole carriers...and us."

Susan braced herself as the missiles roared into attack range. The fleet's point defence opened fire, picking off dozens of missiles before they could pose a danger...

...And then the missiles began to detonate. Laser heads, part of her mind noted, but far more powerful than any humanity had managed to design. Shafts of deadly force lanced out towards their targets, slicing through their hulls and inflicting heavy damage on their interiors. A destroyer blew apart in a flash of light - the first ship to die - followed rapidly by an American cruiser and a French frigate.

"Got a solid lock," Charlotte snapped. The display cleared, revealing twelve heavy starships - battleships or superdreadnaughts - and nine carriers, surrounded by over seventy smaller ships. "They're firing a second spread of missiles!"

And most of our heavy ships are designed to fire energy weapons, Susan thought. Admiral Boskone was reorganising his formation, but the enemy were already pounding the crap out of the screen. *They have an undeniable edge at long-range.*

"Launch our own missiles," she ordered. She doubted they'd score *any* hits, unless the alien point defence was puny, but it would give them something else to worry about. "And prepare to reverse course."

Mason sucked in his breath. "*Courageous* and *Enterprise* have been targeted," he snapped, loudly. "Their screens are moving to provide cover..."

"Alter course," Susan ordered. If the aliens had been watching the fleet from a distance, they might have successfully identified the command ships. Or they might just have been shooting at the carriers. "Bring us about. Prepare to close the range."

She clenched her fists as missiles roared down on the two fleet carriers. Hundreds died, but dozens survived long enough to detonate, blasting laser beams directly into the massive starships. *Courageous* staggered out of formation, plasma venting from her hull; Susan found herself praying that the crew had had enough time to run for the lifepods before the massive ship exploded into a ball of expanding plasma. Seconds later, *Enterprise* followed, the American carrier struggling valiantly until the end.

"Admiral Boskone is dead," Mason reported.

"Enemy ships targeting the Tadpole carriers," Charlotte added. "Our starfighters..."

New icons flared to life on the display. "Commander," Charlotte snapped, interrupting herself, "there are new enemy starships emerging from Tramline Two!"

Well, the morbid side of Susan's mind noted, *that settles the question of whether or not the aliens can use the tramlines.*

"Get on to the fleet command network," she ordered. Losing both of the fleet's commanding officers meant...what? Who was in command? "Find out who's in command!"

"Aye, Commander," Parkinson said.

Susan nodded, then watched grimly as the three starfighter groups collided. The unknowns seemed to be at a slight disadvantage, although they possessed plasma weapons; the missiles she'd launched into the teeth of the enemy formation had all been picked off effortlessly. But the loss of the fleet carriers - the unknowns had blown a Tadpole carrier apart and were now concentrating their efforts on the remaining carriers - meant that recovering the fighter pilots would be far harder...and rearming them would be impossible. The entire formation was coming apart.

It could be a Tadpole in command, she thought, as the sensor display updated again. The unknowns had *definitely* planned the ambush, blocking both the fleet's retreat and any prospect of it charging through the tramline to fight to the death. *Or...*

She shuddered. Was Captain *Blake* supposed to be in command?

"*Belfast* has been destroyed," Mason reported quietly. "*Dallas* has taken heavy damage and her commander has ordered an evacuation..."

Let's hope the aliens are in the mood to take prisoners, Susan thought. *But even if they want to take prisoners, can they keep them alive?*

"Commander," Parkinson said, quietly. "Captain Blake is meant to be in command."

Susan swore. She should have had a contingency plan for *that*, but... but she'd never anticipated every officer above him being either killed or knocked out of contact. Surely there was someone else who could take command? And yet, with the fleet carriers taking a pounding, *Vanguard* was probably the only ship in the fleet that had a reasonable chance of remaining intact. Or, at least, the only human ship.

"They're requesting orders," Parkinson added. "I can inform them that Captain Blake has been...disabled...?"

"No," Susan said. She wasn't sure what to do - no regulations covered this situation - but the fleet couldn't afford an argument over who was in command, not now. "Reroute the fleet command network through the CIC, then update me on the fleet's status..."

She thought, rapidly. The fleet couldn't stay where it was or it would be smashed to rubble, piece by piece. Charging forward into the teeth of enemy fire wasn't an option, not when there was only one battleship and four superdreadnaughts. *Vanguard* and the superdreadnaughts might survive, but the remaining ships would be lost. And yet, there was something odd about the alien formation, something she was missing...

It struck her in a moment of brilliant insight. The unknowns didn't need to worry about trapping the fleet in an inescapable trap; they'd brought more than enough firepower to complete the fleet's destruction. And yet, they'd left the fleet a way out...why? The way to Tramline Three was clear! No matter how she looked at it, the only answer was that the unknowns hadn't figured out how to use the alien-grade tramlines!

"Signal all ships," she ordered. "They are to change course and head directly to Tramline Three."

"Aye, Commander," Parkinson said.

Susan ran her hand through her sweaty hair. She'd either be promoted, if she got the fleet back home, or shot. Or both. The Admiralty would have problems deciding just which charge to put on the execution warrant. She fought down a very childish giggle at the thought, then studied the display. The human starfighters were doing well, very well, but the aliens had the numbers. And it was clear that the only thing holding them back was their technology, not any lack of skill. Given updated starfighters, Susan noted, they'd have a definite edge.

"Order the fleet carriers to take point, escorted by half of the destroyers," she continued, as the display updated. *Vanguard* and the superdreadnaughts would have to take the brunt of enemy fire. Luckily, their armour should be able to resist the enemy weapons. But if there was a *third* enemy fleet, she'd just sent her remaining fleet carriers to their doom. She pushed the thought aside as she considered her options. "And then order the starfighters to engage the enemy formation..."

She swore, inwardly, as the second wave of enemy ships launched a new force of starfighters towards the human ships. "Belay that order," she added. *Vanguard* could shrug off starfighters, unless they were armed with something completely new, but the fleet carriers and the smaller ships were dangerously vulnerable. "Recall the starfighters. They are to provide cover."

"Aye, Commander," Parkinson said.

"The enemy ships are targeting us," Charlotte said. "They're launching another spread of missiles."

And at closer range too, Susan noted. It probably wouldn't make any difference, but it showed just how forcefully the aliens were pressing the advantage. *We may be about to give Vanguard her first real test.*

"The point defence cannons are to fire at will," she ordered. If only they'd been able to link the human and Tadpole ships together! The formation was really composed of two separate formations, barely able to talk to one another! Did the aliens realise it? All they'd have to do was run a tactical analysis and the patterns would be unmistakable. "And try and link our communications overlay with the Tadpole systems!"

"That may cause problems, Commander," Parkinson said. "I..."

"So will a flight of missiles," Susan snapped. And the aliens were launching yet another salvo, targeting the remaining carriers! "We have to stop as many of those missiles as possible!"

"Recommend a hammerhead firing pattern," Mason said. "It might work."

"Do it," Susan ordered.

The captain moaned from the deck. Susan hesitated, unsure what to do. There was a risk of brain damage if someone was repeatedly stunned, but if the captain recovered he could try to retake command. If only he'd had the sense to stay in his cabin, chatting up the prince...

"I'll take him out of here," Prince Henry said. "You concentrate on keeping us alive."

Susan nodded, gratefully.

"Enemy missiles approaching engagement range," Mason said. "Point defence armed and ready...firing missiles."

And see if we can punch holes in their formation, Susan thought. The enemy starfighters were ripping through the formation, despite losing hundreds of pilots to the fleet's point defence. They seemed to have targeted the American carrier *Eisenhower* specifically, although Susan wasn't sure what the Americans had done to piss them off. But then, she had no idea what the contact fleet had done to piss the aliens off either...

"*Eisenhower* has been destroyed," Charlotte noted. "Tadpole-Three is under heavy attack."

"Missiles entering engagement range," Mason snapped.

Susan nodded. Standard laser heads needed to be closer if they wanted to inflict real damage, but the aliens had managed to evade that problem. She wondered idly how they did it, then dismissed the thought. The boffins could figure it out, just as they'd worked out how the Tadpole technology worked during the last war. All that mattered, right now, was saving as much of the fleet as she could...

She keyed her console. "All hands, brace for impact," she snapped. "I say again, all hands brace for impact!"

"Tadpole-Three has been destroyed," Charlotte reported. "Commander..."

Henry felt sweat pouring down his face as he dragged the groggy Captain Blake into his Ready Room, then closed the hatch firmly behind him. He knew he was in good shape, despite spending most of the last decade behind a desk on Tadpole Prime, but Captain Blake felt like so much deadweight. Henry dumped the former commanding officer on the deck, then looked around for something he could use to tie the man's hands. It was *just* possible that the stunner had caused a heart attack, but it didn't look likely. Captain Blake wasn't *that* overweight.

Just stupid and foolish, Henry thought, as he hunted through the Ready Room. It was crammed with junk, but there was no rope, duct tape or anything else he needed. He wound up having to convert a dinner tie into a makeshift rope and using it to bind the captain's hands. *Why couldn't he have stuffed something useful into his Ready Room*?

Captain Blake groaned. Henry contemplated stuffing something into the man's mouth, just to keep him quiet, but it wasn't so easy to gag someone in real life. Stellar Star might be bound and gagged, stark naked, every second episode; real people needed tougher measures to keep them quiet. Besides, stunners posed health risks; it was just possible the captain would throw up, or worse, and he'd choke to death on his own vomit if he was gagged.

I could kill you, he thought, darkly. He'd reviewed the captain's record three times since boarding the battleship, using his access codes to read the classified sections, but there had been nothing to suggest that Captain

Blake was a crawling sycophant. Hell, Henry would have tolerated the sycophancy if Captain Blake had been *competent. I might even be able to get away with snapping your neck right now.*

He scowled. It wasn't likely, not really. But leaving Captain Blake alive created no shortage of problems. His goddamned contacts were likely to demand the XO be hanged for daring to relieve their precious captain of duty. And wouldn't *that* cause problems, when the rest of the navy learned what had happened. The Old Boys Network couldn't be allowed to push a *known* incompetent into command or all hell would break loose.

The captain stared up at him, his eyes flickering from side to side. Henry had never been stunned in his life, but from what he'd heard it was rather like recovering from a three-day bender. It would be quite some time before the captain was ready to cause trouble…he shook his head, tiredly. Admiral Smith would never have reacted so poorly, nor would Admiral Fitzwilliam. If nothing else, Henry was sure he could talk to the latter and work to avert a court martial for the XO. She'd handled the situation poorly, but he had no idea how it could have been handled better.

Accidentally poison the idiot, he thought, *or let him walk out an airlock*?

The entire ship shook, violently. He caught hold of a chair and held on for dear life.

Susan gripped hold of her console as *Vanguard* shuddered. She'd seen the specifications, she knew just how much firepower was needed to punch through *Vanguard's* hull and inflict real damage…she held herself upright, somehow, as red icons flared over the status display.

"Report," she snapped. "How badly were we hit?"

"We took three direct hits," Mason reported. "Turret Six has been disabled and is venting plasma, Drive Two is offline. Engineering and damage control teams are on their way."

"Understood," Susan said. "Helm, how long until we reach the tramline?"

"Ten minutes at current speed," Reed snapped. He sounded badly stressed. "They're gaining on us."

And if we ramp up the drives we leave the remaining carriers behind, Susan thought. The ambush had been *perfect*. *Maybe they haven't picked off the last two carriers because they know we'll be able to move faster without them.*

She scowled. If only she *knew* what the enemy could do...

"Engineering reports that Drive Two is beyond repair," Parkinson said. "The Chief has rerouted power around the fusion core and thinks we shouldn't suffer any major problems as long as we don't lose more reactor cores."

"Understood," Susan said. The enemy fleet was belching another wave of missiles, but steadily drawing closer. She could give them a nasty fright, she thought, if they came into energy weapons range. "And Turret Six?"

"Locked down," Parkinson said. His voice darkened. "There's the prospect of an explosion."

Susan winced. She'd seen those simulations too. *Vanguard* would survive, of course, but anyone in the turret would be vaporised. Unless they managed to vent *all* the plasma in time, which would screw up the sensors on the hull...or if they managed to get out before it blew.

"Have the damage control teams do what they can," she ordered. The remaining hit hadn't done more than scorch the hull; silently, she blessed whoever had designed the compound used to armour the ship. "And see if they can get the crew out before it's too late."

"Aye, Commander," Parkinson said.

And all we can do is keep going, Susan thought. The aliens weren't just aggressive; they were hyper-aggressive. It made her wonder why they hadn't already attacked the Tadpoles. *And hope we reach the tramline before they batter us to death.*

CHAPTER TWENTY FIVE

It happened very quickly.

One moment, George had been sitting at the console, watching the battle with growing horror; the next, she'd found herself halfway across the compartment with only a hazy recollection of white light and no clear idea of what had happened to her. The main lighting had failed, leaving only the emergency lighting casting a baleful red glow over the scene...

She staggered to her feet, stunned. There was a faint whistling noise in the distance, which she knew should alarm her...it was hard, so hard, to think clearly. She rubbed at her ears as she looked around, staring in disbelief at the ruined consoles. There had been a power surge, her dazed mind noted, a bad one. She hadn't seen consoles actually explode outside bad movies and worse fiction.

A groan caught her ear and she turned towards the source. Peter Barton was lying on the deck, his leg lying at an angle that told her it had to be broken. She staggered towards him and saw, to her relief, that he was alive and aware. She'd taken basic medical training back at the academy, but she knew she was nowhere near as capable as a trained medic or the ship's doctor.

"Emergency splints in the cabinet," Barton wheezed. It sounded as though he'd breathed in something harmful, unless her ears were still buggered. "Hurry."

George nodded, then stumbled over to the emergency cabinet, trying to spot the rest of the gunnery crew. Two bodies were lying on the deck, both so badly mangled that she couldn't tell if they were male or female, let alone who they'd been before their deaths. The faint whistling sound was growing louder...it dawned on her, suddenly, that there was a hull breach, far too close to her. Whatever had hit the ship had done *real* damage.

As if you didn't already know that, she thought, as she pulled emergency supplies out of the cabinet. *You need to get out of here.*

She took the splint, a pair of facemasks and a handful of other items back over to Barton, who talked her through the process of securing his broken leg. He was clearly in pain, but he firmly declined her suggestion that he should take a painkiller. George helped him upright once his leg was firmly in place, then helped him over to one of the intact consoles. The red icons flashing up in front of her did not look encouraging.

"The plasma containment fields are fading," he breathed. "They're going to explode."

George stared at him. "Can't you cool them down?"

"Not in time," Barton said. He poked at the console. "We can't vent the plasma either - the control system's fried."

A dull rumble echoed through the compartment. George almost wet herself in shock before realising that someone was pushing their way through the hatch. She breathed a sigh of relief as she saw Simpson, followed by a gunner she didn't know. Simpson strode over to join them; George held Barton upright as Simpson went to work on the console, hoping the older man could find a way to handle the situation. Instead, another panel on the far side of the compartment began to spark, sending smoke drifting up through the air. She couldn't help noticing that it seemed to be pulled towards the hull...

"There's no way to keep the containment tanks from exploding," Simpson said. "And the airlocks leading back into the ship are closed and sealed."

George blanched. She understood - they couldn't risk causing more damage to the giant battleship - but it meant they were trapped. There was no way out of the compartment; they'd have to wait until the containment fields exploded and die. And there was no way to know *when* the containment fields would explode...

"Get your masks on," Simpson ordered. He took charge with practiced ease. "Ms. Fitzwilliam, you're in charge of Peter. Make sure he keeps his mask on too."

"I'm not dead," Barton protested.

"You soon will be," Simpson said. "The compartment's life support is also fucked. What little air we have left is leaking out of the gash in the hull."

George stared at him. "What if we made the gash worse? It would cool the plasma, wouldn't it?"

"Not enough to matter," Simpson said. He gave her a funny little smile. "Nice thought, though."

"We could try to fix the venting system," Barton offered. "Get the plasma streaming out into space."

"I was thinking about getting out over the hull," Simpson said. He removed gloves from the emergency supplies and passed them around. "But we can take a look at the venting system on the way out. Maybe we can fix it."

He paused. "You two, wait here," he added. "We'll clear the way."

"Yes, sir," George said.

Simpson didn't sound optimistic, George noted, as she donned her gloves. Her shipsuit would suffice to keep her alive in space, certainly for less than an hour, but their air supply was very limited. The masks weren't true helmets. She watched the two gunners pull the hatch free, then scramble into the tube. They'd be the first to die if the plasma containment fields collapsed altogether, but Barton and she would die seconds later. She wondered, vaguely, if she'd see a wave of plasma rushing towards her before everything turned black.

The ship rocked, again.

"We're taking fire," Barton said. He sounded more normal now, thankfully. "And we're pushing the drives to the limits."

George glanced at him. "How can you be sure?"

"There's a vibration in the hull," Barton said. He shook his head, slowly. "And to think I was going to ask you out."

George had to laugh. "Is this the point where you ask for a last kiss, which turns into an hour of passionate lovemaking in five different positions?"

Barton's face fell. "You saw that movie too?"

"I think everyone has seen that movie," George said. It had been a major scandal at school when two of the senior boys had sneaked copies into the dorms, but by the time the headmistress found out what was going on just about everyone had seen the movies. "Is there anything Stellar Star hasn't done?"

She shook her head. "Besides, I'm sure even a single position would do worse damage to your leg," she added. "I don't want to kill you."

"But think about it," Barton said. "*What* a way to die!"

George opened her mouth, unsure what to say. If they were about to die, a single kiss wouldn't make any difference one way or the other, but if they weren't...

"There's a way out," Simpson called, his voice echoing back down the tube. "Come along, now!"

"Thank God," Barton said.

George nodded in agreement as she helped him into the tube, then followed him as he dragged himself upwards. She didn't want to die. The temperature was rising rapidly - the bulkheads seemed warmer to the touch - as they hurried onwards, despite Barton's broken leg. Alarms were sounding, a dozen components flashing warning lights as they passed. It wouldn't be long before one of the containment chambers failed completely, starting off a chain reaction that destroyed the turret. Faint wisps of smoke were curling out of some systems, the smoke drifting upwards towards the hull breach. It struck her, suddenly, that some of the automatic sealing systems must have worked.

They must have worked, she told herself. *Or the entire compartment would have vented by now.*

Simpson was waiting for them at the top of the shaft. "Make sure your masks are in position, then hold on tight," he ordered. "We're going to blow the hatch."

George nodded, checking their masks and gloves. The more of her skin was covered, the better. She'd seen vacuum burns during their training simulations. It was like frostbite, she'd been told, only worse. Humans might not explode when they were exposed to hard vacuum, unlike some early movies had suggested, but it was far from harmless. She might survive the experience, only to wind up spending the next two months having her skin regenerated.

"I'm ready, sir," she said.

"Me too," Barton confirmed.

The hatch blew. George hung on for dear life as the remaining atmosphere blasted out of the compartment, picking up dozens of pieces of debris and hurling them into space. Something banged into her leg, almost knocking her free, before the outrush came to an end. Simpson pulled himself forward, careful not to let go of his grip, and advanced slowly out into hard vacuum. George braced herself, then moved slowly forward, handhold by handhold. It felt like it was forever before she climbed out of the ship and onto the hull.

Simpson waved to her, then inched down off the turret - it looked mangled and torn - towards an airlock. George devoutly *hoped* it was undamaged, then glanced at Barton. The wounded man was having an easier time of it, now they were out of the gravity field, but the cold would get them if they didn't hurry. She shivered, feeling the icy grip of death crawling into her flesh, as she hurried down to the airlock. And then she looked up.

She wasn't really sure *what* she expected to see. In truth, space battles looked rather unremarkable if seen with the naked eye. But there were flashes of light, pinpoints that glowed briefly in the darkness, and brilliant flickers of colour as *Vanguard's* point defence engaged the incoming missiles. She hoped - prayed - that they made it back through the armour before a missile struck too close to them. A single hit would be enough to wipe all four of them out of existence. The captain probably wouldn't even *notice* if they died…

He'd probably notice my death, she thought, sourly. *My uncle would probably ask quite a few questions if I died in wartime.*

The airlock loomed up in front of her. Simpson opened the hatch, allowing them to scramble inside and slam it closed behind them. The inner hatch refused to open, but thankfully the atmosphere flowed in, allowing them a chance to relax. But George felt as though she'd never be warm again…

———

"The enemy are closing on the rear," Mason reported. "And they're firing yet again."

We largely classed missiles as useless, Susan thought. *Certainly, when they were fired from long range. But they thought otherwise and the hell of it is that they might be right.*

"Continue firing," she ordered. *Vanguard* hadn't been knocked out, far from it, but she'd taken significant damage and so had too many of the other ships. Only one fleet carrier had survived, the American *Roosevelt*. She had no idea how they were going to recover and rearm the human fighters, let alone the Tadpole craft. None of the escort carriers were capable of recovering more than two squadrons of starfighters. "Time to tramline?"

"Three minutes," Reed said.

They don't know about the second set of tramlines, Susan told herself, firmly. *They'd be pushing the advantage now, if they knew we were going to jump out and escape.*

But her pessimistic side nagged at her. *Unless they jump through the tramline right after us*, it said. *We won't have time to reorganise and defend the tramline.*

She scowled. Defending a tramline was normally impossible, simply because it was difficult to predict precisely where the enemy would arrive. But this time, they *would* have a chance, if they could reorganise the fleet in time…

"Pass the word," she ordered. "The carriers are to keep moving, as soon as we're through the tramline, but the heavy-hitters are to turn and prepare to face the enemy."

"Aye, Commander," Parkinson said.

Mason frowned. "They may overrun us before we reach the tramline," he said. "They're picking up speed."

Susan gritted her teeth. If she had time to rearm her fighters, reorganise her squadrons…of course, the darker side of her mind whispered, as soon as the other commanding officers realised they'd been taking orders from a mere commander, there'd be an almighty row. Her fellow British officers wouldn't be pleased and the Americans would be pissed… she glanced at the display and cursed as she realised that, apart from a

Japanese destroyer, the remaining foreign ships had been destroyed. The once-great fleet had been practically smashed.

If I order every ship to make a run for the tramline, the formation comes apart, she thought, *and we lose our remaining carrier for sure.*

"Commander," Mason said. "The Tadpole superdreadnaughts are altering course!"

Susan stared. The superdreadnaughts were reversing course, bringing their heavy weapons to bear on the newcomers. She reached for the console to order them to get back into formation, but they opened fire before she could saw a word. Their plasma cannons didn't look to be any more powerful than *Vanguard's*, yet they seemed to carry a *lot* of them. Dozens of alien ships scattered as they impaled themselves on Tadpole guns.

"They're buying us time," she said, awed.

She didn't want to watch, but she couldn't look away. Would humans have done the same, if the odds were reversed? Tadpole starfighters were altering course and swooping away from the fleet, moving to protect the superdreadnaughts as they became a magnet for savage enemy fire. And yet, they were clearly capable of taking a pounding. The only one the human race had ever seen destroyed had died when she was rammed by an armoured fleet carrier.

They're drawn to them as if they were moths drawn to a flame, she thought. The enemy had enough ships to split their attention, sending half of them to face the remainder of the fleet while the other half battered the Tadpoles into dust, but they seemed bent on facing the Tadpoles. Were they *such* an aggressive race? *Or are they concerned about the Tadpoles breaking past them and escaping through Tramline One?*

"Order the starfighters to perform a hull landing manoeuvre," she said. The remainder of the fleet was almost at the tramline. "And then pass the word to all ships. They're to jump as soon as they're within the tramline."

And hope to hell we don't have an interpenetration, she thought. It was theoretically possible, if eddies from the tramline knocked one ship into where another was meant to materialise, but she'd never actually heard of it happening. *There are too many ships going through the tramline at the same time.*

"The starfighters have responded," Parkinson said. A dull quiver ran through the ship. "The damage control coordinator reports that we've just lost Turret Six."

"Understood," Susan said. The crew...she hoped they'd managed to get out in time, but there was no way to know. They'd have to do a head-count after the fighting was over, then start searching sealed compartments. "Any further damage?"

"Negative, Commander," Parkinson said. "The seals held."

"Starfighters are landing now," Mason reported. "The enemy starfighters are pulling away from the Tadpoles."

Susan smiled. Unless the enemy had managed to produce a Puller Drive small and inexpensive enough to mount on a starfighter, they were too late. *Vanguard* and the remainder of the fleet were entering the tramline. One by one, starships flickered and vanished from the display as their drives activated. She turned back to watch the Tadpoles, still fighting savagely, and sent them an order to break off. But there was no reply.

"Jump," she snapped.

Vanguard shuddered, one final time, as the display flickered and updated. The new system - UXS-470, according to the survey reports - was as useless as UXS-469, although there was an asteroid belt that would sustain a spacefaring civilisation. There were plenty of groups who'd consider the system a decent home, if it wasn't right next to a race of homicidal aliens who attacked without provocation...

"Bring us about," she ordered tartly, as the final ships snapped into existence. Thankfully, none of the escapees seemed to have rammed one another. "And watch for the Tadpoles. They may get out of the trap."

Mason shot her a look she had no difficulty in reading. *You don't think that's possible, do you?*

She shrugged, then watched the tramline, feeling the seconds ticking by. Any halfway competent tactician knew it was dangerous to give the enemy any time to recover; logically, the aliens should have chased them through the tramline, even though it ran the risk of running into an ambush. The command network was already updating, piece by piece;

the longer they delayed, the worse the bloody nose they'd get when they finally entered the system...

But there was no sign of the aliens.

"They can't use the alien-grade tramlines," Mason said.

We're going to need a new name for them, Susan thought. *There is more than one alien race now.*

She took a long breath. "Stand down from red alert, but remain at tactical alert," she ordered, curtly. "The fleet is to cloak, then proceed to" - she tapped out a location, picking a spot two light hours from the tramline at random - "this location."

"Aye, Commander," Mason said.

Susan nodded, slowly. The aliens might be altering position, moving up or down the tramline to avoid an ambush. Assuming that was what they were doing, the fleet had at least half an hour to hide before the aliens showed themselves. And if they picked a random location, the aliens would have to spend hours looking for them...unless, of course, they had some super tactical sensors that the Royal Navy had never even considered.

And if they have that big an edge, she thought, *they would have kicked our asses.*

Oh, her own thoughts mocked her. *And they didn't kick our asses?*

"And then set up a secure conference for commanding officers," she added, "and invite Prince Henry to join."

"Yes, Commander," Parkinson said.

And hope they don't order me relieved of command at once, Susan thought, silently. *Because just how many regulations have I broken in the last hour?*

CHAPTER TWENTY SIX

"Let me see if I've got this straight," Captain Owen Harper said. The American's accent was strong enough to suggest he was born on New Washington, rather than Earth. "You stunned your own commanding officer and *stole* command of the entire fleet."

Henry winced, inwardly, as Commander Susan Onarina wilted. It was clear she was exhausted, pushed right to the limits of her endurance. No naval officer in recorded history had had to deal with so many problems at once, from relieving her commanding officer for gross incompetence to fighting a running battle to escape from an unexpected threat. He couldn't help admiring her, even though he'd served under both Theodore Smith and James Fitzwilliam. But then, they'd both been secure in their positions when they'd gone to war.

"Yes, sir," Susan said. "That is reasonably accurate."

The assembled commanding officers - or, rather, their holograms - stared at her. Henry wondered, absently, just what was going through their minds. They should be old enough to know that recriminations were pointless, not least because the fleet was still in terrible danger, but he'd been an ambassador long enough to know that some people had no sense of priorities. Questioning Susan's actions could wait until the fleet was safely back home, where the recordings could be analysed in detail...

"You should have passed command to the senior officer," Harper snapped. Henry rather suspected that *Harper* was that officer, although fleet command was something of a poisoned chalice under the circumstances. "You certainly shouldn't have taken command for yourself."

"It would have caused further confusion at the worst possible time," Susan said. There was a curious deadness in her voice, as if she was too tired to feel anything. "And *Vanguard* survived blows that vaporised other ships."

Henry shivered. New Russia had been a curbstomp, but the Battle of UXS-469 hadn't been much better. At least they'd fought back...no, the *Tadpoles* had fought back. And over thirty thousand human naval personnel were dead. God alone knew how many Tadpoles had died in the battle. They'd sailed merrily right into an ambush and escaped by the skin of their teeth.

"That wasn't your decision to make," Harper insisted. "Admiral Pournelle..."

"Was dead," Captain Fletcher snapped. "She did the right thing at the right time."

"She's a *commander*," Harper said. "She isn't even a commanding officer..."

"She is now," Henry said, calmly.

Harper's image seemed to flicker with outrage. "I confess I know nothing about your place in the Royal Navy, *Your Highness*, but I know for a fact that you have no position in the United States Navy," he said. His voice dripped sarcasm. "It isn't your task to retroactively condone her actions."

Henry met his gaze. "I am not speaking in my role as a formal naval personage, Captain," he said. "I am speaking in my role as Earth's Ambassador, with powers granted to me by the First Contact Treaty. All human starships, including yours, are under my authority during any human-alien interactions."

"You are *not* a commanding officer," Harper snapped.

"No, but I *am* the highest authority until we get back in touch with Earth," Henry said, firmly. "There are two precedents, both of which involve American officers assuming command over British and French warships. Your legal officers can find them for you in the records, if you wish to look for case law. Right now, until we return to friendly space, I am officially condoning Commander Onarina's actions and granting her a temporary promotion to Captain."

"That exceeds your authority by quite some distance," Harper observed.

"Actually, there are precedents," Henry said. He silently blessed Janelle for making him study all the little details hidden in the Admiralty's summaries of naval law. "But in any case, the final decision will have to be made by the Admiralty."

He met Harper's eyes, daring the man to object. "Or do you want to push the matter now, when the fleet is still in danger?"

Harper scowled, but said nothing. Henry allowed himself a moment of relief. Harper could have caused a command dispute, even though Henry had a quiet suspicion that the remainder of the American commanding officers wouldn't have sided with him. They knew, even if he didn't, that the fleet had survived through sheer luck. And Susan, regardless of how she'd assumed command, had played a large role in saving their asses.

"I believe you are the senior surviving officer," Henry said, after a moment. "As such, command rests in your hands."

"Thank you, sir," Harper said. He didn't sound pleased. "Right now, our main task is doing as many repairs as we can before we encounter the aliens for a second time. But we also need to decide what to do next."

A holographic image of UXS-470 sprang into existence, showing two tramlines. One led back to UXS-469, where the unknowns were presumably lying in wait; the other led onwards in a dogleg back towards Tadpole space. Henry rather doubted the unknowns would have any problems deducing where the fleet had gone, even if they couldn't follow without heavily modifying their drives. Humanity hadn't had any trouble deducing what the Tadpoles had done, after all. It was merely duplicating the process that had caused so many headaches.

"As you can see, Tramline Two is a standard tramline," Harper said. "The unknowns may well be able to probe back through UXS-467 and UXS-466 to relocate us, if they haven't already surveyed those systems. It would be reasonable for them to attempt to probe for our homeworlds..."

Henry nodded inwardly as Harper rattled on. There were seven transits between UXS-469 and the outer edge of Tadpole space, but it wouldn't take the unknowns long to locate the first settled worlds. Who knew what would happen then? Firing on a fleet of unknown origin suggested a degree of paranoia that worried him. Surely, any *sane* foe would wait until they knew more about their target before launching an attack.

Unless they're so alien that communication is impossible, he thought. It was hard enough to talk to the Tadpoles, despite both sides doing their utmost to make it work. *We might have no choice, but to smash them back to their homeworld and trap them there.*

"And so we'll depart in two days, once the basic repairs are completed," Harper finished. "I believe that gives us the best chance of survival."

He smiled, rather coldly. "I trust that meets with your approval, *Your Highness*?"

"It does," Henry said, hastily replaying Harper's words in his mind. There was nothing wrong with the American's plan, although he would have preferred to start sooner. But recovering and rearming the starfighters was a nightmare in and of itself. "And I believe the Tadpoles will agree."

Harper's eyes narrowed. "Can you explain the plan to them?"

"Yes, Captain," Henry said. "I would suggest, however, that you detach one ship to proceed immediately. The Tadpoles - and Earth - have to be warned that the first contact mission ended in disaster."

"Understood," Harper said. "I'll see to it personally."

He cleared his throat, loudly. "I'm not going to pretend that we didn't just get our asses kicked," he added. "And I'm not going to claim that we didn't just lose tens of thousands of good people when the bastards opened fire. But we survived, and we escaped, and we have the knowledge we need to give those bastards hell, the next time we meet. We'll teach those goddamned fuckers that humans don't come cheap!"

And Tadpoles, Henry thought. In a movie, everyone would have roared their approval, but the assembled commanding officers were too tired to do more than nod. Besides, Harper needed a better scriptwriter. *Right now, we'll be lucky if we manage to get back to Tadpole space before they get a blocking force in place.*

He closed his eyes as, one by one, the images popped out of existence. He'd have to get his staff working on talking to the Tadpoles, explaining what Harper had in mind. And then..."

"Your Highness," Susan said. She sounded annoyed, despite her tiredness. "You didn't have to meddle."

"Yes, I did," Henry said. "The last thing we need is someone insisting that you put Captain Blake back in command."

"I could have talked them out of it," Susan insisted. "I..."

"Maybe," Henry said. "But why take the chance?"

He understood precisely how she felt, but there was no *time*. The fleet couldn't afford any number of the problems facing its command staff, so the least he could do was get rid of one of them. And besides, there *was* case law to suggest he could give generalised orders...although if the fleet ran into worse trouble, it was unlikely the Admiralty would agree with him. But then, if they ran into another enemy fleet before they'd had a chance to reorganise they probably wouldn't make it home anyway.

"You have command of the ship," he said, gently. "I don't know if you'll *keep* it, but for the moment you're her commanding officer. Now, go get a few hours of sleep and then do your job."

"I can't sleep," Susan insisted. "There's too much to do."

"You need to rest," Henry told her. Admiral Theodore Smith had been the same, according to Janelle. "Or you'll fall asleep on the bridge."

Susan snorted. "Get some rest yourself, sir," she said. "And then go make yourself useful."

Henry saluted. "Yes, *Captain*."

Susan was too tired to feel much of anything as she made her way back towards her cabin, stepping aside to allow repair crews to pass as they hurried through the ship. Her head ached and her body felt utterly drained, as if she was on the verge of collapse. She hadn't felt so rotten since survival training on the lunar surface, training that had almost killed her and the rest of her class. But there was work to do before she slept, tasks she couldn't put off until the next morning.

Mason met her at the hatch, looking as exhausted as she felt. "Commander."

"It's *Captain* now, apparently," Susan said. He relaxed in apparent relief. Both of them had known that the other commanding officers might insist on overruling her and reinstating Captain Blake. "Come on inside."

She opened the hatch and stumbled into her cabin, looking longingly at the bed. It would be so easy just to throw herself on the mattress and close her eyes, but she couldn't allow herself to sleep, not yet. There was too much to do.

"Hit me," she ordered. "How bad is it?"

"Turret Six is gone," Mason said, flatly. "Turret Five took a glancing blow, which jammed the rotator system in place, but the Chief is convinced it can be repaired. We vented the plasma from the tanks as a precautionary measure and we'll refill the tanks after the system has been repaired and double-checked. Drive Two is completely screwed; we'll need a shipyard to get the power core out and replaced. And we have three gashes in our armour that we can patch over, at least for the moment. The inner layers held..."

"That's not what I meant," Susan said. "How many *people* did we lose?"

Mason looked pale. "Thirty-seven," he said. "Five gunners were lost in Turret Six, Commander...Captain. It would have been worse if some of them hadn't managed to get out of the section before the tanks blew. Seven others died in Drive Two. The remainder were killed when the ship was hit."

He took a breath. "We also have seventeen injured, ranging from a broken leg to possible brain damage," he added. "The doctor has the wounded in sickbay."

Susan shuddered. It could have been worse; hell, it *had* been worse for the carriers. If there were any survivors, the unknowns would have picked them up. And then...? She had no idea how the unknowns treated prisoners, but judging by their unprovoked attack they weren't worried about upsetting the human race. Or the Tadpoles, for that matter. Did they even *realise* they'd attacked two races, not one?

Tadpole ships look different from ours, even when they fill the same function, she thought, wryly. *Unless our new enemies have no sense of aesthetics.*

"I'll visit the wounded later," she promised. It was her duty, now she was the battleship's commanding officer. "And...and Captain Blake?"

"He's currently in his cabin, under guard," Mason said. "I had a long chat with Major Andres and he agreed that, for the moment, it would be better to keep Captain Blake as isolated as possible. On the record, he doesn't want to rock the boat; off the record, I think he recognises that Captain Blake is no longer the man he once was."

Susan nodded, relieved. The marines weren't *just* assigned to starships to provide boarding parties; they doubled as internal security. If Major Andres had decided to cause trouble, he could have reinstated Captain Blake and thrown Susan in the brig...which would have been disastrous, the next time *Vanguard* went into combat. No doubt Prince Henry's claim to authority would satisfy *his* superiors, at least, that he'd thought he was following legitimate orders. Untangling the whole affair would take the Admiralty *years*.

"I've got half the tactical staff assigned to other duties, but the remainder are already assessing the combat records," Mason concluded. "We should be able to learn more about the enemy soon, I hope."

"Have the records forwarded to Captain Harper," Susan ordered. Mason had to know that she was no longer in command of the fleet. "He's assumed overall command."

She wished that she knew Harper better, but she'd only met him once, back during one of the dinners Admiral Pournelle had hosted. It was hard to blame him for being annoyed at her actions...she shook her head, tiredly. She knew it would be a long time before she trusted the competence of her superiors again. She'd just have to hope that Harper had earned his command, rather than taking advantage of connections. At least his early planning seemed reasonable.

He must have assumed he'd take command, she thought. Hadn't Harper served longer than Captain Blake? *He did some planning before we had the meeting.*

"And ask Prince Henry to join the tactical staff," she added. "He's got more familiarity with aliens than anyone else, even Parkinson."

"The Tadpoles might be nothing like the newcomers," Mason pointed out.

"He still knows not to assume that aliens think like humans," Susan countered. Most of the books she'd read had aliens that were really funny-looking humans. But one of the stories with convincing aliens had been scary as hell. "He'll be good at it."

She yawned, helplessly. *Humanity* wouldn't have attacked a powerful fleet without considerable provocation, particularly one in an unsettled system that was trying to communicate. Or had the aliens thought they were under attack? She vaguely recalled a book - or a movie - about aliens that regarded radio waves as an elaborate form of torture and started a war where both sides had good reason to think the other had shot first.

Mason looked doubtful, but nodded. "I'll see to it," he said. "And, with the greatest of respect, I would honestly suggest you went to bed. You look as if you're about to collapse on the deck."

Susan yawned, again. If she'd been younger, she would have thought about dragging him into bed...she cut off that train of thought before it went anywhere. She was the battleship's commanding officer now, even though there was a very good chance that her court martial would be the shortest formality on record. There was no way she could sleep with anyone, even if it would make her feel *alive*. It would have to wait until she had a chance to go home and visit Sin City...

"Very well," she said. She was definitely far too tired if her mind was wandering in inappropriate directions. "Wake me the moment - and I mean the *moment* - anything happens."

"Aye, Captain," Mason said. He sounded reluctant, which puzzled her until she realised he genuinely cared. "But they didn't follow us through the tramline..."

Susan shrugged. It hadn't been easy to refurbish human Puller Drives to allow them to use the alien-grade tramlines, but it had been done. Humanity's fleet carriers had been ready to use the tramlines within six months of the Battle of Vera Cruz, although humanity had had a boost from a captured alien warship. How long would it take the unknowns? Coming to think of it, had they captured any ships themselves? They'd certainly left thousands of pieces of debris drifting around the red star...

And if one of those pieces of debris happens to include a computer core with an astrographic database, she thought, *we might be in deep shit.*

"We don't know what they might be able to do," she said, instead. Human computer cores were designed to destroy themselves, if their ships were blown out of space. Even a disabled starship should be able to trigger the destruct sequence. And yet, she knew she'd never be entirely sure. "It's better to be careful."

She watched him leave the room, then turned and walked into the bedroom. Too tired to undress, she flung herself down on the bed and closed her eyes. How long had it been, she asked herself, since she'd slept? She knew it was important...and yet, she felt guilty for even *considering* going to bed. The ship needed her. They'd survived their first combat test by the skin of their teeth.

But right now you can barely think straight, she told herself. She'd come far too close to inviting Mason into her bed, a mistake she couldn't afford. *You need to sleep.*

And yet, despite her utter exhaustion, sleep was a long time in coming.

CHAPTER TWENTY SEVEN

"The hatch is jammed," Fraser called. "We'll have to open the door manually."

George nodded, too tired to speak out loud. The moment they'd been rescued from the airlock, the gunners had been sent to help with Turret Five while she'd been reassigned to Fraser and ordered to assist him in searching the remainder of the ship. Fraser wasn't such an asshole any longer, but still…she wished she knew what had happened to the other midshipmen. Some of them were her friends.

She watched as Fraser removed a protective plate and peered down at the innards. The interior airlocks were meant to be sealed, but there were ways to unlock the hatch if one knew precisely what to do. Fraser fiddled for a long moment, then glanced at her and pushed a switch. The hatch shuddered, once, then jumped back just enough to allow her to insert her fingers into the gap. Fraser joined her and, together, they pulled the hatch back and locked it in place. She gasped and almost let go of the hatch as she saw the interior of the compartment. Two dead bodies lay on the deck, one missing a head, while a third man - badly wounded - was lying on top of a console.

"Check him," Fraser ordered, keying his wristcom. "Sir, we have two more KIA and one WIA."

"He's pretty bad," George said. She didn't dare try to move the wounded man. Judging from the way the console was digging into his chest, it might be the only thing keeping the blood in his body. "We need a medic team."

"We need medics," Fraser repeated. He glanced at the wounded man, then grimaced. "Code Blue. I say again, Code Blue."

George shuddered. She'd been taught that Code Blue signified someone who needed immediate medical attention, but during wartime the medical staff might not have time to do anything more than make the victim comfortable and leave him to die. Her tutors had explained that it was the only way to handle the situation - the time taken to save one badly wounded person might be more profitably used to save a dozen people with lesser wounds - but she hadn't been very comfortable with the idea, even when it was purely theoretical. Now all she could do was watch and pray that the medical team arrived on time.

She glanced around, unsure just what had happened to the compartment. One of the enemy laser warheads had struck the hull, not too far away, but the compartment should have been safe. Another power surge? Or had the shock hurled all three of the men across the compartment? The headless man might just have had a terrible encounter with the console…

"One of the segments came loose," Fraser said, pointing. The missing head was lying on the deck, blood pooling around it. "Poor bastard never stood a chance."

George took a deep breath and instantly regretted it, as she breathed in the stench of blood, shit and death. The air filters seemed to have been disabled; they'd known the compartment was still pressurised, but the local life support wasn't functional. *Vanguard* was intensely compartmentalised, she knew. No doubt a strength could turn into a terrible weakness if something went badly wrong.

The medics appeared, carrying a stretcher between them. George watched, unable to tear her eyes away, as they checked the wounded man, then carefully lifted him away from the console and placed him on the stretcher. Fraser spoke briefly to the medic, then beckoned George to take a body-bag and wrap up one of the bodies. George shuddered at the thought of touching a dead man, but there was no choice.

"Take one of the dog-tags," Fraser reminded her, as she zipped up the bag. "We'll hand them in to the XO before we go off duty."

George nodded, then made a careful note of where they'd left the bodies before moving on to the next compartment. It was empty, mercifully;

the compartment beyond was empty, but sealed. The section beyond *that* was exposed to vacuum. They'd have to wait until the engineering crew had time to patch up the hull, she noted, as Fraser called in the report and led her back, deeper into the ship. She'd already had one close encounter with vacuum and she didn't want another.

"They'll send us somewhere else in a moment," Fraser predicted, once they reached a corridor. He sat down, leaning against the bulkhead as he scrabbled in his pouch and produced a chocolate bar. "Here."

"Thank you," George said, automatically. She blinked in surprise as she realised it was one of the bars she'd brought with her, nearly two months ago. It felt as if she'd been on the ship for years. "Have you been carrying it around for months?"

Fraser smiled, rather crookedly. "Grabbed them on the way out of the hatch," he said. "I had a feeling they might be necessary."

George eyed him doubtfully as she opened the wrapping, then munched contentedly on the chocolate. It wasn't a ration bar, a tasteless piece of cardboard that was supposed to include all the nutrients growing spacers needed each day, but it would keep them both going for a few more hours. She knew she needed sleep, yet there was just too much work to do. And besides, they were expendable. Who knew *what* might be lurking in the next sealed compartment?

"We could have died," she said, softly. Fraser was the last person she would have chosen to pour her heart out to, but the words just came bubbling up. "They could have killed us!"

"They did kill thousands of others," Fraser said, quietly. "I was in the tactical compartment, back when it all kicked off. They blew away all but one of the carriers. I don't know if anyone survived."

George shuddered, trying to calculate the death toll. There were at least two thousand *British* crewmen assigned to a single carrier and the American carriers were larger. And that meant…over ten thousand dead, perhaps more. She understood, for the first time, the shockwaves that had echoed through the Royal Navy, after the Battle of New Russia. Meeting a new alien race was one thing, but losing so many carriers so quickly…

"They might have had a chance to get to the lifepods," she said. "They could have blasted free of the hulks…"

"Maybe," Fraser said. He turned to look at her. "Are you all right?"

"I don't know," George said. She had too many conflicting feelings running through her brain and the tiredness didn't help. "Does it get any better?"

Fraser rested a hand on her shoulder, just for a moment. "You learn," he said. He gave her shoulder a gentle squeeze, then let go. "But it never gets easier."

He rose, sticking the wrapper in his pocket. "There are other compartments to check out," he added. "And we may not get any rest until we're dead."

George rose, then followed him through a whole string of compartments. There were no more dead bodies, thankfully, but some of the systems showed signs of damage. Fraser logged it all for the damage control teams; George checked and rechecked his work, sometimes adding her own notes for the logs. They were doing a useful - and necessary - task, she knew, and yet...part of her wondered if it was just busywork. The ship's sensors should be able to keep track of its interior, surely...

"It wouldn't be the first time a computer network was split in two, then refused to reconnect," Fraser said. "The engineering staff may have problems convincing it to reunite."

"Oh," George said. "They're not going to start battling over which of them is the *real* computer, right?"

"You really have to stop watching those movies," Fraser said, although there was an undeniable hint of amusement in his voice. "Real life doesn't work like in the movies."

George smirked. "Really? I hadn't noticed."

Their wristcoms buzzed. "Midshipman Fraser, Midshipwoman Fitzwilliam," a voice said, curtly. "Report to sickbay at once."

"Understood," Fraser said. "We're on our way."

He hurried down a corridor, George following him, looking for the quickest way through the damaged ship to sickbay. A handful of compartments seemed to have been converted into temporary storage spaces for body-bags, the marines carrying them through the ship and placing them neatly on the deck. George wondered, grimly, just what would happen to the bodies, once the ship returned home. Burial in space, like most spacers, or handed over to the families for a quiet funeral?

"This way," Fraser said.

George shuddered as they entered sickbay. There was a wounded crewman in every bed and others lying on mattresses on the deck. A string of others were sitting just past the hatch, clearly too badly wounded to go back to work and yet not badly enough to receive immediate treatment. George saw Barton sitting with them and gave him a wave, receiving a shy wave in return. Fraser elbowed her, gently, as they walked up to the doctor.

"Reporting as ordered," he said, shortly.

"Good," the doctor said. She was a harassed-looking young woman, barely a couple of years older than George herself. The senior doctor was missing, probably in one of the operating chambers. "Midshipwoman, I understand you went EVA. Did you notice any long-lasting effects?"

"No, doctor," George said. "I felt cold, for a while, but nothing else."

The doctor studied her for a long moment. "No numbness? No traces of decompression sickness?"

"I had a mask and a shipsuit," George said. "There was no permanent damage."

"You certainly don't seem to be having any problems," the doctor agreed. "Inform me or another doctor *at once* if you have any problems, even if they seem mild."

"Understood," George said.

She stepped away from Fraser to let him speak to the doctor in private, wondering if he'd give her a hard time - later - if she went to chat to Barton. But he was surrounded by a handful of other wounded men, all seemingly swapping lies about their exploits. She waved at him instead, then glanced into a sideroom. A handful of bodies lay on the deck, half-wrapped in body-bags. And then she froze in horror as she recognised one of them.

"Nathan," she breathed.

She stumbled forward, hardly aware of her movements. Nathan was dead, his face pale; he looked normal until she was almost on top of him, when she saw that *something* had dented the left side of his skull. Blood matted his hair, yet it didn't *look* serious…her head spun, just for a long moment, as she tried to take it in. Nathan had been a friend, a fellow cadet... they'd gone through the academy together. And now he was dead...

"You shouldn't be in here," a stern voice said.

George jumped, then spun around. A dark-skinned man was standing there, carrying another body-bag slung over his shoulder. A marine, she noted; a lieutenant, if she recalled their rank stripes correctly. He placed the bag on the deck, then scowled at her. George nodded, too tired and stunned to argue, and hurried out of the chamber. Fraser met her outside, looking puzzled. She caught his arm and half-dragged him out of sickbay.

"Nathan is dead," she said. She stumbled and would have fallen, if he hadn't caught hold of her. "He...he's *dead*!"

Fraser's eyes went wide with shock, but he showed no other reaction. "He was on one of the damage control teams, wasn't he? He must have been caught in an explosion..."

"The body looked largely intact," George said. She felt herself shudder, again. "He's dead!"

"And it's high time you had a nap," Fraser said. He glanced at his wrist-com. "We've been placed on reduced duty for the moment, as we've been up for hours."

George steadied herself and let go of him. "Can we afford to sleep?"

"Unless you want to start seeing gremlins destroying the ship, then yes," Fraser said. "The XO seems to have decided she can spare us for the next few hours."

George felt almost dazed as they walked back to middy country, barely seeing the crewmen they passed on the way. Nathan couldn't be dead. There had been too much life in him for him to die. And yet, she'd seen the body. Her friend was dead...he'd never joke with her again, he'd never comfort her again, he'd never flirt with every girl he met on shore leave, just to see who'd take him up on it...

"We're here," Fraser said, opening the hatch. The sleeping compartment was deserted, but messy, one of the lockers had sprung over, dumping its contents onto the deck. "Get into your rack and have at least five hours of sleep."

"He didn't deserve to die," George said, numbly. She'd known that people *died* on naval service, but she hadn't really *believed* it, not until now. "He was a good man."

"He was," Fraser agreed, shortly.

"You should have died instead," George said, bitterly. "Why did *he* have to die?"

Fraser's eyes flashed with anger, but he controlled himself. "Shit happens," he said. "A young midshipman, fresh out of the academy, is among the list of the dead. It's a tragedy, but life does go on."

"Not for him," George snarled.

"Tell me something," Fraser said, a hard edge entering his tone. "If he were alive and you were dead, would you want him to waste his time moaning or getting some much-needed sleep?"

George balled her fists. "That's not fair!"

"*Life* isn't fair," Fraser said. "And you are acting like a twelve-year-old schoolgirl because you are tired, cranky and in shock. Now, get into your rack and get some bloody sleep!"

The hatch opened. Honoraria stepped into the compartment. "What's up?"

"Nathan is dead," Fraser said. "And George is taking it badly."

"Shit," Honoraria said. She removed her jacket, hung it up from the railing and clambered into her rack without bothering to undress further. "I'm sorry to hear that, really I am."

"Keep an eye on George, if you can," Fraser said. "I need to do a couple of other things before I hit my rack."

"Yes, sir," Honoraria said.

Fraser pointed a finger at George. "And if I catch you outside this compartment in less than five hours," he added, "I'm going to give you such a clout."

"Believe him," Honoraria said, as Fraser stalked through the hatch. "He'll do it, too."

George scrambled into her rack, pulled her curtain closed and fought hard to keep from crying. Nathan had been a friend, a partner, an ally… and now he was gone. She'd met his family twice, when they'd visited the academy; she'd invited him home, even though he'd been too shy to meet so many wealthy and powerful aristocrats. They'd been close friends, comrades, allies in arms…

It should have been me, she thought, as she closed her eyes. *Nathan was doing so much better…*

The next thing she knew, someone was tapping gently at the curtain. George jerked awake - no one would deliberately wake a sleeping midshipman unless it was urgent - and tore back the curtain. Fraser was standing there, looking pensive. She stared at him in horror, unsure what was going on. How long had she been asleep?

"You're due to report to the tactical section in two hours," Fraser told her. George grabbed for her wristcom and checked the time. She'd been asleep for nearly seven hours, but it felt as if she'd barely touched the pillow before waking up. "And before then, we have something to do."

George swallowed. She'd been rude, very rude, to the first middy. He was quite within his rights to assign punishment duties or, as he'd threatened, give her a clout. But Fraser didn't look angry. Instead, he was holding a box in his right arm.

"I need to go through Nathan's stuff," he said. He opened Nathan's locker as George scrambled out of her rack. "If there's anything you want that isn't intensely personal, you may take it."

"I don't want anything," George said. She rubbed her eyes as Fraser started pulling out Nathan's spare uniforms. "He…"

"Would have wanted you to have it," Fraser said. It was customary to hand out a dead officer's possessions, George recalled, save for anything personal. The remainder would be returned to his family or recycled. "You shouldn't pass up on anything that might be useful…"

George nodded and watched as Fraser found a portable terminal and a handful of unmarked datachips. "Porn, probably," he said, dumping them into the box. "Or Stellar Star. There isn't much difference."

"He wouldn't," George objected.

"Then he'd be the first midshipman not to have a private porn stash," Fraser said. He smirked. "Even the ones more interested in boys than girls have their own stashes."

He picked up a photograph and glanced at it before passing it to George. "That's us," she said, in surprise. The photograph had been taken during a brief excursion to the Apollo 11 park, near Armstrong City. "I remember that day!"

"So did he," Fraser said. "Keep the photograph, if you want."

George nodded, tucking the photograph under her pillow.

Fraser snickered. "Is this yours too?"

He held up a lacy thong. George felt herself blushing as she looked at it, even though it was clearly meant for a woman with a larger behind than herself. Where had it *come* from?

"That isn't mine," she protested. "How…?"

"There's a tradition of keeping underwear as a way of proving one scored," Fraser said, dropping the thong into the box. "It must have been a great lay."

George shook her head. "He had plenty of girlfriends," she said. "Is there anything else?"

"Just a set of handwritten notes," Fraser said. "They'll go to his family, I believe."

George eyed him. "Shouldn't we take the thong out first?"

"Take it and destroy it," Fraser said, passing the box to her. "Unless you want to run a DNA scan to see who it belongs to?"

"No, thank you," George said, primly.

Fraser laughed. "I don't blame you," he said. "Now, go to the wardroom and get something to eat. You're on duty later, remember."

CHAPTER TWENTY EIGHT

"I don't know *why* they attacked," Midshipwoman Fitzwilliam said.

Henry allowed himself a smile. He had no idea why Midshipwoman Fitzwilliam had been assigned to the tactical section, but he did have to admit that she had a decent grasp of tactics and how best to apply the technology at her disposal. Maybe someone was still playing games - or, maybe, she'd been assigned to someone who wouldn't be impressed by her connections. Or maybe she'd been assigned to work with him to keep her busy.

"We may not understand it for years," he said, dryly. The Tadpoles had had a reasonable motive, even if trying to make open contact would have saved considerable bloodshed on both sides. "They may be so alien that we cannot understand them."

"I thought certain concepts were universal," Midshipwoman Fitzwilliam said. "Surely their understanding of the universe can't be that different from ours."

"It depends," Henry said. "There have been human civilisations that thought differently from us, either because they hadn't evolved modern concepts or because they chose to openly reject them. They weren't *alien*, but we still had problems understanding them because we assumed that they thought the same way as us, making their actions completely irrational."

He shrugged. The data was clear; the interpretation was not. A powerful fleet had been attacked in what *had* to be a pre-planned ambush. The enemy clearly hadn't expected the fleet to escape down an alien-grade tramline, but otherwise...they'd been strikingly confident of victory. Henry didn't like the implications. Either the enemy had evolved from something akin to hermit crabs, which attacked anything foolish enough to pass within range, or they'd been utterly confident of victory. And *that* suggested they had a good idea of the power of their enemies.

They might have known about the Tadpoles for far longer than we assumed, he thought, grimly. *And if that's true, they might know about us too.*

"They didn't even *try* to communicate," he muttered. "They just attacked."

They went through the final set of reports, trying to put together a briefing for the captain and her senior officers. Henry had watched Captain Harper carefully, fearing disaster, but apart from a prickly disposition Harper didn't seem to be anything other than a competent naval officer. Two days had allowed the crews to get as many repair jobs done as possible, although launching all of their starfighters was going to be a major hassle. *Roosevelt* and the two surviving escort carriers couldn't hope to launch them all.

And our contingency plans are unlikely to survive their first encounter with the enemy, he thought, checking his wristcom. They had an hour before the briefing, but there was little more to say. *Everything we know about the unknowns suggests that they are insane.*

"Sir," Midshipwoman Fitzwilliam said, quietly. "Can I ask you a question?"

Henry gave her a sharp look. *That* didn't sound like a *normal* question.

"You may," he said.

"My...my friend died," Midshipwoman Fitzwilliam said, slowly. "And I feel...I feel all sorts of things."

Henry lifted his eyebrows. "Like what?"

"Conflicted," Midshipwoman Fitzwilliam said. "I'm saddened he's gone, I miss him; at the same time, I'm angry at him for dying and I'm angry at the aliens for killing him. And I'm feeling numb and yet sorrowful...is that remotely normal?"

"Yes," Henry said. "I lost too many friends during the last war. All you can really do is carry on. The pain lessens, in time."

"But I feel so conflicted," Midshipwoman Fitzwilliam protested. "I don't *feel* normal!"

Henry met her eyes. "How many people have you lost?"

"My grandmother died when I was nine," Midshipwoman Fitzwilliam said, after a moment's thought. "But she was in her nineties."

"And you had time to prepare yourself for her death," Henry said. "Your friend died suddenly, unexpectedly. And so you are conflicted."

He leaned forward, trying to sound reassuring. "You'll miss him, really," he added. It sounded as though the friend had been *more* than a friend, but he didn't want to ask. "I think you'll have days when his absence will be an aching wound, yet it will fade. And then, afterwards, you'll see him again."

"If there is a God," Midshipwoman Fitzwilliam said. "But if there is, why would He allow a new alien race to start slaughtering us?"

Henry shrugged. "There are people who believe that aliens are His children, just as we are, and He loves us all equally, meaning that we have to learn to get along," he said. He'd never considered himself very religious, although watching his children being born had taught him that there were true wonders in the universe. "And there are people who believe that the existence of aliens is a test, a test we have to pass if we wish to survive. Either we make friends with them or one race wipes the other out."

"Like the Survivalists," Midshipwoman Fitzwilliam said. "Didn't they evolve from the Humanity League?"

"Yeah," Henry said. "But they have a point."

Midshipwoman Fitzwilliam looked down at the deck. "Which one do *you* believe?"

"I'm not convinced there is any grand plan," Henry said. He'd grown to loathe organised religion before he saw his first decade. "Just a string of accidents that comprise history. If we'd met the Tadpoles in space, surely we wouldn't have had a war."

He cleared his throat. "And we'd better get back to work," he said. "We have a briefing to attend in fifty minutes."

"And so we're as ready as we'll ever be, outside spending a couple of months in a shipyard," Chief Engineer Alan Finch concluded. "The patches on the hull should keep us going for a while longer."

"Let us hope so," Susan said. She'd inspected the damage over the last two days. *Vanguard* had survived, unlike so many other ships, but not all of the pre-combat simulations had been accurate. "Do you think we can survive another battle?"

"We might have no choice," Finch said. "But there's little else we can do before we go back to war."

Susan nodded curtly, then looked at Mason. He'd handled the military aspect of the tactical analysis while Prince Henry had looked at the other aspects. She wasn't looking forward to this part of the briefing, but it had to be endured.

"Captain," Mason said. He took a breath, then keyed his console, projecting a holographic image of the battle over the table. "At your command, my staff and I have gone through the sensor records and produced a preliminary analysis of alien capabilities.

"First, their stealth system. It appears to be more of a sensor *shroud* than a cloaking device, as far as we can tell; it definitely *looks* to be a blanket covering an entire fleet, rather than merely hiding a single ship. The bad news is that it has none of the weaknesses of a cloaking device; the good news is that it isn't remotely perfect, scattering sensor pulses rather than obscuring them. I believe that extending the drone screen outwards and combining our sensors through the datanet would provide additional warning of any further ambushes."

He paused, then went on. "Second, their missiles. Our general feeling is that they have successfully designed compact missile drives at least an order of magnitude more powerful than our own, although they share many of the same weaknesses. Not least the simple fact that we can track them from launch and project their course. Their warheads, however, remain a more serious problem. We do not, as yet, have any explanation for their improved laser heads."

Reed leaned forward. "Did they not simply scale up a bomb-pumped laser system? That's what the Indians did."

"Not unless they've designed a way to construct a mini-warhead," Mason said. He scowled, darkly. "Their missiles aren't actually any larger than ours, but their warhead yields and ranges are definitely greater. We may need to start targeting their missiles with buckshot, rather than plasma cannons. They can just program their weapons to detonate outside our point defence range."

"Update the programming," Susan ordered. Buckshot was a frighteningly inefficient weapon, compared to plasma cannons, but the projectiles *did* keep going until they ran into something solid. "Can we do anything else about the missiles?"

"Not as yet, Captain," Mason said. "They're really quite determined little buggers. The Americans did try to draw some of them off with ECM decoys, but they didn't take the bait."

"They might have had hard locks on our hulls," Charlotte offered. "The fleet wasn't really trying to hide."

"True," Susan agreed. "Next time, we'll be using our own stealth systems."

Mason nodded, then leaned forward. "There's a more serious problem, however," he warned, his voice growing darker. "Watch the display and tell me what you think."

Susan scowled - she hated guessing games - but watched, anyway, as the ambush played itself out for the second time. One alien fleet coming up the rear, another heading outwards from the tramline leading straight to the alien system...it was definitely a picture-perfect ambush. And yet, coordinating it should have been hellishly difficult...

"Run it again," she ordered, coldly. She felt numb as the pattern evolved in front of her. "I...they have some form of FTL communication."

"Impossible," Parkinson said.

"The aliens coordinated their operations as if there was no time-delay between their two formations," Mason said, flatly. Susan guessed he was as stunned as she was. For all the rumours, no one had ever successfully sent a message at FTL speeds. "If you watch this part of the battle, it's clear the aliens react faster than they should, if they were limited to radio waves or laser communicators."

"If that's the case," Susan said slowly, "they have a major advantage."

"Yes, sir," Mason said. "As yet, we have no idea of the system's range, but we know it covers well over five light-minutes. We have to assume that the *actual* range might be much greater."

Susan nodded. It took between five minutes and twenty-one minutes to send a signal from Earth to Mars, depending on the two planets relative positions. But if someone could halve the time it took to send a signal, they'd have a major advantage. And in a space battle, where seconds counted, it could give them a *decisive* advantage. The more she thought about it, the colder she felt. Upgraded missiles were one thing, but FTL communications?

She tapped the table, meaningfully. "Do we have any clue how they do it?"

"Not as yet," Mason said. "I have teams going through every last recording, but so far they've turned up nothing that might point to how it's done. It's quite possible, I think, that the FTL signals are beyond our ability to detect."

"Wonderful," Susan said, tartly. She knew she was being unfair, but she couldn't stop herself. "Do you have any other pieces of good news?"

"I'm afraid not," Mason said. "Most of the ships that were destroyed during the battle were smashed, but a handful may have left significant chunks of debris behind. Even if the aliens have a habit of shooting at lifepods, Captain, they'll be able to recover biological samples."

Dead humans and Tadpoles, Susan thought.

She scowled. "Does that pose a threat?"

"It would certainly tell them they're facing two races," Mason said. "Beyond that…I don't think it poses an immediate problem. But they would have the ability, at least in theory, to manufacture a biological weapon targeted on us."

"The Admiralty can worry about that," Susan said. She'd heard rumours about just how much research went into safeguarding the British population from genetically-engineered viruses, but she knew very little for sure. Such research was largely considered taboo, after several parties had tried to release such weapons during the Age of Unrest. "Do you think they may have recovered computer cores?"

"I don't think so," Mason said, "but it's impossible to be entirely sure."

Susan waited a moment, then glanced at Prince Henry. "Mr. Ambassador?"

The Prince sighed. "We have no facts, Captain," he said. "There is no logical reason for them to open fire on us, unless they are either inherently aggressive or had strong reasons to believe we were a threat. It's *possible* they thought we were far too close to their homeworld, but we could have haggled diplomatically over who owned UXS-469 or UXS-468. I don't think the Tadpoles would have cared to keep them. They may also be at war already and assumed *we* were allied to that hostile force..."

"Interesting," Susan mused. "Do you have any proof?"

"We know *nothing*, Captain," Prince Henry said. "All we have is speculation. We transmitted the complete first contact protocols as soon as we detected their fleet, which didn't keep them from opening fire. Either there was a terrible mistake or they just didn't care."

Susan closed her eyes for a long moment. Mason had made her rest, but she just hadn't had enough sleep. Nor had the rest of the crew. They weren't exactly inexperienced, yet very few of them had seen actual combat. *Vanguard* had survived her first combat test, but it would be a long time before the scars faded completely.

"Thank you, both of you," she said, opening her eyes. "I assume you've forwarded copies of your research to Captain Harper?"

"Yes, Captain," Mason said. "For what it's worth, the Americans reached basically the same conclusions as ourselves."

Susan looked at Prince Henry. "Do you have any guesses what we'll face in the future?"

"No, Captain," Prince Henry said. "If this was a terrible mistake, they may attempt to open contact and make reparations. Or they may try to occupy the systems past UXS-469 towards the Tadpoles, in hopes of fending off any counterattacks. Or they may simply want to drive us away from UXS-469 and not proceed any further. There's no way to know for sure."

Susan nodded, although her gut feeling told her that the newcomers would go on the offensive, now they'd smashed a major fleet. Whatever they'd *meant* to do, they now knew they were at war against two races, not one. They'd have to keep the initiative or be smashed flat when humanity and the Tadpoles launched a counterattack, after duplicating the alien weapons. Unless, of course, they saw the alien-grade tramlines as a balancing advantage and decided to sue for peace…

"Thank you," she said, again. "Please continue studying the sensor footage. You may find something new."

"I could fly a starfighter," Prince Henry pointed out. "You might find me more useful out in space."

"No," Susan said, quickly.

She shook her head firmly, cutting off his argument. Prince Henry hadn't been a starfighter pilot for thirteen years and she rather doubted he'd kept his skills current. The new generation of starfighters were more advanced than the Hurricanes and Spitfires that had fought the First Interstellar War and he'd need at least a few days in the simulators before he could be cleared for action. Besides, she'd hate to explain his death in action to the Admiralty…

Her own thoughts mocked her. *Along with everything else*?

"Dismissed," she said, rising to her feet. "Mr. Mason, take command. I'll be on the bridge after I finish speaking to the other commanding officers."

———

"The alien FTL communications system changes nothing," Harper said, an hour later. "Yes, I know it's a major tactical headache, but we have other problems."

"Unless the aliens have an FTL drive too," Captain Beasley pointed out. "They've already done one thing we believed to be impossible."

"Then they would have followed us to this system and finished us off," Harper said. "The long-term issue of their FTL communications is something for our superiors to address."

He tapped a switch, activating a starchart. "We have done all the patching up we can do over the last two days," he continued, before anyone else could say a word. "Accordingly, it is now time to proceed back towards friendly space. I've divided the remaining fleet into three squadrons; *Roosevelt, London* and *Vanguard*. *London* will serve as the communications hub with the remaining Tadpole ships, which will be assigned to that squadron. *Vanguard* will take point.

"We will proceed as I have outlined, under full stealth. If we don't encounter the enemy before Tadpole-98, we will reveal ourselves to the Tadpoles at that point and pass on the data we've collected. The Ambassador can head directly for Tadpole Prime while we join the defence force, save for the ships that desperately need a shipyard."

He paused. "If we do encounter the unknowns, we'll do our best to evade contact unless the odds are solidly in our favour," he added. "If they are...well, we need to see if we can get our hands on some of their technology. And I want some payback."

Susan nodded in agreement. *She* wanted some payback too,

Captain Jackson cursed. "And what happens if they have more super-weapons up their sleeve?"

"They are not gods," Harper said. "Yes, they kicked our butts and yes, we're not *used* to having our butts kicked. But they are not so advanced that we cannot beat them. If nothing else, human treachery and sneakiness will win the day."

He tapped a switch and the starchart vanished. "You all have the updated point defence programs," he added. "We should be able to give a better account of ourselves, when we next encounter our new enemies. For now, the fleet will move out one hour from now, in the formation I have designed."

And good luck to us all, Susan thought. *Vanguard* taking point was logical, although she suspected she'd have problems with her subordinates. She might not be a *legal* Captain - and even if she was, she was barely two days into her rank. A destroyer commander might be her technical superior. *Let's hope we make it home safely.*

CHAPTER TWENTY NINE

"Jump complete, Captain," Reed said.

"The cloaking system didn't flicker," Mason added. "We should be invisible."

Should, Susan thought, as the display began to fill with icons. *But if they have FTL communications, what else do they have?*

She told herself, firmly, that there was nothing she could do about it and turned her attention to the tactical display. The new system looked to be habitable; there was a G2 star, a couple of gas giants and at least two rocky worlds within the life-bearing zone. Neither one appeared to be emitting radio waves, but that proved nothing. The enemy might have a system that was undetectable, at least by her technology, or - more likely - the system might have gone dark.

Not that that worked too well during the Battle of Earth, she reminded herself. *Too many people just didn't get the word.*

"We'll hold position here, as planned," she said. Harper was determined not to sail blindly into a second ambush, a determination shared by every other commanding officer on the fleet. "Inform me the moment you detect any artificial emissions."

"Aye, Captain," Reed said.

"One of the planets is definitely habitable," Mason offered, after a moment. "I'd call her a ninety-percent match for Earth."

Susan leaned forward. It was prime real estate, only a handful of jumps from Tadpole - or enemy - space. "Can you pick up any signs of life? Any at all?"

"No, Captain," Charlotte said. "At this distance, nothing smaller than the orbital towers would be visible to passive sensors. The Great Wall of China might as well not exist."

"We could always go look," Mason suggested.

Susan fought down temptation. The prospect of laying claim to an unexplored Earth-type world was not one to be dismissed automatically. Britain's claim would be recognised by both the other human nations and the Tadpoles - and, as the discoverer, *Vanguard's* crew would be entitled to a share of the proceeds. But so close to enemy space, the risk was not to be borne. The priority was to get the fleet home safely, not attempt to lay claim to a world that might well lie within enemy territory.

"Hold position here," she ordered, firmly. "There'll be time to come back and survey the system later."

She kept her expression under firm control, even as she sensed disappointment rippling around the giant compartment. Fortunes had been made by crews lucky enough to serve on starships that had made discoveries - or, in one case, brought home an alien battlecruiser largely intact. Susan was not adverse to risk - she'd picked the wrong career if she wasn't willing to take risks from time to time - but there was little to be gained by risking the entire fleet. Better to avoid contact with the new enemy as much as possible.

And we might discover an enemy colony, she added, silently. *And then we would have to make a very hard choice.*

She gritted her teeth at the thought. There were ROE for peacetime operations and ROE for wartime, but none of the planners had ever imagined the fleet running into an ambush - and then remaining unsure if they were at war or if the whole affair had been a terrible ghastly mistake. The diplomats would find it harder to patch the whole affair up if the fleet found an alien world and laid waste to it, yet if they *were* at war wrecking an alien world would hardly make matters worse. Perhaps it was her duty to check the world for alien life, yet there were no signs of any space-based industry. If the planet was solely restricted to low-tech, bombarding the settlements from orbit wouldn't cripple the enemy's ability to make war…

And you don't have the slightest idea if there actually is an enemy presence on that world, she reminded herself. *The planet might be new and unclaimed.*

"We've picked up nothing," Mason said, fifty minutes later. "The entire system is as dark and silent as the grave."

"Bad metaphor," Susan said, absently. "Communications?"

Parkinson looked up. "Yes, Captain?"

"Order one of the ships to jump back through the tramline and inform Captain Harper that the way appears to be clear," Susan said. Harper would want to sit on the tramline for a while longer, just to check for himself, but afterwards the fleet could proceed onwards to its destination. "And ready a full datapacket for his attention, when the remainder of the fleet arrives."

"Aye, Captain," Parkinson said.

Susan nodded and settled back into her chair as the remainder of the fleet flickered into existence, one by one. Her tactical crews knew where to look, she told herself; the fleet's cloaking systems should render the fleet undetectable except at very close range. And yet the uncertainty created by the alien FTL communications pervaded her thinking. If they could do something that humanity considered to be impossible - *had* considered to be impossible - what else could they do?

They don't seem to have FTL drives, she noted, grimly. *Or else they could have followed us and finished the job. We didn't hurt them* that *badly.*

"Signal from the flag," Parkinson said. "The fleet is to proceed directly to Tramline Two at best possible speed, consummate with keeping us undetected. *Vanguard* and her squadron are to take point."

"Good," Susan said. Harper evidently didn't want to remain in the unexplored system any longer than necessary. "Order the screen to fan out as planned, maintaining a passive sensor watch for any enemy targets."

"Aye, Captain," Parkinson said.

"Helm, take us out on a direct course for Tramline Two," Susan added. "But be ready to take evasive manoeuvres at any moment."

"Aye, Captain," Reed said.

She felt the hull vibrate, slightly, as the drives came up to full power. It might have been smarter, if stealth was their only concern, to dogleg through the system, rather than making a run for the tramline. A single enemy starship, watching their movements from a distance, would have no trouble setting up another ambush if the fleet was following a predictable flight path. And yet, she found it hard to disagree with Harper's orders. There was a chance - a realistic chance - of getting back to Tadpole space before the enemy managed to get a blocking force in place...

Unless they have control of tramlines we don't know about, she thought. *Or if they have something else up their sleeves.*

"Inform me the moment you pick up any traces of enemy activity, any at all," she ordered, after a moment. "I want to know if they so much as pass wind within this system."

"Aye, Captain," Mason said.

Susan scowled, then forced herself to sit back and relax. There was nothing to be gained by panicking - or showing the crew just how nervous she felt. None of her early commanding officers had ever sounded anything but confident, even when their ships had run into dangerous waters. In hindsight, she wondered just how many of them had been faking it. A commanding officer was responsible for the entire ship and all aboard her...

Fake it until you make it, she recalled. It was a piece of advice she'd heard at the academy, back when she'd started. *A show of confidence can often be worth more than actual competence.*

Her scowl deepened as some of the implications sunk in. *And that*, she thought darkly, *probably explains why Captain Blake remained in command for so long.*

"The enemy starfighters are definitely not as good as ours," Lieutenant Shelia Roscoe said, as she brought up the display. "As you can see, they're actually inferior to Mark-III Spitfires; I'd place them as being roughly equivalent to Russian-designed *Katyusha*-class starfighters."

"Except for the plasma cannons," Henry said. The Russians had mass-produced the *Katyusha*-class during the latter stages of the war, sacrificing armour and other essentials for starfighters that packed a nasty punch. "Their plasma cannons are almost as good as ours."

"Yes, sir," Shelia said. She had a faint Australian accent, suggesting she was either a transfer officer or had spent a great deal of time Down Under. "In fact, in some ways, I'd say they were better. Their magnetic containment fields are less efficient than ours, but their cannons actually have a longer range. Useless against starship armour, of course, yet dangerously effective against our starfighters. I suspect we lost quite a few starfighters because the pilots assumed they were out of range."

"Probably," Henry said. He'd been a fighter jock himself and he knew the arrogance that ran through the breed, combined with a grim awareness that death could come at any moment. A starfighter couldn't hope to survive a hit that wouldn't even scratch a destroyer's hull. "It can't be the safest of systems, surely."

"They probably do run the risk of overloading their plasma containment chambers," Sheila said. "That was a common problem with our own upgraded starfighters."

"*Yes*, I know," Henry said, rightly.

Shelia missed the undertone - Henry had nearly been killed when one of the plasma containment chambers had exploded - and carried on.

"Given everything else we've seen, sir, they must have made the deliberate decision to accept the risks," she added. "I do not believe they don't have the ability to make their weapons safer to the user. They chose to sacrifice safety for a little extra range."

Henry couldn't disagree. Civilian firearms, at least in Britain, were designed with all kinds of safeguards built into them, despite objections from owners who believed that disarming the safeguards ate up precious seconds. Military firearms were much easier to use, yet there was no additional *risk* to the shooter. But if it was possible to boost the weapon's range, at some risk to the person who fired it, would the military accept the risk?

It might have to, he thought.

Shelia evidently agreed. "Extending the range of our own plasma cannons shouldn't be hard, but it would mean risking the same problem," she added. "I'm not sure how much we can scale up our guns without running into other issues."

"The boffins will come up with something," Henry said. He was sure of it. The Battle of New Russia had been bad, but the successive engagements had been a great deal more even, once each side knew a little about the other. "And the FTL communicator?"

"Nothing, as yet," Shelia said. "The computers have been sifting through every last byte of data, but they haven't identified anything that might be an FTL signal. It might have been moving too fast for our sensors to detect."

"Or it might have been something our sensors are not *designed* to detect," Henry said. "Do you have any theories?"

"None," Shelia said. "They *may* have solved the problem of producing intensive gravity waves, on cue, but every attempt to do it in a lab met with failure. The gravity wave simply didn't remain in existence for more than a second and, more irritatingly, the range was miniscule."

Henry's eyes narrowed. "On an interplanetary scale?"

"On a lab scale," Shelia said, flatly. "The prospective range, at best, was ten kilometres. It would be quicker and simpler to use radio waves."

"I see," Henry said.

Shelia looked up at him. "Does this tell you anything new about the aliens?"

"Only that their attitude to risk is different from ours," Henry said.

He scowled. He'd been forced to study hundreds of different human societies, back when he'd been preparing for the assignment to Tadpole Prime, even though he'd argued that it was a waste of time at best, openly misleading at worst. The Tadpoles weren't human and trying to judge them by human standards was an exercise in futility. And yet, there had been bits of it that he'd found interesting. The West, the cradle of true civilisation, had veered between being restrictive, to the point of almost being fascist, to being far too permissive and, at the same time, violently opposed to *risk*. Heading off the Troubles - and the Age of Unrest - would have been easy, if the governments had worked up the nerve to act before it had almost been too late.

But they thought they had a great deal to lose, he reminded himself. *It didn't occur to them that they risked losing everything anyway.*

"That proves nothing," Shelia said. "We don't know anything about them, do we?"

Henry shrugged in agreement. There was no hard data on the size of the enemy fleet; therefore it was impossible to say just how badly the enemy had been hurt in the brief engagement. Only a handful of capital ships had been destroyed by the Tadpoles…had they taken out fifty percent of the enemy fleet, ten percent or one percent? There was no way to know. The enemy had lost more starfighters, but that was meaningless. It wouldn't take them long to replenish their losses.

Unless their industrial base is far inferior to ours, he told himself. *But that's an assumption we dare not make.*

"No, we don't," he said, finally. He tapped a switch, bringing up the image of one of the enemy warships. "What do you make of *this* proud beauty?"

"I'm surprised they let you come," Barton said, as George slipped into sickbay. "It's been rather crowded around here."

"*You're* lazing around in bed," George said. She sat down next to him and held out one of the chocolate bars. Fraser had given it to her without an argument when she'd told him what she wanted it for. "I'm lucky to have a few free to come down to see you."

Barton stared at the bar in shock. "Where did you get that?"

"Luna," George said. "It should be edible, I think."

"I should coco," Barton said. He peeled back the wrapping paper, sniffed the brown chocolate and offered her a piece. George took the first bit and chewed it, savouring every last fragment. "You just can't get this in the mess."

George nodded. Cadbury had been in business for centuries, making quality chocolate for rich and poor alike, but whoever was in charge of military procurement had a habit of purchasing supplies from the lowest bidder. Or so she thought. The chocolate bars available in the NAAFI didn't taste anything like as good as civilian chocolate. And she dreaded to think what went into the liquid that claimed to be cola. Only the tea was better than anything available to a civilian.

"Keep the rest, if you don't want to finish it now," George told him. She smiled at his gobsmacked expression. A gold bar would probably have been less surprising. "When are you going to stop lazing around and get out of bed?"

"I should be back up on my feet in the next couple of days," Barton assured her. He tapped the cast on his leg meaningfully. "The doctor says it should be completely regenerated tomorrow, then I just need to walk around until my body remembers how...or something along those lines. I wasn't paying close attention."

"That's something, at least," George said. "Did.... did Simpson speak to you?"

"Smith and Jones didn't make it," Barton said. He looked down at the bed, suddenly a very unsure young man. "I would have thought that nothing could kill them."

"Nathan died too," George said. The pain was still raw, despite working double shifts to make up for the dead or injured midshipmen. But there was nothing she could do about it, not now. Nathan had requested that his body be buried in space, along with most of the other crewmen, yet they couldn't hold a funeral until they returned to friendly territory. "He didn't deserve it."

"Neither did Smith and Jones," Barton said. It struck her, suddenly, that he'd had more time to brood. "How are you coping?"

"Working hard," George said. It was true; Fraser kept her and the other survivors working, even though it was clear he'd been devastated too. "I'm due back in the turrets this afternoon, really; Simpson has been reassigned to Turret Five and I've been spending time with him."

Barton smirked. "Should I be jealous?"

George flushed. "No," she said. She wasn't quite sure how to respond. Barton and she were hardly dating. "No one should be jealous."

"I suppose climbing out onto the hull was a bad idea," Barton said. "But it was the best of a set of very bad ideas."

"Yeah," George agreed. "The doctor said he wants me back here, after we return to friendly space. There might have been other complications."

"There shouldn't have been," Barton reassured her. "He did a full cellular scan on me, seeing I was trapped in bed, and there wasn't any sign of radiation damage. I don't think you had any less protection than I did out there."

George nodded, relieved. She'd taken the precaution of having a number of her eggs removed and frozen - male spacers had their sperm preserved - but the prospect of being accidentally sterilised terrified her. Or, worse, bringing a malformed child into an unfriendly world. She wasn't sure she wanted kids, at least not until she was much older, yet she hated the idea of losing that choice.

And a wave of radiation might just have killed me outright, she thought. There was no shortage of horror stories, although some of them might well have been exaggerated to make sure that prospective spacers understood the dangers of life in space. *Or left me crippled.*

"I'll see what the doctor says," she said. But he was likely right. She hadn't been any less protected than Barton himself. "And..."

She broke off and jumped to her feet as the alarms started to howl. "Crap."

"Good luck," Barton said. She barely heard him as she raced for the hatch. "Hit one of the bastards for me!"

CHAPTER THIRTY

"Captain," Charlotte said, as Susan hurried onto the bridge. "I'm picking up five enemy starships proceeding towards Tramline One."

Susan took her chair and checked the display. *Vanguard* had transited through UXS-471 without incident and entered UXS-472, carefully checking for any signs of enemy presence before starting the long crawl towards Tramline Two. There were actually two other tramlines in UXS-472, but one of them was alien-grade and the other - according to the plotter - should lead *away* from friendly space. She couldn't help wondering, now, if the enemy had started to run ships through the unexplored tramline. It might have allowed them to cut the time to get a blocking force in place.

FTL communications screw up all our calculations, she thought, grimly. *Even with a relay chain, it still takes weeks - at best - to get a signal from one side of the human sphere to another. Here...the aliens might be able to react quicker than us to any potential threat.*

"Make certain of your identification," she ordered, grimly. "Are you sure they're our new friends?"

"I believe so, Captain," Charlotte said. "There's no way to get a close look at their hulls, not at our range, but the power curves and drive fields match those recorded during the first clash. I think there're one heavy cruiser and four destroyers."

"Alert Captain Harper," Susan ordered. *Roosevelt* was twenty light seconds behind *Vanguard*, close enough to exchange signals yet too distant to provide help if the giant battleship ran into trouble. But then, *Vanguard* was probably more capable of handling anything the new enemies had shown than the giant fleet carrier. "And show me their projected course."

She sucked in her breath as the enemy ship trajectories appeared on the display. Unless they altered course, they would hit the tramline and plunge straight into the next system without slowing to survey their current system. But if they *didn't* alter course, they might well pass close enough to *Roosevelt* and the rest of the fleet to pick up *something*, despite the cloaking devices. And then…four ships weren't anything like enough to overwhelm the fleet, unless they had a genuine superweapon, but they *could* shadow the human starships until the aliens assembled a much larger fleet.

But they don't know we're here, she thought, coldly. She tilted her head to one side, considering the different possibilities. *If they knew, they wouldn't be heading right towards us.*

"Record," she ordered.

"Recording," Parkinson said.

"Captain Harper," Susan said. "As you can see, the odds appear to be in our favour. My ship can engage all five enemy craft, aiming to cripple or destroy them. I do not believe that the risks of engaging the enemy openly outweigh the prospective gains. Therefore, unless you order otherwise, I intend to put *Vanguard* and her squadron in position to intercept the alien ships. Please advise within the next ten minutes."

She glanced at Parkinson. "Send."

"Message sent, Captain," Parkinson said.

Susan felt her heart starting to beat faster as she contemplated the options. Evading the enemy ships altogether shouldn't be too difficult, unless the enemy had some kind of sensor system she'd never imagined. But they needed to know more about their enemy and she was in an excellent position to strike them before they could escape. And yet, there might be a handful of other enemy ships nearby, just waiting to see if the uncloaked ships would draw fire. Harper might well have rethought his aggressive approach during the fleet's passage through the last system.

And they came on the least-time course between tramlines, she thought, grimly. *Is that actually a coincidence*?

She scowled as she thought it through. The enemy *had* to know where the fleet had gone, even if they couldn't follow. They probably also knew just how quickly the fleet could move, which would allow them to make some accurate guesses about how far they'd travelled since the battle. And *that* meant they had to have a rough idea that they'd re-encounter the fleet in the current system or the previous one.

Unless they think we snuck back into the first system, after moving down the tramline, she told herself. *But we don't dare count on it.*

"Picking up a signal from *Roosevelt*, Captain," Parkinson said. He smiled. "Message reads: *Proceed in the finest traditions of your service and mine.*"

"In other words, sail into danger," Susan said. She settled back in her chair. "Pass the word to the screen. I want them behind us. Let the enemy ships impale themselves on our guns."

"Aye, Captain," Parkinson said.

Susan glanced at Mason. "Aim to disable the big ship, if possible, but if she keeps firing don't hesitate to take her out."

"Aye, Captain," Mason said. "And the destroyers?"

"Take them out," Susan ordered. The destroyers would have the greatest chance of escaping, once they knew they were under attack. "Don't give them a chance to react."

"Aye, Captain," Mason said.

"Helm, slip us into attack position," Susan added. "Don't let them get even a *whiff* of our presence."

And half of us haven't had time to take showers, she thought, as *Vanguard* altered course and moved to take up her new position. *They can probably smell us.*

She dismissed the thought as the enemy ships grew larger on the display. It looked, very much, as though the enemy hadn't been quite as enthusiastic about starfighters as either humanity or the Tadpoles; instead of developing newer ways to power tiny attack craft they'd spent their time improving realspace drives. Indeed, the more she looked at it, the more she suspected the enemy actually had higher acceleration curves than anything humanity had produced. The Tadpoles had had the same advantage, back in the war, but their starfighters hadn't been noticeably faster…

And better armed, Susan thought. *They slaughtered us at New Russia because we underestimated the threat.*

A thought occurred to her and she smiled, coldly. *Ark Royal* had captured an alien starship and brought it home. Why couldn't *Vanguard* do the same? She had two companies of Royal Marines, men experienced in attacking unwary starships and taking control. And they were ready to dive into a disabled alien craft, gambling their lives that they could capture or kill the crew before they destroyed their own ship.

If we can bring samples of the alien tech home, she told herself, *all of the little irregularities of this voyage will be forgotten.*

"Captain," Charlotte said. "The enemy craft are closing in."

Susan braced herself, pushing visions of fame aside. The closer the alien ships came to the lurking battleship, the greater the chance of being detected. She had no doubt that *Vanguard's* missiles would be completely ineffective against the aliens, if she had to engage their ships at long range. The only consolation was that the revised point defence targeting patterns would make it harder for the enemy to score hits in exchange.

Although they would be foolish to engage us, if they get a look at our hulls before it's too late, she thought. *They could give us one hell of a beating if they decided to close the range, but they'd be wiser to beat a retreat and scream for reinforcements. And they'd get a solid lock on our position in the process.*

"Stand by to engage," she ordered, tartly. "Lock weapons on targets."

"Weapons locked," Mason said. "Multiple targets sighted; main guns primed."

And hope to hell we haven't underestimated them for a second time, Susan thought. *If they can see through our cloaks, they wouldn't keep on coming unless they had a surprise up their sleeves.*

"Twenty seconds to certain detection," Charlotte reported. "Ten seconds to optimum engagement range."

Susan braced herself. This was it, this was payback…the fleet needed a victory, needed it desperately. They'd been the most powerful force assembled in galactic history, as far as anyone knew, and yet they'd been slaughtered by the newcomers. Over twenty thousand personnel - British and American - were dead. Morale was in the crapper and wouldn't climb out, unless something happened to show the remainder of the crew that they were far from ineffectual. They *needed* a victory.

The display flared red. "They have us," Charlotte snapped. "Direct sensor contact!"

"Fire," Susan snapped.

Vanguard quivered, lightly, as she unleashed the full weight of her broadsides. Susan watched, feeling cold merciless delight rippling through her soul, as one of the alien destroyers exploded without altering course or firing a single shot. Her crew had to have been caught completely by surprise. Two more destroyers staggered as they took heavy hits; the fourth started to back off, only to take a hammering from one of the turrets. Seconds later, two of the three remaining destroyers were dead.

"The big bastard is moving forward to shield the fourth destroyer," Mason said. "She's spitting missiles back at us."

"Point defence can handle them," Susan said. She was more worried about the alien cruiser trying to ram *Vanguard*. If the aliens thought they couldn't escape, why *not* try to take out the battleship? "Keep trying to cripple their drives..."

The alien cruiser had a skilful crew, she had to admit, feeling an odd tinge of admiration she didn't like in the slightest. Taken by surprise, crippled in the opening salvos, she still tried to lurch into firing position...and then amble forward, intent on ramming *Vanguard*. But Susan's crew were alert; Reed altered course, smoothly and skilfully, as Mason hammered the alien cruiser into a drifting powerless wreck. And then something exploded within the ship and it came apart into an expanding cloud of debris.

"Shit," Mason snapped.

"Target the final destroyer," Susan ordered. It didn't *look* as though the cruiser had self-destructed, unless something had gone badly wrong. *Human* self-destructs were considerably more powerful. "Take her out before she gets out of range..."

"She's already outside immediate range," Mason warned.

"Order the screen to attempt to intercept," Susan ordered. It was probably futile - the aliens had had plenty of time to signal for help - but worth trying. "Launch a full sensor shell of drones. I want to know if there's *anything* within a light minute of our current position."

"Aye, Captain," Charlotte said.

"Forward the details of the engagement to Captain Harper," Susan added, addressing Parkinson. Harper's sensors would have picked up the brief exchange of fire, but it was unlikely he'd know *precisely* what had happened. "And then advise him to dogleg around our position, just in case the ships we destroyed were bait in a trap."

"Aye, Captain," Parkinson said.

Susan took a moment to think as she studied the expanding cloud of debris. It was unlikely in the extreme that they'd discover an intact computer core within the wreckage, unless the enemy were stunningly careless, but there was a reasonably decent chance of recovering a body... or, for that matter, a book or something else that might assist the xeno-specialists to come to grips with their new challenge. And yet, if the four ships *had* been bait in a trap, remaining where they were was asking for trouble. She'd do better to break contact as soon as possible.

Time to gamble, she thought.

"Raise the Boatswain," she ordered. "Tell him I want every shuttle in space, probing through the wreckage. Draw pilots from other departments, if necessary. They have thirty minutes to sift through the debris and find something - anything - that might be useful. All standard precautions when dealing with xenomaterial are to be observed."

"Aye, Captain," Parkinson said.

Susan settled back into her command chair, feeling relief mixed with fear. The aliens *had* been caught by surprise - their answering fire had been almost pathetically ineffectual - but there was no way to know what their superiors had been planning. Even if they hadn't *intended* to bait a trap, they certainly had an opportunity to do it now. They'd notice they were missing four ships sooner or later, wouldn't they?

Particularly if they expect the crews to report in every hour, she thought. FTL communications messed up *all* of her calculations. The light-speed bubble surrounding every event in space, showing how quickly word spread from one side of a star system to the other, was now meaningless. *They'll know the ships ran into trouble when they don't reply.*

"The shuttles are being launched now," Parkinson reported. "The Boatswain has taken overall command."

"The Main Shuttlebay is being prepped to Code Blue standards," Mason added. "Major Andres has taken command."

"Good," Susan said. She didn't know Andres as well as she'd like, but he was reassuringly competent. If there was any biohazard from the alien wreckage, he wouldn't allow it to threaten the rest of the ship. "Evacuate the surrounding compartments, just in case."

Mason gave her an odd look - she had no difficulty in reading his feelings - but did as he was told. Susan was quietly grateful. Perhaps she was being paranoid, yet she would have preferred to take excessive precautions than accidentally bring a genuine biological threat onto her ship. Or, for that matter, something that wasn't identified as explosive until it was far too late.

And if we do find a piece of alien technology, she reminded herself, *we might not even understand it for years.*

"You remember how to fly this thing?"

"Yes, sir," George said, as she buckled herself into the pilot seat. The shuttle was already powering up, ready to leap out of the hatch and into space. "I haven't forgotten anything."

The Boatswain nodded curtly - she'd really taken too long to get her spacesuit on - then turned to his display and hunted for prospective targets within the debris field. George took the helm, powered the shuttle out into the darkness and steered towards the remains of the alien ships. Great chunks of debris, many larger than the shuttle itself, were drifting through space, rapidly fanning out in all directions. She slowed the shuttle as they approached, turning on the lights so they could see the alien debris more clearly. Much of it looked identical to human debris, right down to the scorch marks.

"One of the shuttles has already picked up a piece of armour plating," the Boatswain said, as she eyed a chunk of debris. "See if you can spot anything more interesting."

"Aye, sir," George said. She would have liked to speak with the Boatswain about other matters - Fraser, Nathan's death - but she knew it would have to wait. "I'll take us further into the debris field now."

She shivered as she nosed the shuttle forward, then cursed as *something* hit the hull hard enough to send shockwaves through the entire craft. The remains of the alien ship were slowly breaking up, spinning out in all directions. She had no idea if it was caused by a collapsing gravity field or something else, but it posed a serious hazard. Standard procedure, from what little she recalled, was to disassemble the debris field carefully - or, if there was no reason to keep it intact, just have it swept up by a mobile recycler. But there was no time to do the former and only the aliens would be interested in doing the latter…

"There," the Boatswain said. He jabbed a finger into the semi-darkness. "Hold still while I take a look at that."

"Aye, sir," George said.

She gritted her teeth as another piece of debris banged into the hull and watched as the Boatswain peered at *something*. It looked rather like a piece of charred meat to her, but the Boatswain seemed *very* interested. And then it occurred to her that the piece of meat was actually a roasted alien and she had to swallow hard to keep from throwing up. She'd had to explore dead hulks as part of her training, yet this was different. This was *real*.

"I'm taking this in," the Boatswain said. He took control of the shuttle's manipulators and went to work. "You are familiar with the Code Blue protocols, aren't you?"

"Everything from an uncontacted alien race is to be kept in strict isolation," George recited, from memory. "Once sealed up, the outsides of the boxes are to be bathed in radiation to make sure that any potentially-hostile germs are destroyed. Crewmen are to wear suits at all times when handling alien materials; any who have any kind of contact are to be held in isolation too."

"Correct," the Boatswain said. He finished using the manipulators to box up the alien remains, then locked them to the hull. "We haven't had any direct contact, but they may insist on us remaining in isolation for a while anyway."

It was hard to keep her expression blank, but George managed it somehow. She understood the need to take precautions to ensure there was no biological hazard, yet the Code Blue protocols were uncomfortably paranoid. She'd spent two days in an isolation chamber in the academy and it had been horrendous, even though she'd *known* there was no real danger. It wasn't something she wanted to do again.

The Boatswain gave her a sharp look - as if he knew precisely what was going through her mind - and then turned his head back to the scanner. "There're a few other pieces of debris that have been marked down for collection," he said. "We'll see how many of them we can snatch up before we have to return to the ship."

"Aye, sir," George said.

She glanced at the live feed from *Vanguard* as she took the shuttle towards the next piece of interesting debris. There was nothing moving within the remainder of the system - at least, nothing that *Vanguard* could detect. And yet, she couldn't help feeling dreadfully exposed - and alone. If the aliens reappeared, she'd have to throw caution to the winds and fly straight back to the battleship..."

"Ah," the Boatswain said, as they approached the next piece of debris. "This may be something *very* interesting."

CHAPTER THIRTY ONE

Susan had taken the opportunity to review the Code Blue procedures during the long trek through unexplored space, but she was still taken by surprise by the level of precautions Doctor Abramson - one of the xenospecialists from Tadpole Prime - had insisted on building into the shuttlebay. The shuttles themselves had been largely removed, allowing the researchers to vent the atmosphere in an emergency, while the hatches had been sealed, ensuring that an explosion would not do significant damage to the ship. If there was any threat, she thought, it would be contained.

And besides, the darker part of her mind noted, *if anyone wants to try to steal an alien relic, they'd find it a great deal harder.*

She glanced at Prince Henry as Doctor Abramson emerged from the airlock, looking dishevelled. The suit he'd worn to examine the alien relics had been bathed with radiation before he'd been allowed to undress, then he'd been checked thoroughly for any *hints* that something had managed to get through the suit and into his bloodstream. There had been no hint that any Tadpole - or Vesy - disease could make the jump into human bodies, or vice versa, but no one dared risk a *War Of The Worlds* scenario.

"Captain," Abramson said. "Mr. Ambassador."

"I don't have long, Doctor," Susan said. *Vanguard* had slipped away from the remains of the alien ships, but there was no way to know when their reinforcements would arrive. "What can you tell me about our new enemies?"

"Something rather unusual," Abramson said, as he led the way into a small briefing compartment. Susan watched, impatiently, as he obtained a cup of coffee from the drinks machine, then sat down heavily at the table. "Something I really wasn't expecting to see."

"Time *is* pressing, Doctor," Prince Henry said. "There isn't *time* for a long examination."

"We're not facing one alien race," Abramson said, bluntly. "We're facing *two*."

Susan stared at him. "Are you sure?"

"Yes, Captain," Abramson said. "The shuttle crews recovered thirty-seven chunks of biological matter - dead bodies - from the remains of the alien ship. Twenty-one chunks belong to members of one race, the remainder belong to another. There's no hint that they originated on the same world. I think we're looking at an alliance."

Prince Henry frowned. "What do they look like?"

"I don't know," Abramson said. "We have some of our computer systems trying to extrapolate what we pulled from the bodies to build a picture of their physical appearance, but so far we don't have a clear idea of what either race looks like. The extrapolation may tell us or it may be completely wrong. As for how they met, how they ended up working together...I don't know."

He took a long sip of his coffee. "I can tell you they're both oxygen-breathers and probably have very similar life support requirements," he added. "They'd need to be quite alike in some ways, just so they could serve together. Unless, of course, one race was the master and kept the other in uncomfortable positions, purely because it could."

Susan nodded. The Vesy weren't *that* different from humans, but they'd find human starships incredibly uncomfortable. And having the Tadpoles on human ships would be incredibly difficult. The two races they were facing now had to be practically cousins, even if they had evolved on different planets...

She looked up. "Are you sure they're actually two separate races?"

"Yes," Abramson said, flatly. He sounded too tired to be annoyed. "The differences between human sub-races are largely nominal. Skin colour, for example, is a very minor difference; there's no reason why two people of different sub-races cannot breed. Even the differences between male and female are tiny. Growing an opposite-sex clone of yourself isn't impossible, merely illegal."

"Yes," Susan said, dryly. If two human sub-races had been unable to breed, *she* wouldn't have existed. "But these are two different races?"

"Yes," Abramson said. "They have nothing in common, as far as I can tell; they didn't even originate on the same planet. I believe one of them is definitely humanoid - there're hints of a torso and legs in the pieces we recovered - but I don't know for sure."

"Two separate races," Prince Henry mused. "I wonder how they met."

Susan snorted. If the aliens were so virulently xenophobic that they attacked strangers on sight, and it *was* one possible explanation for the battle, why would they make friends with another alien race? Unless they thought that humans were repulsively ugly...but they wouldn't even have *seen* humans until after the first contact protocols had been completed, allowing both sides to build up a shared language. Hadn't there been a story where the aliens had started a war because humans looked like monsters to them? She made a mental note to look it up later, then pushed it aside.

"I'll take your word for it," she said, addressing Abramson. "What else can you tell me from the wreckage?"

"Their starship armour is actually a generation behind ours," Abramson said. "The chunks we examined were a step ahead of the solid-state armour that shielded *Ark Royal*, but several steps behind *Vanguard's* armour. However, there are some odd pieces of circuitry running through the hull that have no purpose, as far as we can tell. I've got a team of experts working on it, but given the damage the ship took in the fighting..."

"It may have been wrecked beyond recognition," Susan said. At least they had *one* advantage. The aliens would have problems armouring their ships to match *Vanguard* until they duplicated her armour. But they had plenty of wreckage to play with from the remains of the first battle. "Did you discover any computer cores?"

"No, Captain," Abramson said. "There were pieces of dust within the debris field that *might* have been computer cores, but they were completely beyond salvaging. Even if we had plenty of time, I doubt we could have recovered anything useful. We also didn't manage to locate any books, datapads or anything else that might have helped unlock some of the mysteries."

"So we know very little," Susan mused.

"We know there are actually two races, not one," Prince Henry said. "That's something we might be able to use, later. Driving a wedge into an enemy coalition is a respected diplomatic tactic."

"They were working together, sharing the same starships," Susan pointed out. "We don't share our starships with the Americans, let alone the Tadpoles. And we'd have no difficulty hosting Americans on our ships."

Prince Henry shrugged. "One final question," he said, addressing Abramson. "Is there a biohazard?"

"Everything I've seen, so far, suggests that there is not," Abramson said, stiffly. "However, I would be unwilling to relax the Code Blue protocols until we have completed the final set of tests. The corpses took a pounding from the destruction of the enemy starship and were frozen when the atmosphere failed. It would be better to wait."

"I'm not planning to relax any precautions," Susan said. "Is there *any* kind of threat?"

"As far as we can tell, the wreckage is inert," Abramson said. "What little pieces of trinkets we picked up are charred and broken. But we won't take risks."

"Thank you, Doctor," Prince Henry said. "You can go take a well-deserved nap."

Susan nodded and waited until Abramson was out of the hatch before looking at Prince Henry. "What do you make of it?"

"Two races," Prince Henry mused. "Two races, working together. Two races that decided to attack two more, without provocation."

"Assuming they *knew* they were attacking two races," Susan pointed out. "They didn't open visual communications with either of us."

"Tadpole starships are different from ours," Prince Henry said. "An American starship could pass for a British starship, particularly if the person who saw the ships was unfamiliar with either fleet, but a Tadpole starship would be unmistakeably inhuman."

"Human designers have been producing all kinds of starship designs," Susan said. "All those plans to build a working *Starship Enterprise*."

Prince Henry shrugged. "There are limits to what you can actually build, outside the movies," he said. "And many of those fancy designs are unworkable."

Susan frowned. "Did the Tadpoles provoke them in some way?"

"I wouldn't have thought so," Prince Henry said, after a moment. "They're a careful race, particularly after the war. I don't think they would have lied to us if there had been an…*incident* during an earlier first contact. Unless a rogue Tadpole faction made contact…"

He shook his head. "If that was the case," he added, "surely the aliens would have attacked the Tadpoles long before the survey ships reached their star system?"

"Perhaps," Susan said. "But they might have overlooked the first intrusion. Or warned the Tadpoles that *further* intrusions would not be tolerated."

"They would have told us," Prince Henry said. "They are not a secretive race."

Susan looked at him. "How would you know?"

Prince Henry's voice hardened. "I have lived on Tadpole Prime for the last decade," he said, sharply. "In that time, I have worked with the Tadpoles to smooth out diplomatic incidents that could have easily turned into diplomatic ruptures. I have spoken to triads from many different factions, ranging from ones that respect us to ones that either want to remain isolated or resume the war. And it is my considered judgement, as Earth's ambassador, that they may think differently from us, but they are not inclined to be secretive or treacherous. In many ways, they have upheld the treaty we signed better than ourselves."

Susan met his gaze evenly. "In what way?"

"We delayed telling them about the Vesy," Prince Henry said. "How easy would it have been for them to delay telling us about our new friends?"

"It was *our* survey ships that found them," Susan snapped.

"Our survey ships, which reported in to a Tadpole base," Prince Henry said. "They could have delayed matters indefinitely, perhaps even arranged for the ships to suffer an accident, one that would keep them from returning home. And yet, instead, they invited us to join the contact mission. I do not believe that the Tadpoles had any prior knowledge of the new aliens before our ships found them.

"And it was a handful of *Tadpole* ships that covered our retreat!"

Susan put firm controls on her temper. She was tired and stressed, but she couldn't afford to lose control. "Very well," she said. "I will take your word for it."

"Thank you," Prince Henry said, mollified.

"I'm sure Captain Harper will want a conference call after we link up with the remainder of the fleet," Susan added. "Will you be attending?"

"I think I should," Prince Henry said. "How many others have their doubts about the Tadpoles?"

Susan frowned. It was human nature to search for a scapegoat when things went wrong, even though she knew from bitter experience - and case studies - that things often went wrong through no fault of anyone. The fleet had taken a beating, twenty thousand men and women were dead and they were still deep in enemy territory. It wouldn't be *hard* for the humans to start turning on their alien allies...

Or vice versa, she thought. *Do the Tadpoles blame us for the failure*?

"I'll make sure you are called when it's held," she said. She glanced at her wristcom and swore under her breath. There probably wouldn't be time for a nap, but Mason had insisted that she try to snatch *some* rest before they encountered the enemy for the third time. "And..."

She took a breath. Apologising wasn't something she enjoyed, particularly when her teachers had often ordered her to apologise to children with better-connected parents, parents who could have caused real trouble for the school. Prince Henry's existence pushed far too many of her buttons, even though he'd done his best to escape his birth. And yet, at least in this case, she'd gone too far.

"I apologise for my harsh words," she said.

"I've had worse," Prince Henry assured her. He gave her a charming smile. "I once got a thirty-page document from a Russian diplomat that boiled down to a handful of insults."

"Oh," Susan said. "And what did you send in reply?"

"A fifty-page document arguing over where to eat dinner," Prince Henry said. "It counts as aggressive negotiations."

"So we risked exposure," Captain Haddock said. "We risked exposure for *nothing*!"

"I wouldn't say that," Captain Fletcher said. "We now know *something* about our foe!"

"Two races sharing the same star system is a little unlikely," Captain Drummond commented, carefully. "We may be facing a civilisation with a far larger region of settled space than ourselves."

"Which would give them more flexibility in meeting us, rather than committing themselves to drive the fleet away from their homeworld," Haddock pointed out. "We told them where we were, for what? A handful of pieces of flesh and nothing else!"

Susan closed her eyes in dismay. Captain Harper might be the senior officer, and as such the commanding officer, but he didn't have the rank to keep the other commanding officers in line. The fleet might have scored a minor victory, yet everyone *knew* they were no closer to home - and the aliens might well have a lock on their position. Morale was fading, despite the destruction of five alien ships, because of the unknown. If the aliens could signal at FTL speeds, what else could they do?

"*Enough*," Captain Harper snapped. "We took a calculated risk and it proved worthwhile, I think. The data we have gained may be of limited value at the moment, but it may be immensely important later. More to the point, we also have harder data on enemy sensor systems, starship armour and other details that will be very useful in planning our future operations."

"And we can't bicker in here," Captain Francis said. "This is the war room."

"It's actually a holographic conference chamber," Captain Fletcher said. "I..."

Captain Harper cleared his throat. "The presence of alien ships, emerging from Tramline Two, suggests that the aliens are assembling a blocking force to face us," he said. "We can try to head back through Tramline One, but that opens the prospect of being caught between two fires. Alternatively, we can jump through Tramline Three, yet that would push us further into unexplored space. At best, we'd be adding weeks to our journey."

"And at worst," Captain Haddock added, "we wouldn't make it home at all."

"Correct," Captain Harper said.

He brought up the holographic starchart and twisted it so they could see the fleet's position, relative to the tramlines and the alien debris. "We have no way to know if the alien ships we killed got a warning off or not before they were killed," he said. "As one ship *was* chased and killed by *Vanguard's* escorts, we have to assume the worst. Even a standard radio message would have plenty of time to reach a cloaked ship before we reached the tramline."

Susan could find no flaw with his analysis. If the FTL com, however it worked, was limited to one system, they *might* manage to get inside the enemy's OODA loop, but if it crossed light-years there was no way to avoid the enemy having advance warning of the fleet's intentions. And if *she* was in charge of the enemy fleet, she would have made damn sure there was a cloaked ship lurking near the tramline, just to watch for any unpleasant surprises and pass the word up the chain.

"Therefore, we will do two things," Captain Harper stated. "First, we will dogleg around the system"- the display updated, showing his planned course - "and enter the tramline here, rather than taking the least-time course. It's where they'll expect us to appear. Yes, it will add five days to our transit time, at best, but it gives us the greatest chance to escape detection.

"Second, we will deploy ECM probes on an automated trajectory. Ideally, the probes should pass for the fleet, limping towards the tramline on a least-time course. They may assume we took damage in the brief skirmish or that *Vanguard* was several days ahead of the remainder of the fleet. If they take the bait, they'll be drawn out of position and give us a chance to sneak past them before they realise they've been tricked and double back."

And even if they stay where we think they are, Susan added mentally, *they'll still find it hard to keep track of us.*

"The probes will be rigged with laser-head warheads," Captain Harper said. "Automated systems are far from perfect"- there were some chuckles; automated combat systems had far too many limitations - "but it should give them a nasty surprise, when they swoop down on the drones. It should also destroy the remainder of the drones, just to make sure that no further examples of our technology fall into enemy hands."

Captain Haddock scowled. "Can you guarantee that none of the ECM drones will survive?"

"There are no guarantees in war," Captain Harper pointed out, tartly. "The drones exist to be used, gentlemen. I know there is a risk of losing a drone to the enemy, but it has to be faced."

He paused. "We took a beating, true," he added. "But we just proved the enemy are not gods. They can be beaten. And we will beat them again."

Susan nodded in agreement. The plan was simple enough, yet it would give them the best chance of sneaking through enemy territory and returning to friendly space. Better to lose a few dozen drones than the entire fleet. And, even if a drone were to be captured, standard procedures should keep the enemy from learning anything useful.

And even if the precautions fail, she thought darkly, *they will have had ample time to draw intelligence from the remains of the fleet. They already know more about us than we do about them.*

CHAPTER THIRTY TWO

"Signal from the flag, Captain," Parkinson said. "The last of the drones is in place."

"Good," Susan said. "Any contacts?"

"Negative," Charlotte reported. "The system appears to be empty."

Susan frowned as she studied the display. If the aliens had managed to get a lock on their position, they'd need to act as quickly as possible before the fleet moved. And yet, no further attacks had materialised. Had the handful of ships *Vanguard* destroyed been nothing more than a probe? Or had the aliens been unable to get a larger force into the system before it was too late?

The FTL communications system must have a downside, she thought, mischievously. *Their high command is forced to watch, helplessly, as we slip away.*

She smiled at the thought, then sobered. Having an FTL communications network, even one that operated on an interplanetary scale only, would allow the enemy to coordinate their operations without having to worry about the pesky time delay. It might strip their squadron commanders of some of their independence - *Susan* wasn't sure *she'd* want a superior officer looking over her shoulders at all times - but the advantages would outweigh the disadvantages. And if the system operated on an interstellar scale, the enemy high command would be able to halve the time it took to react to any new threat.

They were ready for us, she reminded herself. *Did they have someone watching when we linked up with the Tadpoles*?

"Signal from the flag," Parkinson said, again. "The fleet is to proceed along the pre-planned dogleg to the tramline."

"Acknowledge the signal," Susan ordered. Captain Harper would probably *love* an FTL communicator right now, even though the three squadrons were slowly drawing closer together for mutual support. "Helm, take us out along the pre-planned course."

"Aye, Captain," Reed said. "Main drives engaging...now."

Susan felt the background hum of the drives increase in power as *Vanguard* moved, slowly, out of position. Any enemy ships expecting the refugee fleet to take a least-time course to the tramline would be circumvented, hopefully without ever *knowing* they'd been circumvented. But the FTL communications mucked even *that* up...the fleet might run into another enemy force that could summon reinforcements to attack the fleet from the rear.

And all we can do is watch for enemy ships, she reminded herself. *And hope we can get back home before it's too late.*

"Signal from the flag," Parkinson said, forty minutes later. "They are ready to activate the drones."

Susan nodded, slowly. The plan was sound, at least in theory, but it was based on a great deal of guesswork. If any of the guesses were wrong, the best they could hope for was that a number of drones had been wasted for nothing; at worst, the enemy would not alter course as planned and the fleet would have to force a crossing of the tramline. The beancounters would throw a fit, she was sure, when they realised just how many drones had been expended, but that was Captain Harper's problem. They were his drones.

You'd think they'd be happier about losing a million-dollar drone than a billion-dollar starship, she thought. *But bureaucratic stupidity is a law of nature.*

"The drones have gone active," Charlotte said. She sounded impressed. "I *know* they're fakes, Captain, and I'd be fooled at this distance. The sensor images are very accurate."

"Clever," Susan agreed. Hopefully, the enemy wouldn't be able to tell that the drones were fake until they closed in on the presumed fleet. "Better than ours?"

"I think so," Charlotte said. "They're certainly more powerful."

"We'll have to trade for the technology," Mason said. "If it isn't shared, as part of the joint defence against the new threat."

Susan nodded, grimly, as the hours passed and *Vanguard* and her squadron slid towards the tramline. Getting the fleet back home, or at least to friendly space, would be one thing, but it wouldn't be the end of the war. She rather doubted the diplomats could patch things up, not after so many people had been killed. Humanity was likely to plunge back into war regardless of its wishes, fighting to protect itself from a coalition of at least two species. Humanity and the Tadpoles, versus…she wondered absently what the aliens called themselves, then shook her head. No matter what the researchers did with the alien biological matter, they still didn't know what the aliens *looked* like.

"Captain," Reed said. "We are approaching the tramline."

"Inform the flag," Susan ordered. In theory, they should be undetectable, but if…she pushed the thought aside, angrily. They had no time for second-guessing themselves. "Tell Captain Harper that we will proceed as planned."

"Aye, Captain," Parkinson said.

"Sound full tactical alert," Susan added. "Bring the ship to battlestations."

"Aye, Captain," Mason said. Alarms howled through the ship as her crew rushed to their duty stations, readying themselves for anything. The status board updated rapidly as the various departments switched to combat protocols. "All stations report combat readiness, Captain."

"Good," Susan said. "Inform the screen that *Vanguard* will make the first transit."

"Aye, Captain," Parkinson said.

"Twenty seconds to the tramline," Reed informed her. "Puller Drive online."

"Take us through," Susan ordered.

She braced herself, unsure what to expect, as the battleship crossed the tramline. The display faded - she felt a moment of panic, convinced that the enemy were at point-blank range - and then rebooted, displaying a G2 star and a handful of planets. There were no icons, enemy or otherwise, at close range, but as the display continued to update a number of other icons flickered into existence.

"They appear to be commercial ships, Captain," Charlotte said. "It's impossible to be entirely certain at this range, but I'd say they were asteroid miners or light freighters."

Assuming that the enemy development patterns match ours, Susan thought. The Admiralty hadn't been keen on building light freighters, pointing out that the operating costs for *bulk* freighters weren't much higher and they could carry more goods. But bulk freighters also made much larger targets. *Those ships might be something we've never encountered before.*

"This could be a Tadpole system," Mason offered. "And we just came in through the back door."

"Not unless they left it off the charts they gave us," Reed said. "This system was marked down for later exploration, assuming that the tramline projections were accurate. Given that it's a G2 star, they may have wanted to steer survey ships away from it."

Because they'd have first claim on any life-bearing world, Susan thought. Prince Henry had argued otherwise, but she didn't see why the Tadpoles wouldn't press their own advantage, if they thought they had an opportunity. *And besides, this system is somewhat off the beaten path, even for them.*

"Drive signatures are rather obscured at this range," Charlotte said. "But I don't believe they're either Tadpole or human. A number of other radio sources are grouped around a planet within the life-bearing zone."

"But no enemy forces within range," Mason muttered. "It's a trap."

Susan glanced at the display. *Vanguard's* screen had passed through the tramline and was fanning out, their passive sensors watching for signs of alien starships lurking along the tramline. The aliens would have to get immensely lucky to have an attack force within range, unless they *had* maintained a hard lock on the fleet. But the opportunity to land a decisive blow from hiding, just as *Vanguard* had taken out the enemy scouts, was fading fast. The battleship might have jumped in blind, but that was no longer the case.

"I don't think so," she said. She studied the system's activity for a long moment. It reminded her of a stage-two colony, one where the planet had been tamed and the settlers were investing heavily in orbital infrastructure. Judging by the source of radio signals orbiting the gas giant, the settlers either had a cloudscoop or were trying to establish one. "I don't think they're lurking in ambush."

She took a breath. "Signal the screen," she ordered. "One ship is to jump back through the tramline and inform Captain Harper, then tell him to bring the remainder of the fleet through as quickly as possible."

"Aye, Captain," Parkinson said.

Susan looked at Reed. "Plot us a course that keeps at least a light-minute between us and any known enemy position," she added. "Do you have a solid fix on the tramlines?"

"Aye, Captain," Reed said. "There're three in the system, one alien-grade."

"We could take it," Mason suggested. "Captain, if they can't follow us through the alien-grade tramlines."

We really do need another name for them, Susan thought. *It isn't as if there's only one alien race now.*

She leaned forward. "Where does it go?"

"Deeper into unexplored space," Reed said. "It's possible there might be another way back to Tadpole space, but we'd add at least a month to our journey."

Susan scowled. The absolute worst case scenario was that the unknowns had departed the scene of the ambush and attacked the nearest friendly settlements. Indeed, given that they'd picked a fight with two races, they would have good reason to seize as much space as possible before the inevitable counterattack. And if that was the case, the Tadpoles already knew something was badly wrong. But the fleet's firepower would be required to preserve as much of their territory as possible.

And going along a predictable course will only make it easier for them to ambush us, she thought. *That too is Captain Harper's decision.*

"The fleet has completed its transit," Mason reported.

"No sign of enemy activity," Charlotte added.

Susan studied the display, trying not to show any tension on her face. The enemy hadn't taken the bait - or had they? There was no way to be entirely certain of *anything*. But they seemed to have entered the system without being detected…

"Signal from the fleet," Parkinson said. "We are to proceed along an evasive course until we reach Tramline Two, at full tactical alert. Captain Harper is calling a command conference."

"Understood," Susan said. She wasn't pleased. Even stepping into the Ready Room, during a tactical alert, felt like dereliction of duty. "Helm, take us out as planned. Communications, inform the screen that I want them sweeping the fleet's path. If there's a single hint of an enemy fleet lying in wait, I want to know about it."

"Aye, Captain," Reed said. "ETA Tramline Two, forty-seven hours."

We could do it quicker if we went on a least-time course, Susan thought. *But the risk is too great to be borne.*

"And ask Prince Henry to meet me in the Ready Room," she added, keeping her thoughts to herself. "I believe he should attend the conference too."

"The question of the hour is simple," Captain Harper said. "Do we take advantage of the opportunity to attack this system or not?"

Henry leaned forward. He hadn't had much time to study the sensor reports, but the long-range passive scans strongly suggested they'd entered a system controlled by the unknown aliens. The odds against a *third* unknown alien race existing in the same region of space were staggering, although he had to admit that the odds had already been beaten once. And the prospect for some payback was tempting, very tempting.

"I would say so," Captain Fletcher said. "They already have a rough idea of our location, Owen, and they have to be rushing forces into position to intercept us."

"I would say no," Captain Darlington said. "Right now, we have a relatively clear path back to friendly space. Taking the time to wreck the system would give *them* time to put a blocking force in our path."

"If there isn't one there already," Captain Fletcher said. "They have to have a good idea of the quickest way back to friendly space."

"Assuming they *know* where we came from," Darlington said. "There was no hint they knew about us until they attacked the fleet. They may have no idea of our ultimate destination."

Henry kept his expression under tight control. He'd wondered if the quickest way to Tadpole space was only accessible through an alien-grade tramline, but a quick check had revealed that that wasn't the case. There was nothing stopping the unknowns from making their way into the heart of Tadpole space, save for their own reluctance to explore. Humanity had had good reasons to establish as many colonies as possible - there was no shortage of groups on Earth that wanted their own homeworld - but the aliens might not have the same urge. Hell, for all he knew, they might be capable of tolerating population densities that would have sparked off social unrest and civil war on Earth.

"It wouldn't be hard to bombard the planet at long-range," Fletcher was insisting. "A handful of kinetic projectiles would do real damage."

"And would be flatly against our Rules of Engagement," Henry said, sharply. He couldn't allow that sort of idea to breed. "Mass slaughter of alien civilians is strictly forbidden."

"They slaughtered us," Fletcher snapped. "What sort of consideration do they deserve?"

Henry took a moment to gather his thoughts. Theodore Smith had forbidden indiscriminate strikes on Tadpole worlds during the war - the *first* war. Even if the Tadpoles had been monsters, he'd said, there was no reason for humanity to turn monstrous too. And besides, ruining a biosphere was easy. A single highly-radioactive warhead would render a world uninhabitable. Turning the war into a mutual rush to commit genocide would have destroyed one race and ruined the other.

"First, we do not know for sure that this system is inhabited by our new enemies," he said, carefully. "I know there are good reasons to believe that that is indeed the case, but we do not know for sure. And if the system is *not* inhabited by our new enemies…well, the last thing we need is more enemies.

"Second, assuming that this is indeed an enemy system, do we really want to set a precedent for planetary strikes? Do we really want the aliens bombarding our worlds with abandon because we bombarded theirs?"

"They ambushed us," Fletcher snapped.

"Yes, they ambushed a military fleet that fought its way out," Henry said. "They didn't slaughter civilians in vast numbers."

"They killed a number of reporters," Captain Haversack muttered.

Henry bit down on the urge to suggest that the aliens deserved commendations for slaughtering reporters - personally, he wouldn't have shed a tear if every damned reporter on Earth died in screaming agony - and leaned forward, willing them to understand.

"We know nothing about them," he said. "Starting a war of genocide is not just evil, it's stupid."

"They might win," Darlington said.

"Precisely," Henry said. "And the third reason, one we should bear in mind, is that yes, the ROE do forbid indiscriminate planetary strikes. We'll be shot as soon as we get home."

"We could sweep the system of its orbital infrastructure," Fletcher pointed out. "*Those* structures would be legitimate targets, would they not?"

"Yes," Darlington said, "but do we have the time?"

He nodded towards the starchart. "Let's not delude ourselves," he said. "Our command network is a mess, many of our ships have taken heavy damage and we have only one fleet carrier. We are in no condition for a stand-up fight against even a weaker enemy force."

"We killed five of their ships," Susan snapped.

"We ambushed them," Darlington said. "Would things have gone so well if the aliens had known we were there?"

"Probably not," Susan conceded.

Henry couldn't disagree. The aliens would have been fools to risk engaging *Vanguard*, but one ship could have tracked the fleet while the others summoned reinforcements…or simply signalled for help, depending on just how their damned FTL communicator worked. *Five* ships could have made sure the fleet couldn't break contact and vanish before it was too late.

Captain Harper sighed. "The decision is mine," he said. "We will evade contact, rather than engaging the system's defences or bombarding the planet."

"Owen," Fletcher said. "This is an *opportunity…*"

"I doubt that destroying the system's infrastructure will make much difference to the enemy's industrial base," Harper said. "If this was one of their core systems, David, it would be a great deal bigger. No, pausing long enough to lay waste to the system's facilities will give the enemy more time to get a fleet in place to engage us."

He tapped the starchart, meaningfully. "We will continue along the planned course, watching carefully for any enemy contact," he added. "It is quite likely we will encounter them in UXS-464, if not sooner. That's where this chain of tramlines links up with the chain of tramlines we used to reach UXS-469, giving them a least-time path to Tadpole space. The sooner we get there, the better."

Henry nodded in agreement. The discovery that they were facing *two* races, not one, meant that the aliens were not xenophobes who instinctively attacked anyone who entered their territory. And the colony world they'd discovered indicated that the aliens were interested in colonisation. And *that* suggested that the aliens would have run into the Tadpoles already.

"I understand that some of you want to take the war to the enemy," Harper added. "And I agree with the principle. But this is not the time."

Fletcher looked disappointed, but he nodded. "If nothing else," he said, "we have an excellent target for any future counterattacks."

"Quite," Harper agreed. "Dismissed."

The images blinked out of existence, leaving Henry and Susan alone. "That was close," Henry said. "I was afraid they were going to attack the planet."

"They might not have been wrong," Susan said. "What if peaceful co-existence is impossible?"

"So far, we have not met a race we could not communicate with," Henry said. If there were two races, they had to have some way to *talk* to each other. "And I find it hard to believe that *any* race could get into space with nothing but instinct alone."

"I hope you're right," Susan said. "But it doesn't look good."

CHAPTER THIRTY THREE

"Wake up," Fraser hissed.

George jerked awake, cracking her head on the overhead as she sat upright. No one, not even Fraser at his worst, would interfere with a sleeping midshipman unless it was an emergency. None of the surviving midshipmen had been sleeping very well - there had been two alerts as the fleet crossed the tramline and left the alien system behind - and their work had begun to suffer.

"Fuck," she moaned. "What's happening?"

"The XO - the *Captain* - just sent a message," Fraser said. He sounded panicked. "She's going to carry out an *inspection*!"

George rubbed her aching forehead, trying to process what he'd told her. There were only five midshipmen left alive and out of sickbay, three of whom were on duty…and the fleet was still deep in enemy space. Standards had slipped badly; the tasks of keeping middy country in order had fallen by the wayside as they struggled to do their duty. It wasn't time for an inspection, surely? It wasn't *fair*.

"Get up," Fraser snapped. "Have a shower, get into a clean uniform and *hurry*! She could be here at any moment."

"Yes, sir," George said.

She swung her legs over the side of the bunk and dropped to the deck, cursing her decision to sleep in her uniform. But she'd been too tired to take off her jacket and trousers, let alone the rest of her clothes. She'd never thought the XO - the *Captain* - was a sadist. And yet, carrying out an inspection now would allow her to see how the midshipmen coped with adversity.

Not well, she thought, as she tore off her uniform and hurried into the shower. She'd need to dump her clothes in the washing basket, even though that would leave her short for a day or two unless the washing was done ahead of time. Drawing another uniform from ship's stores would cost her, literally, while the other female midshipmen wore different sizes. *We've been so occupied with everything else that we've let standards slip badly.*

She washed hastily, cursing the water restrictions under her breath, then hurried back into the main compartment. Fraser was wiping the floor and checking under the racks, trying to sweep up as much dirt and grime as possible. He barely glanced at her as she donned a clean uniform, tossing her a mop as soon as she was decent. George sighed inwardly as she went to work. Standards had *definitely* slipped.

But it wasn't our fault, she thought, numbly. *We've been doing our duty as junior officers...*

"Make sure you look decent," Fraser ordered, sharply. "Commander Bothell would assign demerits for even the slightest problem."

George swallowed. Demerits reflected badly on both the midshipman in question and his immediate superior, the first middy. Fraser was likely to get in trouble if there was something - anything - wrong with her, even though he didn't have the time to micromanage her. Hell, they'd spent more of the last few days out of middy country than in it. But she had no idea if the captain would be impressed by excuses. In all honesty, she rather doubted it.

"It's a bad time for an inspection," she grumbled, as she checked her appearance in the mirror. Vanity was one character flaw she'd never had, thankfully; it wasn't something she could have afforded at the academy, when merely being washed and clean had been hard enough. "Why now?"

"Stow that chatter," Fraser advised. "Grumbling isn't safe anywhere near a senior officer."

"Yes, sir," George said.

It was nearly forty minutes before there was a firm tap on the hatch. George stood to attention, practically bracing a bulkhead, while Fraser opened the hatch. The Captain was standing there, wearing a clean white uniform. George felt a flicker of admiration, mixed with envy. She wasn't quite sure what had happened, when the XO had taken command of the ship, but Captain Onarina was the kind of person she wanted to be. The dark-skinned woman had clearly never let her outsider status turn into a disadvantage.

"First middy," the Captain said. "Midshipwoman Fitzwilliam. May I have permission to enter?"

"Permission granted, Captain," Fraser said. George had to fight to hide her amusement, despite her growing nervousness. The captain might, by custom, be required to ask for permission to enter, but she couldn't imagine any midshipman saying *no*. "Welcome to middy country."

"Thank you," the Captain said. She stepped through the hatch and looked around. "I trust that standards have not slipped?"

"We have done our best to uphold them, Captain," Fraser said. "Two of us died in the battle and two more are still in sickbay, but the remainder of us have worked hard."

"That is understood," the Captain said.

She stepped forward and began to examine the compartment. Her eyes flickered from side to side, looking around almost casually, but George would have been very surprised if she'd missed anything. She took a long look at the two empty racks - Nathan and James had both been killed - and bowed her head, before turning to look at Fraser. He didn't quite flinch under her gaze, but it looked as though he wanted to.

"What happened to their possessions?"

"Ah, we went through them, as per custom," Fraser said. "A handful of their possessions were clearly personal, so we boxed them up and stored them. The remainder were handed out to the other midshipmen."

"Good," the Captain said. "Did you have any problems?"

"None, Captain," Fraser said. "James had a small collection of coins and notes from Earth, which we gave to the purser to add to his account, but there was little else of significance."

Apart from the porn, George thought. She rather doubted the Captain would be surprised - she'd been a midshipwoman too, once upon a time - but she might want to make an example of it. Porn was *technically* illegal, although there were plenty of movies in the ship's database that crossed the line between entertainment and pornography without being put on the banned list. *But she probably doesn't want to know about it.*

The Captain nodded curtly, then peered into the shower compartment. George hoped - prayed - that they hadn't left anything out of sorts, not after her mother had scolded Annie and her for leaving dozens of bottles of shampoo out for the maids to clear up. Annie had protested that it wasn't her job to clear up the mess, which had earned her a week's grounding and a strong lecture from her father. The old man had known how to tear them apart with a few well-chosen words.

"Clean enough," the Captain said, briskly. "Are you coping with your water ration?"

"Yes, Captain," Fraser said.

"Good," the Captain said.

George kept her face impassive. There was no real *need* to ration water for junior officers and crew - the giant battleship recycled everything from human waste to coolant - but she'd been told it helped discipline. Besides, at the academy, they'd been taught to wash in less than a minute. She got three minutes on the battleship.

The Captain stepped into the toilets and examined them, briefly. George silently blessed all the gods there were that they'd had time to clean the toilets, even though it wasn't a task she enjoyed. Personal hygiene had been hammered into their heads at the academy and she knew, she just knew, that the Captain would not have hesitated to issue demerits for poor hygiene. It was unlikely, she thought, that poor hygiene could lead to any serious problems - certainly not like they would have had on a sailing ship - but she didn't like the smell any more than anyone else. Besides, sleeping next to nine other midshipmen was quite bad enough.

"Could do with an extra wipe or two," the Captain said, as she emerged. "Do you have the log?"

"Right here, Captain," Fraser said.

He produced a large leather-bound book from the locker and held it out to her. George had never understood why the first middy was supposed to keep a paper record, as well as an electronic record, but she'd never had the time to discuss it with anyone. It was probably just tradition. She watched as the Captain opened the book, her eye scanning the list of midshipmen attached to *Vanguard* before moving to the last couple of pages. George hoped she wouldn't look back into the past - there were too many notes about *her* demerits, back before she'd challenged Fraser to a fight - but she was out of luck. The Captain was looking all the way back to *her* assignment to the ship.

"You've made a note of my arrival," she said, as she checked the page. "Why?"

"Commander Bothell insisted that I add a note of everything that touched on the midshipmen, Captain, even if it wasn't directly connected to my duties," Fraser said. "He told me that keeping records was vitally important."

"He was a very smart man," the Captain said. Her voice was so dry that George couldn't tell if she was serious or not. "How often did he inspect middy country?"

"Once a month, on average," Fraser said. "It tended to vary. He insisted on inspecting us prior to any shore leave, Captain, and again when we returned to space. His conclusions were noted within the logs."

The Captain lifted her eyebrows. "And what *were* his conclusions?"

Fraser reddened, slightly. "A string of demerits for minor matters," he said. "One midshipman was hauled up in front of…of Captain Blake for possession of illicit substances and summarily dismissed from the service. The remainder of the middies were formally reprimanded for not alerting the XO to the problem and retroactively beached for a month."

George winced. Retroactive beaching stripped a month of seniority from the beached officer, sometimes knocking them back down the pecking order. *That* hadn't been a problem if *everyone* had suffered the same punishment, but it would look very bad on Fraser's record as he'd been the first middy at the time.

The Captain's face twisted. "Illicit substances?"

"Yes, Captain," Fraser said. "Devil Dust and Black Smoke, I believe."

"I see," the Captain said. "And you are sure there are no further… *problems*…with banned substances?"

"Yes, Captain," Fraser said.

George felt a sudden stab of sympathy. There wasn't a ship, she'd been told, that didn't have an illicit still hidden away somewhere, but there was a big difference between ship-made rotgut and hallucinogenic drugs. The midshipman who'd smuggled them onto the ship had to have been out of his mind. And yet, his actions would have presented Fraser and the other midshipmen with a deadly dilemma. Report him to the senior crew, thus earning reputations as sneaks, or keep their mouths closed and pray that nothing went badly wrong. Fraser had been lucky not to be permanently beached.

"Very good," the Captain said. She made a quick note in the logbook, then passed it back to Fraser. "Were there any other serious matters?"

"A midshipwoman was reprimanded for trading her communications minutes with her peers, in exchange for money," Fraser said. There was something in the way he said it that made it sound as though he'd taken care to look up the details earlier. "Another midshipman was put on the carpet for earning excessive demerits from the Boatswain. There were no other matters that weren't handled in middy country."

"I see," the Captain said. Her voice sharpened, suddenly. "Midshipwoman Fitzwilliam, front and centre!"

George took a step forward and snapped to attention, her thoughts flicking back to the daily inspections at the academy. The tutors had been strict; cadets who earned more than five demerits a week for failing uniform inspections wound up spending all of their free time in the gym, trying to work them off. Thankfully, she'd actually spent far too much of her life getting into increasingly awkward outfits. She'd found the naval uniforms to be remarkably easy, compared to the dresses she'd had to wear at court.

The Captain looked her up and down, inspecting her with minute attention to detail. George felt sweat prickling at the back of her neck, but held herself still as the Captain nodded once, then turned her attention to Fraser. The first middy looked frozen, as if he were caught in the headlights of an approaching car, before the Captain took a step backwards.

"Very good," she said. "The compartment could do with a more thorough clean, but that will have to wait until we return home. I trust there have been no matters over the last three months that should have been brought to my attention?"

"No, Captain," Fraser said. "All matters were dealt with in middy country."

The Captain gave him a long look, then nodded. "I'll expect to see the other midshipmen at the next inspection," she said. "You will be given a day's warning, allowing you to rearrange schedules as necessary."

"Thank you, Captain," Fraser said.

George saluted the Captain, then watched as she turned and strode out of the hatch. She let out a sigh of relief as soon as the hatch was closed. The inspection had been unpleasant, but she'd had worse at the academy. It helped, she supposed, that they were expected to have picked up *something* in four years, even if it was just the importance of keeping her compartment clean and tidy. The fleet might be deep in enemy space, with two midshipmen in sickbay, but the Captain would still have been angry if the compartment had been messy...

"That was better than I dared hope," Fraser said. He looked as relieved as she felt. "I was expecting something worse."

"She didn't have the opportunity to inspect the compartment before the battle," George said, trying to find a bright side. "She didn't have anything to compare it to."

"She's also the commanding officer," Fraser said. "There's no hope of appeal if she decided we needed extra punishment."

George nodded in agreement, although she had her doubts. In theory, a junior officer could appeal to the commanding officer if she felt she was being unfairly harassed by her superiors, but in practice it was unlikely the commanding officer would rule in her favour. The starship commander would support his officers unless there was a very strong reason *not* to. And bringing something to the attention of the commander might well be a dangerous mistake.

"I didn't think someone *could* smuggle crap into a ship," she said. "I..."

Fraser's face darkened. "You can't get crap into the academy," he said. "They search your bags and shit before you go through intake processing, then they do it again when you stagger home from Sin City. And if you were caught with something - anything - you'd be removed from the academy at once."

George nodded. She'd never returned to the academy drunk out of her mind, but she knew cadets who had. It was a mistake they never repeated. The tutors put them on heavy duties for the first week after their return, then they had to struggle to catch up with the rest of the class before the exams. Besides, it wasn't as if it was *hard* to take a pill to sober up. It just required a little pre-planning before it was too late.

"But if you go on leave, after you are assigned to a starship, your bags are rarely searched," Fraser added, after a moment. "You could pick up something really dangerous on the planet and bring it back with you. Harry...thought he could get away with it. We were just lucky that he was caught before he went on duty, drugged and stupid."

He sounded pretty stupid already, George thought, but she kept that opinion to herself. She couldn't imagine why anyone would want to experiment with illegal drugs - there were plenty of substances that weren't on the banned list - yet she had to admit there was a certain thrill in doing the forbidden. And it was possible that Harry had tried the drugs on shore leave, become addicted and then convinced himself that he could control the habit, while onboard ship. Fraser was right. The entire crew had been lucky that Harry was caught before it was too late.

Fraser opened the logbook, scribbled a note about the Captain's visit, then looked up at George. "I notice you haven't spent any time on the shooting range," he said. "And your fighting skills are pathetic."

"You didn't knock me out," George pointed out.

"I was *trying*," Fraser said, "to get you to cry uncle. Slamming your head against the deck a few times *would* have knocked you out, unless someone has replaced your skull with metal."

George swallowed. She was proud of what she'd done, but she knew he was right. If he'd wanted to kill her, or simply knock her out, he could have done it easily. And only her stubborn refusal to surrender had earned her some respect.

"We'd better deal with that," Fraser said. He gave her a long look, then glanced at the duty roster. "You have to be in Turret Five in thirty minutes, then you have an hour's free time...meet me at the shooting range at 1750, I think. It's time we brushed up on our shooting."

"I don't think we have a hope of winning the shooting prize," George said. "Don't the marines keep winning it?"

"I wouldn't care to be in *their* shoes if they didn't," Fraser said. "Major Andres is *tough*."

"Yes, sir," George said. She picked up the record book, then frowned as she read an entry from a year ago. "What happened here?"

"We had a midshipman who had a habit of…well, let's just say it wasn't a very pleasant habit," Fraser said, simply. "I had to thrash some sense into his head."

He smiled at her stunned expression. "See you in the shooting range."

CHAPTER THIRTY FOUR

George hesitated outside the hatch leading into the shooting range, unsure if she truly wanted to enter. She'd fired shotguns and hunting rifles long before she'd passed her basic firearms certification course at the academy, but she hadn't really been fond of using weapons on the estate. Shooting wild geese and foxes had always struck her as cruel, even though the former made good eating on a winter's night. There were just too many young aristocrats who took a sadistic pleasure in hunting the fox over hill and dale before finally running the poor creature to ground.

And the foxes also prey on our farms, she reminded herself. Parts of Britain had seen a resurgence in wild animals, after the bombardment. *They're making it harder to feed our people.*

She shuddered at the thought, then pushed it aside. There was no choice, not really; Fraser was the first middy and his word was law, unless she was called away by a senior officer. If she delayed, Fraser would not be pleased…she shook her head at the thought, then stepped up to the hatch and pressed her hand against the scanner. It hissed open, revealing a small waiting room. Fraser was standing there, drawing a pair of weapons from the armourer.

"I assume you've used a SIW-48 before," he said. "It was what they fired at the academy during my time."

"Yes, sir," George said. "We fired the same weapons."

"Probably literally," Fraser commented. "The SIW-48 - the marines call them Black Betties, for some reason - is a very sturdy weapon."

He took the box and led the way into the next room. "Weapons and ammunition are issued if the senior crew believes there's a chance the starship will be boarded," he said. "Right now, guns have been issued to marines and senior staff, but we haven't been armed. That's something that may change in the very near future, so I want you to be ready."

"Yes, sir," George said.

Fraser put the boxes down on the table, then opened one of them, revealing a dull metallic pistol. "I'll spare you the lecture," he said, "as you should have had it drummed into your head at the academy. "Do you remember the four *don'ts*?"

"Don't assume the gun is unloaded, don't point the gun at someone, don't have your finger on the trigger and don't shoot without making sure of your target," George recited. She'd learned that much from one of her uncles, who had threatened to horsewhip anyone who fooled around with loaded weapons. "Is that close enough?"

"Close enough," Fraser agreed. He shrugged. "Obviously, don't point the gun at someone unless you want to shoot them and don't have your finger on the trigger unless you're ready to fire. Walking around pretending to be an action hero is a good way to get kicked off the course, which could put a crimp in your career."

He tapped the weapon in front of her. "Check it's unloaded and safe," he ordered. "And do it carefully."

George nodded, picked up the pistol and checked that the safety catch was on, then opened the magazine to make sure the gun was empty. Some of the instructors at the academy had had a habit of taking a gun, sneaking a blank round into the firing chamber and then issuing demerits to every cadet who didn't recheck the pistol when it was returned to them. She had a feeling Fraser would be doing that too, later down the line.

"Empty," she said, holding it up so he could see into the chamber.

"Very good," Fraser said, dryly. He removed a clip from the other box and passed it to her, sliding it across the table. "Now, load the gun and click the safety on and off."

George frowned, but did as she was told. Her fingers remembered how to use the weapon, even if her mind was a little iffy. Fraser watched her like a hawk, then nodded once the gun was loaded and the safety tested.

George held the weapon, careful not to point it at him, as he removed a second gun from the box and loaded it himself, his fingers moving with practiced ease. He was a great deal quicker than her.

"Keep your weapon in a safe position, then come with me," he ordered, rising to his feet. "I have one of the shooting ranges prepared for us."

"Yes, sir," George said.

She followed him through a hatch into a small airlock, where a handful of ear protectors were hanging from the bulkheads. Fraser took one and passed it to her, then took a second pair for himself. George wondered, absently, how the marines coped when they were firing weapons without protection. Didn't their ears get sore too?

"They learn to cope with it," Fraser said, when she asked. "We can repair damaged eardrums, don't you know? But it's better to use protection when necessary."

George hadn't been sure what to expect from the shooting range, but it turned out to be a long dark room, very much like the one she'd used at the academy. It was smaller - there was only enough room for three or four people behind the safety line - yet the layout was the same. Fraser keyed a switch, activating a set of holographic targets, then winked at her as he took up a firing position. George barely had a second to brace herself before he fired off eight shots in quick succession, hitting all eight of his targets. The holographic images flickered red or yellow as they dropped to the deck.

"If they turn red, you killed them," Fraser shouted. She could barely hear him through the earmuffs. "Yellow means you wounded them. The computers generally assume that all wounds are survivable, unless they're immediately fatal."

"They said that at the academy too," George shouted back. "Does it get more complex?"

"The marines have a much more complicated set-up," Fraser said. "But you won't get to play on that unless you impress them!"

He nodded to the firing line, then reset the display. "Have a go," he shouted. "Fire at will!"

George lifted the gun, braced herself and pulled the trigger. It jerked in her hand; she cursed, tightened her grip and fired again. This time, she hit her target, which flashed yellow as it collapsed. She gritted her teeth, then kept firing, moving her gun from target to target until she ran out of ammunition. Fraser passed her a second clip; she took it, loaded it into the gun and resumed firing. One by one, the holographic targets snapped out of existence.

"Your aim isn't bad," Fraser said, once the last of the targets had vanished. "You could do with holding the weapon in both hands, but otherwise you're not doing badly."

"Oh, good," George said.

"Of course," Fraser added in a more even tone, "if this was a real fight, you'd be dead by now. You take too long to reload."

"I know," George said. She had no fear of firearms - she'd grown up on an estate, after all - but she'd always treated them with respect. Trying to reload at breakneck pace struck her as a good way to have an accident. "I need to practice."

"Practice with a set of blank rounds," Fraser advised. "The marines have practice kits you can borrow."

George blinked in surprise. "Why don't they use them at the academy?"

Fraser smirked. "I was told it breeds complacency," he said. "Personally, I always thought the instructors were leery of accidentally loading a set of blanks when they needed *real* ammunition."

"It would be embarrassing," George muttered. "Now what?"

"Now you fire off a few more rounds," Fraser said. He passed her a fresh clip, which she slotted into the magazine. "And keep shooting until we run out of ammunition."

George wanted to argue, but there was clearly no point. Instead, she took the weapon and fired, trying to get used to the kick. Fraser watched her closely as he passed the ammunition, sometimes offering advice when she hesitated. By the time they ran out of ammunition, George had to admit that she was almost enjoying herself. It helped, she supposed, that Fraser was actually more helpful than her firearms instructors. But then, he wasn't trying to teach a dozen cadets at once, some of whom had never touched a weapon in their lives.

"Not bad," he said, when she was done. He passed her his gun, then smiled in relief as she checked and cleared the chamber. "Take the weapons into the next compartment and clean them, while I mop up the spent casings. They won't thank us for leaving a mess."

"Yes, sir," George said.

She was surprised that Fraser hadn't made *her* clear up the mess, she thought, as she sat back down at the table and dissembled the first pistol. He certainly *would* have done, a couple of months ago, if he'd bothered to offer her some additional lessons in the first place. But then, her lack of shooting time probably reflected badly on him. Middy country needed to compete with every other department on the ship, she decided, as she finished cleaning the first weapon and moved on to the second. Fraser might not have a hope of winning any tournaments - the marines had been shooting their weapons for years - but he might intend to try to come second or third.

"You scored seven hits out of every ten shots," Fraser said, as he stepped through the airlock hatch. "Two thirds of the hits you scored were lethal, which would please your firearms instructor back on the moon. Nowhere near marine standards, of course..."

"Of course not," George agreed. She ran a hand through her sweaty hair. "How often do they come here and shoot?"

"They fire off thousands of rounds a day in marine country," Fraser said. He sounded surprisingly enthusiastic. "And they have some really cool shooting galleries for daily training. They can practice everything from hostage rescue to boarding an alien ship, all without leaving the comfort of their quarters."

George gave him a sidelong glance. "Why didn't you join the marines?"

"My father was a Paratrooper until he got too old to be jumping out of airplanes with the young lads," Fraser said. "He'd have done his nut if I'd joined the marines. He wasn't too pleased about me joining the navy - he spent four months on Vesy when I was fourteen and insisted there was still a role for the Paras - but he figured that command of a ship would be an impressive feather in my family's cap."

"He would have stopped you joining the marines?" George asked. If Fraser's father had been on Vesy a decade ago, he would have been serving alongside Percy and Penelope, her semi-cousins. "Really?"

"They used to beat up marines for fun," Fraser said. "Or perhaps it was the marines beating up *them* for fun. It changes depending on whom you ask."

"I'm sure it does," George said.

Fraser nodded and checked her work. "Good enough," he said, snapping the boxes closed and locking them. "Did you enjoy it?"

"I suppose," George said.

"Good, because we'll be coming back here at least once a week for the next few months," Fraser said. "More, if we can arrange it. After that, I want you continuing to practice shooting on your own."

"Yes, sir," George said. She *had* enjoyed it, after all. "But...what if we waste all the bullets we need to fight, if we get boarded?"

Fraser laughed. "I was wondering how long it would take you to ask that question," he said, dryly. "You'll be surprised by how few officers *think* to ask, despite endless lectures on the value of logistics at the academy."

George frowned, unsure if she should be pleased or embarrassed.

"The short answer is that the machine shop on the ship turns out thousands of cartridges a day," Fraser explained. "Those bullets we expended? The remains get swept up and dumped in the recycler. Give the machine shop a few days and it'll turn out enough bullets to fight a minor war. They're not actually difficult to produce, unlike so many other pieces of gear we need."

"I see," George said. "And what happens if we *do* run short?"

"There's a reserve, around ten thousand rounds," Fraser said. "That reserve doesn't get touched, ever, unless we're being boarded. The marines ensure there's always an ample supply. More advanced weapons, of course, are a little harder, but you'd be surprised at what the machine shop can turn out, if necessary."

He glanced at his wristcom. "I have to be in the tactical compartment in twenty minutes, so I'm going to snatch a shower and then run," he added. "Make sure you snatch a shower too - no one will thank you for stinking up the compartment with the stench of gunpowder."

George winced. "I'd forgotten about that," she muttered, looking down at the deck. She'd meant to go visit Barton, now he was out of bed and on light duty until his leg was properly healed. "But thank you for the lesson."

"Thank me after we start unarmed combat training," Fraser said, darkly. He rose to his feet, carrying the boxes under one arm. "I'd suggest, if you bothered to ask my advice, that you put in more time at the gym too, but that's in your hands."

"I will," George said. "But when am I meant to do it?"

"There will be replacement midshipmen, eventually," Fraser said, simply. "And when there are, you will have more time to develop yourself."

And it's quite possible I'll still be at the bottom of the totem pole, George thought. It wasn't a pleasant thought. She barely had three months as a midshipman and the next class wouldn't have graduated yet. Any replacements would outrank her and probably everyone below Fraser as well. *That won't be pleasant.*

She found herself staring after Fraser, feeling a strange mix of confusing emotions. He was sarcastic and rude, but he was no longer treating her as though she was something disgusting he'd found on the underside of his shoe. Indeed, he'd been almost *civil. And* he'd been a better tutor that she'd expected. There were layers to Fraser, she realised slowly, that weren't apparent on first glance.

Rising to her feet, she stepped out of the compartment and hurried down the corridor, heading to the recuperation suite. Barton had been told to stay there, along with a dozen other crewmen, until the doctors certified him as fit for duty. She wasn't surprised, when she peeked in through the hatch, to see him stumbling backwards and forwards as he tested his leg. The shorts he wore made it obvious that he'd had regeneration treatments. One leg was normal, the skin slightly darker than average; the other was pale, as if it was fresh out of the womb. It would take weeks, she thought, for it to blend into his body.

"Hi," Barton called. He limped towards her, his movements making it look as though he was constantly on the verge of toppling over. "How are you?"

"Tired," George said. She wasn't surprised when he motioned her out of the compartment, even though she had every right to be there. There were five other crewmen in earshot, all pretending not to pay attention. "Peter, I think you look much better."

"That's what I've been telling the doctor," Barton said. "I might not be able to carry a box without crumbling under the weight, but they can strap me into a chair and I can operate the firing system. There's no *need* to stay on light duty."

He smiled. "You could try talking sense to the doctor..."

"And then I'd be told off by the doctor, clouted by the first middy and probably written up by the captain," George said. She'd heard that starship doctors had the right to relieve *captains* of command. Doctor Chung would have no difficulty ordering *her* punished for sticking her nose where it didn't belong. "Do as he tells you."

"It's just *boring* down here," Barton moaned. He struck a dramatic pose, almost falling to the deck. "There's nothing to do, but walk, watch movies and engage in pleasant conversation."

"Sounds wonderful," George said. She didn't know what Fraser would say if he caught her watching a movie, but she doubted it would be anything *pleasant*. "I could do with a break."

"Let me take you to the seashore, when we get home," Barton said. "I used to love walking along the cliffs and admiring the skies, before plunging into the water and freezing to death."

"You didn't die," George said. It was a tempting offer - or it would have been, if she hadn't been worried about where it might lead. A relationship between her and *anyone* wouldn't remain private for long, not given her family. "But it sounds wonderful."

Barton smiled. "Or we could go to the zoo?"

"Maybe," George said. She glanced at her wristcom. "I have to get a shower before going back on duty, but otherwise...I'll see you soon."

"I'll hold you to that," Barton said.

George waved, then hurried back through the corridors to middy country. Fraser was standing in the middle of the sleeping compartment, dressing hurriedly. He gave her a surprised look as she entered and started to undress. Thankfully, she had one spare uniform she could use.

"George," he said. "Where *were* you?"

"With Peter," George said. "I still have time to wash."

Fraser looked doubtful, but he didn't have time to argue. "Don't be late," he said, instead. "I wouldn't want to explain it to your superior."

"I won't," George said. There was something in his voice that bothered her, a hint of...concern? "See you later, sir."

"You too," Fraser said. He sounded doubtful, very doubtful. "Bye."

CHAPTER THIRTY FIVE

"I was surprised when you requested permission to use the simulators," Susan said. "You *are* pushing the upper age limits."

Henry scowled as he clambered out of the simulator. "My former CAG was at least two decades older than me, which didn't stop him having an affair with one of his squadron commanders," he said. There had been more to it than that, he was sure, but most of the details had been heavily classified. "He flew a starfighter during the early battles of the war."

"A very impressive man," Susan said. "And how did *you* do?"

"Not as well as I'd hoped," Henry admitted. He just hadn't had the time to keep up with his flying, not when he'd been on Tadpole Prime. "I'm still rated for flying shuttlecraft, but the new generation of fighters is beyond me. Taking a fighter into combat isn't going to happen."

"I doubt it would have happened anyway," Susan said. "Losing you in combat would have been embarrassing."

Henry shrugged. The Royal Family had always known the value of *appearing* to share the dangers facing the common folk, although it had taken months of arguing before his family would allow him to train as a starfighter pilot. It would have been far safer, they'd tried to argue, if Henry had served as a starship officer instead. The dynasty had to be preserved, even if Henry himself didn't want the throne. But Henry had been pushed too far to care about the survival of the dynasty.

But Susan will have enough problems when she gets home, he reminded himself. *I don't think she needs to lose me too.*

He glanced at the simulator, grimly aware of just how much he'd lost in thirteen years out of the military. His reflexes had once been good - he took some pride in knowing that he'd earned his ranking, despite his family - but now he was too slow. Simulated enemies had always been faster and tougher than real enemies, yet even reducing the parameters hadn't made matters better. He could just imagine what his instructors at the academy would have said, if they'd seen his performance. Or maybe they would have been too disgusted to speak.

"I tried," he said. It was unlikely anyone would allow him back in a starfighter cockpit, but he could dream. "Why do you even have a simulator anyway?"

"The Admiralty likes to encourage crewmen to earn their flight wings," Susan said. "It's supposed to be a new innovation, just in case we need to ramp up the number of fighter pilots in the fleet. Not many have applied to take the exams, though."

"I can imagine," Henry grunted.

He studied the simulator, wondering why anyone had signed off on the idea. They hadn't offered crewmen the chance to transfer to starfighters in his day, although he could see why the beancounters had liked the scheme. He made a mental note to check the Admiralty's records, when he got back to Earth. He'd be surprised if more than a handful of crewmen had *ever* transferred. They had far too much to unlearn if they wanted to be starfighter pilots.

And they're not exactly expendable, his thoughts reminded him. *Starfighter pilots get so much leeway because they're not expected to survive their first deployment.*

Susan gave him a sharp look as they walked towards the hatch. "Why did you want to try out in the first place?"

Henry hesitated, then answered honestly. "I've met too many high-ranking personages who did nothing, but issue useless orders," he said. It struck him that Captain Blake probably fell into that category too. "And too many ambassadors who did nothing but attend diplomatic dinners and stuff their faces while their underlings did all the work. I didn't want to be one of them."

"I understand," Susan said. The hatch hissed open, waiting for them. "Their underlings did all the work?"

"It provides deniability," Henry said. He hadn't liked the concept, when he'd first heard of it, but he'd come to understand its value. "The underlings on both sides work out the treaty, then the higher-ups review it. If they like the treaty, it gets signed into law; if they don't like it, they blame everything on the underlings and assign a different group of underlings to work out a second treaty. Or whatever they're working on."

He shrugged. "The Ambassador cannot walk back his own words without losing credibility," he added, tartly. "But an underling can be sacrificed for the greater good."

"Shit," Susan said.

"There'll be more work for me, both on Earth and on Tadpole Prime," Henry added. "We'd kill for the FTL communications system."

"Maybe you can trade with the aliens," Susan suggested. "We must have something *they* want."

Henry shook his head. "If I was in their shoes, I wouldn't trade FTL communications for anything," he said. "It gives them too great an advantage."

He contemplated the problem for a long moment. If there were two alien races, not one, they must have a way to communicate. He couldn't imagine an alliance without *some* way to share ideas. Hell, if humans had problems running alliances with other humans, he couldn't imagine how hard it would be with two *different* races...

And we're going to have to work with the Tadpoles, he reminded himself. The treaty committed humanity to support their allies, even if human ships *hadn't* been caught up in the fighting. *That's not going to be easy.*

"I think..."

He broke off as the alarms started to howl. "All hands to battlestations," Mason's voice said. "I say again, all hands to battlestations. Captain to the bridge!"

"Crap," Susan said. "Go back to your quarters and stay there."

"Aye, Captain," Henry said.

He watched her striding down the corridor, not *quite* running, then turned and headed back towards his suite. Once, he would have been amongst the first starfighter pilots to be launched into space; now, he was just deadweight. There was nothing he could do to influence the course of the battle, but wait in his cabin and pray *Vanguard* didn't take a fatal hit.

No wonder the higher-ups keep issuing so many useless orders, he thought, darkly. For the first time in his life, he thought he understood them. *They feel helpless to affect what's happening around them.*

"Captain," Mason said, as Susan entered the bridge. "Long-range sensors detected a large enemy fleet heading towards Tramline Three."

Susan blinked in surprise. "Not heading towards us?"

"No, Captain," Charlotte confirmed. "It looks like the fleet is heading directly into Tadpole space. They're barely two jumps from Tadpole-453."

"Show me," Susan ordered. "And forward all of our sensor readings to the flag."

"Aye, Captain," Parkinson said.

Susan leaned forward as a handful of red icons appeared on the display. They didn't seem to be aware of the fleet's presence - she reminded herself, rather sharply, that they were nearly ten light minutes away - but they didn't seem to be searching either. Instead, they looked as if they were launching an invasion. She tapped her display, bringing up the starchart showing tramlines running through the sector. The enemy fleet might have come from UXS-469…or it might have come through another set of tramlines, branching off into enemy space.

We are not dealing with a race that's limited to one star system, she told herself. If she'd had any doubts, and she'd lost most of them after stumbling across the alien colony, they were gone now. *Their civilisation may be as big and powerful as our own - or larger.*

"They'll cross the tramline in two hours, assuming they maintain their course and speed," Charlotte said.

"They're planning to attack the Tadpoles," Mason said. "They *can't* have anything else in mind."

Susan was inclined to agree, although her mind kept tossing up question marks. The aliens weren't *surveying*, unless they'd sent out a survey squadron while the fleet had been putting itself back together; they were launching a full-scale invasion. And that meant…*what*? Had the aliens tracked the survey ships as they retreated from UXS-469? Or had they known about the Tadpoles for *years*? *Humans* would have tried to make contact, she was sure, but aliens might have reacted differently. God knew the Tadpoles had started preparing for war from the moment they'd first encountered the expanding edge of human space.

"They may have stopped looking for us," Mason offered.

"Or we might just have flown past their hunting parties," Susan said. *She* wouldn't have allowed a powerful fleet to remain in her backyard, but the aliens might have different thoughts. Besides, they'd spent the last fortnight dodging the slightest hint of alien contact as they crawled home. "Or their fleet might be trying to sneak up behind us."

"Signal from the flag, Captain," Parkinson said. *Roosevelt* was barely close enough for a real-time conversation. "Captain Harper wants to speak to you."

"Put him through," Susan ordered.

Captain Harper's face appeared in front of her. "Captain," he said. "It appears we have a situation."

"Yes, Captain," Susan agreed. "It looks as though the enemy are invading Tadpole space."

"And blocking our way home," Captain Harper said. "My officers predict they'll be attacking the nearest friendly base within two days, perhaps less."

Susan nodded. "We need to shadow them," she said. "Taking a longer path to the tramline will leave us unable to intervene when all hell breaks loose."

"Precisely my thinking," Captain Harper said. "They would be turning to engage us if they knew we were here."

Unless their concept of tactical wisdom is very different to ours, Susan thought. *She* wouldn't let an alien fleet run around if it could be avoided, but the aliens might believe that the human ships were contained. *Or if they feel they can afford to ignore whatever damage we do in their backyard.*

"I'm detaching a destroyer to race ahead and warn the Tadpoles," Captain Harper added, firmly. "The remainder of the fleet will proceed along a least-time course to the Tadpole system. If the timing works out in our favour, we'll add our weight to the defenders and hopefully give our new friends a bloody nose."

"Aye, sir," Susan said. She couldn't fault his planning, although the enemy would almost certainly reach the Tadpole system *first*. Unless, she supposed, they took the time to survey the two systems between them and their target. "We may have been wrong, sir."

Captain Harper frowned. "What about?"

"They either captured a working database or they knew about the Tadpoles for years," Susan said. "Either way, we have problems."

She scowled at the thought. The Tadpoles had recovered an astrographic database from Heinlein, shortly after the disastrous first contact. It had lacked hard data on everything from defence bases to military technology, but it had been quite enough to point the Tadpoles in the right direction. They'd never had any problems finding targets during the war, while human ships had had to explore their space to locate their bases. Security procedures had been tightened up afterwards, she knew, but a single insecure database could be disastrous if it fell into enemy hands.

"That's not something we can worry about now," Captain Harper said. He cleared his throat, loudly. "The fleet will proceed as I have outlined, ready to engage the enemy when we have a chance."

"And keep a careful eye on its rear," Susan added. "Their blocking force could be sneaking up behind us."

"Indeed," Captain Harper said. "*Vanguard* will continue to take the point. Good luck."

His image vanished. "Stay on course," Susan ordered. "Keep the cloaking device engaged; I don't want a single *flicker* that could betray our presence."

"Aye, Captain," Mason said.

Susan forced herself to relax as the enemy fleet proceeded on its course, *Vanguard* and her screen shadowing them from a distance. There was little else she could do, but wait. The ship was already at full tactical alert, the crews prepped for anything from a direct encounter to another ambush. Further orders would just confuse the issue.

"Assuming they maintain their current course and speed," she said, "how long until they enter Tadpole space?"

"Thirty-six hours," Charlotte said. "Captain, I should note that we have no hard data on their realspace drives. They might be capable of moving at higher velocities than we've observed..."

"Let us hope not," Susan said. *Vanguard* could move faster than the alien starships, assuming the highest speed they'd shown was the maximum, but there was no way to know for sure. It was quite likely that their smaller ships could outrace the giant battleship. If nothing else, they had a higher acceleration curve. "Continue to monitor them from a distance."

"Aye, Captain," Charlotte said.

"Order the beta crews to catch some sleep," Susan added. "I want them ready to take over when the current shift ends."

"Aye, Captain," Mason said.

Susan studied the display, cursing under her breath. She'd have to catch some sleep herself, hopefully before the enemy ships entered friendly space and opened fire. So would the rest of the alpha crew. But she didn't *want* to leave the bridge. There was nothing she could do, yet she couldn't help feeling that leaving the bridge would invite disaster. It was not a rational thought, but nothing she told herself made her feel any better about leaving matters in Mason's hands.

They must have taken the time to sift through the wreckage before dispatching the invasion fleet, she thought. The unknowns could have reached Tadpole space quicker, if they'd departed immediately after the first battle. Unless, of course, the fleet *Vanguard* was shadowing was actually the reinforcements. *There's no way to know just what we're facing.*

She gritted her teeth, then rose. "Commander Mason, you have the bridge," she said. "Keep the screen active and alert me the *moment* you have any reason to believe we may have been detected."

"Aye, Captain," Mason said. "I have the con."

"I'll be in my Ready Room," Susan added. The sofa folded out into a sinfully comfortable cot. "Pass command to the beta crews when shift ends, but make sure they know to alert me."

"Yes, Captain," Mason said.

Susan took one last look at the display - the alien ships were crawling slowly towards the tramline, seemingly unaware of their shadows - and then turned and walked towards the hatch. It would take her seconds to grab her jacket and run back onto the bridge, if the shit hit the fan; there shouldn't be any time for things to go badly wrong. But if the alien fleet was merely the bait in a trap…

All you can do is watch for signs of trouble, she told herself, as she stepped through the hatch and into the Ready Room. She knew she wouldn't sleep easily, but there was no choice. *And if everything goes according to plan, you can catch the enemy with their pants down.*

The ship felt…*quiet*.

George could *feel* it as she left Turret Five and made her slow way back to middy country, too tired to call in on Barton or even pick up something to eat from the wardroom. Crew were talking to one another in hushed voices, as if their words would somehow reach across the vacuum of space and alert the enemy. Something - anything - could be on the other side of the hull, just waiting for *Vanguard* to make a mistake. Cold logic told her that the entire crew could scream in unison and the aliens wouldn't hear a peep - sound couldn't pass through a vacuum - but spacers tended to be superstitious. Making a sound might *just* trigger a disaster.

"Everyone's on edge," Fraser said, when she stepped through the hatch. "How are things in the turrets?"

"The crews want some payback," George said. Simpson had worked everyone hard, training for every contingency he could imagine. George had taken direct control of the main guns, then scrambled to patch up imaginary problems or don a spacesuit before the entire compartment vented. "They're *angry*."

"I don't blame them," Fraser said, shortly. He glanced at his wristcom, then clambered into his rack. "The bastards gave us one hell of a pasting in the last ambush."

"And then we blew five of their ships out of space before they had a whiff of our presence," George pointed out. "We did get *some* payback."

"There's no such thing as enough," Fraser said, darkly. "When are you due back on duty?"

"Just before the jump into Tadpole space," George said. Simpson had told her to get some sleep, then report back in nine hours. It would give her enough time to settle in before the fleet crossed the tramline. "You?"

"Ditto," Fraser said. He met her eyes. "Make sure you get *plenty* of sleep. No sneaking out to visit anyone."

George felt her eyes narrow as he pulled his curtain down. What possible business of *his* was it if she went to visit anyone? Nine hours was long enough to have a proper rest, then go snatch something to eat before the ship went back into battle. But then, the alert could come at any moment. If the aliens detected *Vanguard*, they'd certainly come about to face her before proceeding with the invasion.

She shrugged as she undressed, carefully placing her uniform in the locker where it could be grabbed at a moment's notice. She'd had nightmares about reporting to her duty station in her underclothes - or stark naked - but she doubted any of her superiors would be amused if she did. Besides, spacewalking in a shipsuit was bad enough; spacewalking while naked meant certain death. Stellar Star might have done it, but Stellar Star had the scriptwriter on her side. Real life was nowhere near so cut and dried.

Pity, she thought, as she climbed into her rack and pulled the curtain down. *It would have been so much easier.*

CHAPTER THIRTY SIX

"Captain," Charlotte said, formally. "The alien fleet is about to cross the tramline into Tadpole-453."

Susan sucked in her breath. The fleet had made the first jump while she was sleeping, entering a system the Tadpoles had claimed, yet considered largely worthless. There was no hint the unknowns disagreed. They hadn't bothered to survey the system, but merely headed straight towards the second tramline, the one leading directly into a populated system.

"Inform the flag," Susan ordered. So far, there was no hint the aliens had detected them, but they'd spread out their own screen as they traversed the system. There was no way to know if the aliens *had* caught a sniff of them or if they expected the Tadpoles to be setting an ambush of their own. "And keep us on our present course."

She cursed, again, the stifling lack of information. Did the Tadpoles know the enemy fleet was coming? They must have known *something* was wrong, when the contact fleet failed to report back, but did they suspect the worst? And the ship Captain Harper had dispatched to warn them? Had she made it through the tramlines before it was too late?

"Aye, Captain," Charlotte said. "They'll be through the tramline in twenty minutes."

"We'll be through in two hours, Captain," Reed warned. "If they leave pickets on the near side of the tramline, watching for contacts..."

"We should see them before we enter range," Susan said. She doubted the enemy would bother, not when battles had been won or lost based on the presence or absence of a single ship, but it was well to be careful. "Let us just hope we can get there before they do real damage."

The Tadpoles hadn't said much about their planned deployments, according to the files; they rarely discussed military movements unless they took place in jointly-controlled systems or along the border. Susan didn't blame them, not really; *she'd* have been reluctant to discuss her fleet movements with aliens, no matter how much she trusted them. But it made it impossible to predict what the unknowns would encounter, when they forced their way into Tadpole-453. Had the Tadpoles managed to reinforce the sector, in case of trouble? Or had they stripped the fleet base bare to support the contact fleet?

If the latter, they may ravage all the way to Tadpole Prime before they get stopped, she thought, coldly. *Getting ships from the near border to the other side of their space will be a nightmare.*

"Captain," Charlotte said. "The enemy ships are transiting the tramline."

"Understood," Susan ordered. "Communications, raise the flag. Inform them that we intend to cross the tramline on schedule."

She studied the display for a long moment, trying to consider the options. The aliens would *have* to engage the fleet base, unless they intended to risk leaving it in their rear. And it would take them at least two hours to *reach* the fleet base. Unless, of course, they had a faster drive than anyone had realised...she shook her head, dismissing the thought. If they had a way of moving faster in realspace than anyone else, they wouldn't have ambled their way to Tadpole-453...

"The enemy fleet has completed its transit," Charlotte reported. "This system appears to be deserted."

"Maintain full passive sensor watch," Susan ordered. "We are *not* taking that for granted."

She felt sweat trickling down her back as the fleet crawled towards the tramline. Anything could be happening on the other side, anything at all... and she wouldn't know about it until the fleet jumped into Tadpole-453. Were the Tadpoles ready and waiting...or had they been caught by surprise? The enemy fleet hadn't cloaked, at least. Their approach should not have passed unnoticed.

"Twenty minutes to jump," Reed said. It felt like *hours* had passed on the bridge. "Captain?"

Susan glanced at Mason. "Tactical?"

"All weapons and defences are online, ready to engage," Mason said. "All duty stations are fully manned."

"Take us through the tramline," Susan ordered.

She gritted her teeth. No military force could remain at battlestations forever, no matter what the media or politicians claimed. Being on full tactical alert for so long had drained her crew, even though they *knew* it was no drill. *Vanguard's* crew needed a break, a chance to stand down and relax, yet they weren't going to get it. The only hope of a break lay on the other side of the tramline.

"Signal from the flag," Parkinson said. "Captain Harper requests that we dispatch a screening unit back to update him before the main body makes transit."

"See to it," Susan ordered.

"Transit in ten seconds," Reed said. "Nine…eight…"

The display blanked, for what seemed like an eternity. Susan had a moment - just a moment - to think that something had gone badly wrong, that they were trapped somewhere along the tramline, then it came back to life. Hundreds of icons flickered into existence, all red; one by one, a number started to turn blue…

"There's a battle going on," Mason commented. "The Tadpoles made a stand near the tramline."

Give them time to fall back on the planet if necessary, Susan thought. Five superdreadnaughts, three fleet carriers and nearly a hundred smaller ships were fighting a desperate last stand against the new enemy. *And they will have to fall back.*

"Take us on an intercept course, under cloak," she ordered. The enemy was pushing the Tadpoles back, their starfighters roaming forwards and circumventing the superdreadnaughts as they pressed their advantage against the fleet carriers. "Record a message."

"Aye, Captain," Parkinson said.

"Captain Harper," Susan said. "I intend to attack the rear of the alien formation, using the cloak to remain undetected. I strongly advise you to attach the heavy ships to my command, keeping the fleet carrier to the rear. Please advise me of your intentions."

She tapped her console, ending the recording. "Send the signal to the screen, then dispatch a ship back to alert the fleet," she ordered. "Helm, time to intercept?"

"Seventeen minutes at current speed," Reed said.

"Then hold us on our current course," Susan ordered. The remainder of the fleet started to flicker into existence, one by one. "Do we have an update from the flag?"

"Aye, Captain," Parkinson said. "Captain Harper has agreed to your plan and has attached the heavy-hitters to the squadron."

Susan smiled, rather coldly. *Vanguard* might be the largest ship in the fleet, but she was easily the most junior commanding officer. She had no doubt that protests were already being filed, even though an open command dispute in the middle of a combat zone was a court martial offence. Sorting out the mess was going to keep a number of Admiralty Courts gainfully employed for years.

"Order them to take up position on our flanks," she said. "And make it clear that they are not to open fire without my direct order."

She leaned back in her command chair, feeling the tension fading away as she braced herself for battle. No more sneaking around, no more trying to hide from overwhelming force; this time, there would the beautiful simplicity of a battle, of an engagement that would end with either victory or death. *Vanguard* would finally get a chance to show what she could do.

"The enemy fleet doesn't seem to be watching its back," Mason noted. "They're keeping all their attention on the Tadpoles."

"We could send a message," Parkinson suggested. "Let the Tadpoles know we're coming."

Susan considered it, briefly. There was a chance, a very real chance, that the Tadpoles would accidentally fire on her ships. A cloaked starship was a potential threat, particularly one in the middle of a combat zone or sneaking up to a secure base. But, at the same time, sending a message ran the risk of alerting the enemy ships to her presence. They might not be able to decipher the message - she doubted it was possible, unless their computers were vastly superior to humanity's - but its mere existence would tell them she was there. And then they would either break contact or turn and face her.

"No," she said, finally. "We don't dare send a message."

She sensed Parkinson's concern as she studied the display, but he said nothing. The decision was hers, after all. And if it exploded in her face, she'd be the one who had to deal with the consequences. She glanced at the timer, silently calculating the best moment to open fire, then at the enemy fleet. Charlotte's department was steadily analysing the alien ships; the fleet carriers were instantly recognisable, but the heavy cruisers were rather harder to understand. Some of them seemed to be missile-heavy, others seemed to be crammed with nothing more than plasma cannons.

Interesting that they chose to build specialised vessels, she thought. *Vanguard* was heavily weighted in favour of energy weapons, but she could fire salvos of missiles too. *I wonder what their designers were thinking.*

She pushed the thought aside as they closed rapidly on the alien fleet. "Target the fleet carriers first," she ordered. Like the Tadpoles, the aliens had stationed their carriers towards the rear of their fleet. "And prepare to rip them apart."

"Aye, Captain," Mason said.

"Interesting design," Charlotte said. "They have quite a bit in common with *Ark Royal*."

Prince Henry would love to hear that, Susan thought. Although, if the enemy were more inclined to use energy weapons they probably had good reason to add extra layers of armour to their ships. Human designers had followed the same reasoning. *Are they as slow and cumbersome as the Old Lady*?

"Weapons locked on target," Mason said. "Two minutes to optimum firing range."

Susan braced herself. The enemy had other problems to worry about, but she would be astonished if the fleet managed to get into firing range without being detected. Indeed, even a cursory active sensor sweep would reveal the fleet's presence. No human commander, particularly one who had studied the Anglo-Indian War, would have risked leaving his rear so unprotected. A starship could sneak into firing range and blow a carrier away...

Just as we proved in the war games, Susan thought.

"Fire missiles as soon as they detect us," she ordered. "And engage with plasma cannons the moment we enter firing range. Don't wait for orders."

"Aye, Captain," Mason said.

Susan watched the last minute tick down, then the display flared red. "They have us," Mason snapped. "Firing missiles!"

Vanguard shuddered as she unleashed a full broadside, launching missiles right into the enemy rear. The enemy seemed to flinch - perhaps she was imagining it - as their sensors penetrated the cloaks, their commanders suddenly unsure what to do. Susan had seen simulations where a sudden shock stunned commanding officers, rendering them incapable of reacting…it was good to know, on some level, that the aliens *could* be shocked…

"Increase speed," she ordered. The best countermove the aliens could make, she thought, would be to scatter, making it harder for *Vanguard* to do significant damage. "Open fire on the carriers as soon as they enter range."

"The carriers are launching missiles, many missiles," Mason reported. "Buckshot countermeasures engaged."

Very like Ark Royal, Susan thought. She'd seen the original plans, dating back over eighty years. The Admiralty had envisaged *Ark Royal* as a cross between a fleet carrier and a command ship, but the march of technology had rendered the whole idea impractical. *And yet it might no longer be impractical…*

"Buckshot countermeasures seem effective," Mason added. "The enemy are recalling their starfighters."

"Pass a message to the Tadpoles," Susan ordered. The display blossomed with green icons as *Roosevelt* launched her fighters, then altered course to stay out of the fighting. "Inform them of our arrival, then copy our tactical files to their ships and the fleet base."

"Aye, Captain," Parkinson said.

Susan nodded in relief. Whatever happened, the full story of the ambush and the fleet's retreat through unexplored space would not be lost. The Admiralty would get the full story, including the sensor recordings and the various post-battle analysis reports. God alone knew what they'd make of it, but at least the story would not be forgotten.

"Entering firing range," Mason said. "Opening fire…now."

Vanguard seemed to shudder, again, as her main guns opened fire, sending pulse after pulse of superheated plasma into the enemy carriers. Susan watched, feeling a cold vindictive glee, as the carriers shuddered under the pounding, one turning to bring its weapons to bear while two more tried to head in opposite directions. And then the first carrier stumbled out of line, venting atmosphere and plasma…

"She's trying to come about completely," Mason reported. "I think she's hoping to ram us."

"Launch nuclear missiles," Susan ordered. It was unlikely the enemy carrier could succeed, but she needed to be certain. "Take her out completely."

She glanced at the screen as the alien starfighters fell on *Vanguard*, spitting plasma fire and missiles into her armoured hull. The point defence returned fire, updated fire control programs helping to swat the alien craft out of space. She smiled in relief as the first wave of starfighters retreated, having inflicted almost no damage at the cost of a third of their number blown into dust. But they had picked off a number of point defence weapons…

"Direct hits," Mason said. "The carrier is dead."

Susan glanced at the display, just in time to see a missile lance into a gash in the carrier's hull and detonate. Her internal armour was nowhere near as tough as *Vanguard's*, Susan noted; the first blast set off a chain of explosions that ripped the starship apart. Her companions were trying to escape, but it was too late. *Vanguard* and her screen unleashed a withering hail of fire that wiped out their point defence, then started to hammer deep into their vital innards. One carrier died in fire, the other lurched right out of formation and went dead…

"I can finish her," Mason said. "But there might be no point."

"Leave her," Susan agreed. The hulk looked powerless…and she'd have plenty of warning if the aliens managed to get some of her systems back online. Besides, the chance to actually capture an alien ship was not to be denied. "Detach two probes with orders to keep an eye on her."

"Aye, Captain," Mason said.

He sucked in a breath. "The enemy cruisers are turning back to face us," he added. "They're locking missiles on our squadron."

"Stand by point defence," Susan ordered.

She braced herself, knowing the pause was about to come to an end. The alien starfighters were reforming, half of them running CSP around the remaining two carriers while the other half were angling towards *Vanguard*. They had to know that *Vanguard* had very little fighter cover of her own, particularly with the Tadpoles hastily taking advantage of the sudden change in circumstances to rearm and replenish their own starfighters. But even if they hadn't, there had been no opportunity to plan for joint operations, let alone train for them. It would be a minor miracle if they managed to drive the enemy back out of the system.

They'll still have several possible axis of attack, she thought, remembering the sector starchart. *And even if they didn't, the nature of the tramlines means that putting a cork in the bottle would be damn near impossible.*

"Tactical analysis thinks the aliens plan to break through our formation," Mason said. "They may see us as the weaker target."

They might well be right, Susan thought. *Vanguard* was the toughest ship in the system, but there had been no chance to resupply any of the ships. The former contact fleet would be in deep trouble if it had to fight a long running battle. *We're running out of missiles and our starfighters are short on supplies. The chance to crush us before we can find resupply is one that shouldn't be wasted.*

"Then we'll just have to show them the error of their ways," she said. If the enemy ships were kind enough to enter energy weapons range, which they would have to do if they wanted to finish her off, she was more than prepared to hand out a drubbing. "Stand by all weapons."

The aliens held their fire as they came closer, somewhat to her surprise. They could have started spitting missiles towards her, given their improved range and laser warheads. Were they having supply problems too? Or were they just holding their fire until the chances of scoring a direct hit grew larger? They had to have figured out that their long-range missiles had as many weaknesses as strengths, after the first violent encounter.

"They're launching probes," Mason reported. He sounded perplexed. *Vanguard* and her screen weren't trying to hide. "They may think we have more ships under cloak."

Susan scowled. It didn't make sense. The aliens *had* to have a good idea of just how many ships had escaped their first ambush. They'd certainly had plenty of time to do a count before the fleet jumped out of the system. And, save for *Roosevelt* and the escort carriers, every ship that had survived was facing the enemy now.

"Keep a careful eye on them," she ordered. "Do we have an improved targeting pattern?"

"Aye, Captain," Mason said.

"Enemy ships will be within firing range in seventy seconds," Reed added.

The display sparkled with red light. "Enemy ships have opened fire," Mason said. "I say again, enemy ships have opened fire."

Susan swore. There were a *lot* of missiles heading towards the fleet...

"Fire as soon as they come into range," she ordered. No matter what happened, *Vanguard* was about to get hurt - and a number of smaller ships were about to be blown out of space. "I say again, fire at will."

CHAPTER THIRTY SEVEN

"They're opening fire," Simpson said.

George nodded, grimly. There had been little call for her to do *anything* in Turret Five, save watching as the bridge crew directed the main guns into pouring wave after wave of fire into a trio of enemy carriers. But watching them die had been...*satisfying*, in a dark way. She knew, intellectually, that thousands of aliens had died, yet she found it hard to be sympathetic. The aliens had started the war.

She tensed, despite herself, as the wave of missiles came closer, dozens vanishing from the display as they were picked off by buckshot. It was odd to think that such an inefficient system was capable of taking out enemy missiles, but point defence cannons had a very limited range. And yet the range would have been perfectly satisfactory, against human-designed missiles. She had a nasty feeling that the Admiralty would be ordering extensive research into extending the range of human point defence as soon as they saw the recordings of the first battle.

"*Coventry* is gone," someone said. There was a hint of pain in his voice. "They just blew her to hell."

"Concentrate on your post," Simpson ordered. "The enemy hasn't left us alone..."

Vanguard rocked, violently, as something slammed into the hull. George gritted her teeth, expecting to see consoles exploding into sheets of white fire, but nothing happened. The main guns were still firmly under outside control. She watched, a silent witness, as they turned to bear on their first target, then opened fire. An alien destroyer staggered under the blows, then exploded into a fireball. Another altered course rapidly, trying to escape even as she launched salvo after salvo of missiles towards the giant battleship. But it was far too late...

"Target destroyed," George noted. "That's two destroyers gone."

"Keep your eye on the display," Simpson reminded her. "You never know what will happen."

George nodded, then watched as the next wave of alien starfighters zoomed down on *Vanguard*, their weapons picking off point defence emplacements with practiced ease. A dozen died in the first pass, but each destroyed emplacement made it easier for the bigger ships to score hits on the battleship's hull. Their missiles slammed into turrets, trying to burrow into the armour before exploding. It was hard to see just how much damage they were doing, but she was sure they were wearing the armour down.

Peter will be sorry he missed this, she thought. The doctors still hadn't cleared him for active service, despite his protests. *The turrets...*

She swore as a dull vibration echoed through the compartments, alarms sounding a moment later. "They struck the control link," Simpson snapped. "Take direct control of the turret!"

George stared - how the hell had they done that? - and then did as she was told. The turret was undamaged, thankfully - she didn't want to have to escape into space for a second time - but the laser warhead had definitely cut both the primary and secondary control links to the bridge. Given time, the damage control teams would be able to patch up the wound and re-link the turret, yet she doubted they had time. The alien ships were closing in rapidly.

"Searching for targets now," she said, as the turret began to move under her command. She made a mental note to insist, assuming they survived, that additional control links be fitted to the turret. The Royal Navy hadn't planned for enemies with heavier weapons. "Two cruisers within firing range."

"Engage," Simpson ordered.

George tapped the console. A stream of plasma pulses emerged from the main gun and rocketed towards their target. They didn't move at *quite* the speed of light, she vaguely recalled from her briefing, but nothing larger than a starfighter could have hoped to dodge in time. The enemy starship buckled under the fire, then altered course towards *Vanguard*, streaming plasma all the while. George swore, then kept firing until the starship finally exploded into a fireball.

"Keep firing," Simpson said. "Don't let one of those ships get close enough to ram."

"Aye, sir," George said.

"They're pulling the carriers out, while using the smaller ships to keep us busy," Henry noted. "They clearly don't consider the carriers expendable."

"I would hope not," Lieutenant Felicity Carver said. She hadn't been too keen on allowing Henry to join her in the tactical analysis section, but she'd reluctantly dropped her opposition when he'd made it clear that he knew more about how aliens thought than anyone else on the ship. "It takes us nearly five *years* to build a carrier."

Henry nodded. Starfighters were considered expendable - building a starfighter only took a few months, training pilots took only slightly longer if the course was condensed down to the bare essentials - but he doubted anyone could afford to write off even a single carrier without a very good cause. The loss of five fleet carriers in the first battle was going to have nasty repercussions - Admiral Boskone and Admiral Pournelle were probably lucky they'd both died in the ambush - and replacing both the ships and trained personnel would take years.

Anyone who can throw away a fleet carrier for nothing has to be immensely wealthy, he thought, grimly. *And so far our new enemies don't seem to be that free with their money.*

He watched, grimly, as the battle continued to unfold. The Tadpoles were launching their reserve starfighters, trying to slice into the enemy rear, while the enemy ships were clearly breaking past *Vanguard* and her squadron. They were inflicting damage - they'd killed seven starships and wounded *Vanguard* - but was it enough? Could the enemy afford to write off nearly a hundred ships, just to kill *Vanguard* and devastate the system?

It depends on just how significant this battle is for them, he reminded himself. *Taking the system and destroying the fleet base would secure their lines of advance into Tadpole space, but do they know it?*

"They're brave enough," Felicity added. "That's the sixth ship that's tried to ram."

"As long as they don't get close enough to succeed, it doesn't matter," Henry said. "Let's just hope it stays that way."

"Captain, the damage control parties need more time," the Chief Engineer insisted. "They're already dangerously exposed as it is!"

"They don't have time," Susan snapped back. She cursed the designers and their lack of imagination under her breath. Losing one set of command links was bad enough, but losing two was potentially disastrous. *Vanguard* could no longer coordinate her fire from the rear turrets. "We need to repair the fire control system before we lose coordination altogether!"

She glared at the status display as another wave of alien starfighters screamed down on *Vanguard*, despite the Tadpole starfighters in hot pursuit. They couldn't do more than scratch the hull - if that - but they *could* take out the point defence. And every lost point defence emplacement risked more enemy missiles getting through the defence grid and slamming into the hull.

"We need it now," she snapped. "Tell them to hurry."

She closed the connection, then looked at Parkinson. "Ask the Tadpoles to keep pushing at the alien rear," she ordered. A thought struck her mind and she smiled. "Helm, ramp up the drives and take us straight towards the alien carriers."

"Aye, Captain," Reed said.

Susan nodded, grimly. Unless the aliens had *really* improved their drives, their carriers didn't have a hope in hell of evading *Vanguard* before it was too late. And the smaller ships wouldn't be able to stop her from destroying both carriers.

"Try and get a wireless command link into the turrets," she added. Deprived of the united command and control system, the turrets were engaging targets independently. "Issue verbal orders, if necessary."

"Aye, Captain," Mason said.

Susan cursed the designers - again - under her breath. The concerns about an enemy hacking the wireless command network were valid - command networks had been hacked during the Age of Unrest, sometimes with disastrous results - but she rather doubted the aliens could hack into her ship while she was underway and turn off the weapons. Unless, of course, the aliens had *yet another* surprise up their sleeves. *Vanguard* depended on hardwired command networks and the aliens, by accident or by design, had managed to cut them. She'd have to make sure that extra armour was buckled onto the ship during the refit.

And that will be the least of our problems, she thought, as the alien craft launched another spread of missiles. Her point defence fire was starting to slack, although the screen was doing what it could to thin the herd. *At this rate, they're likely to batter us into a hulk…*

"The enemy carriers are picking up speed, but they're not going to escape," Charlotte reported. "Their starfighters are returning, however…"

"Hold your course," Susan ordered. She was surprised the aliens hadn't ordered the carriers to scatter, making it harder for *Vanguard* to chase them both down. But then, they probably couldn't have escaped in any case. "And…"

She broke off as the display updated. "Report!"

"The first carrier is altering course and heading back towards us," Charlotte reported, slowly. "I think the second carrier…confirmed; the second carrier is altering course and trying to make its way back to the tramline."

They're going to try to ram, Susan thought, grimly. The aliens might not know how *Ark Royal* had died, but they were certainly intent on repeating the feat. *A carrier might just survive long enough to do it too.*

"Alter course," she ordered. *Vanguard* was faster, but evading the carrier might prove tricky if her crew remained firmly in control. "All weapons are to engage the carrier."

"Aye, sir," Reed said.

"She's the largest target," Mason said. "The gunners are bound to go for her."

"Pass the word," Susan ordered. "Send runners, if you have to. Get them shooting at that damned carrier!"

She gritted her teeth as the carrier slowly turned to face *Vanguard*, spitting out a series of missiles. The aliens were determined, she gave them that much; *she* would have ordered a retreat by now, at least long enough to regroup and re-evaluate the situation. But they were still fighting, willing to sacrifice a carrier to destroy *Vanguard*...

They may not have a choice, she thought. *They must have realised that they can't hope to save both carriers.*

"The enemy carrier is entering weapons range," Mason said.

"Fire," Susan snapped. "And alter course!"

"Aye, Captain," Reed said.

She gritted her teeth. The aliens had trapped her into a death ride...no, she'd trapped herself, even though she should have known better. Guiding the carrier into ramming *Vanguard* would be far easier than evading the carrier. *Vanguard* might be faster, but turning around would be harder...

"There's a runner at the hatch," Simpson shouted. "Turn all of our firepower on that damned carrier!"

"Yes, sir," George snapped.

She looked for targets, then opened fire, aiming at the carrier's hull. There was no way to tell what would explode when hit and what wouldn't, but blasting the carrier's point defence to hell would give the missile batteries a chance to score hits themselves. The aliens had done it to *Vanguard*; the least she could do was return the favour and do it to them. A chain of explosions flared up on the alien hull; she targeted their missile launchers and hammered them, but there was no major explosion. Nukes didn't detonate if they were hit with a hammer - or even with a plasma bolt.

"They're going to ram us," Haverford breathed.

"As you were," Simpson snapped. "Route all power to the main guns; *kill* that bastard!"

George nodded, barely able to breathe. The main guns were battering the enemy carrier, blowing chunks off its armour and digging deep into its hull, but it wasn't enough to stop the craft. She was still coming...George jammed her fingers down on the console, despite knowing that there was a very valid risk of overheating the guns and causing an explosion, one she knew she wouldn't survive. The enemy carrier was still coming...

"They're launching missiles," Simpson said. "Let the nukes get inside the wanker."

"Aye, sir," George said.

She couldn't quite believe what she was seeing. The enemy carrier was dead, it had to be. No one could have survived the holocaust she'd unleashed. And yet, it was still coming, driven by a mindless indomitable will. A solid mass that threatened to take *Vanguard* with her to hell. And...

The first of the nukes detonated. For a horrified moment, she thought the carrier would *survive* several nukes detonating inside her hull before a chain of explosions ripped her apart, scattering a cloud of debris into space. A number of starfighters roared past, several fleeing to the final carrier while others hovered for a long moment before turning and hurling themselves on *Vanguard*. After what the carrier had taken, their attempts to ram were almost meaningless. The battleship barely noticed the impacts.

"We got her," Simpson said.

George nodded, unable to speak. How much firepower had the enemy carrier soaked up before she'd finally been blown to hell?

"Start emergency coolant procedures," Simpson added. "We don't want an explosion now."

"Aye, sir," George said, shaking herself. Her body was drenched in sweat. The gunnery crew looked terrible and she was pretty sure she didn't look any better. She ran a hand through her short hair and recoiled at the oily feel. "What if we have to keep firing?"

"Then we may be in some trouble," Simpson admitted. He sounded as if he wanted to snap at her, but he was too tired to muster the energy. "But we will *also* be in some trouble if the guns explode, so start cooling them down."

"Aye, sir," George said.

"They were prepared to throw away a carrier to stop us," Felicity said, shocked.

"They didn't have a choice," Henry said. The remainder of the alien fleet had broken off the engagement, retreating back towards the second carrier and the tramline. They'd done a great deal of damage, but there were evidently limits to the losses the unknowns were prepared to take. "We would have killed both carriers if they'd tried to run."

He scowled as he reran the sensor records. It was impossible to be sure, at least until the post-battle assessment teams started to work their way through the derelict alien carrier, but it looked as though the enemy carriers had heavier armour on their prow, rather than trying to protect their entire hulls. That explained why the first carriers had been killed so easily, he decided, while the final carrier had taken one hell of a pounding before it had been blown into debris. Indeed, given the hyper-aggression the aliens had shown, it suggested that defence was not a priority for them.

"They may never see themselves as standing on the defensive," he mused. "I wonder how their ECM compares to ours."

"Standing on the defensive almost certainly means accepting defeat," Felicity said, primly.

"I was taught that at the academy, but it isn't true," Henry pointed out. "Taking the offensive only works if you have enough *firepower* to take the offensive. Pausing long enough to gather the firepower may make the difference between success and failure."

Felicity said nothing, but she certainly didn't *look* if she believed him.

Henry shrugged. "Things seem to be winding down," he added. "We'll complete our report later, I think."

"Break off the pursuit," Susan ordered. The final alien carrier - and its escorts - were well on their way to making their escape. "Warn Captain Harper to stay out of their way."

Mason blinked. "Captain, we could kill them..."

Susan had to fight down the urge to bite his head off. He was right, in a sense, *provided* she was willing to gamble that she could kill the remaining carrier before it rammed *Vanguard*, destroying both ships. But she wasn't. She'd come far too close to losing everything in the final moments before the carrier had been blown to dust. All of a sudden, she thought she understood just how Captain Blake had lost his nerve. Coming too close to utter disaster could break a man.

Poor bastard, she thought, feeling a flicker of sympathy. She still disliked him for not having the courage to seek relief, but she understood him a little better now. *Maybe they'll just let him retire into obscurity.*

"Let them go," she ordered. Neither the remains of the contact fleet nor the Tadpoles were in any state for a prolonged fight. They'd just have to hope that their reinforcements were closer than the enemy reinforcements. Surely, the Tadpoles would have sent for aid as soon as they received the warning. "Transmit a full copy of our records to the Tadpoles and another to Captain Harper, then prep the marines to board the drifting carrier."

"Aye, Captain," Parkinson said.

Susan nodded, grimly. The carrier might just have answers for them, starting with a look at the face of the enemy - both faces of the enemy. And who knew? They might recover an intact database or a piece of enemy technology. Even a damaged piece of scrap would be useful, if studied in the lab. Getting accurate data on enemy armour, if nothing else, would be very useful.

"And get the damage control teams working on the hull," she added. At least they had a hardwire connection back, although she wasn't sure how long it would last if the ship had to go straight back into battle. "We need some point defence emplacements repaired..."

"Captain," Parkinson snapped, interrupting her. "I'm picking up an emergency message from Captain Harper! Hostiles - *multiple* hostiles - transiting the tramline!"

CHAPTER THIRTY EIGHT

"Confirmed," Charlotte said, grimly. "Fifty-seven starships have just entered the system, nine of them heavy cruisers."

"No carriers," Susan mused. Her heart sank. No carriers meant no more starfighters, but neither of the defending fleets had many starfighters left either. "Were those the ships hunting us, do you think?"

"Could be," Mason said. "But the timing would seem to mitigate against it."

Susan nodded, slowly. The enemy had presumably dispatched a fleet up the chain to UXS-470, once they'd noticed their scouting squadron had gone missing. Getting that fleet back to Tadpole-453 in time to make a difference would be tricky, unless the fleet had been lurking in one of the connecting systems, planning to ambush the contact fleet when it passed. But no matter how she looked at it, she couldn't see how the enemy had managed the timing. It was far more likely that the newcomers had been intended as reinforcements for the first invasion fleet…

She shook her head, pushing the thought to one side. "Raise the flag," she ordered. "Advise Captain Harper to join the other carriers, then ready ourselves for a last stand."

"Aye, Captain," Parkinson said.

Captain Harper might have other ideas, Susan thought, *but what*?

Gritting her teeth, she worked her way through the possible options. Retreating - abandoning Tadpole-453 - was possible, but the fleet was so badly battered that they'd be fighting a running battle all the way to the tramline. Even if the Tadpoles joined them, they'd be a battered shell by the time they reached safety…and she couldn't blame the Tadpoles for being reluctant to concede the fleet base. Quite apart from losing their logistics base for the sector, they'd be exposing a large population to the horrors of occupation…

The unknowns didn't look like water-dwellers, she thought. It was impossible to be sure, but the final reports had been fairly certain that the newcomers - both sets of newcomers - were land-dwellers. *The Tadpoles might be able to remain undetected if they stay under the water.*

"Message from the Tadpole CO," Parkinson reported, suddenly. "They're requesting us to join their fleet and fall back on the fleet base."

"Forward the message to Captain Harper," Susan ordered. It was *his* decision, although the honour of the Royal Navy - and the human race - called for standing shoulder to shoulder with their allies. "Tactical, time to intercept?"

"Thirty-seven minutes, from the moment they leave the tramline," Mason said. "They're not moving."

"Must be plotting their next move," Parkinson muttered. "They couldn't have been expecting to lose so many ships in the early stages of their invasion."

And rearming their starfighters, reloading their missile tubes and so on, Susan thought. *They have all the time in the world to prep for the next battle.*

She glanced at the status report and gritted her teeth. The damage control teams were doing the best they could, but *Vanguard* really needed six months in a shipyard. Her point defence was almost gone, her main command links were badly battered and a second fusion core was on the verge of shutting down. She was proud of her crew, proud of their work, proud of their slow journey back to safety, but she knew it might all be for naught. The new enemies had caught them with their pants down.

At least we bled them badly, she told herself. *And we made them suffer for what they did to us.*

The first true battle of the war might be lost, she knew. *Vanguard* and her consorts - and the Tadpoles - would fight to the bitter end, but they'd lose. And yet, the enemy would be badly hurt and the Admiralty, alert to the scale of the threat, would have plenty of time to mobilise its forces. The boffins would go to work improving humanity's weapons and defences, perhaps even duplicating the damned FTL communications system, and the newcomers, whoever they were, would be driven back to their homeworlds. Who knew? Maybe, after a few bloody noses, they'd sue for peace?

They weren't interested in trying to talk to us, she thought, numbly. *And yet there are two races, not one. How do they talk to each other?*

"Signal from the flag, Captain," Parkinson said. "We are ordered to join with the Tadpoles in defence of the fleet base. *Roosevelt* is on her way to link up with the Tadpole carriers."

"Send him an acknowledgement," Susan ordered. "Helm, take us to the fleet base."

"Aye, Captain," Reed said.

She watched, numbly, as the combined fleet slowly fell back on the planet. The Tadpoles weren't wasting their time, she noted; they were forwarding starfighters from the planetary defence stations to their carriers, prepping them for a potential offensive. They'd be out and ready to kill, having learned how best to use their advantages, when the newcomers launched their attack. And they were even running resupply convoys up to the fleet...

They won't have anything we can use, Susan thought. The contact fleet's handful of logistics ships had been blown away in the first few seconds of the ambush, while human and Tadpole missiles were incompatible. *There's no way to replace our losses.*

"The enemy fleet is moving, Captain," Charlotte reported. "They're heading directly towards the planet."

"Understood," Susan said. She felt a surge of cool resolve. Everything had just become a great deal simpler. They would fight until they were overwhelmed, clawing the enemy as badly as they could before they died. "Time to intercept?"

"Forty minutes," Reed said. "We should have time to take up position before they reach us."

"Then keep us on our present course," Susan ordered. "Copy our final records to the flag, then have them forwarded to a destroyer. At least the Admiralty will know what has happened here."

She wondered, briefly, if she should make an announcement to the crew. The history of the Royal Navy was *crammed* with dramatic sayings that had gone down in history. But she couldn't think of anything. There were a dozen commendations she wanted to make too, praising officers and crew who'd gone above and beyond the call of duty. And yet, it hardly mattered. They weren't going to survive long enough for the messages to be received and confirmed by the Admiralty.

And the opportunity to recover that hulk is gone, she thought, morbidly. She thought about dispatching an assessment team anyway, but they wouldn't have time to make any discoveries before the aliens caught them. *We're back to square one.*

"Inform the crew of the situation," she said, finally. "And tell them that we will engage the enemy in forty minutes."

George sat on her chair, hugging her legs. It didn't seem *fair*, somehow. *Vanguard* had been through hell - the ambush and the long crawl to Tadpole-453 - and she deserved a break. Her crew deserved a chance to relax, a chance to actually recover from their endeavours...but now they were all going to die. She knew they'd fight to the last, yet she couldn't convince herself that they had a hope in hell of survival. The enemy had them pushed against the wall.

Uncle James was in bad places too, she reminded herself. *And he managed to survive.*

She swallowed, even though her mouth was dry. Uncle James Fitzwilliam had had both luck and skill on his side. *Vanguard's* position was nowhere near so encouraging. There wasn't a single ship bearing down on them, but a whole fleet. *Vanguard* had superior firepower, yet there were too many alien ships to destroy before they tore the battleship apart, or disabled and boarded her. She touched the pistol at her belt, knowing all too well what it meant when crews were issued firearms and ammunition. The command staff were expecting unwelcome visitors.

"The guns should be recharged in ten minutes," Simpson said. "We'll have plenty of time to engage."

George nodded, not trusting herself to speak. They could fight back, but it wouldn't last long enough to keep them alive. She wondered, suddenly, if anyone would notice if she ran down to the recuperation room and kissed Peter Barton. Would anyone give a damn if they were about to die?

But you can't abandon your station, she told herself, as she sat up and checked the command links. They had been repaired, but they wouldn't last indefinitely. *It's time to prepare for the final battle.*

She hoped that her uncle would know what had happened, that he'd know she died bravely...but she knew she'd never know. She'd recorded one last message for her family during the last transit, a brief message telling them she loved them and wishing them the very best in the future... there was no time to send a final message. All she could do was pray.

"The main control system is online," she reported. "We will be ready to engage the enemy when the guns are charged."

"Good," Simpson said. "And now we wait."

Henry knew, all too well, that war had many twists and turns, that battles thought won could be lost in a split-second, if the odds shifted with terrifying speed. And yet, he couldn't help feeling a bitter frustration when he studied the display. The newcomers had taken immense losses - losing so many carriers *had* to hurt - but they were still coming.

Let this be their Stalingrad, he thought, darkly. *Let them waste all their mobile fleets on us.*

He shook his head, cursing the odds. Maybe the aliens had been dared into a death match, maybe they *had* wasted all their carriers in their attempt to take Tadpole-453, but he doubted it. Two intelligent races *had* to have a large civilisation, one easily big enough to produce far more carriers and other warships. *Vanguard* would hurt the enemy badly, he was sure, but they'd be back. Tadpole-453 would merely be the first world to fall as the invasion continued to dig deep into Tadpole space.

But we'll have time to come to their aid, he told himself. He'd recorded final messages for the Foreign Office, the Prime Minister and Janelle, the former two making it clear that humanity had a treaty obligation to assist the Tadpoles. *Can they fight two other races at the same time*?

He sighed, grimly. He'd sent a private message to Janelle, warning her to take the kids and leave Tadpole Prime. There was the very distinct possibility of Tadpole Prime turning into a war zone - the Tadpoles might be able to hide below the waves, but the human settlers couldn't - and he wouldn't risk exposing his daughters to *that*. There was the very real danger of having them pressed into the Line of Succession - he hoped Janelle would have the moral courage to refuse when the time came - but even that was better than being caught up in the fighting. This new race might even toast planets for fun!

"Mr. Ambassador," Felicity said, breaking into his thoughts. "Look!"

Henry turned to peer at the display - and stared.

"Captain," Charlotte snapped. "I'm picking up a message from the emplaced sensor buoys. Seventy-three ships are entering the system from Tramline One!"

Susan blinked in surprise. Tramline One led deeper into Tadpole space; surely, even if the enemy had found a way to circumvent Tadpole-453, they wouldn't be sending their ships through the tramline to assist the invasion force. No, a fleet coming from that direction *had* to be friendly...

"Get me an ID," she snapped. "Who *are* they?"

"Working on it," Charlotte said. There was a long pause. "They're friendly, Captain; their IFF codes mark them as Tadpole ships!"

"They must have dispatched reinforcements," Mason breathed. "And they got here in the nick of time!"

Susan nodded, curtly. The enemy could finish off the contact fleet and the system's defenders, but they'd be destroyed in turn by the newcomers. Five carriers, seven superdreadnaughts and over a dozen mid-sized cruisers - escorted by entire *fleets* of starfighters - were a damn near irresistible force. There was no hope of the enemy pulling off a victory now, unless they had reinforcements of their own on the way. And even then...

Let them engage, she thought, nastily. *We'll bleed them and the Tadpoles will crush them.*

She studied the red icons on the display, wondering just what was going through the alien minds. Press the offensive, despite the shifting odds? There had been human societies where that had been the only right answer, despite the potential for catastrophic defeat. Or fall back, conceding defeat and preserving what remained of their mobile forces? *She* would have withdrawn at once, even if she'd known that far greater reinforcements were on the way. It wasn't as if the combined fleet was in any condition to take the offensive.

Choose, you bastards, she thought. *Choose and get it over with!*

"They must know the reinforcements are coming," Mason said. He sounded torn between hope and fear. "The ships aren't cloaked. They'll be picking up traces of their presence, won't they?"

"They should," Charlotte said. "I think..."

She broke off. "Captain, the alien ships are reversing course," she reported. "They're heading back to the tramline."

So there are limits to their aggression, Susan thought. On the display, the alien craft were slowly turning in a long arc that would eventually take them back to the tramline. *But even a very aggressive man can see the dangers in picking a fight with someone stronger than him.*

"Order two of the screen to cloak and shadow the alien ships," she said. "I want to know if they either reverse course for the second time or link up with reinforcements."

"Aye, Captain," Parkinson said.

Susan watched, grimly, as long hours passed. The alien ships didn't slow down; they crossed the tramline and vanished, jumping out of the system without even bothering to drop mines or do anything else to delay pursuit. Not that it would have slowed down a counteroffensive for long, she knew, but at least it would have counted for *something*. The shadows vanished through the tramline too. She had no doubt that the Tadpoles would start picketing the next system as soon as they could.

"Order the crew to stand down from battlestations," she said, once the final alien craft had vanished. "The marines are to prepare themselves to board the drifting hulk."

"Aye, Captain," Mason said. He smiled as the lights returned to normal. "Do you think the Admiralty will be paying out prize money?"

"Let us hope so," Susan said. She had a nasty feeling she'd need money for the legal defence fund. Now the battleship had returned to friendly space, she'd have to report to the Admiralty Post on Tadpole Prime and make a full confession. Did saving *Vanguard* from an alien ambush compensate for relieving Captain Blake of command? "Inform Captain Harper that we intend to board the hulk, then move us into position."

"Aye, Captain," Reed said. A dull whistle ran through the ship as the drives engaged, suggesting that one of the drive field nodes was out of alignment. "We'll be near the ship in ten minutes."

"Hold us at a safe distance," Susan added. "Just in case the hulk isn't quite as dead as she seems."

"Aye, Captain," Reed said. "We should have no difficulty keeping our hull safe."

Susan nodded, then rose. "Commander Mason, you have the bridge," she said. She had a multitude of reports to write, starting with commendations for officers and crew who had performed well. "Inform me if the situation changes."

"Aye, Captain," Mason said. "I have the bridge."

"I think I've got emotional whiplash," George said, as she stepped through the hatch into middy country. "Is that normal?"

Fraser looked up. "Walter bought it," he said, as if he hadn't heard what she'd said. There was a grim note to his voice. "He was attached to one of the damage control teams when it was too close to a direct hit."

George swallowed. Midshipman Walter Haworth hadn't been a close friend, but she'd liked him. There just hadn't been the time to get to know the young man as well as she would have liked…

"I'm sorry," she said. Fraser was clearly saddened at the death. "He was a decent man."

"He was," Fraser agreed. He produced another plastic box and passed it to her. "I think he would have been promoted at the end of this cruise. He'd shown that he could handle the tasks put in front of him..."

He sighed. "Maybe the paperwork was already done," he added. "They'll bury him as a lieutenant."

"I hope so," George said. Her problems seemed minor, somehow. "He deserved better."

Fraser nodded, then started emptying Walter's locker. George watched, shaking her head in some amusement, as a handful of paper letters were deposited into the box, followed by a set of intimate photographs of a green-skinned woman. She couldn't help blushing as she looked at them, wondering just who she was. When had Walter had a chance to meet a woman from the Eden Colony?

"She lived on the moon," Fraser said. "Walter met her during a pub crawl and they became intimate. She was a runaway from the Eden Colony, I think."

George looked up at him. "Were they going to get married?"

"I don't know," Fraser said. "Her skin...far too many people make assumptions about her, based on the colour of her skin. It wouldn't be hard for her to have the tint removed, but she kept it. I don't know why."

"They're meant to be devoted to pleasure," George recalled. "Is that true?"

"I've never been to Eden," Fraser said, curtly. He finished dumping personal possessions into the box and sealed it. "But they were *very* sweet together. The battle was won, George, but the cost was still high."

"Yes, sir," George said.

CHAPTER THIRTY NINE

"The face of the enemy," Henry said.

It felt strange to be back on Tadpole Prime, after wearing shipboard uniform for the last two months, and stranger still to see men in shorts and women in bikinis staring back at him. A handful of officers from the fleet, looking disgustingly out of place in shipsuits, seemed unsure just what to do with themselves. He *had* advised Captain Harper and Susan to wear something more suitable for the swimming pool than the briefing room, but both of them had seen fit to ignore him. They'd be sweating like pigs until they returned to their ships.

He pushed the thought aside as he studied the alien body, one of many recovered from the dead carrier. The alien was shorter than he'd expected, with a fox-like face covered in fur and dark beady eyes. He - the xenospecialists thought he was a male, although the genital region was thoroughly mangled - had clawed hands, muscular legs and what *looked* like a retractable penis. They hadn't even *begun* to unravel the complexities of the alien biology yet, but Henry couldn't help thinking that the aliens would be formidable opponents, if he had to face one hand-to-hand.

"We recovered seventeen bodies in reasonable condition," he continued. "There's a full briefing packet in the datanet, but we still *know* very little about them. For one thing, we don't know what the second race looks like, even though we recovered biological traces that suggest that both races serve on the same ships."

A Russian held up a hand. "You recovered no bodies?"

"No *intact* bodies," Henry confirmed. "The researchers *may* be able to deduce an approximation of what the aliens look like, from the biological samples we've recovered, but so far they haven't produced any meaningful results. All they can really say about the second species is that it definitely didn't evolve on the same world as their allies."

He took a breath. "Furthermore, we were unable to recover any samples of alien technology," he added. "The carrier was so badly damaged that most of her systems were destroyed, either directly by *Vanguard* or through a form of limited self-destruct. Our researchers have been able to tell us...*interesting*...things about their hulls, but very little else. Their FTL communications system, for example, is still a total mystery."

"The evidence is purely circumstantial," a Chinese representative said. Henry couldn't help thinking she looked good in her bikini. He reminded himself, firmly, that he was a married man. "There may be no such system."

"The evidence is quite strong," Captain Harper said, firmly. "They reacted impossibly fast, *unless* they had some way to send messages at FTL speeds."

"And the first contact mission was botched," the representative continued. "The fleet should have been more careful."

Admiral Liberec cleared his throat. "I have reviewed all the sensor recordings from the moment the fleet entered UXS-469 to its hasty jump to UXS-470," the Frenchman said. He sounded rather irked by the remark. "The analysts on Earth may find something I have missed, but for the moment I believe that the contact fleet did everything right. There was no reason to think that the fleet wasn't alone in UXS-469, or that the unknown aliens intended to launch a surprise attack. Watching the fleet, even stalking it, would have made sense; launching an all-out attack intended to *destroy* the fleet speaks of hostile intentions. There is nothing *innocent* about their activities."

He took a breath. "Furthermore, two successive attempts were made to hail the aliens when they jumped into Tadpole-453," he added. "They did not respond. We have to assume that they are hostile, irredeemably hostile, until proven otherwise."

"Correct," Henry said. "The Tadpoles have formally activated the mutual assistance clauses in the treaty. Please inform your governments."

He kept his face expressionless with an effort. None of them would be very pleased at having to inform their superiors that a whole new war had broken out, but there was no choice. They *had* signed the treaties, after all. And besides, fighting the enemy outside human space was better than fighting them in the skies of Earth. He could only hope that human governments would see it that way.

But we lost over twenty thousand personnel in the first battle alone, he thought, numbly. *No government could afford to ignore such losses.*

"I will be returning to Earth to brief my government personally," he concluded. It wasn't something he was looking forward to, but he really had no choice. "If any of you wish to depart on *Vanguard* or her escorts, please inform her commander before her planned departure date."

The room emptied rapidly, diplomats heading back to their apartments to go through the full set of reports, line by line, before writing messages to their governments. Henry spoke briefly to Captain Harper - who would have overall command of the remaining human ships, at least until Earth dispatched someone more senior - and then headed home himself. The skies were already darkening, casting long shadows over the settlement. He couldn't help thinking that it was a portent of change to come.

Janelle met him at the door, wearing a pair of bikini briefs and nothing else. "The girls are with a friend," she said huskily, as she pulled him into an embrace. "And I've missed you."

"I've missed you too," Henry said. He kicked the door closed as they stumbled onto the sofa, his hands already fumbling with her briefs. "It's been far too long."

Afterwards, with the rain pelting down from the dark skies, they sat together and went through the reports. Janelle was cleared for everything, up to and including MOST SECRET: she was, to all intents and purposes, his naval attaché. He listened to her reactions, scribbling down notes to himself; he'd have to take them - and her - back to Earth. There was no way he was leaving his family on Tadpole Prime.

"The girls will hate it," Janelle said, when he broached the subject. "This is their home."

"Tadpole Prime isn't *that* far from the front," Henry pointed out. He wasn't fool enough to think he could dictate to her. Janelle had an inner core of strength that made her surprisingly formidable. "The aliens could attack this planet at any moment, love, and the settlement is a strikingly obvious target."

Janelle ran her hand through her long dark hair. "It won't be easy for them to settle on Earth," she said, "particularly if some bastard tells them about their heritage. They grew up *here*."

Henry nodded. His daughters hadn't even passed their first decade, yet they already spoke several languages and chatted freely to everyone. Tadpole Prime was *safe*, safe in a way Earth wasn't. He didn't want to send them to boarding school on Earth, not when they'd probably be bullied merely for having close ties to the crown. But keeping them on an estate wasn't a good idea either. Hell, they'd have to get used to cold weather. Tadpole Prime was hotter and wetter than anywhere in Britain.

"I hope it won't be for long," he said, finally. "But they can't stay here."

Janelle scowled, but didn't argue. She knew as well as he did just how rapidly the fronts could shift, just how quickly a safe haven could turn into a death trap. Earth herself had been attacked during the war. The new aliens, whoever they were, might think nothing of scorching an entire world.

"Then they go somewhere safe and *isolated* on Earth," she said, finally. "Somewhere under heavy guard."

"They will," Henry said. He gritted his teeth. An asteroid settlement would be better, but his children didn't know how to live on one. "And I'll make sure the reporters don't get anywhere near them."

He scowled, bitterly. The hell of it was that he doubted he could keep that promise. Three young girls, heirs to the throne even if their father had refused to stay in the Line of Succession…they'd be hounded by the media on Earth. Tadpole Prime was *private*; reporters were rarely allowed to visit, certainly not for such a minor matter. And yet…he was damned if his daughters were growing up in a goldfish bowl. His childhood had never been private. And his sister had had it worse.

"See that you don't," Janelle said. "I'll geld any reporter who looks at them funny."

Henry smiled. "You would, too."

He reached for her and kissed her. It wouldn't be long before the girls came home, it wouldn't be long before they had to tell their children that they were going away for a while, but he refused to waste a single second. They'd be far too busy on Earth.

———

"You know," Fraser said. "This place is paradise."

George gave him a sharp look. Tadpole Prime was uncomfortably hot, after spending her life in Britain, Luna and *Vanguard*. She'd borrowed a swimming costume from one of the settlers and slathered her exposed skin in suntan oil, but it wasn't enough to make her feel any better about the environment. But, she did have to admit, white sands, blue waters and green tropical trees were quite spectacular.

"It's too hot," she said, finally. She sighed as she shifted, feeling the sun beating down on her skin. "Why do you like it?"

Fraser laughed. They'd been lucky enough to win a few hours of leave on the planet, although the permission had been hedged with so many warnings and restrictions that she was reluctant to risk going for a swim. The Tadpoles might have cleared the nearby waters of anything dangerous, but their definition of 'dangerous' was very different from humanity's and she'd seen too many nasty-looking critters crawling along the shore.

"The dress code," he said. "Have you seen how many topless girls there are?"

"And shirtless men," George countered. "I think they don't notice, these days."

She smiled, inwardly. It had taken her months to get used to undressing in front of her male comrades - and watching them undressing in front of her - but now the thought of doing anything with a bunkmate was unthinkable. They were her brothers and sisters, to all intents and purposes; she knew better than to even *consider* a relationship. And, on Tadpole Prime, the settlers were so used to near-nudity that they simply ignored it.

Probably a good thing too, she thought. *Not all of the men and women I've seen look good in shorts or bikinis.*

"All the more for us," Fraser announced, cheerfully. "You think I could talk one of them into bed?"

"This isn't a normal shore leave outpost," George said. From what she'd been told, there were brothels and bars in every *normal* shore leave outpost. "You have to be careful who you approach."

"I can try," Fraser said. His eyes swept the beach, past the point where a number of crewmen were kicking a ball around the sand up to a handful of young ladies, sunbathing near the waters. "You want to see if you can find someone too?"

George shook her head. In truth, she just wanted to relax and unwind. Nathan was dead...and she knew she needed to come to terms with it, something she couldn't do until she took the remainder of his possessions back home. And then there had been the other losses...she leaned back and closed her eyes, wishing she could forget about everything. But she knew that wasn't possible.

"Hey, George," a voice called.

Her eyes snapped open. Barton was standing there carrying a ball under his arm, wearing a pair of shorts and nothing else. His leg was still inhumanly pale and there were a handful of dragon and whale tattoos on his chest. She smiled at him, despite the brilliant sunlight. It was good to know that he'd recovered from his stay in sickbay.

"I nicked a ball," Barton said. "Want to come play with it?"

George hesitated, then rose. Maybe it would be fun. She'd played on beaches as a child, although *that* had come to an end when she'd turned thirteen. Her mother had wanted to be damn sure that George would turn into a sweet little girl, just waiting for a handsome man to marry her. *That*, at least, hadn't worked. She wondered, as she grabbed for the ball, just what her mother would think of her now. Playing ball on the beach with a crewman of no family name? It would give the older woman a heart attack.

And if it gave my headmistress a heart attack, George thought, remembering Mrs Blackthorn and her insistence on proper deportment at all times, *I wouldn't mind in the slightest.*

"You're good at this," Barton said, after an hour of tossing the ball around. Fraser had vanished long ago, perhaps to woo the settler women. "Want to go exploring?"

George considered it, briefly. There was little to explore, she thought; the settled island wasn't much larger than Skye, if warmer and far wetter.

The settlement itself was fenced in, although they'd been assured there was nothing on the island that posed a threat to careful explorers. It wasn't the most reassuring statement she'd ever heard.

And if you do go with him, she asked herself, *what do you do if he tries to kiss you*?

She cursed, then looked up. "I need to be back on the ship within twenty minutes," she said, glancing at her wristcom. Being late wouldn't impress the Captain, particularly when there were hundreds of others waiting patiently in line for their chance to relax in the sun. "But we can go get an ice cream before it's too late."

"Of course," Barton said. "You know they give ice cream away for free?"

"Very few people here to buy it," George guessed. Producing ice cream by the bucket would hardly be *difficult*. There was a large farm on the other side of the human settlement, raising sheep, cows, chickens and pigs. "They probably made it for us specially."

"I hope so," Barton said. He held out a hand. "Let's go."

"I have reviewed your logs, Captain," Colonel Hoffman said. He was the embassy's current military attaché, Susan had been told, although he was British Army rather than Royal Navy. "I confess that there are strong reasons to support your actions and strong reasons to lock you up and throw away the key."

"Yes, sir," Susan said, shortly. She couldn't help feeling embarrassed - she was wearing her uniform while he was wearing shorts - but she hadn't been able to bring herself to walk into the office in a swimming outfit. "I understand."

She sighed, inwardly. She'd expected a senior naval officer, but apparently Commodore Chambers had been attached to Admiral Boskone when his carrier had been blown into dust. There had been so many dead that she hadn't even noticed at the time. Hoffman was in command until the Admiralty sent out a replacement. And, given that there was a war on, it might be months before the replacement arrived.

"Captain Harper has signed off on *Vanguard's* return to Earth," Hoffman continued. "Your ship requires repairs, does she not?"

"Yes, sir," Susan said. "Earth or Britannia are the only places *Vanguard* can be serviced properly."

"Then I think it would be best if you took her back to Earth," Hoffman said. "For what it's worth, Captain, I believe you did the right thing. I will appraise the Admiralty of my feelings, but they may not pay much attention to me. The Army wouldn't be too charmed if a naval officer presumed to tell them their jobs either."

"I understand, sir," Susan said. She sighed, out loud this time. At least she'd have command until the battleship reached Earth, plenty of time to make basic repairs, analyse the sensor records and make recommendations for future modifications. "And thank you for listening to me."

"I wish it were under better circumstances," Hoffman said. "Half the diplomats and their families will be travelling with you, Captain. I'm not quite sure what I should be doing, if the shit hits the fan."

"This settlement is a rather large target," Susan agreed. It wasn't the only one - Tadpole Prime was surrounded by more asteroid colonies and industrial nodes than Earth - but it was certainly the largest visible settlement on the ground. "Are you planning to make a stand?"

"There's very little in the way of actual weaponry," Hoffman admitted. "Counting everyone with military training, I have forty-seven men who can be armed with rifles. It would be fewer if the Americans didn't insist on teaching kids to shoot in school. Even so, a single KEW would blot the settlement out of existence. I have a feeling that evacuating now might be the best possible choice."

He shrugged. "But you don't need to worry about that," he added. "Best of luck with the Admiralty, Captain."

"Thank you," Susan said.

She saluted him, then walked out of the door and up to the shuttlepad. *Vanguard's* shuttle was sitting there, waiting for her. She waved to the pilot, motioning for him to wait as she turned to survey the settlement. The handful of white buildings stood out like sore thumbs against the greenery, making easy targets if anyone gained control of the high orbitals.

But they would have problems finding the Tadpoles, she was sure. Even the best orbital sensors couldn't detect underwater cities.

And it all looks so peaceful, she thought. The waves lapping against the white beaches seemed harmless, even though she *knew* there were thousands of dangerous creatures lurking below the waves. *What will happen when the aliens arrive*?

She took one last look, then stepped into the shuttle. "Take us back to orbit," she ordered, as she buckled herself into the seat. Tadpole Prime was noted for heavy turbulence. She'd been lucky enough to have a reasonably gentle flight, but some of the crewmen had staggered out of their shuttle swearing never to fly again. "We're going home."

CHAPTER FORTY

"Jump completed, Captain," Reed said. "We have entered the Sol System."

Susan nodded. "Transmit a full copy of our records to Nelson Base," she ordered, "along with the datapackets from Tadpole Prime."

"Aye, Captain," Parkinson said.

"Very good," Susan said. She rose. "Commander Mason, you have the bridge. I'll be in my Ready Room."

"Aye, Captain," Mason said. "I have the bridge."

Susan could have sworn the temperature was dropping as she walked through the hatch and into her Ready Room. They knew - they all knew - that it was time to face the music. Susan had done her best to protect her subordinates, but even a cursory investigation would turn up the simple fact that mutiny had been discussed - and that none of the officers involved had reported the matter to higher authority. Prince Henry's authority might turn out to be spurious, at best.

She keyed her wristcom as soon as she sat down behind the desk. "Midshipman Fraser, Midshipwoman Fitzwilliam, report to my Ready Room," she ordered.

The two junior officers, if matters had been arranged to her satisfaction, should have no trouble in coming at once. She waited, idly scanning a datapad until the door buzzer sounded, then keyed the switch to open the hatch. It hissed open, revealing both of the midshipmen. They both looked understandably nervous. A summons from the Captain was almost certainly bad news, even though Susan had been doing most of the XO duties as well as serving as commanding officer.

"Stand at ease," Susan ordered, as they stood to attention in front of her desk. They relaxed, so slightly the motion was barely noticeable. "There are matters we need to discuss."

She waited, wondering if one of them would say something, but heard nothing. It was hard to blame them, really. She was so far above them that even being *right* wouldn't be much of a defence, if their commanding officer took offense. One day, they'd be XOs and captains themselves, she was sure. She hoped they wouldn't forget what it was like to be a junior officer when they pinned the command star to their collars.

Susan cleared her throat. "Midshipwoman Fitzwilliam," she said. "Gunnery Officer Fitzroy Simpson has put in a request that you be formally commended for your actions in the Battle of UXS-469. I have reviewed the records and chosen to grant his request. A special commendation will be entered into your file, which will be taken into consideration when the promotion board meets to discuss your future."

Midshipwoman Fitzwilliam's face showed a multitude of different emotions. Pride, sadness...a kind of shame, something that would have made no sense if Susan hadn't caught the look she'd shot at Midshipman Fraser. They definitely *were* getting along better since the fight, Susan thought; it would be a shame if a commendation, one that was worth a full *year* of seniority in middy country, came between them. But, right now, it couldn't be helped.

"I have also entered your name into the logbook as a potential recipient of the Victoria Cross, although *that* matter will have to be decided at a far higher level than mine," Susan added. It was true enough, but there were too many nominations from the contact fleet for her to be sure that George Fitzwilliam would have a chance at an award. "However, even being *considered* for the medal will be a feather in your cap."

She met Midshipwoman Fitzwilliam's eyes. "Congratulations!"

"Thank you, Captain," Midshipwoman Fitzwilliam stammered.

Susan nodded, then looked at Midshipman Fraser. "Commander Mason and Lieutenant Reed have both spoken highly of you over the last month," she said. "In addition, Chief Finch has insisted that you be commended for your work on the damage control parties, during the Battle of Tadpole-453.

I have looked over both the recordings and the records and I find that a commendation is nowhere near enough for your services. Therefore, I am promoting you to Lieutenant, effective from midnight tonight."

Midshipman Fraser's mouth dropped open. "Captain?"

"I am promoting you to Lieutenant," Susan repeated, with some amusement. Midshipman Fraser had clearly spent *years* convinced that he wouldn't be promoted. Susan still had no idea why he'd incurred the hostility of a senior officer, but it hardly mattered. Midshipman Fraser had done well over the last year. "You can pick up the uniform from ship's stores now, if you wish. They're expecting you."

"Thank you, Captain," Midshipman Fraser stammered.

"A formal commendation has also been added to your file," Susan added. "As it is quite likely that you helped save the ship, I have recommended you for both the Victoria Cross and the Sinclair Award. Chief Finch has counter-signed the latter."

She smiled at them both. "I have no idea what will happen after we reach Earth," she concluded, "but I wish you both the very best in your future careers. Dismissed!"

"Thank you, Captain," Midshipman Fraser said. "I..."

Susan shook her head in amusement as Midshipman Fitzwilliam helped Midshipman Fraser out of the Ready Room. Midshipman Fraser wouldn't be *Lieutenant* Fraser until midnight - a legal fiction to allow him to celebrate with his former bunkmates before he moved to his new quarters - but he would *stay* a lieutenant. Susan might be put in front of a court martial board and shot; Fraser couldn't be demoted without good cause. Even if the Admiralty tried, they'd have to explain it to Fraser's supporters on the ship.

And the Sinclair Award is only handed out by engineers, she thought. *Chief Finch's endorsement will make damn sure he gets it.*

Her wristcom bleeped. "Captain," Parkinson said. "We've picked up a secure message from Earth. We are to head to Titan and enter orbit until we receive further orders. A team of investigators has already been dispatched."

"Understood," Susan said. Two hours to Titan, she thought; two hours before she had to face the music. "Inform Commander Mason that he is to set course for Titan at once."

"Aye, Captain," Parkinson said.

"I'm a lieutenant?"

George had to smile at Fraser's shock. "Yes, you're a lieutenant," she said. He'd been babbling in shock all the way back to middy country. "Well, technically you're still a midshipman until midnight, but..."

"Oh, shut up," Fraser said, without heat. "I'm a lieutenant!"

He sobered. "But where will I go now?"

George shrugged. Fraser, at least, wouldn't have a problem being promoted up the ladder on *Vanguard*. He'd been first middy, after all; there had been a distance between him and his bunkmates, no matter how much they might have wished to deny it. But he'd grown friendlier after they'd fought...maybe he'd be better on another ship. And yet, she didn't really want to lose him.

They stepped into the sleeping compartment, which was empty. "We would normally have a small party," Fraser said, softly. "But I really don't *feel* like partying, you know?"

"You can at least have a drink," George said, after a moment. "There's some rotgut hidden away in the locker, isn't there?"

"The Captain knew it was there," Fraser said. "She was a midshipwoman herself, once upon a time. I think she'd know precisely where we hide shit."

George flushed. "Is that a bad thing?"

"Depends," Fraser said. "If it causes problems, then it's a bad thing; if it doesn't, it's tolerable."

He sat down on his bunk, staring at the bulkhead. "George...can I tell you something important?"

George frowned. That didn't sound good.

"Yes, she said, finally.

"You and Peter, Peter Barton," Fraser said. "You've been spending a lot of time with him."

"We're friends," George protested, although she knew that wasn't entirely true. "What I do with him is my own business."

Fraser looked up at her. "Not if it affects the ship," he said. "George, you're a midshipwoman; you'll grow into an officer soon, unless you fuck up so badly it can't possibly be concealed. Even now, you are his superior..."

"Technically," George said.

"It isn't *technical* and you know it," Fraser said. "Yes, you shouldn't be issuing him or Gunner Simpson orders because you know much less than they do, but you're still their superior officer. In two years, perhaps less, you'll be a lieutenant. At that point, you'll be issuing orders to your lover."

"He isn't my lover," George insisted.

Fraser scowled. "Is he going to be?"

He tapped his foot on the deck, impatiently. "I understand the urge for companionship," he said, "and I understand the desire to have...intimate relationships with someone. But a relationship between an officer and a crewman, a man who will be under the officer's command, can fuck up everything. You could compromise yourself so badly that you'll be disgraced and your career will come to an end."

George bit down the response that came to mind. She *liked* Barton, she liked spending time with him, watching movies or just chatting about the future. And they had been discussing plans to take their shore leave together, when they finally returned to Earth. She hadn't kissed him yet, but she knew in her bones that it was just a matter of time. It was easy to imagine kissing him under the moonlight on some tropical resort...

"You have to be careful," Fraser told her. "If you are caught, if you are lucky, the two of you will be summarily reassigned to different ships. If you are unlucky" - his voice hardened - "you'll be dishonourably discharged from the service. Maybe that won't be a problem for you, with a wealthy family, but what will that be like for *him*?"

"That's below the belt," George snapped.

"I'm glad to know some of my lessons took," Fraser said. He reached out and patted her shoulder. "If you want to get fucked, go to Sin City. There's no shortage of dicks on legs ready to give you a damn good hammering. Safe, clean and discreet. But if you want companionship, stay friends for now."

George stared at him. "That's..."

"Crude?" Fraser asked. "Yes, it is. It's also true."

He rose. "You've gone too far already, I think," he said. "He doesn't think of you as an officer, but a potential lover. It's not going to be easy to assert yourself later. My very strong advice would be to call it off, now."

George watched helplessly as he strode out of the hatch, leaving her alone. She didn't want to admit it, but he was right. A relationship with a crewman under her command could destroy her career…and, despite herself, she knew her uncle wouldn't save her if she disgraced herself so blatantly. He'd be far more likely to leave her as an object lesson to the next generation of midshipmen.

Shit, she thought, staring down at the deck. She felt miserable, torn between two different urges. *What the hell do I do now*?

"Captain, we have entered orbit around Titan," Mason said, through the intercom. "A shuttle is en route and the occupant has requested that you meet him at the airlock."

"Understood," Susan said. "How long until he docks?"

"He'll be at Airlock One in ten minutes," Mason said. "Captain…"

"I'll be there," Susan said, cutting him off. She didn't want to hear any commiserations or anything else, not now. She'd done everything she could to ensure that the consequences, whatever they were, fell on her shoulders alone. "Thank you."

She cut the connection and rose, taking one last look at the Ready Room. Most of Captain Blake's clobber had been moved out, giving her space to actually *work*. It was *hers* now, but not for much longer. She would be surprised if she was allowed to return to duty in less than six months, assuming she wasn't summarily discharged. Someone else would sit in the command chair, someone else would take command of the ship…although it would be months, at least, before the battleship was fit for combat. She'd made sure that the list of repairs was in order.

At least I had a chance to send a message to father, she thought, as she walked out of the compartment and down towards the airlock. *He'll hear it from me first.*

She stopped outside the airlock, just as the red light flicked green. The hatch opened a second later, revealing a grim-faced man wearing a Commodore's uniform, escorted by two military policemen. Both of the redcaps wore holsters at their belts, the flaps unbuttoned. It was not a reassuring sight.

The Commodore stepped forward. "Susan Onarina?"

"Yes, sir," Susan said. No rank...that didn't bode well. "Reporting as ordered."

"I am Commodore Douglas Archer, Royal Navy Military Police," Archer said. "It is my duty to inform you that I am taking you into custody, pending a full investigation into your conduct on HMS *Vanguard*. You have the right to remain silent, but any and all cooperation you offer between now and your formal hearing will be counted in your favour. Do you understand me?"

"Yes, sir," Susan said.

"As of now, you are relieved of command," Archer continued. "You will be held on my shuttle until you can be transferred to RMP Titan. Although you are not technically under arrest, I would advise you to comport yourself as though you are. A legal officer will be assigned to you at Titan; until then, you may not talk to anyone save for myself and other RNMP personnel. Any attempt to do so through any means will result in you being restrained and held in a cell, rather than reasonably decent quarters."

He nodded to his escorts. Susan briefly considered resistance, but she knew it would be suicidal. Instead, she let them search her with practiced ease, then lead her through the hatch and into the shuttlecraft. Inside, a handful of officers - an emergency command crew, she realised - eyed her curiously as she was marched through the craft and sat at the far end, one of her escorts sitting near her.

Behind her, the hatch slammed closed.

End Of Book One

HMS *Vanguard* And Her Crew Will Return In:
Fear God And Dread Naught
Coming Soon!

If You Liked Vanguard, You Might Like…

ADMIRAL WHO

(Luke Sky Wachter)

A member of a disgraced and ridiculed royal family, Prince Jason Montagne has never had any real power—until his honorary military position suddenly becomes a hands-on job! The newly-minted, unqualified admiral is at the helm of a poorly crewed ship with the galaxy at his feet in this entertaining adventure.

Chapter 1: Changing of the Guard

My name is Jason Montagne Vekna, Governor of Planetary Body Harpoon, Vice Admiral in the Multi-Sector Patrol Fleet, a Prince-Cadet of House Montagne, and a sometimes-struggling college student. And this is the story of the craziest week of my life.

———

Being a member of Planetary Royalty has its perks, but it isn't all it's cracked up to be. The bright lights, flashing cameras, and flashier titles usually just amount to nothing more than a glorified prison sentence. For instance, I had been granted the title and rank of Vice Admiral in the Multi-Sector Patrol Fleet. Sounds great, right? If you looked at the official chain of command, you would see that I was the commander of an entire Fleet sent out to guard the borders of the Confederated Empire. In reality, I commanded nothing at all—that was Imperial Rear Admiral Arnold Janeski's domain, which was fine by me.

I spent the majority of my time aboard ship working on Tabulated Planetary Service/Statistics reports, otherwise known as TPS/S. Homework, in other words, for my distance learning program, which applied toward my degree in colonial administration. It was my dream to renounce my citizenship, and become an administrator in a new frontier colony; I was never actually involved in fleet operations. The 'fleet,' such as it was, consisted of fewer than twenty ships, and was spread out over seven parsecs of space. We controlled our section of the border by performing routine patrols as individual units, or at most, penny packets of two ships.

The only thing I actually controlled was the workstation and terminal in my stateroom. To make certain I understood my position in this fleet (as if I'd ever forget), the real Admiral had stationed two Imperial Marine Jacks decked out in full power armor outside my door, as an Honor Guard. They escorted me wherever I went, and were with me whenever I was outside my quarters. This was the only place I had any real privacy during the cruise.

I was sitting at my workstation, pounding away on a particularly tricky problem of resource allocation for a new colony in the early stages of settlement, when Admiral Janeski's voice sounded from the speakers in my cabin.

"Governor Montagne to the Flag Bridge, Governor Montagne to the Flag Bridge immediately; this is the Admiral," his sharp voice boomed through my room's speakers.

I dropped the cup of tea I had been sipping as I jumped out of my seat, having heard my name on the ship-wide intercom for the first time I could recall. *This can't be good*, I thought.

I was aboard the *Lucky Clover* as a face-saving piece of interstellar politics between the parliamentary government of my home world, Capria, and our good friends from the Empire of Man. My planet was part of a vast Confederacy, which had functionally merged with the Empire about fifty years earlier, to create the Confederated Empire. The Empire had 'asked' (a much gentler word than 'demanded') that the individual world states in our sector of the Confederacy second ships from our individual System Defense Fleets over to the Imperial Rim Fleet. We were supposed to help patrol the borders of the Confederated Empire while the regular units of the Imperial Fleet were siphoned away from Rim Fleet. Those assets were then re-assigned to a Battle Fleet on the other side of the Empire, where there was a real war raging with the Gorgon Alliance.

But a battleship—even an outdated one, like the *Lucky Clover*—represents a significant financial investment (not to mention its symbolic value), so Capria insisted on maintaining some measure of official control over it, even if it was just on paper. This is where my Vice Admiralty comes in.

It might seem like it would be a prestigious position, but the ruling families of Capria disagreed. Since there was no real power or prestige to be found in such a role, there wasn't exactly a line forming around the corner with eager applicants.

The job was eventually given to the Montagne Branch of the Royal Family, who quickly assigned the position to someone they felt best represented the spirit of the post. They needed someone who was not powerful enough to cause any real problems, yet high-profile enough to serve as a proper figurehead. Someone charismatic enough to step in front of the cameras when it was time for a press conference, but too inexperienced to really understand what was going on without a script in front of him. In other words, they volunteered me for the job.

After gathering all of the bits and pieces of my ridiculous court attire, I bolted to the door and de-activated the locking mechanism. I planned to finish assembling and adjusting my wardrobe en route to the Flag Bridge since it was a poor idea to keep Admiral Janeski waiting.

As soon as I cleared the doorway, the two Marine Jacks grabbed a hold of either arm, and despite my bewildered protest that I could easily walk under my own power, they frog-marched me down the corridor.

My quarters were those of a former Flag Lieutenant's and were on the same level as the Flag Bridge. So in almost no time I was through the first pair of reinforced bulkheads leading inside. The first set of pressure doors closed behind us and the second opened as I was unceremoniously pushed onto the Flag Bridge.

Opening my mouth to protest this rough treatment, I took one look at the Admiral's tight-lipped face and snapped my teeth together with an audible click. Glancing down, I started buttoning my formal jacket, embarrassed at the disheveled appearance I presented in front of this most formidable Imperial Officer.

"Governor Montagne," he said, acknowledging my presence with a nod. "It seems we have a bit of a situation."

Admiral Janeski insisted on referring to me by my gubernatorial title, probably because he felt it best personified me in his eyes. Sure, I was Governor of Planetary Body Harpoon; it's true. But the full truth about Harpoon is that it was nothing more than an irregular asteroid, barely larger than this ship, on an elliptical orbit around Capria's sun. About a year ago, I discovered a pair of illegal miners operating there. After I went to the authorities, I couldn't even get a parliamentary court to rule that I should receive a portion of their profits (which would have then been used to offset the costs of my tuition), let alone evict them and their mining operation from the asteroid itself.

"What happens to be the problem, Admiral?" I asked, suppressing a desire to run a hand through my hair and gulp through sheer force of will. When combined with the iron-clad media training every royal of my home world is taught from birth, I thankfully managed to abstain from any other unseemly behaviors. Our training was rigorous, because we didn't want to embarrass ourselves or the government in front of the public—especially the members of government who held our purse strings—and in this case, my training did a good job of settling my flutters. I couldn't imagine what problem could exist that the admiral would need my assistance with, but I was willing to do my figurehead best and help out however I could.

The Admiral ignored me and produced an official-looking paper scroll covered with seals. He cleared his throat as he prepared to read the document.

I quickly schooled my features. This, at least, would be something with which I was familiar. Receiving and listening to speeches from foreign dignitaries, while maintaining an appropriately stoic and regal appearance, had been one of the primary skills taught in royal finishing school. Well, that and making our own speeches in return, of course. We weren't really taught that much about the policies, politics, or inner workings of the planetary government, nor did we have much say in such matters.

Instead, we were taught how to—and how not to—behave at formal state functions, and also how to receive and entertain important galactic visitors. We were really nothing more than the glorified butlers of our parliamentary government.

"By order of Magnus Gaius Pontifex, Triumvir of the Empire of Man, having received the advice and consent of the Imperial and Republican Senate; all ships, officers, personnel, and portable assets belonging to the Empire of Man—excepting certain diplomatic envoys and delegations—are hereafter ordered to immediately withdraw from the Spineward Sectors of the Confederated Empire. All military assets are to be redirected to those provinces along the Gorgon Alliance front, as quickly as possible—."

I leaned back, my eyes widening. "What!" I burst out, unable to restrain myself—and not incidentally, cutting the Admiral off midsentence. "You're stripping the Spine of all Imperial assets? What about the Rim Fleet?"

Fixing me with a thousand-meter stare which froze me in my tracks, he stopped the next words halfway up my throat. After a brief—but sufficiently reprimanding—pause, the Admiral continued through clenched teeth, "This proclamation is not yet finished." His eyes seemingly bored holes through my skull, as efficiently as any cutting torch.

Realizing how badly I had broken protocol by cutting off an Imperial Admiral—while reading an official proclamation from the Triumvirate of Man, no less—I nodded, despite the thousand questions still bubbling up inside me.

The Admiral cleared his throat and continued. "In addition, all assets belonging to the Empire of Man, the Triumvirate and the Senate, which cannot be easily transferred out of the indicated sectors, but which represent a military or technological asset of strategic importance, are to be destroyed. Also," he continued grimly, "all private Imperial citizens are urged, for their own protection, to abandon the Spineward sectors of Confederation Space. Imperial forces will no longer be able to offer an adequate level of protection from piracy, and other acts of vandalism, nor to provide any form of emergency service until further notice."

So saying, he rolled up the proclamation and placed it back inside an official-looking engraved wooden box.

Swaying where I stood, I was completely stunned. This was a complete violation of the Union Treaty, which established the Confederated Empire, and permanently allied both the Confederation and the Empire for time and all eternity.

"What about the Union Treaty...What about the rights of the Spineward Sectors to Confederated Empire protection?" I managed to sputter out. "Aren't we still a part of the Confederated Empire, with the right to equal protection, under the United Space Sectors and Provinces Act?" I ground to a halt, my mouth opening and closing as the potential implications of the Rim Fleet withdrawing from this specific sector of space really started sinking in.

The Admiral shook his head. "All of those are very interesting questions; questions to which I'm sure you'll eventually receive answers. But at this specific moment, they are the wrong questions to be asking. What you should instead be asking—or, at the very least, considering—is what I'm going to do with all the Imperial officers and personnel currently serving in this ad-hoc patrol fleet, and whether or not I am planning to turn the entire fleet toward Empire Space."

I blinked. The thought hadn't even occurred to me. He could certainly do it; not only did he have the personnel to man the ships, but he also had enough Imperial Marines to seize the vessels by force, if necessary.

"I can see you hadn't thought about that yet." Again, he shook his head, but this time his upper lip curled as well. "Taking control of this fleet and transferring it to the Empire would be no problem at all." He snapped his fingers for emphasis and snorted, then shook his head in negation. "However, I am no pirate, and even if I were, this outdated tech is hardly worth the effort. The cost of upgrading this poor excuse for a star fleet to battle-ready condition would be economically unfeasible. Fortunately for you—but, unfortunately for this patrol fleet—that means that a short while from now, you are going to be in full operational command of this fleet...such as it is."

I gasped in dismay, nearly overwhelmed by the weight of his words. Feeling lightheaded, I carefully walked over to the nearest workstation on the Flag Bridge and collapsed into its form-fitting chair. "There's no way I can actually take command of this Battleship, let alone act as a real Admiral for the entire fleet!" I blurted, verbalizing the first thing to enter my brain.

The Imperial Admiral shook his head dismissively. "You've no choice but to fulfill your duty. Political expediency may have placed you in ceremonial command of this patrol fleet that's true. Unskilled and unfit as you are, you'll no doubt make a hash of it. However, it is still your duty to carry out the stated will of this fleet's collective governments, and complete its mission and intended purpose before returning safely home."

"Of course, I'll make a hash of it," I muttered. "I have no actual training in space force operations." Then another thought came to me and I jumped out of the chair. "I could be thrown in jail just for taking real command of the fleet; I might even be charged with treason against the Planetary Parliament!" I paced back and forth. "They never actually meant for me to command this fleet; you're supposed to do that." I finished, unable to stop myself from glaring at the Imperial Admiral accusingly. "That is your job, Admiral." I flared as only someone already facing the prospect of an unpleasant execution can.

Turning his back, the Imperial Admiral activated the forward view screen. "That *was* my job," the Admiral corrected me with military precision. "I have since been reassigned by the Triumvir. You can do your duty and take command of this fleet, or you can let someone else do it for you. Whatever happens to the fleet after I step out this ship's airlock is no longer any of my concern." He gestured to the main view screen, and one of the many Imperial Technicians assigned to the Flagship shunted a sensor feed through to the screen. On it, an Imperial Command Carrier appeared, and according to the estimated course shown on the screen, it was due to dock with our aging Battleship within the hour.

"The Imperial Command Carrier, *Invictus Rising*, will be docking with us shortly," explained Admiral Janeski. "At that time, I will transfer my Flag, and all Imperial personnel currently onboard this ship, to the *Invictus Rising*. Any other personnel who choose to sign on with the Empire of Man's space fleet prior to undock will also transfer to *Invictus Rising*. After that, this ship—and its remaining personnel—will be exclusively under your command."

Unable to think of any protest I could utter that would convince an Imperial Admiral to disobey the direct order of an Imperial Triumvir, I slumped back in my chair, overwhelmed by the enormity of what was happening. The entire Spineward sectors of Confederation space were being abandoned, in favor of protecting the Empire's Provinces along the war front.

Careful to make no sudden motions which might upset the Imperial Jacks stationed in the room, I watched blankly as the Imperial Command Carrier came closer and closer. My mind numb, all I could manage was to stare at the screen. Not only was my home world's sector being stripped of protection, but on a more personal level, I was in deep, deep trouble.

Fifty years ago, members of my planet's royal family—specifically those royal members belonging to the Montagne branch of which I was a reluctant part—had temporarily seized power from the Parliament in a bloody coup. The coup was ultimately suppressed, by elements of the Confederated Empire's Rim Fleet, some months later. And by suppressed, I mean bombarded from high orbit until even the rubble was rendered unrecognizable.

The current parliamentary government had sent me out here, knowing with total certainty that I'd never have any hint of real authority within an Imperial Fleet; I was just here to look good on camera, and show how important supporting the Empire was to our planet.

When they found out things were otherwise, heads would roll—perhaps even literally—and it was quickly sinking in that almost certainly one of those heads would be my own. I would never be allowed to renounce my citizenship and leave for a new colony, not after this! I would be carefully watched for the rest of my days, and if I was very unlucky, I could even be permanently assigned to the royal retreat, which wasn't so very different from an actual prison sentence. Consumed with these thoughts, the hour until docking passed by like a dream.

When the *Invictus Rising* actually docked with our ship, I imagined I could feel the whole world shudder along with the ship. The next two hours also passed in a blur, as Admiral Janeski ordered the entire crew confined to quarters, and then started transferring all the Imperial personnel off ship, along with the equipment they had brought with them. After that, he ordered the main Imperial database wiped, and prepared to leave the Flag Bridge for the last time.

The Captain of the Battleship, also an Imperial officer, soon arrived on the Flag Bridge. Together, the Captain and Admiral ceremonially cased the Admiral's Flag, which was a metal standard made of Duralloy, and had been personally given to the Admiral by an Imperial Triumvir when he had made Flag rank. When that task was complete, they began to leave.

As they pivoted on their heels and took the first step towards the door, I wondered if this was it. I quickly realized that yes, it was, and they were just going to walk off and leave me with this terrible mess. Unsure if I was supposed to do anything other than just watch them leave the Flag Bridge, I was suddenly reminded of the many holo-vids I'd watched back home, where the departing Captain or Admiral would ceremonially turn the command codes and keys for the ship over to the new officer about to take command of the ship. Finally seeing something I could do, my royal training kicked in and quickly I cleared my throat.

The Admiral glanced back in my direction. Seeing him look at me, my courage went up a notch, and I hopped out of the chair, drawing myself up to full attention as I did so. I resolved to play this thing out just like I was a real Royal, about to receive actual command of a space fleet. "Admiral Janeski, I am prepared to receive the command key and codes for both the Flagship, and Patrol Fleet, at this time."

The Captain looked at Janeski, who in turn looked at me with narrowed eyes. Then, after taking two abrupt strides, the Admiral stopped in front of me and produced a clear crystal from a vest pocket on the front of his uniform. Slapping it in my hand, he turned and strode out of the Flag Bridge and off the ship, without further ceremony. The Captain, with the corner of his lip, pulled up in a sneer, drew out a similar crystal and tossed it at my feet before following the Admiral.

Janeski was already gone, but the sneering Captain hadn't yet left when my mouth took over. It must have been the stress because my mouth just took over. "I wouldn't want to keep you from your date with the waste recycler, you Imperial coward," I said in my most polite tone and gave a slight bow. The Captain stopped in his tracks and whirled around on me.

"What did you say, boy," he barked, and stomped across the deck plates toward me, stopping literally inches from my nose.

I did my best to keep defiance out of my voice and suppressed the urge to gulp. "It's an ancient Caprian saying, customarily offered when ancient sea vessels would cast off their lines and head off to war," I lied through my teeth.

The Captain narrowed his eyes, and for a moment I was afraid he had actually understood what I'd said. But after an uncomfortable moment or three, he slowly turned and proceeded down the corridor once again.

I breathed a sigh of relief; it's nice knowing a secret language almost nobody in the universe even knows exists—at least, nobody outside of your immediate family. It allows all kinds of liberties at times like these. Like I said before, it's not like Royalty isn't without its perks; but just what had I been thinking, poking him with a verbal stick like that?

As quickly as that, I was the Master and Commander of an entire fleet of warships. At least briefly, I was in total control of my own fate and my destiny was entirely in my own hands.

What could possibly go wrong?

APPENDIX
GLOSSARY OF UK TERMS AND SLANG

[Author's Note: I've tried to define every incident of specifically UK slang in this glossary, but I can't promise to have spotted everything. If you spot something I've missed, please let me know and it will be included.]

Beasting/Beasted - military slang for anything from a chewing out by one's commander to outright corporal punishment or hazing. The latter two are now officially banned.
Binned - SAS slang for a prospective recruit being kicked from the course, then returned to unit (RTU).
Boffin - Scientist
Bootnecks - slang for Royal Marines. Loosely comparable to 'Jarhead.'
Bottle - slang for nerve, as in 'lost his bottle.'
Borstal - a school/prison for young offenders.
Clobber - stuff/junk.
Donkey Wallopers - slang for the Royal Horse Artillery.
Fortnight - two weeks. (Hence the terrible pun, courtesy of the *Goon Show*, that Fort Knight cannot possibly last three weeks.)
'Get stuck into' - 'start fighting.'
'I should coco' - 'you're damned right.'
Kip - sleep.
Levies - native troops. The Ghurkhas are the last remnants of native troops from British India.
Lorries - trucks.
MOD - Ministry of Defence. (The UK's Pentagon.)
Panda Cola - Coke as supplied by the British Army to the troops.

RFA - Royal Fleet Auxiliary

Rumbled - discovered/spotted.

SAS - Special Air Service.

SBS - Special Boat Service

Skive - Avoid work

Spotted Dick - a traditional fruity sponge pudding with suet, citrus zest and currants served in thick slices with hot custard. The name always caused a snigger.

Squaddies - slang for British soldiers.

Stag - guard duty.

TAB (tab/tabbing) - Tactical Advance to Battle.

Walt - Poser, i.e. someone who claims to have served in the military and/or a very famous regiment. There's a joke about 22 SAS being the largest regiment in the British Army - it must be, because of all the people who claim to have served in it.

Wanker - Masturbator (jerk-off). Commonly used as an insult.

Wanking - Masturbating.

Yank/Yankee - Americans

Printed in Great Britain
by Amazon